I0607217

Brighton Ho!

Edward Arno

Victory Rose Press
Burbank, California

Copyright © 2010 by Edward Arno.

All rights reserved. No part of this publication may be reproduced, distributed or transmitted in any form or by any means, including photocopying, recording, or other electronic or mechanical methods, without the prior written permission of the publisher, except in the case of brief quotations embodied in critical reviews and certain other noncommercial uses permitted by copyright law. For permission requests, write to the publisher, addressed "Attention: Permissions Coordinator," at the address below.

Edward Arno Victory Rose Press
4206 W Victory Blvd
Burbank, CA 91505
www.edwardarno.com

Publisher's Note: This is a work of fiction. Names, characters, places, and incidents are a product of the author's imagination. Locales and public names are sometimes used for atmospheric purposes. Any resemblance to actual people, living or dead, or to businesses, companies, events, institutions, or locales is completely coincidental.

Book Layout ©2013 BookDesignTemplates.com
Cover graffiti by kcigam
Edited by Bertha Garcia

Ordering Information:
Quantity sales. Special discounts are available on quantity purchases by corporations, associations, and others. For details, contact the "Special Sales Department" at the address above.

Brighton Ho! / Edward Arno. -- 1st ed.
ISBN # 978-0-9996465-3-3
Library of Congress © TXU 1-688-070

Dedication to
My Grandchildren
Laura, Joshua, Melissa, and Zak

CHAPTER ONE

Naked Presumed Dead

James woke to the high-pitched scream of a young lady. He couldn't see her or move to see where she was. His eyelids wouldn't open and for a few seconds, he wondered if he had gone blind. He tried to move his arms and legs but nothing happened, his entire body seemed numb. The screaming stopped and was followed by a few sobs before it began again. In the semi-silent moment, he heard the crashing of waves on stones. The odd cry of a low-flying seagull some-where nearby, then the screaming girl again. James wanted her to stop screaming, he wanted to hear the other sounds. Why could he hear the waves was this some kind of music? CD playing relaxing opus to calm those around? It wasn't working for this girl, whoever she was. He shouted "shut up" and for a few seconds, she did. He felt elated she heard him. He shouted "help me". There was no response, only an-other high-pitched scream.

He didn't realize he lay naked on the stony Brighton beach. His left groin stabbed several times. Unlike the four other adolescent men who found themselves in this predicament, he had not bled to death. His clothes were folded and placed neatly just above his head. The wound to his groin had congealed and dried.

The girl stopped screaming when a male voice told her to calm down. She sobbed a little and then stopped. The man spoke, his voice had an edge to it.

"Control Wilcox here, it's another naked male body, send the team."

James heard the words naked and male body. Was he lying somewhere naked on his stomach or his back? He hoped no one was around with a camera or video camera taking pictures. These days they ended up on Facebook within minutes of events happening. If only he could move, or speak. He tried to shout again, but nothing happened.

He lay listening to the voices around him talking about another poor sod dead. He wasn't dead couldn't they see that he was alive only he couldn't move. Why couldn't they see his chest moving as he breathed?

The sound was of the stones moving and crunching grew as more people arrived. They talked about keeping people back and stopping the press from coming down on to the beach. Someone said they should put a screen around the body. It would be in the newspapers, his mother would see it. If only he could remember what happened. How did he get here according to those speaking without clothes on?

He had arrived in Brighton two days earlier to turn an old hotel into a luxury apartment complex. Moving into a small quiet flat on the Old Stein on six months rental agreement. Then yesterday he went for a walk, and that is all he remembered. What happened to me? No one answered. They all thought he was dead. He was three weeks away from celebrating his twenty-fifth birthday, and he wanted to celebrate it. He wasn't dead, just unable to move. Dead people get taken to the morgue placed in a refrigerator waiting for a post-mortem. They cut you up in a post-mortem and he was still alive. He also hated the cold, and being stuck inside a cold refrigerator would be hell for him.

More people arrived. A powerful male voice seemed to have taken command of the situation. Seagulls gathered a few yards away like vultures waiting to pick at the corpse.

"Put the screen up as quickly as you can. A crowd has gathered on the prom. It's bad enough he was dead without people seeing him naked."

"I'm not dead," screamed James, but they didn't hear him.

"Sergeant the police surgeon has just arrived."

"Good, the quicker we can get his corpse out of here the better."

"Help, I'm not dead," James's frustration grew, how could he let them know he wasn't dead.

"Morning Sergeant Barnes, so let's look at this body. Male and naked."

The Police surgeon knelt beside James.

"So what do we have here, male between twenty and twenty-six of age? Approximately five foot ten inches weighing one hundred and forty pounds. Slim with no distinguishing marks."

He took out of his jacket pocket rubber surgical gloves and put them on. Touching James's stomach, it surprised him to see it was still warm. He looked at the wounds in the groin moving James penis out of the way.

"There are six stab wounds, this is consistent with the other dead men." He moved the leg a little and looked at the stones beneath.

"Not a lot of blood," he said.

Something instinctively made him pick up James' hand and feel for a pulse. He carefully placed the hand down and took off his right-hand rubber glove and touched the throat.

"Blanket and an ambulance now," he shouted, "This one's not dead, didn't one of you morons think to check for a pulse?"

James screamed, "thank you," but they didn't hear him.

They placed a blanket over James's naked body as the doctor checked his eyes. It surprised him to see a sparkle in the eye.

"Looks like they drugged him, I think he may hear what we are saying. He is just paralyzed."

The Doctor leaned forward and whispered into James' left ear. "This paralysis shouldn't last too long. We will get you to hospital to check over your wounds, you may not know but they stabbed you in the leg several times. Then we just wait for your recovery from the drug."

The ambulance men arrived and placed James on a stretcher. He couldn't feel what was happening, but the change in sounds told him he was being moved. They placed him in the ambulance and the doctor stood at the door.

"When you get to the hospital ask them to run a test for drugs. They gave him some kind of drug and it would be useful to know what it was."

"I'll follow in my car."
He closed the ambulance door, watching as the siren roared as it raced down the street.
Detective Inspector Neal Gladstone turned from watching the ambulance drive away. He beckoned for his second in command, Detective Sergeant Thomas Hoffman, to join him. They walked away from the taped off area.

"First, I want a twenty-four-hour guard put on that young man. He is our first break in this case. Next, I want every inch of this area examined. Anything they find I want to see."
"No problem Neal, I've had his clothes bagged."
"Good, get them to the lab. I'm going to the hospital, I want to be there when he recovers. And get a statement from the girl. Why was she on the beach so early in the morning? It's not even seven o'clock yet, and they found him over ninety minutes ago."
"I'll call you in an hour and give you an update on what we find on the beach."
The Inspector drove to the hospital and parked. He hoped they could find out from this young man who was behind the murders. Two police officers sitting outside the room stood up as the Inspector approached.
"Find out who will have access to him from the hospital and get a copy of their ID. Doctors and nurses, I give no one else access without my permission. Do you understand, treat this man as though you are protecting the Queen herself."

The two officers nodded and discussed who should get the information from the hospital. The Inspector opened the door and entered the room. James was lying in bed, he had several tubes attached to his arm. A nurse stood on the other side of the bed. She looked up as he entered.

In a low voice, almost a whisper she said, "can I help you?"

He took his warrant card out and showed her. She read the card carefully and nodded for them to move closer to the door.

"I'll get the doctor."

She left the room, returning immediately with a tall, thin male doctor. Inspector Neal showed the doctor his warrant card. The doctor took him by the elbow and led him out of the room.

"He is conscious but unable to speak. We are waiting for the results of the tests we ran. I think they have given him some form of flunitrazepam, also known as Rohypnol."

"The date rape drug?"

"We think it is a recent version of it as it paralyzed him."

"How about the stab wounds?"

"Lucky for him none of them cut the Femoral Artery. If they had, he would have been dead by now having bled to death."

"Hopefully he will tell us what happened to him."

"Very unlikely, he may in time remember, but the one thing about the drug is it blocks the memory."

"I hope not we need to catch whoever is doing these murders, and he is the only one other than the murderer who knows."

"Do you know his name?"

"A picture business card in his pocket said his name was James Matthew Pidgley from Birmingham. We have the local police going to the address on the card."

Inside the room, the pain spread on the inside of James's left leg. He had been told someone stabbed him and assumed this was the place. He could feel his skin on the back of his hands. The sensation in his body was returning. He drifted off to sleep hoping this was some kind of nightmare and he would wake up soon.

Matthew Pidgley arrived at the hospital, a tall man going grey at the temples. Like his son, he was a handsome man who dressed immaculately. The two police officers stopped him from entering James's room. One officer took him to a small office just down the corridor.

Detective Inspector Gladstone dragged his tired body from the hospital canteen to meet a man claiming to be the victim's father.

Matthew had a built-in dislike for all policemen. As Inspector Gladstone entered the small office, he felt the hairs on the back of his neck stand up. The Inspector didn't help himself with his opening remark.
"So you're the man claiming to be our victim's father."
"I'm not claiming I am, here is my passport and James's birth certificate. The Birmingham police suggested I bring them for identification."
The Inspector looked at the documents, they seemed in order. If this man was who he claimed to be, and he didn't let him see his son, he could cause trouble.

"Seems in order, understand Mr. Pidgley, your son
has been a victim of a murderer. He is lucky, the
other young men died."
"That inspector is what we the public pay you to
solve. Now if I may see my son."

The Inspector stunned by Matthew's remark and without saying another word showed him to James's room.
He told the two officers that Mr. Pidgley senior could
have unlimited access to his son.

Matthew sat by James's bed as the nurses and doctor
entered and left the room. The Inspector entered two
hours later, a little more refreshed and less belligerent.
"How is he, Mr. Pidgley?"
"The same according to the doctor, it could take
hours or days for the effects of the drug to wear
off."
"When did you last have contact with your son?"
"Yesterday lunchtime he called and said he was go-
ing for a walk. James liked to know his surround-
ings so he would walk around the district
familiarizing himself."
"He hadn't been in Brighton very long then?"
"Less than a day."
"I didn't know that. Was he here on business or just
a holiday?"
"Business for about six months."
"What kind of business if you don't mind me ask-
ing?"
"My son is part of the family property company he
was here to oversee the conversion of a hotel to
luxury apartments."
"Did he say where he was going for a walk?"
"Not exactly along the seafront, I think."

"Thank you, Mr. Pidgley, if there is any change in your son's condition please notify the officers outside the room. I need to talk to him, we need to stop whoever is committing these attacks."

Matthew sat with his son through the night, sleeping occasionally in the chair. The first few rays of dawn broke through the vertical blinds in the room. He rearranged the items on the bedside table. Replenishing the water in the glass and straightening James's mobile and watch. He picked up the pen and placed it on top of a small notebook. He couldn't remember a time when James hadn't a pen and paper somewhere near him.

Taking his son's right hand, he held it. Hoping and praying there wouldn't be long-term damage to his brain. The little finger wriggled, then stopped. Matthew touched it and watched to see if he moved again.
    "James, this is Dad if you can hear me move your little finger again."
Matthew waited, but the finger didn't wriggle or move. He fell into a light sleep to wake with James's thumb caressing the back of his hand.
    "James can you hear me?" There was no reply, "James, if you can hear me press my hand with your thumb once for yes and twice for no. Do you understand?"
James pressed the back of his father's hand once.
    "Thank God I thought we had lost you. Do you know who did this to you?"
Pressing his thumb twice, James then relaxed his hand.
    "Sorry, your tired, rest and we will try again a little later. I love you, son." Matthew kissed him on the forehead.

Matthew left the room. The two police officers were still outside the door.

"My son is sleeping."

He passed through the reception area. Another police officer was behind the counter with the young receptionist. A woman in her twenties is talking to them and getting upset because they won't let her see someone.

"Listen to me, I was the person who found him on the beach, I want to see him."

"Sorry Miss but only the family is being allowed to see him."

She made a grunting sound and walked over to a row of chairs and sat down. Matthew hesitates for a few seconds before approaching her.

"Sorry to interrupt but did you say you found someone on the beach?"

"Yes, a naked man, I just wanted to know how he was."

"Why don't you and I get a cup of tea in the cafeteria. If it's the same person, I think it is my son you found."

They sat at a table by a window looking out on to a small courtyard. Several nurses stood outside smoking. Matthew had never had a problem with the awkward silence when first meeting someone. The young lady tried several times to speak but seemed to have difficulty working out what she should say.

"My son is getting back to normal. The doctors think they gave him some drugs."

"It was horrible I thought he was dead. I was walking home from my boyfriend's home. Well, ex-boyfriend! We had just split up and I just wanted to get home. I saw something lying on the beach, so I looked and saw your son. He was naked and had a wound on the inside of his leg."

"Did you call the police?"

"No, I just screamed, and this man came out of a hotel. He ran over to me, saw the body and ran back to call the police."

"My boyfriend talked about the other victims last night. He said it was more likely a girl who did it because of the knife wound to the inside leg. We argued."

"Is that why you broke up?"

"No, he wouldn't make love and he said we couldn't because I had given him gonorrhea. I said no way I hadn't been with anyone else. Then he hit me and I left, telling him I never wanted to see him again. Sorry, I shouldn't have told you. It's my business, I just needed to tell someone sorry."

"It's all right, I understand."

"My father will say as he always does, I told you he was a loser but will you listen?"

"He only says that because he cares."

She sat composing herself again, taking a white handkerchief out of her handbag. She twisted it in her hands, then after folding it carefully replaced it into her handbag.

"I'm on the beach screaming and the police arrived. At first, they thought your son was dead too. Then this doctor came and said he was still alive, and they raced him off to the hospital. They kept me at the beach asking questions for over three hours. I think I told them about me, Collin and gonorrhea. So embarrassing."

"I think maybe, just to be on the safe side, you should get tested. If your ex-boyfriend has it, then he could have passed it on to you."

"I never thought of that, I'll go see my doctor. Then I suppose I should see my parents."

"You don't live with them?"

"No, they have a house in Surrey. I came down here to work for my uncle."

"I don't know your name."

"Julia Brooke, what's your son's name?"

"James and I'm Matthew."

"It's nice to meet you, Matthew. Would you give James a message for me?"

"I am sorry they won't let you see him. They have two police officers sitting outside his door."

"I understand I heard a policeman on the beach say he could be the most important witness in the killing of those other men."

"I know little about the other men whom they murdered."

"Me neither, I need to visit my parents. Thank you for talking to me. This is my card you can get in touch with me if you need to see me at my uncle's place."

Leaving the cafeteria, she turned at the door and waved. Matthew brought himself another cup of tea and the fish special of the day. He picked up a newspaper someone had left on a chair. Returning to his seat, carrying his tray of food. He suddenly remembered she never told him what was the message for James. It was the early evening edition of the local paper. Daniel Stratton wrote an account about James being found alive. It was a very short piece about James, but made longer by an attack on the police for not catching the attacker. Alongside the article was a picture of James lying naked on the beach. Superimposed over the genitalia was a large black shape. Matthew knew the original picture would somehow find its way onto the Internet. At least from the distance, they took the photo, James wouldn't have to worry much as it was impossible to tell it was him lying there.

Detective Inspector Gladstone entered the cafeteria talking to DS Hoffman. He seemed very animated and was gesticulating with his hands flamboyantly. Seeing Matthew, he said something to DS Hoffman before joining Matthew at his table.

"Mr. Pidgley, how is your son?" Without waiting for a reply, he continued, "The hospital rang and said he had regained consciousness. We need to talk to him as soon as we can."
"James had regained his senses, but his speech doesn't seem to work very well."
"I'm sure he will tell us what we need to know."

DS Hoffman arrived at the table carrying two cups of tea and two very large pastries. Inspector Gladstone took the largest of the pastries. He ate it as though he had missed several meals over the last few days.

"I have just met the young lady who found James."
"Julia Brooke! Seems to be on the level," said Inspector Gladstone, stuffing the remains of his pastry into his mouth.
"I found her a little tense and felt she was hiding something, but I couldn't work out what it was."
"Her title, I suspect."
"Title?"

"She is the Honorable Lady Julia Brooke, the present Lord Cobham's granddaughter."

"I see that explains a lot," said Matthew, sipping at his tea.

"I think it is time we had a chat with your son."

"I'm not sure you will get much out of him his speech hasn't returned."

Detective Inspector Gladstone and Detective Sergeant Hoffman stood on one side of the bed. Matthew sat in a chair on the other side, holding his son's hand.

Inspector Gladstone leaned forward, his face a few inches away from James's face.

"Mr. Pidgley, I am sorry to bother you while you are recovering. I'm sure you understand the quicker we get your side of what happened, the quicker we can apprehend the culprit."

The smell of coffee from his breath made James turn his head towards his father. Matthew didn't realize why James looked at him. He assumed he was looking for help.

"The Inspector is right James so if you can remember anything try to tell him."

"I cart remama emyfink," said James out the corner of his mouth.

"What did he say?" asked the Inspector.

"I'm not too sure, but I think he said he couldn't remember anything."

"Do you know who did this to you?" probed the Inspector.

"Noooooooo."

A nurse entered the room. She took one look at the police and left. A few minutes later the Doctor entered. The Inspector was leaning over James again, his face much closer to James this time.

"You will not get much out of him today Inspector. The drug they gave him affects the vocal cords more than any other organ. If he remembers anything it could be as long as a week before he can speak properly."
"If you say so Doctor, Mr. Pidgley, may I have a word with you outside."
The inspector left the room expecting Matthew to follow. He returned as Matthew had continued to sit holding his son's hand.
"If we could have that word now."
Matthew followed the inspector into the corridor.
"The doctor just told you it could be weeks before his speech returns."
" I understand that now, Mr. Pidgley. I was speaking to some colleagues in the Midlands. I was wondering if you thought this had anything to do with the death of the clown. I know it was a few months ago, but your son was in the center of the murder."
"James involvement because he was living inside the Winter Quarters of the Circus."
"I see."
"I believe this is the fourth or fifth attack and in the other cases murder. So how could those attacks if similar to James's attack be anything to do with the death of a clown?"
"We have to look at every possibility when we have several murder cases. If your son remembers anything please get in touch with us. I'm sure as a father you understand the need to catch this monster."

"The moment he tells me something about the attack and how he ended up on the beach, I will contact you."

The inspector nodded his head. Opening the door, he indicated to the Sergeant to follow him. Matthew watched as the two men walked down the corridor. Matthew's dislike of the police hadn't changed over the years. These two policemen seemed only interested in protecting their pension and arresting anyone whether or not they are guilty.

He returned to the room and sat down next to James.

"Don't worry about them?" said Matthew

James became alive. His head moved and pointed to the bedside table with his mouth.

"You want some water?"

James moved his head slowly from side to side.

Matthew looked puzzled, "Not the water."

He picked up the watch and showed James the time. Once again James moved his head from side to side. Matthew picked up the mobile phone and James gently rocked his head up and down.

"You want to call someone?"

James moved his head to say no. Matthew opened the phone and showed the display screen to James. The smile crept over James's face, scaring Matthew.

"It's okay, dad, I'll explain later."

"You can talk?"

"But I'm not letting them know."

"You're are really my son."

"All our lives we have been treated like criminals by the police. You and grandfather taught us never to trust them. I haven't, even though I have met a few nice coppers."

"When did your voice return?"
"Not sure, only I knew if the cops thought I could speak they wouldn't have left me alone."
"True, so how do you feel now."
"My arms and hands have feeling in them. My legs don't but I can feel my toes if I move them."
"Well, that's an excellent start."
"Dad, I want to get out of here, I think my legs will be back in the next few hours. Would you go to the flat and collect me some clothes?"

Matthew opened the cupboard and took out the plastic bag the police had given the hospital. He showed them to James.

"That is what I was wearing I don't want to put them on again until we have washed them."
"Where are the keys to the flat?"
"They must be in the trouser pocket."
Matthew opened the bag and searched the pockets and found a set of keys. Then closed the bag.
"We will go through your clothes later, who knows what we may find."
"Hopefully a clue to what happened to me."

Matthew left James trying to get the feeling back in his legs. If only he could remember what happened he would relax. How did he get himself into this predicament? He recalled getting up yesterday and eating breakfast. He made a few phone calls and arranging a meeting with the contractors in the morning at the hotel. He had lunch at the corner sandwich shop. Then his mind went blank as a foggy mist clouded over. It started after lunch. A flash of light followed by swirling stars made him put his hands to his face and rub his eyes. He had just seen a glimpse of something, but he didn't know what it was. Hopefully, the images would return.

When Matthew returned James was sitting up in bed eating his midday meal. He placed the paper carrier on the bedside table and sank into the chair.

"I brought some briefs, jeans, a shirt, socks and a pair of trainers. It surprised me at how messy your flat was."

"What do you mean messy?"

"It looked like a tornado had been through it. I always remembered you were the tidy child."

"I am, my flat was very tidy when I left it."

"Then someone has broken in and ransacked it."

"Broke in?"

"Not exactly, I would say they had a key and let themselves in."

"At least there was nothing of value."

"What about your computer?"

"Hidden as all my valuables are."

"I'll clean up after we leave the hospital, I'll call the owner's agent and get a locksmith to change the lock."

James finished his meal, at least what he could eat. Matthew took the tray out of the room. When he returned James was standing by the bed. He takes a few steps, unsteady at first but after a few paces gained his balance.

"I think I'm ready to go home."

"The nurse just told me the doctor will be here in half an hour. We can ask him to release you."

"Dad while you were at the flat, I was thinking about yesterday. Whatever happened started after

lunch. I can remember up to then, afterward is just
a blank."
"You may never know what happened, according to
the doctor."
"I hope I do, can you imagine missing part of your
life and not knowing what happened. It will not
happen to me."
When the Doctor arrived, he examined James and
seemed very pleased with his progress.
"Doctor, I would like to go home."
The Doctor looked at Matthew, hoping for a disap-
proving look. He didn't get one, only one of Matthew's warm smiles.
"Mr. Pidgley, I'm not sure you are ready."
"I am sure doctor I want to leave the hospital and
my father is here to look after me."
"If you promise to take it carefully for the next
three days, I will discharge you. We need the bed.
I'll fill out the paperwork, the nurse will bring it to
you. James you were very lucky less than a centi-
meter was all that was between you and a cut to the
femoral artery."
"I think I have some powerful guardian angels
looking after me."
"You must have." The doctor left.

James picked up the bag his father had brought his
clothes in and entered the private bathroom. He didn't
shut the door completely but took a quick shower, trying not to get the dressings in his groin wet. He returned to the room refreshed and dressed.

The nurse came with his discharge papers. She asked if
she could just check his dressing one more time.
James dropped his jeans, and the nurse inspected his

dressing. He looked at his father, who was trying to hide a laugh.

She handed him a bag containing fresh dressing for the next three days. They left the room thanking her, Matthew still trying to control his laugh.

As they walked down the corridor, one of the police officers raced after them.
"Where are you going?"
"Home."
"Does the Inspector know?"
"I don't think so."
"Then you can't leave."
"What do you mean I can't leave? Am I under arrest?"
"No, you're not under arrest."
"Then there is no reason I cannot leave. I am a free man to do as I please."
"But the inspector will be mad."
"I already think he is," said James as he and Matthew continued down the corridor.
The other officer joined his mate. "I think we should call the Inspector before we get blamed for him leaving."

They called the Inspector on his mobile, but it rang and rang. After several minutes they gave up and rang the police station.

Matthew and James arrived at the one-bedroom flat James had rented while he supervised the conversion of the hotel. A man in his fifties sat on the top step leading to the flat. He stood up as they climbed the stairs. The man's blue overalls stained with grease and metal fragments.

"Mr. Pidgley?"

"Yes," answered Matthew.

"I'm the locksmith, the owner said someone broke in. It won't take long to change the locks."

"They didn't break-in, they used a key and walked in."

"We get that a lot these days an old tenant keeps the key and returns a few months even years later. Most landlords don't change the locks."

Matthew opened the door to the horrific mess. Whoever had broken in had opened every drawer and cupboard, the contents thrown onto the floor.

"Drugs."

"Sorry," said James.

"They were looking for money to buy drugs. Brighton is full of it now, almost as bad as Edinburgh."

"Well, they didn't find any."

"That's why the place is a mess. If they don't find money quickly, they ransack the place to see where you have hidden it."

"In the bank."

The locksmith changed the lock and handed Matthew two keys. He stood inspecting his work before slowly collecting his tools together. James watched as the man left and wondered why he had hesitated before leaving.

Matthew closed the door and picked things up off the floor.

"Strange how he didn't want to leave."

"Not really, he was hoping for a tip or a cup of tea."
"We'd better clean up."
"You're doing nothing but resting I'll clean this
mess I want you to think about what happened. I'll
make a cup of tea and then we go through what you
remember."

James sat by the window looking out onto the Old
Steine. He had read when the hurricane hit Brighton
in October nineteen eighty-nine; it blew all the trees in
the square down. It must have been a mess, like his
apartment was now.

Matthew returned with the tea, they both sat by the
window looking at the Victorian water fountain.
"Tell me how your day started yesterday."
"After eating breakfast, I went to the hotel and meet
the contractor. We talked for about an hour. I left
and walked along the seafront."
"Did you meet anyone?"
"Yes, an old man staying at the Grand Hotel. He
told me about the night the Bomb went off, almost
killing Margaret Thatcher. He said he was standing
right where he was now when the whole building
seemed to explode out. It reminded him of the war.
People were running all over the place until the police came."
"Why was he outside the hotel yesterday?"
"He left Brighton just after that, his wife said it
wasn't a safe place anymore. They moved up the
coast to Hastings. He hadn't returned to Brighton
since. He said he just wanted to see. I remember
saying goodbye to him and after that, my mind
goes blank."

"Whatever happened took place in the afternoon.
Sit here while I clean unless you want to lie down."
"I'm fine here, I enjoy looking out of this window
and watching night arrive."
Matthew spent the next hour and a half cleaning the
place. After he had finished, he cooked a meal, and
they ate, not speaking very much.
"I think I'll hit the sack pop."
"You take the bed I'll sleep on the sofa."
"No way I'll take the sofa."
"Listen, son, you had a nasty shock you need your
bed."
"Compromise we both sleep in the bed. It is big."
"Okay, you go I'll clean up these dishes and join
you shortly."

When Matthew entered the bedroom, James was sleeping. The soft pattern of his breathing reminded Matthew of James when he was a baby. He would lie on
Matthew's naked chest and breathe so gentle he often
wondered if the boy was still alive. None of Matthew's other children did that.

James had fallen asleep quickly. He was exhausted,
his body felt heavy.

The hand clutched his tightly and led him down a long
dark passageway. They emerged into a cavernous hall
with neon lights and mirror balls high in the ceiling.
People were drinking and smoking. Several girls were
dancing in the center of the room. James was handed a
glass of liquid he wasn't sure what it was. He sipped,
and the hand dragged him over to another part of the
place. The waiters were wearing black bow ties and
white Speedo swimming trunks. As one of them

passed James, a woman grabbed the waiter's buttocks and squeezed. The waiter waited while the woman stroked and touch him. Once she had finished, the waiter moved on. A topless girl offered him some hors-d'oeuvre, her naked breasts resting on the silver salver. Everyone seemed drunk or drugged out of his or her mind.

A man in a Butler outfit shouted orders and everyone left the room. The hand dragged James to join the others. They sat down at an enormous table. A woman was making sure it was a boy girl boy girl seating arrangement. She moved several of the men who had sat down together. James couldn't find a seat and stood by the window. The people around the table were hammering their knives and forks on the table. A gigantic man with an enormous stomach picked up a carving knife and sharpened it. The double doors at the other end of the room opened. Two of the waiters pushed a cart into the room. On it was a huge dish with a dome cover. The people around the table clapped as they wheeled it towards the man with the carving knife.

The man with the knife stood behind the cart. The room became silent as everyone looked at him. He nodded his head, and the waiters removed the dome cover. The people stood up and clapped. James couldn't see what was on the dish. He pushed toward the cart and saw himself lying naked on the dish. The man with a knife was about to cut into his inner thigh.

He woke screaming, his entire body shaking. Matthew switched on the light and took his son in his arms to calm him down.

CHAPTER TWO

Party House for Sale

Matthew wiped the back of James's neck with a cold, wet flannel. He had calmed down since waking, but the horror of his dream persisted. Matthew sat on the edge of the bed and coaxed the dream out of him. James reluctantly told his dream and went into a shaking fit.

"You went to a private party."
"How do you know this was just a dream?"
"No, your memory is recalling some of what happened. The other is your imagination running away with itself."
"How do we separate fact from fiction in a dream?"
"Only take what obviously could be true. The party, yes that happened with men and women skimpily dressed, possibly. You naked on a silver salvo ready to eat, never."
"Okay let's say I went to a private party. There must have been several parties going on in Brighton."
"On a Monday night at the end of the season. I think not most people would have work the next day."
"If you're right, how would we find out where it was and who gave it."

"That part is simple."

"Since when have you become a skilled detective?"

"Since your mother brought me the complete DVD set of Midsomer Murders."

"I didn't think you like television."

"I don't, but that is a brilliant series."

"So how do we find out where the party was and who gave it?"

"Waiters."

"Waiters how will they know?"

"From what you have described it was a very elaborate party. Therefore, it is likely they had waiters in Speedo swimming trunks or not."

"That makes sense, can we do it in the morning?"

"I hope so, let's get some sleep and begin our investigation later today."

James quickly fell asleep. Matthew took more than half an hour before he dozed off. Neither of them woke when the alarm clock buzzed into life. Who switched it off, it would be one of those mysteries plaguing many families.

They woke at around nine. After a shower and break-fast, they began their search for the waiters. Matthew had collected the name of four agencies supplying waiters and waitress for private parties. The first three seemed angry, almost accusing James and Matthew of trying to steal business from them. Miss Dorsey, a forty-five-year man-eater, managed the fourth domes-tic help agency. She seemed so muddled and con-fused. Her office was at the top of a flight of stairs above a wine shop. It was one room and acted as a waiting room and office. Several men sat in chairs near the door. Matthew assumed they were waiters waiting for assignments. She invited them to sit down on two-kitchen chairs placed in front of her desk. James had to move a very large overfed tomcat that hissed and spat at him. She had heard there was a party on Monday night. Didn't know who gave it or organized it. They left the office climbing down the stairs, James brushing the overlong cat hairs off his jeans.

"At least we have a confirmation there was a party on Monday night."
"If we can believe that scatty woman."
"Not as scatty as she seems James, she was hiding something."
"What do you mean?"
"She was acting, and not very good at it. Let's get a coffee and rethink our strategy."

They sat opposite the Dorsey Professional and Domestic Agency. Matthew had picked up the local paper and was reading it as he sipped at his hot coffee. James stared at the agency, watching as several young East European men climbed the stairs. As an English born Romani, he was aware of the influx of the wandering refugees gracing the shores of Britain. Unlike some, he didn't care if they were here or not. He had hated closed borders. Therefore, refused to say they should deport illegal immigrants. He was so focused on the doorway to the agency. He didn't see the man approach.

He stood in front of James and smiled. Matthew put down his paper and smiled back. James seemed a little confused how to react. Matthew recognized him as one of the men who had been sitting inside Miss

Dorsey's office. Matthew gestured for the man to sit at the table. He hesitated and looked around.

Realizing the man's problem Matthew stood up, taking the man's elbow to guide him inside the café.
"Let us move inside, I think it may be a little more private."
Before James could protest, they had gone into the café.
"Let's have some more coffee, James could you get, I don't know your name."
"Pasha."
"Pasha I'm Matthew and this is my son James. Let us also have some more coffee."
James felt pushed out and went over to the counter. Looking back at his father, who is already talking to Pasha. When James joined them, Pasha is explaining he is from Bulgaria.
"So why did you want to speak to us," asked James.
Pasha looked at Matthew and lowered his head. James went to speak again, Matthew spoke first.
"Pasha my son is a little impatient please forgive him."
Pasha nodded and gave Matthew a mouth twitch for a smile. The waitress arrived at the table and placed three mugs of coffee in the center. She gave Pasha a side-glance, hoping neither James nor Matthew saw it. Matthew was prepared and expected some communication from her. He had noticed when they entered; she had glanced at Pasha and a strange nod of the head.

"You were upstairs at Miss Dorsey's office when we arrived?"
"Yes, I heard you ask about a party on Monday night."

"My son went to this party and met a girl. He is too shy to ask her what her name was. So, we are trying to track her down," said Matthew.

"There were a lot of girls at the party."

"Do you know who the party was for?"

"No, I and the other waiters procured were taken to this house."

James had become frustrated and asked in a forceful tone, "Do you know where the house was?"

"Yes, it is in the local paper." He pointed to the paper Matthew had been reading. Picking it up, he searched through until came to the estate agents adverts. He folded the paper in half and pointed to the house. Matthew looked at the advert and gave a low whistle when he saw the price they were asking for the house.

"We are sorry to ask you all these questions, but can you remember what happened at the party?"

"There was a lot of drinking and drugs. Some men played with the girl's others played with the boys. The waiters along with the waitresses were told to go a little further than just serve if someone wanted it. I didn't, I'm not into sex with men and they kept trying to take down my swimming pants."

"It didn't sound like you had fun at the party."

"No, but they paid well, they had to, so we keep our mouths shut if we see something."

"And did you?"

"Nothing worth blackmailing someone. I need to get going, I hope you find out what you are looking for." Pasha stood and hurried away from them. He didn't look back, disappearing from view.

"James you will not get any information from people if you attack them. You need to be a little more subtle."

"I just want to know what happened to me. Never have I have not been in control."

"I understand but I think there may be something more sinister behind you being found naked and stabbed."

"Sorry, so what's next?"

Matthew opened the paper and looked at the estate agent advert Pasha had pointed out. It was a sizeable house with six bedrooms, each with a bathroom. The kitchen was the size of most people's sitting rooms. The price tag of two million two hundred thousand pounds reflected this.

"It's a good job your mother isn't with us. If she saw this house, she would want to buy it."

Matthew handed James the paper and watched as his son read about the house. James gave all the expressions of a surprised person. The low whistle at the price brought a smile to Matthew's face.

The waitress came over to the table and picked up the coffee mugs. She hesitated before returning to the counter. Matthew followed and leaning on the counter asked, " Do you have something you wanted to say?" Turning her face expression showed anger.

"Why do you speak with the waiter?"

"My son met someone at a party and the waiter was there."

"You English men are all the same, no respect for us foreign workers. If not for us, you get no food or coffee."

"I'm sorry you feel that way. I thought we showed Pasha great respect, even though he couldn't help us."

"Whatever."

Matthew joined James at the door.

"There goes her tip."
"I would not give one, anyway. Let's see the estate
agent and James let me do the talking."

Millar and Rogers Estate Agents' principal office stood
on North Street between an American Style Pizza restaurant and jewelers. The shop front displayed various
residences for sale. They sold a few with red labels attached stating the property. Matthew opened the door
and expecting a tinkling sound to find none. The girl
sitting at the first desk inside by the door looked up at
him. She smiled her white teeth seemed to fill the pe-
tite mouth.

"Good morning, sir."

Matthew nodded and deliberately stood in front of
James. Veronica Lloyd had just celebrated her twenty-
first birthday. With the money from her family, she
had given herself a complete makeover. Only it hadn't
lasted and her hair was now back to dyed blonde
stringy style. Her faded yellow dress resembled a po-
tato sack. To make matters worse, for her, the strap on
her Divina of Paris left shoe had snapped in half.

"How can I help you?" She said as she forced a smile.
"I would like to talk to someone about this house."
Matthew showed her the advert in the paper.
"That is a lovely property, sir, our Mister Gammon is
overseeing the sale of it."

She removed her shoes. Walking barefooted across
the room to a desk at the back of the shop. Matthew
couldn't see whom she was talking to as double computer screens on the desk hid who was sitting down.

James had moved from behind his father and was looking at the various properties the Estate Agency had on its sales roster. Veronica returned to her desk, made herself comfortable before looking up at Matthew, and smiled. She saw James standing by the window and called out to him.

"Please do not remove the cards." She picked up some papers from a pile and straightened them. Then nonchalantly addresses Matthew.
"Mister Gammon will be with you shortly."
James joined Matthew in the center of the shop, awaiting Mister Gammon.

Sliding from behind the computer screens on his desk. Mike Gammon stood five foot eight inches tall and brushed a speck of dust off his trousers. He was very particular about how he looked. At thirty-one, he knew he wasn't as wealthy or prestigious as he had wanted to be. He placed the palms of his hands on the side of his head. Flattening his greased hair, wiping his hands on the back of his trousers. He made a comic move of pulling himself up straight in the hope it would make him look taller. Walking towards Matthew and James, the slight swagger in the walk reminded James of Los Angeles gang members he had seen on a documentary.

"Sorry awfully sorry to keep you waiting." He said in a fake minor public-school accent.

James smiled to himself, he knew the type immediately. Mike Gammon was a showman, a wannabe. An obscure cologne covered his unchanged underwear and lack of body washing. He would tell everyone it was very expensive and from Berlin. Everything he did

was to impress, and for some, it would work very well.
During the ninety eighties, he had watched as his older
brothers trying to get away with the less hygienic hab-
its and attitude. Their father had quickly caught on
and chastised the brothers. Mike had quickly learned
how to cover the truth from his family and friends.

"Miss Lloyd said you were interested in the house on
Brighton Road."
"Not exactly, we were wondering who gave the party
there last Monday night."
"Party, sorry, but I'm not sure I understand. Are you
saying there was a party at the house?"
"Yes."
"I do not know of a party, the house is empty. Miss
Lloyd, do you know anything about a party at the
Brighton Road house?"
Veronica stood and faced them, "No Mr. Gammon, the
house is empty."
"Sorry, gentlemen, it seems you have the wrong infor-
mation."
James went to speak but a quick look from Matthew
and he stopped.
"Sorry to bother you we must have the wrong house."
"Why are you interested?"
"The caterers were so good, so a friend told us, and we
wanted to know who they were."
"I see, well I am sorry I wasn't able to help you."
Mike stood at the glass door and watched as James and
Matthew walked down the street.

Without turning his head to look at James Matthew
said, "Don't speak or look at me just keep walking."

They reach the end of the line of shops and turned the corner. Matthew kept walking and James who had stopped ran to keep up with him.

They sat on the seafront bench looking out to sea.

"He wasn't telling the truth."

"That's what I thought, he also watched us walked down the street."

"Hence the reason I told you not to speak or look at me."

"So, what now?"

"I think we should pay a visit to this house, who knows what we might find. And if someone comes, we can say we are thinking of buying it after all it is for sale."

Matthew parked the car a little away from the house, pointing toward Brighton town center. He sat in the car and looked up the road and checked the mirrors before he climbed out. James didn't need to ask why they had parked away from the house. His father had taught all the children of the family about being cautious. The house stood back from the road, the privet hedge blocked a view from the road. The driveway twisted to the left and on each side was a newly cut lawn. They approached the solid oak front door. On each side of the door, two six-foot-high, two-foot-wide windows gave a view into the hallway. An empty bottle of Champagne stood beside the door. James peered inside through a window. The place was a mess, with plastic cups and bits of garbage over the floor. He could just see into the first room; a chair was on its side next to a table.

"Looks like they haven't cleaned the place since the party."

Matthew rang the doorbell, and they waited for someone to appear.
"Let's look around the back."

They walked to the side of the house and opened a tall
wooden gate. This led to a small courtyard with the
garage on one side of the house. At the other end, they
had erected a glass conservatory. It still housed plants,
some, thought Matthew, looked like orchids. They
had used the pots as ashtrays. The doors into the conservatory inside the house were open. They could see
into the dining room. A very long, highly polished table were worse than what they had seen in the hallway.

They continue around the glass conservatory and into a
back garden. A door at the back of the house opened
and a small, possibly East European woman appeared.
She is carrying two very large and overfilled black
plastic bags. Seeing Matthew and James, she drops
the bags.

Instinctively James ran and helped her pick them up.
One of them had opened, and the contents had spilled
onto the ground. Using a paper plate, James tried to
scoop the rubbish back into the bag. The woman
stooping to help kept looking at Matthew. She neither
smiled nor frowned, just stared at him.

Matthew was aware of her looking at him. She was a
small woman, about fifty years old. Her hair, although
long, pulled back and wrapped into a bun. She didn't
wear makeup, except for a very faint touch of red lipstick on her small thin lips.

Once the rubbish was inside the bag, she tied it and
tried to drag it over to a large bin at the side of the

house. James took the bags off her and carried them to the bin. He placed one inside and the other on top, as the bin was now full.

She stood watching before turning towards Matthew. Straightening her dress and pushing back a non-exist- ence strand of hair off her face, she walked toward Matthew.

"Hello, how may I help you?" She said in a deep East European accent.

"We came to see the house my son said he had been here and said it was an exquisite house."

"It was until those animals had a party."

"Party?"

"Yes, the other night and now I have to clean up the mess."

"I'm sorry to hear that. You would think the own- ers would have more sense than to make a mess of the house while they are trying to sell it."

"It wasn't the owners." She walked back into the house, leaving the door open. Matthew and James followed her into the kitchen.

"You and your son like a cup of tea?"

"That would be very nice."

"I like you. You have very good manners for a rich English man."

Matthew didn't reply and watched as she prepared a pot of tea.

"I am Lenora Fedorov from Russia, I was the own- er's housekeeper until they left. Now I just keep the place clean until someone buys the place."

"It's a pleasure to meet you, Lenora, I'm Matthew, and this is my son James."

James stood leaning against a wall, trying to see if he could remember entering the kitchen the night of the party.

"I am not happy having to clean up this mess, bottles, cigarette end. White powder and used condoms everywhere."

"Didn't they pay you to clean up?"

"Oh, he gave me twenty pounds, that's all a miserly twenty pounds."

Matthew produces a twenty-pound note out of his pocket and hands it to Lenora. She takes it and pushes it into her pocket. Matthew clears a chair in the kitchen of rubbish and sits Lenora on it. He nods to James to continue making the tea. Matthew pulled one of the other chairs closer to Lenora and sat down facing her.

"If it wasn't the owners, whose party was it?"

"Those men who came here with him said at first they were thinking of buying the place. Then one of them said his son would like to have a party here. They gave Mike five hundred pounds. He gave me twenty, cheap bastard."

"Do you know who the men were?"

"Oh yes I know them, it was the rich man and his son from Hove. The one who owns all those restaurants and supermarkets. With him was the real nasty man who sold drugs. I know he sells them, I saw him once selling. When I worked in the Lanes in a little café, he would come and sell his dirty stuff to the school kids."

"They came here and met someone they gave him five hundred pounds too."

"Did I not just say that, and I have to clean the place up."

"Do you know the names of these men?"

"Yes, I know their names."

"Could you tell us?"

"You want to know who they were, why didn't you say. The rich man is Peterson-Jones hyphenated, he says. What does that mean, I ask myself?"

"The other men, who were they?"

"The nasty man was Gordon Tuff, I heard him introduce himself to the cheap bastard, Mike Gammon."

"Why are you only cleaning the place now, the party was two days ago?"

"Because I have more important work to do first in other houses. They pay me good, not a lousy twenty pounds. I go tell the owners about Mr. Gammon."

"Don't do that Lenora, I will talk to Mike and make him pay you properly."

"You do that for me?"

"Yes."

"You are so kind can I help you now."

"Could we look over the house now we are here?"

"Sure, no problem, it is in a mess but you know that."

"We will start at the top and work down."

"I make a fresh pot of tea for us when you come back."

Matthew and James left the kitchen and standing in the hallway looking up the stairs.

"What does she mean she'll make a fresh pot we haven't any tea yet?"

"Just an expression."

James ran up the stairs two at a time. He stopped a few steps from the top. His heart pounding, he had a flash of being there before. Each step had a candle on it in a tall glass vase. He was holding on to the belt of a small fat man who was pulling him up the stairs. A girl was behind him pushing him, her hands dug into his buttocks.

"Problem?"

"No, I just had a vision from the other night. If Gordon Tuff is a short fat man, then he was who I was with."

They looked into each room, James standing in the doorway before venturing deeper into the room. After each room, he shook his head. Matthew entered the main bathroom, it was as Lenora said a mess. Cigarette ends, and other burnt objects were all over the room. The bathtub had used condoms and the wrapper they came in floating on a few inches of water. Someone had written in brown lipstick on the mirror, "Karen Gooding is a good fuck. Signed Brighton and Hove football team."

James had not entered and stood in the doorway. He felt nausea rise inside, something bad had happened in this room and he didn't want to remember. Matthew watched him and knew this could be an important breakthrough to his memory.

"Close your eyes. Good, now I will lead you into the bathroom. When I tell you, open your eyes and let the images come to you. It may be painful, but I think this room has a lot to do with what happened to you."

James closed his eyes, for as long as he could remember he trusted his father. The man had always been there for him and never led him into danger. Matthew took him into the center of the room. He stood behind his son and placed his hands on the boy's shoulders.

"Ready?"

James nodded his head and tried to relax.

"Open your eyes."

James stood for a few minutes before opening them. He looked around the room, nothing came into his mind. He shook his head and then sat down on the closed toilet lid. Suddenly he was in the room, several people were also in the room with him. A man with greasy hair and terrible acne was leaning over the countertop sniffing a white powder through a rolled-up five-pound note. An older man was kissing and playing with a very drunk girl against the window. Her Skirt was pulled up and her panties around her ankles. James's vision seemed blurred, and he felt very drunk. He wanted to vomit. He lifted the toilet seat and kneeling on all fours vomited into the bowl. The door of the bathroom opened, and another couple entered. The man who was snorting cocaine straddled James so James couldn't stand up. The man pushed the girl, so she was sitting on James's back. At first, James was sure what was happening, then he realized the girl was lying on his back, her legs in the air held by the man who was straddling him. The man was raping her. She looked about twelve years old. Each time the man pushed into her, James vomited.

James rushed from the room and gasping for air held onto the stair banister rail. Matthew had followed and held his son.

"Try to calm yourself, don't talk, just breathe and
relax. You can tell me what you saw once you
have settled."
"I need to get out of this place."
"Let's go then."

When they arrived in the kitchen Lenora was scrub-
bing the floor. Matthew thanked her and they left via
the front door so as not to cross over her washed floor.

Once outside James took deep breaths and slowly relaxed. They walked to the car and Matthew helped
him into the car. A car had parked a little up the street.
It hadn't been there when they arrived. Sitting in the
car, Matthew stared at the other car. It looked as
though it was empty, but when they came out of the
driveway, he saw someone slip down in the driver's
seat. As they drove slowly away from the curb Matthew sees a man's head pop up in the rear-view mirror.
He drives cautiously, allowing the driver of the other
car to catch up with them.

James realizes what his father is doing and position
himself to get a look at the other driver. They drive
around and around a roundabout until they are level
with the other car. Matthew suddenly turns up a one-
way street, the wrong way. The other driver follows.
Matthew quickly U-turns and returns to the roundabout. The other driver isn't as fortunate as they were
facing the wrong way with several cars trying to pass
him.

"Did you get a look at the driver?"
"Yes, but I have never seen him before."
"So, what happened in the bathroom?"

"I was in there vomiting people were having sex and snorting cocaine. Then this man arrived with this pubescent girl and raped her."

"Sorry to put you through that, I think from now on more of what happened will return. You may not like what you remember, but I believe it's always best to get it out. Nothing worse than a festering memory."

"At least this time you were with me."

"I think we should see Mike Gammon again, that estate agent has some explaining to do."

Matthew parked the car close to James's rented flat. He checked the street to see if anyone followed them. After circling, he reversed in between two vans. They walked to the estate agents, James looking cautiously around. He waited outside while his father entered the shop. Veronica Lloyd stood just inside and when she saw Matthew, she became tense. After a few words, she relaxed and then gave Matthew directions. When Matthew shook her hand, she became a little giggly and became bashful.

"He has gone for lunch Veronica has just told me where he normally eats. We'll take our lunch with Mr. Gammon."

They walked up the road and into the Lanes, passing the antique stores and tourists traps. Mike was sitting outside a small café eating his lunch. James took the chair to his left and Matthew to the right and sat down at his table.

"Mr. Gammon, how nice of you to invite us to have lunch with you," said Matthew, catching the attention of a waitress.

"I didn't I was just leaving."

"I think you should stay. We don't want the owners of the Brighton Road house to hear about your side line. Now, do we?"

Mike sat back in his chair as he looked at Matthew, then James. He knew from their expression they meant business so he would have to play along with them. The waitress came over and they ordered lunch and a pot of tea for three.

"What do you want to know?"

"Mike, I can call you Mike, I hope so. My son and I would like to know everything about the party. From the beginning."

"I think you know some of it."

"Maybe but better to tell us than the police. If you cooperate with us, then we can make sure no one else finds out about it."

"Okay, Hector Peterson-Jones wanted to give a party for his son. He and a guy called Gordon Tuff came to see the house saying they were thinking of buying it. After I had shown them over the place Gordon said he would like to rent the place. He offered me five hundred pounds rental fee in cash. Can you imagine no one needed to know?"

"You took the offer," said James.

"Damn right I did, and when they said I could go to the party, it was the icing on the cake as they say."

"What was the party like?" asked Matthew.

"Wild even for Brighton. Drink, drugs, and every kind of sex you could think of."

"Who organized the party?"

Mike looked at James before he answered. A slight grin appeared on his face.

"Gordon and his girl, you know that already as you were there with them. Plastered or stoned out of your head, but you were there."

"Who was the girl?"

"Don't know her name but someone called her the fix-it girl. Evidently, she fixed things for people. Whatever they want, she would get for them. She was all over you I thought Gordon would punch you but I think he could see it was her not you. He pulled you apart when she took your pants down. Everyone thought you would have sex with her, a demonstration. Only Gordon stopped it."

Matthew looked at his son and raised his eyebrows. James gave a nervous cough and looked up the lane.

"Gordon just kept giving you drinks and moved you around the house. I thought it was strange the way he did it. He was making sure everyone at the party saw you."

"Then what happened?"

"They left, leaving you behind in the hands a of waiter. I had just met this girl called Charlotte who was willing. As they were leaving Gordon spoke to a waiter gave him something and pushed you into the arms of this waiter."

"Do you know which waiter it was?"

"No, they all look alike and I'm not into men, so I don't notice other guys."

"Nor am I," said James indignantly.

"Didn't say you were, as I'm going upstairs another waiter comes over and says he knows where you live and would take you home. They place you on a sofa in the hall's corner and continue serving drinks to the other guests. When I come down after my fun with sweet Charlotte you had gone."

"Is there anything else we should know?"

"Don't think so."

"That leaves only one thing then."

"What's that?"

"Mike, what would the owner of the house say if he found out you have rented the place out for a party. Not asking their permission or given any of the rental fees."

"Are you going to tell them?"

"We are not but your cleaner might, you pissed her off with the twenty pounds you gave her. Especially as she knows you received five hundred."

"How does she know that?"

"Next time you do business I suggest you make sure no one is around to listen."

"Shit."

"It's very easy to sort out. When we left her, she was working very hard cleaning up the mess. I think you should give her one hundred and fifty pounds. It's more than she would expect and she would be your best friend."

Mike sat thinking about it and sipped on his cup of tea James had just poured for him.

"I'll see her, I need the place clean for tomorrow as I am showing it to a buyer."

"If you think of anything else about the party, phone us." Matthew handed him a business card.

Mike took it and placed it in his back pocket.

They watched as he walked up the lane, the swagger still in his step.

"What do you think?"

"He wasn't telling us everything, but he will and soon I think."

They finished the tea, and Matthew paid the waitress.

"Let's walk along the seafront, the journey you took, and seeing what you remember."

As they walked the King's Road, Matthew didn't speak but looked around at the buildings on one side, the sea and stony beach on the other. He always loved the seaside but never understood why. As a child he didn't go to the coast and as an adult had only been once before. The silence between him and his son felt comfortable. He enjoyed walking and not talking, just being together and soaking in the scenery and atmosphere. Passing the entrance to the pier tempted him to run into it. Leaving James standing wondering what he was up to. He would have if they had been on holiday or just a day visit. They had a mission and he must keep focused on it. Looking at James and seeing he was deep in thought. He didn't ask a question he felt he needed to ask.

James stopped and looked up at the Grand Hotel. He shook his head and continued to walk.

"Remembered something?"

"Sort of, when I passed the Grand, an old man was standing looking up at it. He suddenly started telling me about the night they tried to assassinate Margaret Thatcher. How he had rushed from his home to see the damage."

"To some people, events like that have an incredible effect on them. He possibly was revisiting the air raids of the Second World War."

James nods and then looked over the railing and down on to the café area below. Even though this was out of season people were drinking coffee. Maybe someone from the party might recognize him and talk to him.

He didn't think he would remember anyone from that night.

They continued and stopped at the War Memorial for those who fell in South Africa at the entrance to Regency Square.

"They were some punks sitting at the foot of the monument. They were making a joke because it said a memorial to the Boar War. They thought it was boring and therefore came out with these jokes about the war being boring."

"Schools need to educate the young about our history."

"I don't think these guys ever went to school. Anyway, an old man came by and he gave them hell for sitting on the steps."

"At least we know you got this far."

"I continued and I think I turned off somewhere."

"Let's keep going, it may come back to you."

As they approach Montpelier Road, James slowed down and suddenly stopped. He pointed up Montpelier Road. They walked along the road, Matthew looking at the houses converted into flats and hotels lining the street. At Western Street, James turned right again something was drawing him this way. He had a strange feeling something would appear somewhere along this street. He walked faster and faster until he ran. Once outside a line of shops he stopped. His father hadn't followed at a fast pace. He walked at the pace they had been going until he reached James. He could see James was suddenly very excited, something had awakened in him. Hopefully, a memory of what happened.

They ambled, James looking into each shop before moving onto the next. At the Music Room shop, he smiled and leaned against the glass window. The banging on the window brought him back to reality. Matthew knew he would have to be patient before James related what he had remembered.

"Ready to tell me?"

"I remember being here and this girl came out of the store. She was the girl you looked at, but not knowing why. Anyway, she followed me, so I stopped. She told me she was looking for a place to have a party. I said I didn't know anywhere. Then she suggested we have a coffee."

"And you being the gentleman I brought you up to be, then you took her for a coffee."

"You got it in one. She asked me what I was doing in Brighton. I remember I was being careful so only told her I was overseeing the conversion of a hotel. She asked if we had already started the work. I said no. She stood up and asked me to take her there."

"So, you took her to the hotel?"

"On the way she called someone and asked me the address of the hotel. When I gave it, she seemed to freeze for a second. Then we continued to the hotel. A man was waiting outside, he was greasy and fat, I felt very uncomfortable being with him."

"Do you think it could have been this character Gordon Tuff we have been told about?"

"I don't remember his name. It was just after we had gone inside, I felt strange. Everything was different with loud voices, colors, and even how people looked."

"Do you think she slipped something in your coffee?"

"She could have, I left to go to the bathroom before I finished my coffee. On returning to the table she said Drink up, let's look at your hotel. So, I did, and now I think about the coffee suddenly tasted bitter."

"When we purchased the hotel, the former owner was so glad to get rid of the property. I was a little suspicious. You said there had been squatters, who are they and are they still there?"

"Do you think this could have something to do with the hotel?"

"Keep an open mind. I think you will remember a lot more now you have a starting point to fix things too."

"I'm not sure I want to."

"Maybe not but a least we know a little more. So now we know why you went with them, you really didn't have a choice. I also think we need to find this girl, she is the key to it all at present."

"Should we look at the hotel?"

"Not yet, I think I need whatever is happening there to continue unabated. Then we might catch them at it."

"What do we do next?"

"We need to find the waiters who were at the party. One of them knows who you went off with."

CHAPTER THREE

Waiters and Waitresses

Matthew had taken a nap after returning to the flat. Extensive experience had taught him if he would be up late into the night, then he needed to rest during the afternoon. After an augmentative time trying to work out whom they should search for first. They compromised and said 'the fix-it girl' was more important than the waiters. They began by going to the pubs frequented by the young wan-a-be hip crowd. James had remarked it was a mistake to even try those places. As this girl wasn't the type to go to such common pubs. The more exclusive wine bars and public houses. Although shed a little light on the people whom she would associate with didn't bear fruit.

One of the very upmarket wine bars with an overweight bouncer on the door. Proved to be the end of their search for her. James asked the barman if he had heard of this girl. The bouncer appeared and escorted them out of the place. He grunts in some almost undistinguishable language, "Don't come back."

Disheartened and feeling cold from the sea breeze as they walked along North Street. They built most of the shops and restaurants without an alleyway beside them. The Poochi Inn restaurant had an alleyway running up its left side. James and Matthew walked past, both looking down the alleyway. James stepped back and looked again at the waiter Pasha was leaning against the wall smoking a cigarette. Pasha walked down the alleyway and smiled at James.

"Hello again."
"Hello, Pasha, we have been looking for you. We need to ask you some more questions. I'm sorry, but it is important."
"I understand, but I am working now."
"Can we meet you after you have finished work?"
"Sure, I'll meet you by the bandstand on the promenade. At about one when I finish here. Is that okay?"

James nodded and held out his hand. Pasha shook it, and the smile on his face broadened.

"Pasha, we will see you around one o'clock."

Matthew was silent as they continued to walk along the road. He stopped at an Indian restaurant, saying he was hungry.

"Why didn't you say I'm starving too but thought you weren't hungry."

They ate and then sat drinking coffee, knowing it would keep them both awake.

"I thought you did well talking to Pasha, he is a slippy customer. I don't trust him, I'm not sure who's side he is on."
"I think we should try to find the other waiters and I thought he might know who they were."

At twelve forty-five, they sat on the promenade bench
with its glass cover on the back and sides. The waves
lashed the stones on the beach, sounding like a slow
heartbeat. Matthew listens to the rhythm, feeling his
body relax. James relives the nightmare of lying on
the beach unable to move and speak. Impatience gets
the better of him and he keeps looking at his watch.
At one fifteen, he sighs.

"He is not coming."

"He will."

James wants to pace about, his impatience getting the
better of him. Walking towards them is a man
hunched over with a hood covering his head and face.
As he nears them, he looks around before slipping into
the seat next to Matthew. Pasha removes the hood.
The smile he gave James earlier returning to his face.
James sits next to his father so they are both facing Pasha.

"You think I not come and see you, correct?"

"Not really, I believed you would," said Matthew,
hoping James wouldn't say anything.

"Please understand I have to be very careful. I am
a married man with a baby girl. The people you are
seeking are very dangerous."

"We understand and only want to find out who the
girl was or the names of the other waiters so we can
ask them."

"I know who the girl is by sight, but I don't know
her name. She is a girl who would never talk to me
unless she wanted a drink."

"Do you know where she might hang out?"

"No, I only see her at very rich people's parties

when I work at them. She never goes to the restaurants I work at."

He gives a list of the other waiter's names and James
writes them down in his little notebook.
"I must go now my wife will worry if I am too late.
Be careful they are terrible men."
"Where will we find the other waiters?"
"They all meet at Cristo's near the station, it is the
only place open all night. Goodbye and good
luck."
They watch him run across the road and up a side
street. Both lost in thought from what he had said.

Cristo's was a very seedy run-down café. The smell of
fried food and dirty oil permeates the air. Three other
customers, each with empty cups. They didn't look
homeless, only people with a home not worth going to.
The condensation is running down the café window.
A woman sitting next to it had written on the window:
"bollocks to you."

Matthew ordered two teas in large mugs. No one
looked up or questioned why they are there. They sat
facing the door to watch who came in or left. Several
men entered, nodded to the man behind the counter.
They cross the café and entered a stairway leading to
the floor above. Matthew picks up his mugs of tea and
heads for the stairway. The man behind the counter
calls to him.
"Hey, that's out of bounds to you."
Matthew returns to the table when the door opened and
several more men enter. One of them smiles at James
and shakes his hand.
"Hi, again my name is Filippo, you remember me?"

James remembers seeing the man's name on Pasha's
list of waiters.

"You were at the party?"

"Se, sorry, yes. You enjoy the party I hope."

"It was okay."

"Sorry I interrupt you and your daddy."

"How do you know he is my daddy?"

"James, he thinks I'm your sugar daddy."

"What? Filippo this is not my sugar daddy but my
actual father."

"Really, he is a very handsome man."

Matthew blushed and asks Filippo to sit down with
them.

"Sorry did I embarrass you?"

"It's okay, so you were at the party with my son?"

"I worked your son he partied very much."

"So, I've heard, did you see who took him home?"

"No, he was the fix-it girl and Mr. Tuff for part of
the night, then they left."

"You know the fix-it girl?"

"I know who she is but not her name, no one knows
her name. Is that who you are looking for?"

"Yes, and who took my son home?"

"You come upstairs with me and we ask the other
waiters."

They walk towards the stairway. The man behind the
counter looks at them.

"It's okay, they are my friends."

He nods and they follow Filippo upstairs. Entering a
room filled with tables and chairs, several groups of
men are around the room. To the one side, a counter
like the one downstairs has a beautiful teenage girl
working behind it. Filippo showed them to a table in
the far corner. Four other men sit talking in inaudible

voices. They look up as Filippo approaches, and it surprised them to see Matthew and James with him.

Matthew catches the reaction of one of the waiter's at seeing James. When Filippo introduces them to each waiter but only one seems reluctant. His name is Romeo, and he doesn't look them in the eye when he shakes their hand.

"They need our help. James would like to know who took him home after the party, and they also want to find the fix-it girl."

The reaction from them was what Matthew had expected. He knew it was hard to get others to talk.

"I'm thirsty, do they serve beer in here?"

"Yes, but in large tea mugs, because they don't have a license to sell it."

"Okay, who would like a beer then."

The waiter's faces changed, and they all order a beer. Filippo and James went over to the counter, returning with large blue and black mugs full of beer. After the second beer, the waiters seemed to have relaxed a little, and each talked about where they came from and how long they had been in Britain.

"You do not get as drunk tonight as you did at the party," said Alfredo, a small fat man from Spain.

"Was I very drunk?"

"Very drunk and the girl she kept trying to take your clothes off. Only the man stopped her," laughed Rene, spilling beer on his white shirt.

"I don't remember."

"That is because they kept putting drugs in your drink. They did it with everyone."

Matthew looked at the waiters. Only Romeo hadn't joined in the conversation. He was the one they needed to talk to privately.

"Gentlemen who is this fix-it girl who wanted to strip my son naked."

"She is like the ghost in our minds, she is illusive. We see her at all the rich parties, but I heard no one call her by her name."

"She is always with Mr. Tuff."

"That is because she is his girlfriend."

"Or the wife."

The waiters all laugh.

"She is not his wife."

"True, she does not act like a wife, so free and always trying to take men's clothes off."

"Did any of you see who took my son home?"

They shook their heads, either they did and didn't want to say, or they genuinely didn't see.

"That party was a bad one, everyone tried to touch you. They grabbed at you as though you were just a slave."

"We were to most of them, they the rich people think we are just scum."

"One lady she tried to grab my cock, but I was wearing a crouch box. She was so angry she throws her drink at me. I moved, and it went all over the floor."

"Crouch box?"

"I think he means a cricket box, protection and support for the genitals dad."

"That was nothing this man dragged me into the toilet and tried to make me suck him."

"Did you?"

"No."

Matthew looked at James until he felt it was time for them to leave.

"Gentlemen it has been a pleasure meeting you I think my son and I need some sleep now."

The chilly night air with the smell of the sea hit them as they left the café. James turned to walk towards his flat. Matthew guided him the other way and into an alleyway.

"We need to wait one of those waiters knows a lot more. He is scared to talk in front of his friends."

"Really which one?"

"You didn't notice?"

James shook his head, "I was wondering what happened to me. The talk of those waiters made me wonder if they raped me."

"You'd know if they raped you, but you better get a check-up, anyway."

Sitting on the plastic dustbins in the alleyway, they waited and watched. Each time they heard the café door open, Matthew peered around the corner of the building and looked to see who was leaving. James fell asleep, waking himself each time his head hits the wall behind him.

"Now you realize why I took a nap this afternoon." They heard the café door open again and Matthew looked to see the four waiters they had been talking to leaving together. He beckons James to join him. The four waiters saunter down the road, unaware of Matthew and James following them.

Alfredo and Filippo take a side road, waving goodbye to their friends.

Rene hugs Romeo and opens the door to a house converted into bed-sits. Matthew suddenly walks faster. He knows Romeo will want to get home quickly after leaving his friends. Realizing James and Matthew were following him and runs down the street. At a cross street, he turns left. James sprints down the alleyway while Matthew continues to follow Romeo.

Romeo looked behind him, seeing Matthew following. He ran into James as he stepped out of an alleyway.
    "Please don't hurt me," he begs.
Matthew catches up, he is out of breath and stands trying to control himself by taking deep lengthy breaths.
    "Romeo, we don't want to hurt you but we know you remember a lot more and can help us solve the problem."
    "I know nothing."
    "Two days ago they found a man on the beach naked."
    "Yes, I heard."
    "It was my son James and we need to find out who did that to him. It was after the party."
    "You were the naked man on the beach?"
    "Yes, Romeo, if you know something please talk to us."
Romeo stood looking at them, "no bull, you were the man on the beach?"
    "Yes, and unlike the others I didn't die."
    "Come, follow me."

Romeo's bed-sit would have, at one time, made up slum living. It was cold and damp, the old-fashioned gas fire even though he had put it on full burn gave very little heat. He made them a cup of instant coffee using condensed milk out of a tin. The room was sparse with furniture and so Romeo sat on the edge of his bed while they occupied the two chairs at the cheap wooden table. He sipped his coffee before looking at them.

"Please understand not that I don't want to help you, I am scared. I am illegal and every time I see a white man, I think he is from immigration. They come to take me away and send me back to my country."

James looked puzzled with a name like Romeo he had expected the man to be Italian.

"We will tell no one, I promise."

"I have been anxious since that night so many things happened at that party I didn't like."

"You mean the drugs and sex."

"No, I can handle those things. It was what people were doing and saying."

"Tell us from the start what you can remember."

He sipped his coffee and then bit on his lower lip. Matthew knew he would need to be very patient with this man if he would get the complete story.

"My son and I will not interrupt you, we may have a few questions afterward."

"The party started like any other, people arriving getting drinks and food. After about an hour more people arrived including Mr. Tuff and the girl. She was holding on to your arm and kissing your cheek. You were very drunk. I saw you during the evening and they kept giving you drinks. Then they left and one of the security men took you to a room, I think."

He sipped his coffee again, staring into the gas fire.

"When I had a break, I went to the room where we had put our coats and bags. Alfredo was with me

opening the door I saw Mr. Peterson-Jones and another man talking. They were in the dark so when
the door opens it illuminated the room. You were
lying on the floor and they saw you. We closed the
door saying sorry and went back to serving people.
Alfredo went off with some man, so I was left to
work our two rooms alone."

He stood up and made himself another coffee. As he
sat down, he shuddered and then looked at them both.
"A little later I was outside collecting glasses when
I hear the man who had been with Mr. Peterson-
Jones. He was telling someone to dump the body.
I assumed it was you."
"Hence the reason it shocked you to see my son to-
night."
"Yes. After the party was over and we were clean-
ing up the glasses and things I saw two of the secu-
rity men carrying a tablecloth out to a car. It
looked like it had something or someone inside it."
"Do you know who the other man was?"
"No, I have never seen him before."
"What did the men who took the tablecloth out look
like, can you describe them?"
"Filippo is always taking pictures, and he took one
of us before the party. In the background, you can
see the two security men talking."
He opened a wooden cigar box on the bedside table
and took out a photograph. He handed it to Matthew
without looking at it.

The picture was of the five waiters smiling and two
other men standing in the background. Matthew examined the picture and smiled to himself. He handed
James the picture.

"Can we get a copy of this picture?"

"I will ask Filippo for another copy, please take mine. If it helps, I would be happy."

"It helps."

"The obese security man was the one who brought the drugs to the party. I know he works for the man whose party it was."

"You didn't see who took my son?"

"No."

"When you heard about the body on the beach, did you think it was someone who went to the party?"

"Not at first, then someone told me it was a guest at the party."

"Is that the reason it scared you when you saw my son in the café?"

"Yes, when you are a waiter, you see lots of things and learn to keep your mouth shut tight."

"Because you thought you had seen him being carried out in the tablecloth?"

Romeo nodded and emptied the last of his coffee.

"You look exhausted, we will leave you now and let you get some sleep."

"Thank you, I am sorry I cannot help more."

"You have given us a lot and we will always be grateful. If we can ever do anything for you, let us know."

Out on the street, James could hardly contain himself. They hurried away from Romeo's flat. Matthew stopped around the corner and peered back to see if anyone entered the place. After a few minutes, he and James returned to their flat.

Once inside and lying in bed, Matthew spoke, "The name of the security company in the photo is the same as the one we used to remove the squatters."
"It's the same and I'm not sure they did an expert job."
"Why do you say that?"
"Tomorrow, sorry later today I want to go around to the hotel, I think the squatters are back."
"Have we paid them yet?"
"No, and they may not get paid until the squatters are out."
"Let's get some sleep and go over what we found out in the morning. When you get to my age, you need your sleep."

The black clouds of the storm rolled in off the sea. It didn't rain until eight-thirty in the morning. By the time James and his father had woken, the rain was beating hard against the already soaked ground. They ran to the little café still serving breakfast. When they ordered eggs and bacon the waitress looked at the clock on the wall. It was five minutes to eleven, and breakfast stopped being served at eleven. She took the order, muttering something about idle rich and breakfast at all times. Neither James nor Matthew could make sense of what she had said.

"One day dad I will live in a country where it's sunny all the time."
"You could join your sister in California."
"If she is still living there, wasn't she moving somewhere."
"From Kansas to California and she said it was her last move."

They ate breakfast and thanked the waitress. She gave them her blank look as though words meant nothing to her. They left the café forty-minutes later and walked towards the hotel. The rain had eased a little and was now an irritating drizzle. On this dull, miserable day, the place looked dull and horrific. They had boarded all the lower windows, the only way to enter the building was through the front. James pushed open the door for the second time in a week. It wasn't locked. They stood in the atrium and listened to the sound of the building. Someone was running somewhere above them. The timpani of dripping water seemed to be everywhere. They climbed the stairs to the third floor and stopped to listen. Just the sound of water torturing the interior of the building echoed around the place. Whoever had been in when they arrived had hidden themselves. Walking the empty corridor of the third floor, Matthew opened several of the doors and looked into the empty rooms. They descended to the floor below and did the same again it yields nothing.

On the first floor, they checked each room. Several had boxes and a few had bags inside. Someone was using the place. There were four more doors to open and James felt they could skip them. Matthew didn't and opened the door at the end of the corridor.

The young twelve-year-old girl sat naked on the dirty mattress. She was bruised and several cuts on her body were bleeding. The man stood in the bathroom doorway, his brown trousers undone. Sexual intercourse had just taken place. The girl sobbed softly, looking scared as Matthew stared at her.

The speed his father took to cross the room and attack the man shocked James. He called the police on his mobile, telling them where they were and which room they were in. Matthew had forced the man to the floor and was beating him, the punches pounding the man's face and chest. It took James a lot of effort to remove his father from on top of the man. Matthew stood beside the man. James found a dirty towel in the bathroom and gave it to the girl to cover herself with. She continued to sob softly, looking with her big blue eyes at the men in the room.

The man tried to stand up as the heel of Matthew's right foot swung backward and into the man's groin. The squeal from the man sounded like a pig being led to slaughter. When the police arrived, James took charge and explained what they found. He said nothing about his father attacking the man. Only they had to pull the man off the girl and restrain him. The ambulance men took the girl away with a policewoman holding her little hand.

The man became belligerent and police had to use force to handcuff him and take him out of the hotel. Matthew gave a statement and then sat on the top step waiting for James to give his.

"I think your father is very upset about what you found," said the police officer taking the statements.
"Yes, it seems to make him furious. Child abuse has always been one of his hates."
"Did you know the place was being used for such practices?"

"No, and we paid a security company to clear the
place and keep it empty."

"They didn't do their job."

"Luckily we start the conversion next week."

The police officer left and James sat next to his father
on the top step.

"Dad, what happened in there, I thought you would
kill the man."

"I wanted to."

"Why?"

"Something is best left unsaid."

"Stop treating me like a child, I want to know
why," said James, raising his voice.

"You won't like the truth."

"Let me be the judge of that. All our lives you
have protected us from sharing what you feel inside. Maybe if you explained it wouldn't be so
painful anymore."

Matthew sat silently on the step. He always knew that
this day would come. He never expected it to with
James and prayed he would never have to tell any of
his children.

He looked at James and knew he would have to speak
up this time. This his seventh child would not be
fobbed off with lies.

James lowered his head. The words choked in his
throat as he said to them, "Sorry dad, I didn't mean
to pry."

Those few words hit Matthew in the heart. He had
brought up all his children to show respect. Maybe he
needed to do the same. The tears formed and ran
down his face, dripping on his already wet coat.

"It's hard to talk about something you have always felt ashamed of. Even though you know you weren't to blame."
He took a deep breath and spoke slowly, looking straight ahead.
"My father, your grandfather, wasn't a rotten man. Why he did what he did only he will ever know. Times were very hard, and we Romany's found it hard to get work. He took his anger out on me. At first, it was the constant beatings. Like that girl, they left my body bruised and bleeding most of the time."
Matthew swallowed, holding back his tears. His voice cracked, and he spoke in a strangely unfamiliar voice.
"Then on the day when I was with him, this man said, 'what a cute little boy'. Dad was drunk and when the man offered him money for me, he took it. My life became hell, I was ten years old, and these men used me. Dad took the money and spent it on the family, no that is not true he spent it mostly on women and drink. I became the bread-winner and if I objected, he beat me. That was the reason I left home at sixteen, I couldn't take it any-more. And when I saw that girl, the memories came back."
They sat, each with his thought. For the first time James understood his father. He placed an arm around him and hugged him.
"Now I understand why you never hit us. All the other kids at school thought you were the best dad in the world because you never spanked us."
"No, child needs smacking if the parent from the start shows the child how to behave, it's unneces-sary."

"Thanks for telling me."

"I'm not angry at my father, not now. I hated him for a very long time until your mother pointed out that if he hadn't used me, the family would have starved and been homeless."

"That's very little compensation for what you had to endure."

"All this excitement has made me hungry, let's get some lunch."

"I'll phone that security firm and tell them we will not be paying their bill."

"Don't do that, not yet anyway. I think that firm knows something with what was going on and what happened to you."

James was in the bathroom. He needed time to control his anger. His grandfather had been so gentle and kind to him as he grew up. All the time his father had suffered at the man's greed. It was a strange age growing up in Birmingham after the Second World War. He had never suffered the prejudice his family had endured. There was hatred and someone had to be the scapegoat. The Romany gypsies had no real defense and took the brunt of the anguish. His grandfather must have carried the guilt, hence his love and kindness to the grandchildren.

James's mobile rang in the other room. Matthew looked at it for a few seconds, then flipped it open.

"Hello, Mr. Pidgley," said a voice pronouncing each syllable of the name in a Scottish accent, "Kenneth Muir of ING Securities here. I heard we had a minor problem at the hotel. Those squatters must have returned."

"Or never left," said Matthew softly.

"Sorry I did not hear that."

"I said you're probably right."

"Aye, I think so. We should meet and go over the place again to see how they got in. Would four o'clock today suit you?"

"Yes, my son and I will meet you at the hotel at four."

Matthew closed the phone before Kenneth Muir could reply.

James entered from the bathroom wearing a bath towel. His wet black hair glistening, stressing his hazel colored eyes.

"Who was that?"

"Kenneth Muir."

"What did he want besides not being paid?"

"We are meeting him at the hotel at four today. He wants to find out how the squatters re-entered the hotel."

"As if he didn't already know."

"I don't want you to antagonize him. He will know who the fix-it girl is and if he was at the party, he may know what happened to you."

"I wish I could remember who I saw."

"Like my past it sometimes good we don't remember everything."

"At least we have the picture Romeo gave us. Maybe Kenneth will tell us who the ING security guards were."

"Or he will clam up."

"He likes to be called Kenny and has a quick temper."

Matthew had insisted on standing facing the sea and taking deep breaths before they approached the old hotel. Kenny Muir was standing outside the hotel. It was the first time Matthew had seen the man. As he always said first impressions show if a person has something to hide. Some men should never wear suits, and Kenny was one of those men. His over testosterone body looked awkward in the off the peg suit. He must have spent hours at the gym and on body enhancing powders to get the muscles. The seams of the suit on his upper arms and thighs stretched to almost breaking point. His head was round, the hair closely cropped at the side and short and spiky on top. As a child, Matthew had fought not to have the common short back and sides haircut that was so popular in the nineteen fifties. Today the young and trendy middleaged embraced the fashion.

As they approach Kenny turned and seeing them gave a broad false smile. Another of Matthew's beliefs was never to trust a man who smiles when you first meet him. The person would con you or had some very important information to hide from you. Over the years he had found estate agents and used car salesmen perfected this approach when meeting people. They thought it made them look friendly and open. He supposed to the great ignorant public it did.

"James, and this must be your father?" Kenny held out his hand to shake Matthews. James took the hand first and squeezed it as he shook it.
It surprised Matthew after he had shaken the man's hand. He had expected a firm handshake, so a little surprised by the effeminate, weak hand placed in his.
"It's not a delightful day today. So Mr. Pidgley senior, what do you think of Brighton?"
"Call me Matthew, I have always liked Brighton, maybe not some people who live here."

"Aren't most places like that?"

"Yes, but in Brighton, it conjures up devious Bankers and Murderers."

"You've been reading too many crime thrillers."

"Maybe, shall we start the business we are here for?"

"I was thinking we could start checking from the top and work down floor by floor."

They climbed the central staircase to the top floor. The lifts weren't working as they had shut the power off. The rooms on this floor were small and shared bathrooms. Although for James the view out of the windows was the best the place could offer. They opened each door and entered the room. Some had recently been occupied but were now empty.

Matthew took out a small notepad and wrote the condition of each room. James had already made a list, and Matthew could then compare the damage. The bathroom at the end of the corridor to the left of the stairs had water running into the bathtub. It hadn't overflowed but was very close to doing it. James turned the tap off and pulled the plug.

They descended to the floor below. These bedrooms all had en-suite bathrooms, and it took them some time to check each room. They had locked one door, Kenny produced a set of keys and opened it. The room was empty and was clean. The last door to open on this floor was the one they had found the girl in. Both Matthew and James took deep breaths as Kenny opened the door and walked inside. The mattress was still on the floor and the bathroom was empty.

Kenny looked at Matthew, then asked James, "This is the room they found the child in?"

"Yes, according to my friends in the police force, someone beat the shit out of the man before they arrived."

Matthew didn't answer and wondered why security men always claim to have friends in the police force who tell them things.

"Really, we know nothing about that," replied James, not looking at his father.

"According to one of my policemen friends, the rapist had a record for child abuse. He'll have a hard time inside a prison."

"If he reaches there," said Matthew as he left the room.

James looked at the mattress, something was between the wall and what would have been the top of the bed. He leaned over and pulled a small soft brown badly worn teddy bear. He looked at it as the emotion welled up inside him. It must have been the girls. He carefully placed it into his pocket. He would find a way of getting the teddy bear to her.

Matthew had already taken the stairs to the floor below and was standing outside one room. The floor below was the premier floor when the hotel was in its heyday. These rooms not only had bathrooms but compact sitting rooms. Each suite had a name straight from the Victorian era. The Royal room was spacious and was in excellent condition. The room with the name 'The Grand Tour' attached by one screw to the door was not in such a pleasant condition. Someone had made holes in the walls. The next en-suite known as the Imperial was the largest of the rooms. Kenny opened the door, and they all entered before halting just inside.

The two bodies lay on the floor side by side. The younger of the two men was naked. His left hand cupped in the other man's right. His slightly red ginger-colored pubic hair was bloody. The stab wounds to his groin visible from the doorway.

"We had better check to see if either of them is alive."

Matthew showed for Kenny to check. The man tiptoed across the room and knelt beside the naked youth. His hand touched the white neck. He repeated it on the suited man. Returning to the door, he shook his head. Matthew left the room, calling the police on his mobile. Kenny also left making a call to someone. James looked around the room until he realized the windows on the side facing the street were fully open. The breeze blew into the room and James smelt the aftershave cologne one of the dead men was wearing. He had smelt it before but couldn't remember where.

Standing looking at the two bodies, he knew this is how he must have looked on the beach. Naked for all to see. He wished he could cover the naked man. He had not taken in the other man and now took a step forward to look at him. He estimated he was about six foot four, tall and overweight. The pinstriped tailormade suit was very expensive. The black leather belt and the top of the trousers lay open and pulled down to the ankles. The hole in the head's front showed they had shot him. The clothes of the naked man weren't visible. James skirted around the bodies and checked the other rooms to see if they were there. It surprised him not to see them.

As he returned to the doorway, he saw the man was in his late teens or early twenties. The other man looked just over thirty.

He could see the hole in the man's head as he passed the bodies. It looked like an exit wound, but he was not an expert on it. His friend and sister's boyfriend Trevor had shown him pictures of bullet wounds. Trevor was a filmmaker who had spent hours making sure of accuracy in such situations.

Matthew returned and led him out of the room, closing the door as he did.

"The police are on their way."

Kenny had gone ashen white, the blood drained from his face.

"You okay, Kenny?"

"I will be."

"You know the men?"

He looked at Matthew, a shocked expression on his face.

"Aye, we have a contract with a businessman and that is his son."

James spoke before realizing he should keep quiet.

"Julian Peterson-Jones?"

"Aye, that's him."

"I think we should all wait for the police," said Matthew, realizing this could be a splendid time to ask those questions about the party.

"Maybe we could wait in the reception area," said James.

"Aye, that would be better than outside."

The reception seems dark and cold compared to the room the bodies were in.

On the way down to the reception, Matthew had

thought about how to approach Kenny regarding the party.

"Sad Julian should die so quickly after his birthday."

"Aye, he had a party on Monday to celebrate."

"You were at the party?" asked James.

"We do all the security for Mr. Peterson–Jones."

"And Gordon and his girlfriend now what's her name. They organized the party."

"Patrice. She did most of it and Gordon brings the entertainment."

"And what do you bring?"

"We just make sure there is no trouble."

"Was there any at the party?"

Kenny gave Matthew a quizzical look.

"If that is Julian upstairs then he upset someone, maybe at the party."

"There was one man with Gordon who seemed out of it but after they left, he quiets down. I think he went home with a waiter. There were a lot of poufs at the party. Julian was how can I say this bisexual he likes alternative people around him if you know what I mean."

"Did his father know?"

"I don't think so, but I wasn't part of the elite team that works with Mr. Peterson-Jones."

"Elite team."

"Our boss, Jonathan Dase-Pollock, handles the Peterson-Jones account himself. He handpicks the men who work on it. I'm not one of them he picked."

The front door of the hotel bust open and four police officers entered

CHAPTER FOUR

Double Murder

Matthew told a police officer where they could find the bodies. Two officers stayed in the reception area with them while the others climbed the stairs. The awkward silence and the glances from the police officers made Kenny uncomfortable. James and Matthew ignored them and were leaning on the reception counter.

The policeman ran down the stairs. He took the other two to the side, speaking to them in a whisper.

The tall, thin officer approached Matthew. He looked like a schoolboy.
"If you gentlemen could wait for the Detective Chief Inspector Greenwell to arrive."
"How long before he arrives?" asked Kenny, who had become very nervous.
"Not sure, sir."
"I'd better call the office and let them know what's happened."
Kenny walked toward the street door as a policeman blocked him from leaving.

Matthew and James watched him as he explained to
someone on his mobile phone what was happening.
Whoever he was speaking to was asking a lot of questions and seemed to make Kenny even more nervous.
Kenny undid his shirt collar the sweat beginning to
gather around it. The man couldn't handle stress without breaking out into a panic attack.
Kenny finished the call and return to the reception
counter. He placed his head on it as though the world
had just collapsed.

"Problems?"

"You could say that my boss is not the easiest man
to deal with. And as the Peterson-Jones are his big-
gest client, it's worrying."

"Why is it worrying?"

"They employ the company to protect the Peterson-
Jones family and property."

"If one of them gets murdered, it doesn't look too
good."

"True."

"Did Julian have a bodyguard?"

"According to Jonathan, that's my boss, Julian had
a bodyguard so where is he?"

The door opened and a tall grey-haired man entered.
The Police officers walked forward towards him,
showing respect. They spoke, then the policeman
pointed to the three of them.

"I'm Detective Chief Inspector Greenwell and I
will be in charge of this case. Which of you found
the bodies?"

Kenny looked at Matthew and James before speaking, "We all did together."

"What were you doing in this old building?"

"These gentlemen own it and we had problems

with squatters. We were doing a walkthrough to see where they were getting in."

"Okay give the officer over there your names and how we can contact you. I will need you to come down to the station later to give a formal statement."

The officer took their names and phone numbers. Then asked them to report to the police station at seven that evening. Matthew and James left the hotel first. Kenny seemed to hold back before he exited.

"Can I call you later, I think I may need your help."

"Anytime you want Kenny."

They watched as he walked down the street. A car pulled alongside him and he climbed in. Before he closed the door he looked back at them. James made a mental note of the car number, then saw his father writing it down in his little notebook.

"I think we need something to eat. By the time we have finished it would be time to go to the police station."

The police station on John Street looked more like a cheap hotel than a police station. If it didn't have the blue sign saying POLICE and the communication post on the roof, it could be.

The police had separated them into the interview rooms. Neither James nor Matthew knew if Kenny had arrived. When Matthew asked the police officer at the front desk he shrugged his shoulders in reply. James had sat in several Police station interview rooms before. The first time he had been very nervous, now he relaxed. He knew what to expect from the interviewing officers. The door opened and DCI Greenwell entered, followed by another man.

Greenwell sat down opposite James while the other man sat to the right of Greenwell.

"Mr. Pidgley I am Detective Chief Inspector Greenwell and this is my colleague Detective Inspector Gladstone."

"We have met before," said James. Remembering it was Gladstone who had spoken to him after they had found him on the beach.

Greenwell looked at DI Gladstone and wondered why he hadn't been told he had met James before.

"I'm not a man to beat about the bush, Mr. Pidgley. I know all about your past and your involvement in other crimes. If you hadn't been on the beach naked and stabbed, you would be my number one suspect. I don't like people interfering with police business. Hope I make myself clear."

James didn't answer but just looked blankly at the man.

"I shall leave you now to give your statement to DI Gladstone. But I warn you if I find out you have been meddling in police inquires. I will come down on you like a ton of bricks."

"Is that a threat, Detective Greenwell?"

"Take it any way you like."

"Then I shall have to consult my lawyer."

"As you wish, I warn you."

DCI Greenwell stood and left the room. The police officer just inside the door relaxed after he had left.

James smiled, "Not a very popular man."

DI Gladstone didn't respond. Turning to the police officer asked if he could rustle up some tea for them.

The officer nodded and left the room.

DI Gladstone checked to see if the tape machine was running or not and removed a cassette from the recorder.

James took a pen out of his pocket and twisted the end. He waited and then looked at his mobile phone. He put the pen back into his pocket and closed his mobile phone. DI Gladstone looked at him, wondering what he was doing. James decided not to tell the policeman he had just checked to see if any microphones were listening to their conversation. It was a device a friend had given him when he was working in Great Malvern. If there had been a microphone, his mobile would have texted him a message saying, 'silence boy'. The mobile phone had not sent him a message.

DI Greenwell leaned forward and in a soft inaudible voice said, "I too know all about your past, and for me, if you continue investigating it's okay. The police in Birmingham and Great Malvern had given up, but you continued and found out the truth."
"It's hard to believe a policeman these days."
"The difference is if you find out something you will share with me. You can ask people questions I cannot."
"True but giving information works both ways."
"What would you like to know?"
"Anything you can tell me about those other men who died on the beach. Then what you know about the two men we found today?"
DI Gladstone sat back in his chair as he looked at James, then at the contents of the folder in front of him.

"I think the first thing is why you didn't die like the rest. It has left us all puzzling."

"Me too."

"Then a very diligent policewoman searching the beach area found the broken blade of a knife. Whoever stabbed you broke the knife, hence why the cuts weren't deep, and it didn't cut any major blood vessels."

"At least I have something to be grateful for."

"All the men were naked between eighteen and twenty-five years old. Except for the last one like you they had piled their clothes above their heads. Now the naked man you found today there was one strange thing, he had false teeth."

"Strange for someone so young."

"They raped the victim."

"By the other man?"

"Not sure we are waiting for the Post Mortem results to know, but it looks like it."

"Were any of the other men?"

"No. They executed the man in the suit."

"How?"

"Looks like they shot him in the back of the head while kneeling."

"Sounds like a scene from a gangster movie."

"He was a like gangster, well more of a bully from what I have found so far."

"Do you know who they were?"

DI Gladstone referred to the folder and produced a piece of paper.

"The naked man is unnamed. The other man was Julian Peterson-Jones. He was the son of a very rich, powerful local man. Hence the pressure is on DCI Greenwell."

"Still doesn't give him the right to be offensive."

"I agree, but he always is."

DI Gladstone handed James the folder and sat back, watching him as he read the few papers it contained.

"Why are you telling me, my experience with the police has been a very negative one in sharing information?"

"James, when you have Romany blood inside your veins it is hard not to know which side your bread is buttered."

"You're a Romany?"

"Yes, my grandparents on my mother's side of the family gave up the traveling life. My parents made sure we didn't get affected by the prejudice."

"You know we are Romany or you wouldn't have told me."

DI Gladstone nodded and then gave James a broad smile.

"Do you speak Romani?" asked James.

"Sadly, no I wish I could. My wife calls me the wanderer because I like to be out and about, I love the countryside."

"Me too."

"My mother talked a lot about the life and her parents and why they gave up the road."

James sat looking at the man, he had noticed the change in the face, from a hard detective to a soft human being who cares.

"What was your mother's maiden name?"

"Glover they mainly lived in the Kent area."

"Fruit picking."

"Until the East Enders from London came and took over."

"I have an uncle who said the Londoners were a vicious lot of thugs. But I think he was talking about the bankers."

"That was what my mother also said, and one reason her grandparents gave up the road."

"I'm not sure why my grandparents gave up the road, I must ask my father."

"My father was a military man and forbade my mother to talk about that side of our family history. She would tell me stories when she could. It was our secret. After my father died, she told me the complete truth."

"Did you like your father?"

"Not really, I feared him like everyone else."

The officer returned carrying a tray with mugs of tea, Gladstone's attitude changed.

"Now Mr. Pidgley, I need to know what happened today when you found the body?"

It took James another hour to tell DI Gladstone what happened and sign his statement. As he was leaving DI Gladstone shook his hand, a business card hidden in his hand. At the front desk of the station, James asked if his father had finished giving his statement. The police again shrugged and continued with his work.

James stood outside the police station and called his father's mobile. There was no reply, so he walked back to his flat. He expected to see his father sitting on the sofa when he arrived. To his astonishment, he found a note hastily written.

'Sorry James but your mother has taken ill and I need to get back to Birmingham. I'm taking the nine-thirty

to Victoria train, then the last train to Birmingham.
I'll call you when I get home.'

James looked at his watch. It was only just nine if he
ran, he could make it to the station before the train left.

He ran through the streets of Brighton as fast as he
could, then stopped why hadn't he used the car. He
continued and after several near misses with cars and a
man on a bicycle; he arrived at the station. It was just
nine twenty-nine as he ran along the platform looking
into the train for London. He couldn't see his father as
he peered into the carriages. The train pulled out of
the station and he sank to his knees.
Out of breath and tired, he walked out of the station
and into the woman. It surprised her.
She smiled and then realized he didn't recognize her or
remember her.
"You don't know who I am," she said.
"Should I know you?"
"I found you on the beach."
James thought she found me naked on the beach. According to the police she was a member of the aristoc-
racy.
"Sorry it took some time to get my sight back and I
remember little."
"It may be an agreeable thing you don't remember,
it must have been horrible. It was for me."
"Seeing me naked you mean."
"No thinking you have found someone dead. I'm
Julia Brooke."
She held out her hand and James shook it. He felt
awkward and looked at the ground. She was an ex-
quisite woman, and he always had difficulty talking to
ladies like her.

"You look as though you have been running."

"I was trying to catch a train."

"Were you going somewhere?"

"No, my father was on it and I missed him, he was going home. My mother has taken ill."

"Sorry to hear that, maybe if you had a cup of tea or something it would restore you to normality."

They sat in the little café by the train station drinking a cup of tea. She looked at him. He was for her very handsome, if a little shy. Neither of them wanted to speak first. Finally, James plucked up courage and spoke.

"You know my father and I found two bodies today."

"Really where?"

"In a hotel, we are converting into flats."

"How horrible, finding you was bad enough without finding two dead people."

"Sorry, you had to find me."

"Do you know who they were, the people you found today?"

"Only one of them Julian Peterson-Jones."

"Jules is dead."

"Yes, did you know him?"

"Yes, because his father knows my father. I went to his birthday party on Monday."

"Was it a delightful party?" asked James, trying to hide his surprise.

"Expensive I hate it when money is thrown away. Patrice Sickle organized it. I went to school with her at Cheltenham Ladies College."

James went silent. He didn't know what to say.

"Sorry I sound like such a snob and I'm not really. My grandfather is Lord Cobham and when he dies my father gets the title. Sadly, no money to go with it, grandfather was a spendthrift. Then when you get people like Jules throwing money around like water, it makes me very mad."

"I was at the party you know."

"Jules birthday party on Monday? I didn't see you, I don't think."

"Patrice has a boyfriend, Gordon."

"The dealer."

"Yes, well, somehow and I'm not sure how I ended up with them and at the party."

"They are a dangerous lot. Into many things, so I have been told. The trouble is, it's how those people make money and power."

"Don't I know it."

"Did you know the chief constable's son and daughter were at the party? So was a minor Royal. That's why I went to the party because I thought if they go then there can be nothing wrong with it."

"I still don't know why I ended up there. Or how I became naked on the beach."

"You should try to find out."

"Maybe. I must ring home and see what's happening to my mother. I completely forgot about it."

"That's my fault. Let me get us another cup of tea while you phone home."

She left the table and went over to counter. James dialed the family home and waited for someone to pick up the phone.

"Pidgley residence."

"Who is that?"

"Peter, who's speaking?"

"Peter its James, what's happened?"

"James, is dad with you?"

"No, he is on his way back to Birmingham."

"Good, Mom needs him."

"She fell and broken her pelvic bone, I think."

"How did she fall?"

"That's just it, we don't know. Ann thinks she may have blacked out. Trevor wonders if she had a brain aneurysm, then fell."

"She okay now?"

"Yes, they are doing many tests and she can't move."

"Give her my love and tell her I'll call tomorrow."

"When are you coming home?"

"Not sure, why?"

"Because we all want to know why you were naked on the beach."

"Later Peter, dad will update you all on that matter. Bye."

He closed the phone as Julia returned carrying two mugs of tea.

"So how is your mother?"

"Broke her pelvic bone, my brother thinks."

"Painful and I can see why your father rushed home."

They sat drinking the tea James glanced out of the window and saw Romeo walking by. The waiter seeing James then Julia nodded but using his right hand gave a sign as though he was applying the brake. James wasn't sure what that meant, it would mean another late night waiting for Romeo to finish his work.

"Drinking all this tea has made me hungry."

"It not supposed to, I read in a ladies' magazine if you drink a lot of liquid before a meal you don't eat as much."

"Maybe I have eaten little today."

"I am not surprised by what's happening to you. It must be nice to have the support of your family around you."

"I have an extensive family, five sisters and four brothers."

"I have one brother, Giles. My grandfather controls the family, he is a Victorian tyrant."

"I didn't know people like that still existed."

"James in the world I grew up in, it's all about power and status."

"Then I must think myself lucky, our family is very democratic. Along with my father and three brothers, we run the family property company. Hence why I am here, we are converting a hotel into flats."

"Oh, that's why you were in the old hotel when you found Jules's body."

"Yes, and the poor boy with him."

James sipped at his tea and listened as his stomach rumbled. He looked up and saw Julia staring at him. She suddenly busted out laughing, pointing at his stomach. He blushed at first, then laughed.

"I think you need to eat something."

"Will you join me?" She looked away as though she would refuse. He continued, "I hate eating alone and I like..."

"I would like that if you really want it."

"I wouldn't ask if I didn't."

"I don't eat meat. I'm not vegetarian, I eat fish but not meat."

"Then it's Riddle and Finns on Meeting House Lane."

"Oh yes, I love their Roast halibut with a mushy pea puree."

"For me it's the Goan fish curry."

"I've never tried that."

They left the café and walked toward Meeting House Lane. James was normally a very observant person but didn't notice the man slip into the unlit doorway. He watched as they walked and talked along the street. Once they were forty yards ahead of him, he stepped out of the doorway and followed. He kept pace with them as they walked. Stopping to peruse a shop window when James turned and looked behind. He wasn't sure if James realized he was being followed. As they entered the elegant entrance of Riddle and Finns the man increased his pace. He slid into the shadows across the street to watch for them to leave. Taking a chocolate fruit and nut bar out of his pocket, he broke off a piece. Sucking on the chocolate until only nuts and raisins remained.

James and Julia sat towards the back of the restaurant. Neither seemed to mind and relaxed looking at the menu. Even though Julia had decided beforehand what she wanted, she scanned to see if she might change her mind.

Placing the menu on the table, she looked at James.

"Why did you keep looking behind you as we walked here?"

Without looking up from the menu he replied, "I thought we were being followed."

"Were we?"

"Not sure, if we were, they are good at hiding."

"Possibly my father, he doesn't like me to wander too far from the family home."

They ordered their food, and both seemed lost in thought. Julia had said she just wanted water. James hesitated whether to have a glass of wine or a beer. He chose to just have a glass of water.

After Julia had returned from the ladies' toilet, she seemed to be full over with questions.

"What have you found out so far about how you ended up on the beach?"

"Not much only I seemed to have been at the party with Gordon Tuff and Patrice Sickle both of whom I don't know."

"You've never met them before?"

"No, that's the strange thing, how did I meet them and why did I go with them?"

"I don't remember seeing you at the party, but I saw Patrice and Gordon."

"When did you see them?"

"I arrived late, and they were thinking of leaving."

"I think I was in some bedroom asleep or unconscious, but I'm not sure."

They finished the meal and Julia refused coffee, saying she should get home. After James had paid the bill, they walked through The Lanes to the place where she was staying. He was sure they were being followed, but just couldn't see who it was. He had noticed through the meal Julia had asked the questions. When he asked her a question she didn't reply or gave a very vague answer. She suddenly stopped outside a very expensive apartment complex. James could see it had a night porter on duty who was staring out at them as they arrived.

"Thank you for an enjoyable meal."

"My pleasure."

"Maybe we will see each other again."

"I hope so…" James became awkward and stood on one foot while the other was a few inches off the ground. He lost his balance and fell a little towards her. She instinctively grabbed at his arm to help. They were now very close. He could feel the warm breath exhaling from her thin lips. Julia kissed him gently on his lips. He didn't pull away but placed his hand behind her head and pulled her into him. The kiss continued until a motorist driving by honked his car horn.

She pulled away, looking into his eyes. She quickly kissed him again and ran into the building.

"I'll call you…" he called after her.

How could he, he didn't know her phone number? What a stupid thing to say. She must think him an idiot.

He stood looking at the building and saw a light open several floors above him. He wandered towards the sea. As he crossed the road to stand on the promenade above the beach. He knew someone was watching him. He quickly turned and saw them draw back into the shadows. Looking back out to sea and watching the surf crash on the stones, he thought about Julia. She had asked too many questions and given him very little. He had seen her replace her mobile into her handbag when she returned from the ladies' toilet. It was then she began her questioning him about what he remembered. If they sent her to find out what he knew, he didn't care, she had kissed him.

He hadn't felt the touch of a woman's lips on his since he broke up with Vicki two years earlier. It was such a wonderful feeling he wished the driver of the car hadn't honked his car horn and broken the spell.

Walking towards the pier, he ran down the steps to the lower promenade. The cafés were closing up or had already closed for the night. He slipped into a patch of darkness, his breathing quickening. His heart pounding as he watched to see if his follower had succumbed to follow.

He waited, but no one came by. He stepped out of the shadow and a girl with her Mohican hair styled boyfriend squealed.

The boy looked at James and shouted, "Fucking pervert."

He walked the other way, hoping no one had heard the boy's comment. As he climbed the steps to the upper promenade, he saw several people below looking at him.

The text message on his mobile beeped, and he looked at the message. *Thanks for a beautiful evening, Julia. Call me.* He smiled and remembered the kiss. How had she known his phone number he hadn't given it to her? There were just too many unanswered questions about Julia Brooke.

He wasn't sure how he would lose the person following him, but he needed to before he met Romeo.

As he walked, he looked for a place he could hide from someone and then make his escape. He watched as the man entered the public toilet but didn't exit. James sat on one of the many seafront beaches. Out of the corner of his eye, watched as men entered the toilet but didn't come out.

He stood and walked into the toilet to his surprise it was empty. He walked around and found the other exit. He quickly took it and ran as fast as he could up the street and into the darkness of an alleyway.

After a few minutes, he saw a man exit the toilet in a hurry looking up and down the street. The man raced to the corner of the street and looked in every direction. James didn't recognize him as the man was wearing a hat and a scarf wrapped around his face. For one moment James thought the man would walk up the street toward him. The man re-entered the toilet and didn't reappear. James sensing the coast was clear stepped out of the alleyway and ran up the street. He wasn't sure when he would meet Romeo since the waiter had very odd hours of work. He would just have to be patient, he told himself as he sauntered towards the all-night café.

As he approached the Queensbury Arms pub, he saw a small crowd gathered outside. The pub was closed, but the people were still partying. He tried to pass them, but a small sylphlike girl grabbed his hand and danced around him. He turned and tried to pull away. A young brightly costumed man took his other hand and danced with him. Seeing this, the others in the crowd joined in so James was pulled and pushed in several directions. The dancing became intense and faster. As though a gust of wind blew down the street the dancers including James fell to the floor. James found himself on top of several people. Hands were all over his body, touching him. There was a flash of a camera and then another as someone had taken a picture. James tried to free himself by pushing the various hands away.

He finally could stand as the sylphlike girl kissed him on the check. Suddenly several others joined in. The camera flashed again as several young drunk men kissed James's face. He pushed them away and ran up the street. The sylphlike girl gave chase, but after he was several yards ahead of her, she stopped and returned to the others.

James stopped at the top of the street and looked back at the crowd. He tried to see who the photographer was, but no one was taking pictures. Arriving outside all night café, he peered inside through the window. The place was empty, not even the local homeless had appeared tonight. He ordered a mug of tea and sat by the door so he could see when Romeo entered. Two of the regular waiters arrived and the man behind the counter told them no one was upstairs. They ordered tea and sat looking out of the window, talking in inaudible voices.

The man with the hat and scarf who had been following James parked his car a little way from the all-night café. He had driven past and seen James sitting by the door. At first, he sat looking at the place, his hands rubbing the steering wheel for comfort. A large delivery van arrived parking on the opposite side of the street blocking the view of the café. He waited to see if it would drive away. After fifteen minutes, he realized it would stay there until morning. The man climbed out of the car and locked the driver's door. He then checked all the other doors and the boot.

Light from the all-night café spilled across the street. Not wanting to risk being seen in the light by James, the man backtracked and ran down the street. He found a cross street running to the next parallel street and up it. At a cross street, he ran back to the street with the all-night café on it. He was only a few yards from the café and looked for somewhere dark to hide.

He panicked when a group of waiters suddenly appeared and passed him. One of them looked at him and gave a brief nod as though he knew him. The man hurried away and stood forty yards from the café in a doorway.

As the tide returned on the seashore, the smell of the sea would travel back up the draining system and filter into the town. The man was standing in a doorway with a drain in the gutter just in front of him. The smell of the sea oozed out, and he coughed. It was an intense, nauseating stink. The man brought vomit up into his mouth from his stomach several times. It would only be a matter of time before he couldn't contain it anymore.

As the remains of his lunch wretched up and into his mouth, he grabs the scarf from his mouth. The camera he had been holding in his pocket fell to the floor. Before he could pick it up, his lunch returned to the surface and spewed over the road. He heaved several times before controlling himself. Picking up the camera and wiped it clean of dirty dust and his vomit before returning it to his pocket. A woman walking her dog across to the other side of the street had to stop the dog from getting a taste of the man's lunch.

James ordered another mug of tea and a bacon sandwich, unaware of his follower's plight. He returned to his seat and looked out of the window indoor. Had he misunderstood what Romeo meant, and he wasn't coming to the café tonight. Filippo arrived but was in a hurry to climb the stairs to see James as he entered. James looked at the time on his mobile. It was already one-thirty. He ate his bacon sandwich and drank the remains of his mug of tea and left the café.

He would walk around seeing if Romeo's light was on his bed-sit. The man with the scarf and hat almost missed seeing James leave. He was trying to rid himself of three stray cats who having licked up his vomit found his shoes and trouser bottoms interesting.

He saw James walk behind the parked van and kicking the cats away with the toe of his shoe and ran after him. James heard the footsteps and turned to see a man dart behind the van. Had his mysterious follower returned? He slowed down and checking in shop windows and a glance behind now and again. He concluded he was mistaken and returned to his normal pace and onto Romeo's.

To see if Romeo's light was on, James would have to pass the front of the building and peer up the side of the building to the back. The light wasn't on and James felt let down. He looked up again and this time the light was on. Running back to the main door and pushing the button on flat thirty-six. He tried several times before the buzzer unlocking the door engaged.

The automatic hall light illuminated as he entered. A flash from outside made him turn back and look at the door. He had been seeing flashes all night. Maybe it was lightening. He raced up the stairs to Romeo's not sure of the welcome he would get.

The man was still following James had just taken a snapshot of the front of the building. He knew he had enough evidence and decided not to wait around for James to leave. He felt the brush of something against his leg and looked down one cat had followed and was licking at the turn up on his trousers. He tried to kick it away, but it had attached itself to the trousers. Two cats seemed to fight over the right of ownership were attacking his other trouser leg. He tried to kick them away, then noticed he had attracted about ten others, all starting to bear down on him. He ran, the cats hanging on the trousers as he raced up the hill. The other cats gave chase, and soon cats and stray dogs were pursuing him. An animal fight followed him back to his car. Miss Dora Coventry looking out of the window saw the strange man with the animals and called the police. She reported a cat thief in action.

The police officer sent to investigate missed the strange man by a few seconds. He relieved himself of his cat posse and gets into his car. The cats scratched at the door and one climbed onto the bonnet. He drove away with the cat sliding off, unaware if he had run over it or not.

Romeo opened his door as James reached the top of the stairs. He smiled when he saw James.
    "I'm making some tea, would you like a mug?"
    "Yes, please."
James entered the small bed-sit and sat on one of the two chairs. Unlike the last time his father and he had been there, the room was warm.
Romeo placed a large mug of tea on the table while holding one in his hand. James took a sip.
    "I think I miss understood your gesture earlier to-day. I thought it meant to see you later at the all-night café."
    "No, sorry, I didn't want the lady to see me."

"Julia, you know her?"

"Yes, she is part of the crowd of the man who gave the party."

"Well, she told me she knew him, but I'm not sure she has much to do with him."

"Oh yes, I have seen them on dates having dinner several times. I think she likes him because she was always kissing him when I see them."

"Are you sure? He didn't kiss her?"

"No, I never saw him kiss her, always she kisses him, I think she may be dangerous."

"You know he is dead?"

"Who is?"

"The man whose party it was."

"No, when?"

"My father and I found him earlier today with another man."

"Was he dead too?"

"Yes."

"Do you know who he was?"

"Not yet, but I will. Do you think it might be one of your waiter friends from the party?"

"Maybe, but they weren't my friends."

"What else can you tell me about the honorable Julia."

"She takes drugs or has done in the past. I think she was selling them too. I went with a friend to a nightclub and she was there. She kept going into the ladies' toilet with other girls."

"A sure sign of a dealer."

"You like her?"

"Yes, very much, and I thought she liked me."

They sipped tea, James looking into the red-hot ceramic gas fire. Romeo seemed to be off in some

distant land thinking about his family, thought James.
It must be hard not to see or even communicate with
them.

"Do you speak to your family?"

"My cousin has a computer in his home. My
mother will visit him and I will email her from the
library. I have one friend who has a computer in
his flat and I have Skyped my mother. It's a free
telephone on the internet."

"I don't know what I would do if I couldn't contact
my family."

"I have some news for you."

"Nothing bad I hope."

"That depends on how you look at it. I found out
who took you away from the party."

"Who?"

"The rich man's son in his car. Rene remembers
seeing you being helped into a car and the rich
man's son also getting into it."

"I wonder what happened afterward?"

"Rene said you were unconscious."

"That may have been the best thing."

"I'm glad he is dead, he was a nasty man."

"What do you mean? Was he a dealer too?"

"No, I think he was the boss and not just drugs,
other things too."

"Like what?"

"James, drugs aren't the only things smuggled into
Britain."

"People."

"How do you think I got here?"

"They smuggled you in, when, how?"

"I've said too much sorry, no more questions."

"Sorry, I shouldn't pry."

"It's okay, please forget what I said. You must go now I need to sleep I have three shifts tomorrow."
"Why three?"
"I need to pay off my debt."
"Your debt for what?" James looked around the bed-sit there seemed nothing of value in the place.
"It is very expensive to come to Britain."

CHAPTER FIVE

Mike Gammon's Dilemma

The fire had engulfed the offices of the Dorsey Professional and Domestic Agency. It shocked the people arriving for work or for their early morning breakfast. To see the top of the building a charred black mess. Streets around the fire-damaged property were closed to the public by police. Several rumors had circulated among those watching the fire brigade. The number of bodies found differed from who you spoke to?

Mike Gammon arrived for work to find his normal route barred. He didn't like things to change too much. It heightened his normal irritable state. He found his favorite café already full of people who couldn't get to their place of work because of the street closures. Joining a line of people waiting to get served, he tried to find out what had occurred. Listening to the various accounts being spouted by the other customers in the line. The realization of which property was burnt sent him into a panic. His boss Jonathan Dase Pollock owned the burnt-out building, and he was the letting agent. He would lose commission if he couldn't rent it.

Leaving the line, he ran to the blue and white police tape surrounding the property. The rookie constable listened intently to what Mike had to say but wouldn't let him cross the police tape to see the damage. Frustrated, he ran around several streets until he found a way to the estate agent's offices.

Veronica sat painting her nails with purple nail polish. She looked up as he fell into the office, tripping over the welcome mat.

"What's happened?"

"It's on fire."

"What is?"

"Mr. Dase Pollock's property."

"His lovely home is on fire."

"No, the Dorsey Agency building."

He picked up the phone and dialed the home of Jonathan Dase Pollock. The phone rang several times before the answering machine kicked in. He didn't leave a message pressing the disconnect button and trying Jonathan's mobile.

The phone rang and once again the voice messaging system started.

"Jonathan, it's Mike the Dorsey agency property is on fire, please get back to me as soon as you can."

"You're serious and I was thinking it was one of your jokes."

"It is serious Veronica. Now you're in charge here, call me on my mobile if Jonathan gets in touch with you."

"I suppose so, what if someone comes looking for a property to buy?"

"Take their phone number and I'll call them later."

He ran back to the police barrier and watch to see whom was in charge. A uniformed sergeant seemed to order the constables into position. He finally caught the attention of the sergeant.

"Sorry to bother you at such a very busy time."

"Yes, sir, what can I do for you?"

"I'm from Dase Pollock Enterprises, we own the property on fire."

Mike produced one of Jonathan Dase Pollock Enterprise's business cards and handed it to the officer. The officer raised the blue and white tape, letting Mike get closer to the burned out building. From behind the tape, it was hard to see what had burnt. As Mike came around one of the fire engines, he could see the top part of the building had completely been burnt. They had saved the lower offices from the fire. Although inside everyone was dripping with water used to douse the fire. A man in a black and grey checked suit approaches them.

"Sergeant it seems no one was inside and the fire started in the offices on the first floor. I have asked the arson investigators to confirm my findings. I would check to see if anyone saw anyone running away from the property."

"Would you like to see upstairs?"

It surprised Mike when the sergeant asked him. They took him to the stairs leading up to the first floor. The walls were black from the fire. He stood at the top of the stairs and looked at the damage. It burned everything. The filing cabinets were now twisted, melted metal. Their contents destroyed.

He returned to where the man was standing. A woman and man had joined him and were deep in conversation as he approached.

"This gentleman may help you."

"Mr. Dase Pollock?"

"No, I represent his company. Mike Gammon," he handed them his business card.

"Jocelyn Gilbride and Paul Nielsen immigration services."

"Immigration?"

"Yes, we have a few questions for Mr. Dase Pollock. Do you know where he might be?"

"Sorry I don't, I have been trying to contact him myself. Is there anything I can help with?"

"I think we should talk to Mr. Dase Pollock," Jocelyn handed a card to Mike, "When you contact him, please ask him to get in touch with us."

Mike looked at the card with the government official seal embossed on it when he looked up, they had walked away. Calling Veronica, she told him Jonathan hadn't been in touch. Mike tried Jonathan's mobile number again, only to get the voice message. Jonathan Dase Pollock had always been very secretive telling Mike just enough about where he was and what he was doing to stop him from asking too many questions.

CHAPTER SIX

Family Discord

James sat reading the newspaper after taking a shower. His morning was slow. His only meeting of the day was at the planning office regarding the permits required to start the conversion. He scanned the paper and let his mind wander after seeing an advert for Romeo and Juliet by the Brighton and Hove Players. Romeo had given him the best news possible. At least now he knew who had taken him away from the party. Sadly, Julian Peterson-Jones was no longer alive to tell him what had happened. Maybe the person driving the car would know and Julia would know who drove Julian around. It would be important to find out more about Julia and Julian's relationship. Was Julia trustworthy, what had made Romeo so suspicious of her? He would ask Romeo the next time they met. He lay back and closed his eyes then, remembering the kiss she had given him. It had been some time since a girl had kissed him in the way she had. His entire body had felt excited by it. Few girls had made him feel that way. He usually took a long time to get into a relationship. He had often wondered if that's why they didn't last long. The girls felt he wasn't interested when all the time he was trying to be romantic and woo them. One girlfriend had told all her friends he was a proper gentleman. It gave rise to the rumors he was gay. It took several months to dismiss that myth. He had nothing against gay people, men didn't attract him sexually. Although he preferred the company of men more than women. This was as he surmised was because he just didn't know how to talk to women. His sisters had dominated him growing up, and when he opened his mouth to speak, they usually made some jokes at his expense.

Julia had struck a note his heart had melted. This was for him a dangerous time if he let his heart rule, he would forget everything he was there to do.

His stomach rumbled as hungry banged its drum inside him. Walking down to the old town, he found most of the properties were closed. They shut his favorite café without a notice on the window telling the customers why. Finally, he found a cafe open and joined a line to order and then find a seat. A loud noise outside distracted a couple that would take a table by the window. They moved to the door to see what was happening. James slipped quickly into a seat and showed to the waitress this is where he was sitting. The couple returns and finds James sitting at the table. Too polite to say anything, they step to the side and wait for another table.

Mike Gammon after he had searched around for a café open entered the establishment and seeing it was full was leaving. He saw James sitting by the window, an empty seat at his table. He orders some food and crosses to join James.

"Just returning the favor, I hope you don't mind."
James smiles and nods, extending his hand for
Mike to sit down.
"They are very busy today. My usual breakfast
place wasn't open."
"The town is in chaos, but this happens."
"Too many visitors?"
"No, the fire."
"What fire?"
"One of our buildings caught fire and because of
the difficulty in getting close to it the police and
fire brigade close all the streets around here."
"Hence why the other café wasn't open."
"Possibly. I can't get hold of my boss to tell him
what's happened."
"He won't blame you for the fire, will he?"
"No, but he also owned the business destroyed.
Well, his wife ran it, although she used her maiden
name."
"Double blow."
Their food arrived, James ordering another pot of
tea.
"Mike, do you know who Julian Peterson-Jones's
driver was?"
Mike looked at James suspiciously, wondering why he
had asked that question.
"I've found out I left the party with Julian and his
friends, I want to thank them for looking after me.
His driver might know who they were." James
hadn't mentioned the beach and was hoping Mike
had forgotten what happened to James.
"Well, you can't ask Julian."
James played dumb so Mike continued, "He's dead,

they found his body in the throes of some sex
orgy."
"Really where."
"Some seedy run-down hotel, I think."
"What about his driver?"
"Don't think he's dead. Oh, you mean, who was
it?"
"Yes, I would like to thank him."
"Don't know his name but he works for Lexington
cars in Hove. He always had the same guy driving
him around."
"Thanks, I'll see if I can find him."

James looked at his watch and realized that time had
raced by. He had about fifteen minutes to get to his
meeting at the town's planning office. He paid the
waitress and ran back to the flat. Hesitating at first, he
took the car, as it might just be quicker than walking.
It would be several hours before he realized his mistake. Because of the fire, several roads had been
closed, and it took him a lot longer than ten minutes to
get there. Finding a parking space was also difficult
since he had never had the problem before at the town
planning office. He ran up the stairs to the reception,
apologizing to the receptionist and telling her he had
an appointment with Mr. Denton.
   "I'm sorry, sir, but Mr. Denton is with someone
   just at the moment if you care to wait."
James sat on one of the long bench seats and waited.
He looked at his watch fifteen, then thirty minutes
passed. He picked up a magazine someone had left
and read. When he looked at his watch again ninety
minutes had passed since he had arrived.

A man crossed to the receptionist spoke with her before approaching James.

"I'm Mr. Denton, how can I help you."

"I've come about the Bumbery Hotel conversion."

"I was just talking to Mr. Pidgley about that."

"Mr. Pidgley, but I'm Mr. Pidgley."

"Then it must be another Mr. Pidgley. He went over the documents and made the few changes we required and signed them."

"What other Mr. Pidgley?"

"The one who's just left I told him he could have the permits in a few days…"

"You say he just left."

Mr. Denton looked over the banister and down towards the entrance door.

"That's him leaving the building now."

James looked down and saw a man leaving the building. He raced down the stairs two at a time, almost falling at the bottom. He ran out into the street to see the man climb into a car. James ran to his car and climbed in. He started the engine and cut up another car, leaving the car park. The man was about five cars in front of James when they stopped at a traffic light. James jumped out of his car and ran towards the man's car. The lights turned green and running back to his car, the drivers behind him had honked their horns. Black clouds gathering over the sea, night had arrived early.

The man had turned on to Marine Drive and was leaving the town. James ran through a red light to catch up with the man. Several cars had squealed to a halt to avoid hitting him. The driver was heading toward Rottingdean after passing the Brighton Marina. Although the road was dual carriageway, the traffic was heavy at first, then thinned out and James found himself behind the man's car. He tried to pass him, but the man wouldn't allow him to overtake, swerving in front of him each time he tried. A sports car came up behind James and letting the driver pass James tailed him. It was too late for the man to stop James as he came along. In a rash moment, James turned his steering wheel and forced the man off the road onto the grass verge and cliff top.

Neither man opened their car doors, James expecting the man to drive away. The other driver turned off his engine and slowly opened his car door. James did the same but left the door open just in case he would have to give chase again.

The light had faded, so it wasn't easy to see who the man was at first. The man walked his head down towards James. A car doing a U-turn on the road suddenly illuminated them. James stood with his mouth open in surprise. His older brother Brian looked at him. Neither spoke, James still in shock and his brother looking at him in disgust.

"You idiot, you almost killed me."

"Brian, what are you doing here?"

"I came to take over?"

"Take over what?"

"You're no longer in charge down here. The board relieved you of your responsibilities. You might as well pack up and go home."

"When did the board decide?"

"This morning I called an emergency meeting."

"Why wasn't I told about it?"

"Oh, James, read your emails more often."

"Did dad agree?"

"After what happened to our mother, he had no choice."

"Sorry I don't understand."

"James' mother had a stroke because of you."

"Me!"

"For her, it was the last straw. You have embarrassed the family for the last time."

"How did I embarrass the family?"

"First you entangled the family in that solid little murder in Birmingham. Causing dad to get arrested. Then you created the mess with those dreadful circus people in Malvern. We almost lost money on those houses we were building because of that. Now you get a picture of yourself naked on the front page of the national newspapers. I'm not sure what kind of pervert you are, what sexual deviation you like to practice. But to indulge in homosexual orgies and bring the family's name into disrespect was just too much for our mother."

"What homosexual orgy?"

"Well, that's what happened at the party down here, wasn't it? I wonder if it involved you in the disgusting events that happened in my hotel."

"Brian, what are you saying?"

"You caused our mother's stroke."

"Me, I'm calling dad."

"Don't bother, I have a note from him and a letter from the board. It requests you relinquish all your responsibilities down here immediately and hand over to me."

James leaned against the car, holding the two pieces of paper Brian had handed him. He looked at his brother and realized his appearance had changed. It was no

wonder he hadn't recognized him at the council offices. Brian was fatter, not just a few pounds at least
one hundred. His suit was too tight, the obesity falling
out where possible. The collar of his shirt dug into the
neck causing the collar wings to stick up at an odd angle. The body had blown up without the owner noticing the change. Brian had brushed light brown hair
from the right side to cover the large bald patch. Brian
was old before his time.

"Brian, why are you doing this?"
"To save our family from your disgusting perversi-
ties. You have always been in trouble ever since
you were a little child. I didn't want you to be part
of the family company from the start. The others
fooled said I had to give you a chance."
"Why wouldn't you give me a chance? What have
I ever done to you?"
Brian didn't reply. The look of hate on his face was
enough for James.
"My brother hates me."
"You were always a snotty know it all, kid. Our
parents ignored the rest of us when you were born.
Even the younger ones became second best to you.
Mother and father treated you like a little prince.
Mother even called you her 'Little Lord Fauntle-
roy' we all made fun of you because of it. The
Aunt Eileen called you her Little Lord Fauntleroy,
and I was the one she liked, not you."
"And that was my fault?"
"You took advantage of it, never trying to be like
the rest of us. Rubbing our noses in where we
came from."
"You mean our Romany roots."

"We are not Gypsies, our grandparents just moved about the country looking for work."

"You're denying our ancestry."

"James it never happened."

"Tell dad that."

"He knows he just played along with your fantasy."

"Do Donald and Peter think the same as you?"

"Hence the reason they agree to remove you from the project. You and your claims to gypsy heritage always embarrassed them. You are the only one who hangs onto this. Our wonderful grandfather gave up traveling, so how does that make you a gypsy?"

James looked at Brian in disbelief. His brother had turned against him.

"You're jealous. So, what did you say at the board meeting to get my father to turn against me?"

"I told them the truth and showered the pictures. How you are wasting the family's money showing off to strange women. Going to a foreign waiter's bed-sit in the early hour and not leaving for some time having endless gay sex with him. Do you have to pay him for it?"

"That was you following me?"

"I have been watching you for the last few days. If you had done your job, these despicable men wouldn't be dead on my property."

"You said it again your property. Don't you mean the family's property."

"Without me, this family would be nothing."

"Dad was here with me, what about him?"

"Our father worried like the rest of the family. He was trying to keep our name out of the newspapers again. What you have done, embarrasses us all?

James collect your things and leave you're finished.
At the next board meeting, we will vote you off and
ask you to resign from the company."
James had become angry. He wasn't sure if it was to
do with Brian's denial of the family roots. Or the way
the whole family seemed to treat him.

"Forget about the next board meeting if that is the
way you all feel then I resign now."

"I'll put it to the board, I suggest you make it official by putting it in writing."
Brian opened his car door and sat inside. He rolled
down the window.

"Maybe you shouldn't go back to Birmingham. I
think if you just disappeared it would make the
family happy. If you think of changing your name,
I know an excellent solicitor who can help you."
He rolled the window up and drove off the grass verge
and back on the road.
James leaned against his car and looked out to the sea.
The black clouds had gathered closer, making the light
dim. The first drops of rain fell. He climbed into the
car and switched on the inside roof light.

He looked at the letters Brian had given him. He
opened the one from the board. It simply read *the
board has requested James Pidgley relinquish all responsibilities towards the Bumbery Hotel Conversion
project. Effective immediately. Signed Matthew,
Brian, and Donald Pidgley.*

He crumpled up the letter and threw it into the back
seat of the car. He hesitated before opening the other
letter from his father. He had always had great respect
for his parents and if they ever asked him to do something, he always obeyed. He read the typewritten note.

Dear James, Brian presented a very sad picture to the board I had no choice but to accept his findings. I agreed with their decision and request you to comply with it. I hope you will understand. Matthew Pidgley.
It was unsigned, and his father always signed his letter to the family with Dad.

The rain lashed at the roof of the car. For a few seconds, James felt like driving forward over the top of the cliff. He looked at the letter again, his father hadn't written it, this was not his words.

He hadn't realized his brother and sisters hated him. Then he remembered times when they would go out to play and not tell him. Or they wouldn't include him in their games. He would have to sit and watch them. They never invited him to take part in the Christmas or birthday gifts for his parents. The signs had been there, but he had not seen them.

His mobile beeped. He had received a voice message.
"James its dad I don't think this is the time to talk maybe tomorrow but not now. I am so worried about your mother. Good luck."
He replayed the message and saved it. His father had rejected him, now he was on his own.
He dialed his father's mobile. It rang and someone answered, then closed it. He tried the family home phone, it too rang, and no one answered.

He drove off the grass verge and back to Brighton. Sitting outside the hotel, he wondered what he should do. Climbing out of the car, he ran to the front entrance. Standing in the darkness was a tall heavyweight man who stepped forward as he approached.

"Can I help you, sir?"

"I'm James Pidgley. You're not the usual security man from ING."

"I'm not from ING sir, we have replaced them and I have instructions not to let you in, sir."

"Who from?"

"Mr. Brian Pidgley."

"I see,"

James didn't feel like becoming entangled with this man. He walked back to the car and drove to his flat. At least he had paid for three months in advance. They wouldn't throw him out.

He lay on the bed looking at the cobwebbed ceiling. His family had turned against him. He rolled over on to his stomach and fell asleep.

The morning light had illuminated the room for several hours when James opened his eyes. For a few seconds, he felt the paranoia of being paralyzed on the beach. He lifted the bedsheets and looked at his legs, shaking them hard. Relaxing his head resting on the soft down pillowcase. The full force of what had happened occurred to him. His brother had turned the entire family against him. He was alone now. He could turn to no one for help. Brian had declared war he would have to fight back. If they wanted him out, then they would have to buy him out and it wouldn't be cheap. He would need money to survive and look for another job. Then again, would it be worth dashing up to Birmingham to see the family? Maybe he could talk them round Donald and Peter were reasonable guys. How could he prove Brian's allegations had no foundation? His father was here when some of it happened. Yes, this is what he would do once he got out of bed. He was a Pidgley, a fighter for justice.

He sat at his computer looking at his emails eating hot buttered toast. The familiar sound of ping told him he had email. He instantly knew who it was from. Only Brian would have an email address of mrdirector@pidgleyproperties.com. He opened the email hoping it had all been a mistake and Brian was apologizing. Brian had sent the wording for James' resignation letter. He threw down the remaining piece of toast and typed a reply. Brian had only emailed James. Knowing how it would annoy him, James included all the family members in his reply. He wrote, *Brian if you want me out of the company then you must buy me out. The price is half a million pounds in cash. James.*

He pressed send and then had a sudden feeling of remorse wash over him. He had always been so impetuous maybe he should recall the message. Before he could, the reply came back. *In your dreams, loser.* Brian hadn't included all the family members with his reply. James included them again and put them on the bcc line, hiding them from Brian's view. He replied *I don't have dreams only goals my feet are firmly on the ground. You have too many airs and graces. Trying to be a middle-class snob who denies his Romany heritage.*
He closed the computer before they could send a reply. He showered and left the flat.

The rain from the night before had cleared the air and given the place a fresh smell. It was only James's mood that was dark and depressing. He couldn't believe his family had rejected him. They had hated him all this time and said nothing to his face. Or was it Brian had convinced them and they believed him. After all, it was only Brian's word. He remembered how Brian would convince everyone what was true, even if it wasn't. The man was a skillful manipulator, a champion slimeball. James sat on the seafront bench and dialed each of his brother's and sister's mobile phones. Each time he went into voice mail. Even his sister Ann who was usually the brunt of the family anger didn't pick up the phone. He had once saved her life, and now she didn't want to speak to him. He sank his head into his hands. The despondency was too much to handle. They didn't want to speak to him. Even his father who he thought had formed a special bond with had said not now. Falling into a pit of self-pity, he recalled his childhood and the problems he endured.

His father had given Brian the task of looking after James as he grew up. Frequently, James had given Brian his homework to check. Later, when he asked for the homework back, Brian denied any knowledge of it. Money disappeared and Brian had blamed James although there was no proof. Broken windows and crockery all blamed on James. How many times had his brother and sister gone to the cinema without him or bluebell picking for their mother? He had finally resigned himself to being alone after they had all gone to Cannon Hill Park for a boat ride. Brian had told everyone he had asked James who said he didn't want to go. When their mother confronted Brian he denied ever saying it. Brian always had an excuse why James wasn't with them. *I couldn't find him. He is always hiding somewhere.* Or he told them James didn't want to play their games, they were too rough for him. He's just a mommy's boy usually followed this. He became the sulky child of the family according to Brian, who said it enough times for everyone to believe.

He felt the emotion well up inside him. Had his mother and father treated him differently than the others? His siblings had always objected and taunted him for being a dutiful boy. Doing what he was told. He hadn't seen it that way with such an extensive family. Not wanting to put more pressure on his parents than necessary. The writing had been on the wall, he just hadn't seen it. He sat down on a bench.

He dialed his father's mobile number, then closed it before pressing send. Placing his mobile on the seat next to him. Standing, he shouted at the wind and sea. "Well sod them." The old couple walking hand in hand stopped, looked at him and then swerved to avoid him. The man turned back and looked at him after they had passed. James said, "Sorry." They didn't hear and continuing their walk. His emotions erupted, and the tears ran down his unshaven face.

He took a few steps and leaned against the turquoise rusting cast iron waist-high railing. He breathed the sea air, hoping it would clear his sad mood. A seagull landed on the railing and hopped towards him. They looked at each other in the eye. It was as if the seagull was trying to say something only words didn't seem to be the right way. James shouted at the bird, more out of anguish than hate. "Why? What did I do wrong?"
    The bird replied by squawking and then hopping up and down. James laughed. The old couple was returning and seeing this display shook their heads and walked faster.

"See what you did, you scared the old folks,"
laughed James.
The bird squawked again and then pecked at his right
webbed foot. James took several deep breaths and
wiped his wet face. The seagull took flight and soared
into the air. His overfed body was almost too heavy
for the wings to lift him. It reminded James of a
jumbo jet trying to take off its fat belly full of people
struggling to leave the ground. He watched as the
bird, once in the air streams, glided across the sky with
grace. Several other gulls joined the display, perform-
ing acrobatic twists and turns.

The birds seemed to line up facing the promenade,
hovering in anticipation. Looking along the promenade, he saw a woman about twenty feet from him.
She looked like a bag lady searching for her plastic
bags. Taking a flat squashed box out of a bag, she
opened it. The yellow-colored cake threw into the air
as she gave it a hard toss from the box. The cake
landed on the stony beach. The seagulls dived towards
it, a few at first, then at least fifty appearing from nowhere. A feeding frenzy began and James watched in
amassment at the velocity of the cake consumption.

A small, thin seagull hopped on the outside of the
feasting group. The other birds pushed him away. He
tried again and this time a very large fat dark grey seagull physically attacked the smaller weaker bird. Each
time the bird tried to get to the cake, the bully bird
chased him away. In the frenzy, a piece of the cake
threw into the air and landed a few inches away from
the smaller, weaker bird. Without hesitation, the bird
seized it and flew into the air. The bully bird and the
other birds didn't see what happened and continued to

devour the cake. James in his excitement for the smaller, weaker bird shouted out. "Yes." The other birds gave flight at the sound and flew into the air. The smaller, weaker bird landed close to James and ate at the cake. If a bird could smile. James was sure this one had a grin on his face. Ten feet away the large bully bird landed and hopped towards the smaller, weaker bird. Seeing this, James skirted around the cake eating seagull and chased the bully bird away. He watched as the smaller bird finished the piece of cake. Then a seagull flew into the air and out to sea. Looking back at where the bag lady had thrown the cake, it shocked James to see nothing left. It had been completely eaten. No wonder the seagulls were getting fatter, they were constantly being fed by visitors or locals.

The sky above the sea was clouding over once again. Another rainstorm was on its way. His grim mood returned and the indulgence of self-pity took control. Why had his father rejected him so suddenly? Or had he in the voice message he said later because I'm worried about your mother. May he hadn't rejected him and Brian had lied again. He would call his father later in the day on the pretext to see how his mother is. He wanted to know that, but he would use the opportunity to gauge the atmosphere. Finding out what Brian had been saying would tell him how much damage control he would need to do. Who could he call, the best person was Anne, but she seemed to have sent James to Coventry? Trevor, Ann's boyfriend, would talk to James. It was James who had arranged for Trevor and Ann to meet. He would call him tonight and hopefully he wouldn't be with Anne when he called. Watching the small, weaker seagull had somehow given James a direction to go. Slowly and in the full procession of the facts, that is what he needed to fight his bullying brother. He had already made a few mistakes. He shouldn't have started that email tit for tat. He looked out to the sea and sighed. Why was he so impetuous all the time? Had he not learned to control himself?

The driver stepped out of the black limousine. He bent down and removed a fleck of dust from his polished shoes. His drill sergeant would have exploded at such disrespect for neatness. Standing straight, he checks his suit for any bits of cotton or dirt. He rubbed his shoes on the back of his lower trouser legs. He wished the car company had a uniform rather than suits and ties. It must have been something in the old days when chauffeurs for the rich had to wear a uniform. He felt comfortable in a uniform, and people respected men who wore a uniform. He missed his army days. They were for him the best days of his life. The thrill of the war, of being the victor and making the weaker do his bidding. Those Iraq's and Taliban's had no clue how to fight. He and his squad had taught them a lesson a few times. Now he was nothing, a nobody just a driver of the rich not even the famous. He needed to change, that is what he needed to do, something to make everyone look up to him.

James was unaware of the driver approaching him. His self-pity mood was still riding its course. The driver spoke, making James hold the railing tighter.

"You want to talk to me?"

"Depends on who you are."

The driver points to the car.

"Were you Julian Peterson-Jones driver?"

"I was for my sins."

"Do you know who I am?"

"Sure you're the drunken party animal who almost got buggered by Julian."

"You know he's dead?"

"And his bum boy."

"You don't like homosexuals?"

"I've nothing against queers if they pay me to drive them around. Julian paid me well to keep my mouth shut."

"I just want to know what happened to me the night of his party."

"Besides getting hammered, but if you hang out with Tuff and Miss Fix-it, that's what will happen to you."

"I mean when you and Julian drove off with me."

"You want to know if Julian fucked you arse."

"He didn't I know that."

"Then you've nothing to worry about."

"Just tell me what happened after you drove away from the house."

"You, Julian, and his bum boy were in the back of the limo. I think you were lying on the floor completely out of it. Julian had got Tuff to give you something."

"Like a date rape drug?"

"Something, with them I never was sure what drug they use. Anyway, the bum boy gets Julian all hot and excited. So Julian told me to stop, and they just pushed you out into the road. A lucky escape."

"Lucky."

"Julian was a very vicious man who liked to inflict pain. I have on occasions had to clean up the blood from his fun in the back of the car."

"Fun?"

"He would have me drive him to a club pick up some young impressionable man. They would start in the car and if it were over quickly, I would drop the kid off and drive Julian home to his flat."

"You didn't mind?"

"He paid me very well and I just take orders."

"Why have you told me all this?"

"A mutual friend said I could trust you."

"Who would that be?"

"I'm going to the Marina and then a brief boat ride. Why don't you come with me I think you might learn something?"

"What how to get dumped at sea?"

"That will not happen to you, you know too much. I can tell you my theory about who murdered Julian and why."

"Before we go, why are you going?"

"Julian may have been a sadistic queer, but he was a friend to me. Helped me out a few times. I only drove him around at night. What he did during the day is what this is all about. I want to know because I think they set me up."

"Where do I fit in?"

"After we dropped you off you ended up on the beach naked. When Julian saw the picture of you, he was so mad he hadn't fucked you. Anyway, he knew why you were on the beach naked it's all connected."

"I'm not homosexual."

"Doesn't matter to me. So, you in for the boat ride?"

"What have I got to lose, and you seem to know a lot more than you're letting on."

Brian watched as James climbed into the car, sitting in the front next to the driver. He took several photographs before the car drove away. Standing next to the bench, Brian looked out to sea and watched the seagull's aerobatic display. The mobile phone rang on the bench. Brian bent down and picked it up. The caller was Dad announced on the phone's screen. He pressed ignore and closed the phone. Placing it in his pocket, a grin becoming an evil smile on his face.

CHAPTER SEVEN

Smuggling

They sat in the limousine at Brighton Marina.
"Look it's simple Julian was into some heavy shit.
Not drugs, I know that for sure, but something.
Anyway, you overheard something the night of the
party, and they, whoever, you panicked them.
Somehow you survived so now they are looking for
another patsy and I think it is little old me."
"Because you kept Julian's secrets, they think you
know everything and therefore a threat to them."
"Correct in one."
"You don't know who they are?"
"Not the major players, hence why I'm here be-
cause I think I will find out a little more."
"Who invited you?"
"Ah, that's a good question. Julian's father asked
me to take Julian's place."
"So the father knows what it's all about."
"Possibly but he thinks I do."
"Does he know about me?"
"He thinks you and Julian were working together
because of what happened at the party."
"Sorry, you've lost me."

"That's right, you can't remember what happened. Maybe the best thing."

"He told me to come and get you to take control of the situation as Julian's business partner."

"Why would he think I was in business with Julian?"

"Two reasons first they were using your hotel for whatever they were doing and therefore you must know about it. Second, Julian told his father he had met a brilliant businessman. When Julian kissed you at the party, you were out in front of everyone. They all thought you were his business partner."

"I see guilty by ownership and a kiss."

"Where did he kiss me?"

"I think you were in the dining room."

"No, not what place, where on my face did he kiss me?"

"You will not like it, it was full on the lips, very passionate."

"Hence why so many think I'm gay."

"Look your safe old man Peterson-Jones wants nothing to happen to you. He told me to bring you to see him once this minor job's over."

"And what is this minor job?"

"We go out to sea, pick up a small cargo and bring it home."

"Then we will know what Julian was into and why they murdered him."

"I hope so, whatever happens, I'm on your side."

"What is your name and give me your actual name, not one made up."

"Bradley Quinn. Most people call me Brad."

"Not the Mighty Quinn."

"When I was in the army, they called me pussy and

I didn't understand why. Until this sergeant told
me in the olden days a woman's vagina they called
a quinn."
"I bet you hated that."
"At first but after a while I just let it go. Then
when someone new came along, I would say it was
because I liked women so much."
"And do you like women?"
"Oh yes, very much, I've nothing against gay men
or women. Like you, I'm just not into it."
"Well, Brad let's see where this takes us."

Parking in the grey concrete multi-story car park on
the first floor. Brad had driven into a parking space
with the confidence he wouldn't have trouble parking
there. His mobile phone rang before stepping out of
the car. He pushed the button on the radio before answering. Climbed out of the car, leaving James inside
it.

*The Prime Minister said he had every confidence in
the Chancellor. Breaking news, we are getting reports
of eighteen bodies being found in a container in Do-
ver. We believe the dead were all men and died of suf-
focation. They had covered the air hole in the
container they were traveling in. The Home Secretary
said they would carry a full investigation into the
smuggling of illegal immigrants out after this tragedy.*

Brad returned to the car and turned off the radio.
James climbed out of the car and followed Brad into
the marina. They walked in front of the restaurants
and shops to the other side of the marina.
"Why didn't we park at that end of the marina?"
"Just following instructions."

They took the wet sloping ramp on to a lagoon. James's foot slipped as he stepped onto it, and he grabbed the red handrail. The boat was large with a seating area in the stern as you step onto the boat. Steps to the left led to a small upper deck. On top was the customary radar and communication equipment. This was a very expensive boat and carried a small life raft at the stern. Going through the glass sliding door, he found himself inside a luxury craft. A skillful designed white curved sofa with mahogany wood furniture. He could just see below and into a bedroom. Growing up, he had never had the desire to go to sea, and he didn't get excited at the prospect now. A woman was in the kitchen area serving a man with a bottle of beer. Another man joined them in the kitchen and asked for a glass of red wine. Brad introduced himself and said something James couldn't hear about him. The man with the beer raised it as an acknowledgment to James.

Brad returned to James, "This shouldn't take too long before we set sail according to Derek."

"Do you know where we are going?"

"Just out to sea and then back."

The boat moved and James left the cabin and went onto the lower deck. He sat down on the blue and white striped cushion of the built-in sofa. The boat made its way gentle between the other craft moored in the marina. Brad joined him and stood looking at the various boats moored in the marina. Just as they turned to head out to sea, another boat came very near to them. Julia Brooke was standing on deck talking to a man. He wasn't sure if she saw him because the man suddenly grabbed her and held her close. Her line of sight obstructed. The man in a suit and tie. His face was youthful, for someone in his early forties. The grey hairs at the temples and deep lines of his forehead showed he wasn't as young as he looked. His right hand was on the back of her head and held it in place. He didn't want her to see who was on this boat. It didn't look like they had kissed, but James wasn't sure. He felt angry, betrayed, had everyone in his life deserted him.

The crewman who had raised his bottle of beer to James appeared from inside the cabin.
"Want something to drink?"
James looked at him and shook his head. He was still feeling annoyed at being emotionally played by Julia. Brad grinned and disappeared inside the cabin. James must keep Brad in his sight at all times. He could see him at the bar area talking to the middle-aged lady. He looked back to where Julia's boat had been before it had disappeared. Why was he so angry they weren't in a relationship, was he foisting his family problems onto everyone he knew? The lady came from behind the bar carrying a tray of food. She approached James outside. He had noticed everyone inside had taken the food, so he took two pieces. Brad was behind her carrying two unopened bottles of water.
As they traveled out into the English Channel Brighton seemed so far away. The rain clouds that had been gathering earlier had dispersed. There were very few small boats out on the sea. To the northeast of them was a boat similar to the one he was on. Other than a few actual yachts were sailing to the west of them. The boat movement stopped, and he heard the engine go silent. They had moored and close to the major route for the gigantic cargo ships. From a distance, the ship didn't seem too big. As it came closer, he

realized how big it was. The height of the ship surprised James. They covered the deck in containers six
high. He had seen nothing like it before. How could
such a heavy cargo stay afloat? He wished he had paid
more attention when Mr. Hancock had talked about
Archimedes and his theory. The ship moved grace-
fully through the water. The two shiny anchors sticking out from the bow of the ship. The bridge was so
high the people inside behind the glass windows were
tiny. The ship's siren boomed out as though it was
calling to the smaller craft. Or was it saying I'm big-
ger than you get out of my way?

He watched as it sailed on to a port to unload. He
wasn't sure why, but his family problems returned to
his thoughts. He had realized the problems go back a
long way. At school, some older boys had bullied him
and he wondered if Brian had egged them on. Most of
the boys were Brian's friends. He had heard Brian's
voice when they tied him upside down in the boy's toilets. His feet lashed to the cistern, his head just above
the water in the bowl. They had removed his trousers
and underpants. Someone had drawn a face on his
groin area. The choice for the nose was obvious.
Many of the boys in the school had arrived to view his
predicament. It was only when the teacher on the
playground duty arrived he was released from his embarrassment.

"Penny for your thoughts," said the middle-aged
lady joining James on the sofa.
She was smoking a cigarette and blew the smoke
away from James.
"I was thinking about how cruel families could be
to each other."

"We hear all this talk about family values today.
For me, no family has value if they treat each other
badly."
"Sounds like you are speaking from experience."
"I am. My family were very destructive and as al-
ways it had to do with money."
"Jealousy I think is the monster in our family.
Well, maybe I'm best out of it. My grandfather
would say give them enough rope and they will do
the rest."
"He was possibly right. I noticed you weren't
drinking alcohol would like some tea or coffee."
"No, thank you, I have this bottle of water."
"Wise move, you can never be too careful among
strangers."
"Or friends and family."
"I'm Joyce Janson, the Captain's wife and bottle
washer. Did you know that girl?"
"Which girl?"
"When we left the marina, I saw your face when we
passed the other boat. The girl who had the man
draped all over her."
"I know her, but I didn't know she had a boy-
friend."
"Oh, he wasn't her boyfriend."
"How do you know that, do you know her?"
"Never seen her before, it was the way she reacted
to him. If he meant anything to her, she would
have responded to him, but she didn't."
"Meaning what?"
"Either she was doing someone a favor or he had
something she wanted and it wasn't sex."
"Perceptive."
"A lifetime of watching people."

"I need to do more of that and not let my emotions run my life."

"Emotions mean you're alive and humans don't give them up. Just learn to control them if you have too. As for watching people, I think you're very good at it."

"Sorry I don't understand."

"Yes, you do a watcher knows when others are watching them. You have a very cute face, but the teenage boy look has gone. You may fool the unobservant."

"Then we are just the same."

"The same but different."

"You said the captain of this vessel was your husband."

"Sort of we never married. He was already, she won't let go. I think she hopes he will be very rich one day and she can go after the money."

"Not being married doesn't bother you."

"It did once, but not anymore."

A ship passed them with the name Grimaldi Lines painted on the side of it. James gave a laugh as he watched the vessel.

"Something amused you?"

"I was thinking about the Titanic."

"I think our boat is a little small and we are at the wrong end and not moving."

"I know, but it is ironic how such an enormous ship could sink after hitting an ice cube. Do you think she saw me?"

"Oh yes, and her thought wheels raced."

"If we meet again, she'll ask a lot of questions."

"You expect to see her again."

"Have you seen Brad?"

She didn't react to him not answering her question.
Then lit another cigarette.

"I think he is down below listening to the radio.
So, you're Julian's replacement."
"I sort of became involved."
"Were you and he…?"
"No, this is purely business."
"He gave me the creeps the way he looked at peo-
ple, especially men."
"Did he ever bring any of his friends along?"
"Once and only once the captain soon put a stop to
his games. He had this adolescent boy, I think he
may have been underage. Anyway, they made out
on the upper deck and with the ship's passing. It's
the last thing we want to do is bring attention to
ourselves."
"Stupid I'd call it."
She stood up and put one foot through the glass sliding
door. Turning back, she said, "if you want anything,
just ask."

He looked at another ship passing. It wasn't as big as
the previous one, but still could have crushed this vessel to pieces. The containers line the deck and a tiny
figure stood on a white tower looking down at them
through binoculars. Joining a merchant ship was like
joining the French Foreign Legion. Either you were
running away from something or desired only the company of men most of the time. The thought of being
alone now, his family had rejected him, made him
shudder. Maybe being alone, independent, would be
the best thing. He relied on his family too much; he
needed his space to make his own mistakes. Brian had

been right, even if he had done it in such a spiteful
way.

"Bullshit," he shouted at the wind.
Alone now without his family. He couldn't call them
just to say hello what's going on. His life would be
very miserable from now on until he removed the anger and hate in his mind. Brad interrupted his self-ar-
gument by shouting at someone inside the boat. James
stepped inside, letting the glass-sliding door shut behind him. Brad was pointing a finger very close to one
of the crew's faces. Neither man wanted to back
down. Brad was about to speak when James shouted
loudly at him.
"Brad shut it and get on deck."
Brad looked at James's hatred fill his face. He lowered his finger and obeyed. The crewman watched
and relaxed after Brad had closed the sliding door.
"Thanks."
"What was it about?"
"All I said was the army is a load of pussy boys and
he exploded."
"He was in the army in Iraq and saw several of his
unit killed by a roadside bomb."
"That explains it."
"I believe we don't want to bring attention to ourselves, so I ask you and the others calm down."
"What about him?"
"I'll deal with him."
James looked at Joyce, who smiled and nodded her
head. The man who Brad was about to punch may
have been in his late forties but had a very athletic
body. The only feature to make him stand out in a
crowd was his scar running from his left ear to his
nose. The other man involved in the argument was in

a cheap off the peg suit. He was not a crewman. From the way he looked at James, he was very nervous and seemed to want to talk to James. He moved forward, holding out his hand for James to shake.

"I'm Read Simpleton that's Read with an a.
Thanks for intervening it could have got very nasty."

Read suddenly stood sideways as though he was letting James see his profile. He turned to face James again and pulled his jacket sleeves up. On both hands, he had tattoos of doves with love under the one on the right hand and hate under the other.

James just nodded and went outside to join Brad, who was pacing up and down on the small deck.

Brad put his head in his hands before sitting up, wiping his face.

"Sorry man, I just lost it."
"I understand, but we have got to be very careful."
"I know I just don't like people criticizing the army."
"Oh, that load of pussy boys," James punched Brad on the shoulder.

Brad gave a laugh.

"Julian said he thought you were an exemplary man, and he was right."

James didn't respond he changed the subject, "who is Read Simpleton?"

"Not sure, he would be on board when Julian took these trips. Seems very nervous though, and he kept saying he would be glad when it was over, and he was back on dry land."

"Did he give any clue to what we are here for?"
"No, but it's not drugs, I'm sure of that."

"Why do you keep saying that?"

"No guns, if it was drugs then everyone would have a gun."

"You don't have one?"

"No, Julian hated guns so he wouldn't let me carry one."

"So what are we smuggling?"

"Maybe stolen art. Once when I picked up Julian, he had a large flat package. Looked like it was a picture to me still in its frame."

"Did he like pictures?"

"He said he had a Picasso, but I never saw it."

The sun was setting as though the sea was swallowing it. James had seen photographs, but nothing seemed to compare with the actual thing. For him, the sunset was more spectacular than sunrise. The light was fading quickly. The boat suddenly moved in the semi-darkness, James wasn't sure of the direction. Had they already picked something up Brad and the crewman altercation a clever diversion?

Against the dying light, the small cargo ship seemed huge. They motored around the ship to the side, away from the coastline. James and Brad came down on the lower deck. Pulling alongside the cargo ship, two men raced down the metal ladder and jumped on the boat. Read had appeared and let the men pass inside before turning to James.

"Remember me."

He jumped on the metal ladder and ran up it, stopping at the top to look back at James.

A crewman had taken the two recent arrivals below into the bedroom. James and Brad sat looking out of the window as the boat motored away from the cargo ship. James stood suddenly and stepped out onto the lower deck. Brad had followed, not sure why James had acted so quickly. They both looked at the small cargo ship. The splash in the water was the only noise they heard.

"What did you see?"

"A naked man falling into the water."

"Who?"

"I don't know, but I can guess."

They returned inside. The temperature outside had changed and the warmth of the cabin was very welcoming. James sat on the other side this time the small cargo ship behind him. He could just see into the bedroom. The recent arrivals had taken off their clothes and stood nervously in cheap underwear briefs. They gave each man a brown paper package. They changed into the suits looking at themselves in a mirror. The smile grew on each man's face.

James turned to Brad, "Get it."

"Yes, but what about..." James had placed his finger to his lips.

"It must be worth it."

The captain appeared from the bedroom. He was in his late fifties, a thin grey-haired man. The deep lines of life's worries imprinted into his face.

He gave James an envelope and answered the question, "ten thousand pounds per person for you."

The two men entered from the bedroom, adjusting their suits by brushing down the front of the jacket. Joyce handed them a drink each and in some foreign language, James didn't understand, then gestured for them to relax. They sat next to each other, looking from one person to the other in the cabin before relaxing back into the seat. The captain handed them

British passports. Placing their drinks on a table, they open the passports and looked at the pictures. Both men smiled and showed each other the photos.

James sat back in his chair and watched the two men. They had been laborers, their hands rough from hard work. The sun had burnt deep into the skin. It must have taken them a long time to collect this money. Unless there was another reason they had money. James looked at his watch, he didn't know what time Muslims took prayers only they did it five times a day. One man caught James staring at him. He raised his glass as though giving a salute.

"Are you muslims?" he asked.

The man seemed surprised but answered in a deep accent, "muslim?"

"No, we are Christians."

James wasn't sure if he believed him, it was the expression they would teach a terrorist. Also, why had he assumed they could be Muslims and therefore they were terrorists? How he had become conditioned by the television. It was what Brian had done with the family. Pounded into them one way or another until they couldn't resist anymore and believed.

It would take a long time to convince his family he wasn't the nasty guy. It would be so easy to take a simple innocent event and make it a horrific criminal tragedy. Having dinner with Julia and passing her a clean napkin. If they photographed it in a certain way, it could look as though he was passing her drugs or money. Brian had been working on his plan for some time.

The captain appeared again he spoke to his wife then the two men.

"Let them leave first, best to get them away from the boat. We have someone picking them up."
"No problem, Brad has our instructions so I shall sit back and relax."
Brad looked surprised, then smiled.

They entered the marina and moored at the same place they had left. James watched as a crewman while tying up the boat was looking around to see if they were being watched. He signaled to the captain who took the two men on to the lagoon. James realized this must have been the most dangerous part of the operation. If the police arrived, they were all sitting ducks. The captain shook both men's hands before handing them over to a West Indian in the same tasteless suit they were wearing. The captain watched until they were off the lagoon before entering the cabin.

"We have completed our part, I think we should cool the operation for a while."
"No problem, I'll tell my partners, Captain."
After an awkward goodbye, James and Brad walked back to the limousine.
Brad was looking around to see if they were being watched. Once inside the car, he relaxed.
"I don't think anyone was watching."
"Sorry to disillusion you, but we had two sets of eyes watching. I think you may have to lose the official one before we see the boss."
"Shit, I didn't see anyone."
"That's because you were looking for them. Drive slowly, I want to see who it is that's watching us."
"Where were they?"
"Do you remember the couple kissing by the black Anchor outside the restaurants?"

"They were watching us?"

"No, the old man who was trying to take a picture of them."

"Did he get a picture of you and me?"

"No, he hadn't taken the lens cap off."

"Who was the other?"

"They were much more discrete. It was a man I saw earlier when we left for our brief trip."

"A problem?"

"Not at present."

They drove along Marine Drive towards Brighton town center. Brad was keeping a steady pace, trying to see if they were being followed. It wasn't until James smiled and made a grunting sound Brad saw the car pull out of the side road.

"Who are they?"

"Not the police, I'm sure of that, can you lose them?"

"Sure, we will change cars at the garage. We enter by the front and leave via the side entrance."

The switch was smooth, and James had to hand it to Brad; he knew how to handle this situation. They circled before heading to Hove.

"Whom are we meeting with?"

"Mr. Peterson-Jones?"

"So he is the boss man."

"No."

"He just asked you to bring me to see him when we returned."

"Correct."

"How many times do you think they did this run?"

"I brought Julian here last month, fifteen times, and it was twenty-three times the month before."

"You knew what was going on?"

"Not really I guessed when five men got off the boat who hadn't got on it."

"They must have been making a lot of money."

"Julian was paying me five hundred a day to drive him about."

"So, your rich now?"

"My bank account is. How did you know they gave me instructions to take you to see PJ?"

"Someone went to an inordinate length to plan this operation. I have an envelope with money in it in my pocket. They gave it to me, and you didn't ask me for it. Therefore, you knew what we would do once we had docked."

"Smart that's what you are."

The Peterson-Jones house in Hove was a nineteen fifties red brick. The house was sizeable, standing in its own grounds. They drove up to the front door, James checking to see if anyone had been following them. Brad sat in the car while James rang the doorbell. A woman who could have been Lenora's sister opened it. She showed James into a sitting room with a cocktail bar by the French windows. They decorated the room in nineteen sixties-style plastic furniture. After the woman had left James looked carefully at the furniture. This wasn't reproduction, it was the genuine thing from the period. The high stool in front of the cocktail bar would have graced any nightclub of the period. As James turned around to look at the rest of the room, he saw the alcove with its waterfall and mini fountain.

Mr. Peterson-Jones entered wearing a brown suit, blue shirt, and gold tie. He nodded at James and went behind the cocktail bar. He poured himself a large brandy before turning to face James.

"I don't want to know details, just that the operation went smoothly."

"It did. The captain would like to cool it for a while."

"Not my problem, this was my son and your business."

"May I offer my condolences?"

"Thank you, my son was a fool, but at least he wasn't selling drugs."

"They gave me an envelope."

"Yours to keep I only want this one to go off smoothly for my son's name."

A phone rang in the hallway and Peterson-Jones left to answer it. James took out the envelope, taking out five hundred pounds. He placed the money in his trouser pocket, returning the envelope to his jacket inside pocket.

"Sorry about that, thank you for your help, I don't think we need to meet each other again."

He took James to the front door and opened it. James held out his hand to shake Peterson-Jones. The man just closed the door.

Brad looked up as James sat in the car. He handed Brad the five hundred pounds before putting on his seat belt.

"Thanks," Brad assumed it was from Peterson-Jones, "did you get anything out of this?"

"Yes, lots of information about what happened to me."

"But not who left you naked on the beach and stabbed you in the balls."

"You know about that?"

"But not who or why?"

"You have a theory?"

"Not really and no proof."

"Was Julian the boss of the people-smuggling?"

"I don't think so he tried to make out he was Mr. Big of Brighton, but I think someone else was pulling his strings."

"Why was I picked to go on this brief excursion and by who?"

"Peterson-Jones called the office and said he had a job for me. He told me who I was to pick up and take. Then this other man came and gave me detailed instructions about you. I already knew you from the party."

"How do you know it was Peterson-Jones?"

"The girl in the office said that's who called."

"So you're not sure if it was him and the other man, what did he look like?"

"Dressed in a very expensive suit and handmade shoes. He was old, about forty, with grey hairs in his sideburns. It was the deep lines on his face that made him look scary."

"Have you seen him again?"

"At the marina when we arrived, but he disappeared."

They drove back into Brighton and stopped outside James's flat. Brad handed James a business card.

"My mobile phone number and call if you need me. It won't cost you anything, I think I may need your help soon."

"Why?"

"Not sure, but I have the feeling they have followed us, and I think it may be the police."

"Where did they pick us up?"

"At Peterson-Jones's house, no one was following before we arrived."

James dialed Brad's number and waited for it to ring. Brad answered, then put the information into his mobile contact, as did James.

Climbing out of the car, James carefully looked around. A car had stopped a little way up the road with two people inside. James climbed the steps to the flat's street door. He pretended to open it and stood watching Brad drive away. A car passed and James called Brad on his phone.

"You are being followed by a blue car with chrome bumpers registration ST59BJD."

James ran down the steps and across the street. Hiding in a very dark doorway. His instincts had been right as soon as the blue car was out of sight four police cars came racing down the street. Several officers ran up to the front door and forced it open. He watched as the officers returned to the street empty-handed. Except for one car with two police officers inside, the others drove away.

James stood still, his heart thumping in his chest. He waited for fifteen minutes before deciding to slip away.

The street was empty and if he stepped out of the shadow, the officers would see him. He needed a diversion to his surprise and disbelief it came from the old lady in the basement flat. She ran up from her basement carrying a pan obviously of hot oil and on fire. She tripped and then slipped, the burning oil splashing over the front of the police car.

The old lady screamed, and the police officers jumped out of their car. It engulfed the police car in flames.

One of the police officers helped the old lady up from the ground and led her to safety several yards from the car.

James took the opportunity of this slip out of the shadow of the doorway and up a side alley.

The sound of a fire engine always brought onlookers, and James passed several people trying to find out where the fire was. He kept to the side roads and alleys walking around for a short while before returning and entering the flat complex from the back. He had checked out all the entrances and exits when he moved into the flat. Very few people knew you could enter the place from the back alleyway. Deciding to check if the police were still watching the front of the flat. He walked out of a side road into the major road and stopped dead. Quickly retreated into the side road. Brad's car had stopped in the middle of the street. They blocked it on all sides with police cars. Police officers were all over it. There was no sign of Brad.

James wondered if Brad would talk and tell them about the boat trip. He may have been very loyal to Julian and not reveal anything about the man and his exploits. Brad hardly knew James, he may squeal to protect himself. James watched as the police systematically examined the car. A police car drove away, then stopped. In the back James could see Brad. Their eyes met and James put his finger to his lips. Brad nodded, then showed his hands in handcuffs. Brad mouthed something to James who read it as don't worry.

Sitting on a bench on the promenade, he ate his fish and chips. He hadn't eaten all day and had a headache

from it. The sea was calm, the slight waves gently lap-
ping the stony seashore. At least it didn't look like
rain, although the air had gone cold with several gusts
of wind off the sea. Looking along the promenade, he
could see the lights of the pier. He needed to take
stock of his situation. But only after he had gone
home and had a good night's sleep. The walk back to
his flat seemed to take forever. He was getting colder
and his headache was throbbing. He passed the end of
his street with the fire engine and police outside his
flat. He entered the narrow alley and then into the
back garden of the flat complex.

He prudently opened the door and stood inside listening to the sounds of the place. He could hear the television from the first-floor flat. The man must have
been deaf because he always had it blaring at full volume. He climbed the back stairs, once used by the
servants when the place was a house. He would have
to take the main stairs to reach his flat. He stopped at
the doorway from the servant's stairs onto the second
landing and listened. All seemed silent as he pushed
the door a little and peered into the darkness. What
had happened to the lights? On the first-floor, sensor
lights would pick up if someone moved. You had to
switch on for the upper two floors. They would automatically switch off after a few minutes. He stepped
on to the landing and stealthily climbed the stairs. On
the next landing again, he stopped and listened. He
could still hear the old man's television, but nothing
else.

He tried to look up the stairs to see if he could see
someone outside his flat. As he stepped onto the first
step the wooden board creaked. His grandfather had

taught him to use the side of the steps as they rarely
made a sound. He took each step slowly and stopped
to listen before moving onto the next. His inner in-
stinct was telling him someone was there. He reached
the bend in the stairs and peered into the darkness
above. If only the man hadn't played the television so
loud, he could hear if someone was breathing. He took
two steps at a time he needed to get into the flat as
quickly as he could. Once on the landing, he hurried
to his door. He fumbled in his pocket for the key, then
dropped it. Like the big drum in the marching band,
the sound echoed loudly. In the darkness, on his hands
and knees, he searches around the floor for the key.
Finding it next to the pair of shoes. He couldn't tell if
they were male or female shoes. Quickly picked up
the keys and opened the door. The other person followed him into the flat. He didn't put the light on.
Crossing the room, he closed the heavy curtains. He
had noticed if they were closed correctly you couldn't
see if there was a light on from the street. He switched
on the small table lamp. Grabbing a towel he had
thrown over a chair and stuffed at the bottom of the
flat door.

Someone had placed a grey silk scarf over the lamp,
making the room darker. He looked around the room
to see who else was with him. The room seemed
empty. Sitting on the sofa and closed his eyes to ad-
just them to the light. He sank back onto the sofa; he
didn't care anymore, his headache was throbbing. The
hands touched his head and massaged it. Laying back,
he let the hands gentle ease away the tension. From
the touch, he knew whoever this was, they would not
hurt him.

The hand massaged the back of his neck until the tension disappeared.

"Thank you."

The person came around the sofa and sat down next to him. He opened his eyes and looked into the eyes of Julia. She smiled.

"Julia you're the last person I expected to see."

"Did you think it was a policeman?"

"No, I don't know, maybe. I just knew I wasn't in danger."

"How?"

"I couldn't smell it."

"Can you smell danger?"

"Dogs can and I think I can, but I'm not sure how to describe it."

CHAPTER EIGHT

The Becks

Julia made a pot of tea while James continued to rest on the sofa his eyes closed. He wasn't sure what he would say to her. It wasn't as if they were in a relationship, not even dating. His body ached, he needed to sleep. He felt her sit on the sofa, although he couldn't tell how close she was to him.

"I missed you."

"You surprise me, Julia." A coldness to his voice.

"Why what have I done?"

"Nothing to worry about."

"I saw you on the boat."

"I saw you too with your boyfriend wrapped around you."

"He wasn't my boyfriend, just a real creep. A friend asked me to go with her on this little cruise. As soon as your boat came into sight, he grabbed me and held me. He told me not to move as he didn't want someone on your boat to see him."

"I see what happened, then you made love."

"No," she shouted, "why are you being so beastly?"

He didn't reply, not sure why he was being so crass towards her.

"Did you enjoy your cruise?"

"Well, that's it, we followed your boat out to sea and then he watched it though some very high-powered binoculars."

James stopped feeling supercilious and leaned forward. Realizing he had shown too much attention to what she had just said, he poured the tea into the mugs. He handed her a mug of tea. She looked at him, not sure if she wanted to take it from him.

"Sorry for the bitchy comment."

She took the tea, relaxing into the sofa. James didn't want to ask her what happened next. If he showed her, he was interested she may ask him questions, and he wasn't in the mood to answer any.

She sipped the hot tea and then continued, "he was speaking to someone on a radio the entire time he was watching your boat. It looked like he was giving instructions."

She looked at James to see if he was interested. He nodded his head and waved his hand for her to continue.

"I sat on the deck and pretended to enjoy myself, but I couldn't stop watching him."

"What happened then?"

"Once it got dark, he changed to night sight binoculars. Then you went to the other side of the cargo ship and he became very excited. Well, it looked like you were next to the cargo ship, but by that time it was hard for me to see."

She sipped her tea and stared at the blank wall opposite her. James noticed for the first time how perfect her lips were. They were so natural looking without lipstick, he just wanted to kiss those lips.

"I heard him say terminate and dump."

"Meaning what?"

"I don't know, but we suddenly lifted the anchor and came back to the marina. I thought we would go on somewhere, but as soon as we docked he just disappeared."

"What was his name?"

"They introduced him to me as Karl Vektar, but he wasn't Karl. I know him, well knew him. Daddy did some work with Karl several years ago and he came to our house. So, I got to know him. Then he left Britain and went to Guinea-Bissau and died."

"What from?"

"Daddy said he contracted some disease. His wife had the body flown back to England, and they buried him in Kent."

"I wonder who this man is?"

"I don't know but I know he isn't a friendly man. He has a very cruel smile."

They continued to drink the tea in silence. James was becoming obsessed with her lips and was concentrating on them when she spoke. He didn't hear her question when he refocused, he saw her staring at him.

"Sorry I was just..."

"I asked you why you were on your boat."

"Not sure they asked me to go in place of someone. Another dead man."

"What happened?"

"We went out to sea, I'm not sure why. Then they thought there was a problem, hence why we went close to the cargo ship. Everything was okay, so we came back to the marina."

"Two strange boat trips."

"What happened to your friends?"

"They weren't my friends. My mother asked me to

go along. She always did that when they needed someone to make up the numbers. Endless dinner parties with boring people."

"Parents can be strange sometimes."

He noted the contradiction she had made at first it was her friend who asked her to go now it was her mother.

James placed his mug back on the tray and sunk back into the sofa, his hands splayed out on each side of his body. Julia touched his hand and stroked it. He wondered if she had touched him when he was naked on the beach.

"What are you thinking?"

"I'm still trying to work out how I became naked on the beach."

"I wasn't screaming because you were naked. I thought you were dead."

"You've seen a lot of naked men?"

"One or two."

James blushed and wished he hadn't asked the question.

"You have a very nice body."

"So, do you."

"You haven't seen me naked."

"True, but I have a good imagination."

She coughed as she took another drink of tea, spilling some on her blouse.

James took a tissue from the box on the coffee table and tried to wipe it up on her chest.

Realizing what he had done pulled back and blushing once again, "Sorry I…"

Before he could finish, she kissed him.

They parted, looking into each other's eyes. He took her tea mug, placed it on the coffee table. Then gently pulled her towards him. Kissing her softly on the lips.

Those perfect shaped lips. He held the side of her
face. The softness of her skin coupled with the sensu-
ous smell of her body he became aroused. He pulled
away abruptly.

"Sorry I got carried away."

"It's okay with me."

He sat back on the sofa when she sprang forward and
straddled him. She sat facing him, her knees pressing
into his thighs. He looked closely at her face, the soft
blue color of her eyes and the pinkness of her lips. He
wanted to bite them. She leaned forward and kissed
him, her tongue teasing a little into his mouth. She sat
back, and he leaned forward, kissing her neck. The
wetness from the split tea was still visible on her
blouse. He kissed the spot, then licked it. She threw
her head back and made her breasts rise. He kissed the
crevasse between them, cupping each one in his hands
gently. He undid the buttons on the blouse, then continued to kiss the top of her breasts. His mind raced
ahead and panicked. Would he be able to undo the
clip on her bra without making a complete mess of it?

Sensing his panic, she arched her back outward, and
the bra fell forward. He lifted each breast out of it. He
kissed the left one and saw the nipple become erect.
He licked it before sucking gentle on it. She moaned
and put her hand on the back of his head so he couldn't
move from this position.

It had been so long since he had touched a woman in
this way. She must feel his erection underneath her.
She guided him to the right breast, lifting it with her
hand so he could position his lips on it. His heart was
beating fast and his breathing became heavy. He suddenly stopped and looked at her. He didn't have a

condom. For the first time in his life, he had made no preparation for sex. All those years in the Boys Brigade in Birmingham and told to be prepared what for they never told him. He had assumed it meant for moments like this. Now he wasn't.

She arched backward, almost falling off him. He grabbed her sides and held as she bent backward. From her handbag, she produced a strip of three condoms. She handed them to him as though she had read his mind. He took them in his teeth and then holding her firmly stood up, carrying her into the bedroom.

The sun pushed through the closed curtains, giving a pastel brown glow to the room. It was morning, and he was lying naked next to a naked woman. The three used knotted condoms lay on the floor.

He had read somewhere in one of his sister's magazines that most people after casual sex regretted it. He wanted it to never end. To him, he had performed above and beyond what a woman could expect from any man. To him, it wasn't just sex; it was lovemaking. He felt it had restored his manhood, at least in his mind. She lay next to him, her gentle rhythmic breathing comforting his troubled mind. He needed to use the toilet slipping gently out of the bed so as not to wake her.

In the bathroom, he took a bath, being quiet as he could. He wrapped a towel around his clean body as he entered the bedroom. The bed sheets were in disarray, her clothes no longer hanging off the end of the bed. She had gone. He raced to the door to the flat and opened it. Listening, he couldn't hear anyone on the stairs. Closing the door and locking it. Back in the bedroom, he collapsed onto the bed. He rolled over and looked at the pillow where she had placed her graceful head. A few strands of her hair were still clinging to the white cotton pillow fabric. He moved the pillow to smell and touch it.

The note had fallen behind the pillow and onto the bed. Picking it up, he read it, then lay back onto the bed and kissed the note. He read it again, '*Parting is such sweet sorrow, that I shall not say farewell till it be tomorrow. When we meet again beneath the great oak tree. Three times the day is not enough till then.*'

James studied the note. It was a strange note for someone to leave. He knew the Shakespeare part, but the rest made little sense. She was leaving him a message. Was there a grand oak tree in Brighton? He had never seen one or heard of one. What did she mean by three times the day? If it were anything to do with their love making, she wouldn't have said three times a day. He made the bed and dressed, needing to get out of the flat just in case whoever was searching for him returned.

Entering the alleyway from the back door, he peered into the street. They parked the police car at the end of the road. Hesitation on what his next action should be, he stepped back into the alleyway just as several cars arrived. Quickly climbing out of two of the cars, four men ran into his flat building. He turned and ran to the other end of the alleyway and out into a side road. Hurrying so as not to draw attention to himself. Circling, using side streets until he was in the alleyway opposite his flat building. Several people had gathered after a woman had screamed from his building.

James stood behind two very large building site workers. Watching as the four men who had entered the building ran out. Chased by a screaming hysterical mid-forties woman from flat number nine. Dressed in a heavy dressing gown and fluffy bunny slippers, several of the onlookers laughed.

The police arrived and the four men ran down the street. Several police officers gave chase. One of the four men fell over and two of the police officers fell on top of him. This delighted the crowd who had gathered to watch. James wasn't sure if they applauded the man for getting caught or because the police officer fell over. A car with two men still sitting in it slowly backed up the road. The policemen didn't notice. Wondering how crimes could ever get solved if the police were so unobservant.

One of the building site workers called over to a policeman.
    "Hey, George, what's up?"
The police officer strolled over to the building site workers. He shook the man's hand.
    "Mark, what you doing here, not working?"
    "Yeah around the corner in an old hotel."
    "Four men broke into that building, not sure why, but we caught one of them. Funny, we were here last night looking for someone who lives in a flat in the building."
    "You didn't get him?"
    "Nope, strange, those guys were breaking into the guy's flat."

James sunk back into the alleyway. These guys were after him too.

Strolling backward down the alleyway so no one noticed. The policeman had peered into the alleyway. It would only be a few minutes before he realized who James was.

Sitting in a deck chair on the stony beach, James looked out at the receding tide. It was a sunny day and several families had gathered on the beach to enjoy themselves. He had placed his deck chair near a family. Close enough for anyone watching to think he was part of the family without invading their space. The mother of the family had noticed him arrive. She had watched him and realizing at least what he was; she spoke to one of her eleven-year twin boys.

The boy appeared beside James in one hand, a paper napkin folded around a sandwich in the other hand, a soft drink. He held them out for James to take. James looked over towards the mother who was smiling and nodded her head. James took them from the boy.
"Dad said, why don't you come and join us."
The boy said in a cockney accent. His tight blue jeans made his legs look even thinner than they were. Disappearing under the oversize black tee shirt with the red lettering. Telling the world, he was for sale, price, one trillion pounds. James smiled, at least the boy had a sense of humor. His denim jacket looked like a hand-me-down from an older brother, and this too was a size too large for him.
James looked at the family. It could be a suitable cover for the afternoon. He stood as the boy folded the deck chair and walked over to the family. James followed the sandwich and drink in his hands. The boy placed the chair next to his mother and then stood back, waiting for James to sit down.

The mother spoke, "You look so lonely just sitting there."

Her cockney accent didn't seem as pronounced as the boys. James smiled at her. This was a better cover than he could have expected.

"Just came down for the day from London," said James in his broad Birmingham accent.

Although he normally didn't speak with the accent he had since a little boy been able to turn it on.

"Well, you make yourself comfortable I'm Sharon and that great lump over there is me husband Dave."

Dave nodded his head and then took a drink from his beer bottle. James ate the meat paste sandwich and listened to the family talk. They were from the East End of London and in Brighton for a week's holiday. Dave leaned back in his deck chair and closed his eyes. The black grease under his fingernails told James the man worked either in a garage or in a factory on heavy machinery. He wore an American baseball cap on his head advertising the New York Yankees.

The boy who had given James the sandwich gathered up the other children and led them down towards the water's edge.

Sharon shouted after him, "Garrett you watch those kids"

The boy waved his hand mumbling something to himself.

Sharon then looked at James, smiled and said as though it was so natural to say, "you on the run."

James looked at her. It surprised him at her forthrightness.

"It's okay, we understand. I meet Dave while visiting my father in Pentonville. Now I have half my family in the clink."

James decided not to lie, "yes, but I'm not sure who I'm running from."

"Not just the police then?"

"I know the police would like to talk to me. The others I think would like to kill me."

"What have you done?"

"Nothing I think it is what I saw or heard which has put me in danger."

"And you don't want to tell anyone."

"No, although I think it's all related to the murder of someone."

"Nasty murder."

"How did you know I was on the run?"

"The way you looked around when you arrived. Then you sat close to us, but not close enough to interfere with us. From the road, it looks like your part of our family."

"I was that obvious?"

"No, but when you have done it yourself you know what to look for."

James relaxed back into the deck chair. He had kept the Birmingham accent and hoped he didn't forget to use it.

The scream from the water's edge woke up Dave and had Sharon standing up. The family's children ran back to Sharon. A thin eight-year old girl stood in front of her mother dripping wet and beginning to shiver.

"Garrett I told you to look after them. Emily it's okay baby we'll get you dry."

Sharon opened a bag she had beside her deck chair and
took out a bath towel. The girl undressed. James
looked the other way.

It was Dave who broke the silence, "something up
they're clearing the beach. Are they looking for
you? Garrett show this gentleman the way to our
hotel. Better use the pier okay."

Garrett nodded, tapped James on the shoulder and
walked towards the pier. The tide was flowing back
in. Under the metal pier, Garrett suddenly climbed up
the metal struts. James followed him until the smell of
the boy's trainers hit his nostril. Once they were at the
top instead of going towards the shore, the boys
headed out to sea. It amazed James at the boy's agility
as he climbed along under the pier. The waves were
crashing below as they continued out towards the end
of the pier.

The boy swung onto a metal ladder and climbed up on
the pier itself. He stopped at the top, his hand held out
to stop James following. The boy then climbed on the
pier deck, his handheld over the side still in the halt
position. The metal ladder had thin round metal steps
and after a few minutes hurt the calves of his legs.
James looked up at the boy's hand, hoping he would
give a signal for him to come up. When the signal
came James didn't see it immediately as he was looking down at the sea the tide was getting higher.

Once on the pier deck, the boy kept very close to
James looking around as they walked down it towards
the shore. The boy had guided him onto the other side
of the central glass windbreaker. Most of the other
people on the pier had gone to the other side to look
over at the commotion below.

At the entrance to the pier, several police officers stood by police cars. Garrett grabbed James's hand and pulled towards the roadway.

"Come on," he shouted, "I want a burger you promised if I went to the end of the pier with you."

The police officers gave a quick look at them and then back to the beach. The boy ran across the road, pulling James with him.

"You're one smart kid."

"Got to be if you live in Hackney."

"What age are you?"

"Twelve same as Fenton."

"Your twin?"

"Yep."

They arrived at the holiday flatlets. The owner had done little to maintain his or her property. The paint was peeling from the wooden window frames and off the front door. Garrett took James to the side of the building and then to the back. Pulling on a rope, the metal fire escape ladder descended.

"Third-floor landing. See you there."

James climbed, he wasn't sure why he was putting so much trust in this family. They somehow remind him of his own family. The family who had just turned their backs on him and abandoned him.

Garrett opens the fire escape door and stood to the side to let James past him into the corridor. The inside of the building was in better shape than the outside.

Garrett passed James the boy's way of walking was the imitation of the American gang member. It was the depiction of a hard man from so many terrible Hollywood films. James wanted to laugh out loud. Twelve-year-old Garrett had suddenly become a cartoon figure of himself.

The door of one flat was ajar, James watching the comical Garrett didn't notice the two men inside arguing. A third man caught sight of James in a mirror and smiled. He peered into the corridor and watched as James and Garrett entered the holiday flatlet. Closing the door, he dialed a number on his mobile phone.

Inside the flat, Garrett collapsed onto the sofa and switched on the television. He flipped through the channels, unable to find something he liked. James stood by the door awkwardly, not sure what he should do. He had left his fate in the hands of this family he didn't know. Why had they suddenly helped him? His hands became sweaty as he felt the panic surface inside him.

Garrett continued to flip through the channels, his attention span being very short on anything he didn't like. He gave a side-glance at James and then returned his attention to the television. Trying to relax, James crossed over to the window and gazed down into the street. The window was on the side of the building, looking towards the pier. James could see the police cars and a sizeable crowd. He could imagine the chaos of everyone trying to get a glimpse of the police activity. His hands were still sweaty, and he searched in his pockets looking for a handkerchief. He knew he was only sweating because he wasn't in control. Grabbing at the thin cotton curtains and wiped his hands. He gave a glance at Garrett to see if the boy noticed anything.

Garrett's mobile phone rang.

James became very tense he was a rat caught in a trap. Garrett answered monosyllabically to the person on the other end. When the conversation finished, he returned his attention to the television. Staring at him,

James realized the boy would say nothing. What had he been thinking to let himself fall into the hands of this family? That was the point he wasn't thinking. Too much had occurred in the last twenty-four hours for him to have a proper thought.

Sitting at the end of the sofa, he looked at Garrett engrossed in the television. James wouldn't sit for hours watching endless, mindless television programs. He would rather read a book or talk to someone. Garrett watched a World Wrestling Association program recorded in Atlanta, Georgia. As a little boy, James had stayed with his grandmother, who had been a fan of the British wrestling programs. He hadn't liked them, as they were for him so phony. Garrett was wriggling his body in simulation with the wrestlers.

The noise of two men arguing in the next flat became louder. Garrett responded by turning up the volume to drown them out. For a brief second James thought he heard his name, then one voice sounded familiar. Garret continued to turn up the volume. James stood by the wall and listened to where had he heard the voice before. He became frustrated because he couldn't understand what was being said. Was it in English he just didn't know? The voices stopped and someone knocked on the door. James ran to the bathroom, positioning himself so he could see through the crack of the door.

Garrett still watching the television, opened the door. A small middle-aged woman stood there saying something to him and waving her index finger at him. Garrett nodded, closed the door and returned to the sofa. He lowered the volume on the television.

James sat on the toilet with the lid down. This was ludicrous. He was a sitting target for anyone after him. Why were they after him, what had he done or seen which made him a threat to them? The police knew hence why they were chasing him. He needed to get away from this place and find somewhere to hide and think things through.

He returns to the living room Garrett was still watching the wrestling. James stood by the door into the corridor. He wasn't sure what he should say.

"Tell your mother and father thanks for me."

"Dad told me to tell you to stay put. He has a plan, or at least a way you can hide for a few days."

"You spoke to your father?"

"He called me."

"What did he actually say?"

"He said, tell James to stay in the flat as the cops are all over the place looking for him. Then he said, we will be back in half an hour with fish and chips."

James hesitated before opening the door. Garrett turned from watching the television as he spoke with new authority in his voice. No longer the twelve-year-old boy, but a grown man on a mission.

"If dad says he has a plan, he will have, that's why he is not in prison. And why I and Fenton have stayed out of the long arm of Lilly law."

James let go of the door handle. Something in the way the boy spoke made him feel a little less uneasy.

"Dad's a genius at escaping situations said he watched too much telly as a kid. I use that as my excuse when mom goes on about me watching too much telly."

James returned to the sofa. He was still anxious about the situation, but something in the boy's voice made him want to stay.

"It's cool we're the Beck's of Hackney."

The boy seemed so confident as he spoke; it reminded James of himself at that age. The television program went to a news flash.

"The police in Brighton are looking for several men in connection with the murder of Supermarket owner's son." The announcer then described the men, one of which could have been James. Followed by pictures of two of the men the police were searching for. James recognized them as the men who had been sitting in the car outside his flat during the last invasion. They could hear screams and laughter. Garrett turned off the television.

"There here I'm starving," he said as he ran to the door.

James didn't have time to go to the bathroom, instead he crouched down behind the sofa. He was too scared to look up as the family entered the flat.

The door slammed shut and Dave grabbed Garrett by his tee-shirt.

"Where's James?"

James peered over the back of the sofa. Garrett seeing him pointed with his child's finger. Dave looked over to the sofa and seeing James let go of the boy, smiling when he saw James. Garrett stepped away from his father and stood next to Fenton. For the first time, James could see they were twins. Not identical, but from a short distance, it would be difficult to distinguish between them.

James stood up. He was ready for any confrontation from the family.

"Problem Dave?"

"No, I just told the boy to make sure you stayed, it's not safe for you out there right now."

"Let me get the food sorted out Emily you can come and give me a hand."

James watched as a girl he hadn't seen before followed Sharon into the kitchen.

Dave took James by the elbow and guided him over to the window.

In a whisper, he said, "Sorry about that but when you're trying to teach your kids to do the right thing. You have to be a little brutal."

"Dave, why are you helping me?" Dave turned and walked over to the dining table and sat.

"Fenton, what did that copper tell the woman?"

Fenton stood by his father. He spoke to the table, not looking at anyone.

"The copper said you were from a Birmingham crime family. Involved in the smuggling and mortgage frauds. You're one of us and we the Beck always help our own."

"So what happened on the beach?"

Dave didn't realize James didn't acknowledge where he was from or that he was part of a criminal family.

"After you and Garrett left, we settled down to wait and see what would happen. Suddenly the police were all around us. Sharon offered them a sandwich, I think it was meat paste well that was the only one left. Anyway, they got a little over-aggressive and asked where the fugitive was."

"I pointed at dad and said he was," said Fenton, falling to the floor laughing. Garrett joined him on the floor, laughing.

"I think one copper believed him until this toffy nosed bugger in a suit said it's not him. Anyway, in the commotion of searching our things they upset the food bag."

"It didn't contain food anymore on account we had to eat it all," said Sharon entering from the kitchen carrying plates of fish and chips.

From the floor still laughing Fenton said, "then this big-footed copper stood on the bag and mom screamed at him."

"I told him he had just trodden on our dinner. The toffy nosed guy took out his wallet and gave me forty pounds. So enjoy the fish and chips and a nice dessert for after," said Sharon.

They sat around the cheap MFI table and ate the food. Fenton and Garrett disappeared into the kitchen, returning with cans of soda and two bottles of beer. They gave Dave and then James the beer.

The men in the next flat argued again, the shouting getting louder and louder. Dave rose from his chair and thumped on the wall. It took several thumps before the men stopped shouting.

"Bloody foreigners, always making a noise day and night. I don't think they sleep."

"Not the same men, they keep changing," said Sharon.

"How do you know?" asked James.

"Emily said she saw the ones who were here when we arrived leave with a suitcase."

"James I've nothing against foreigners, I just think if they come here, they should learn the language and not be so noisy. I'm not racist or anything."

"We don't vote National Front although a lot in the

East End do," said Sharon collecting the empty plates.

She disappeared into the kitchen, followed by Emily. The noise from the men next door had stopped again James tried hard to remember where he had heard the man's voice. It wasn't long ago, more than a day, but he knew he had heard that voice.

Sharon returned from the kitchen carrying a tray with a large chocolate fudge cake on it.

"Compliments of the local police force."
Fenton and Garrett laughed it was an infectious laugh. Within seconds everyone around the table was laughing. James wasn't sure why, but it helps break the tension building up inside him.

The sound of the building fire alarm broke the merriment as it screeched out. The family moved as though an army on maneuvers. They gathered a few things together and headed for the door. James sat motionless, he was not sure what to do. He felt as if the hope of the world drained from him.

Dave turned to Sharon, "Shock reaction just grab him."

Sharon snatched at James's left wrist and pulled him from the chair. Emily stopped in front of her mother, ran back to the table and picked up the chocolate fudge cake. Dave felt the door before opening it. The corridor was full of smoke. A man was blocking the way to the nearest fire escape and pointed Dave to take the family the other way. Once they reached the bend in the corridor, the smoke was thinner. Holding onto each other, they ran towards the open door of the fire escape.

James had woken from the temporary freezing of his mind and helped Emily down the metal stairs. The sound of the fire engines some distance away seemed to relax most of the residence.

Dave led the family away from the other residents. He counted each member of his family and then kissed Emily on her cheek. She stood holding the cake in both hands, a smile on her face. Standing at the back of the other residents. James watched as those left inside the building climbed down the metal fire escape. He hadn't realized how many people lived inside the building. He searched to see if he recognized anyone. In his mind, the man's voice seemed to resonate.

The firemen arrived, guiding the building residents away from the fire escape. James and the family stood at the entrance to another alleyway running behind the building. All eyes were on the fire escape as a fireman appeared carrying a woman over his shoulder and down the fire escape. Spontaneous applause erupted from the other residents. Emily had grown tired of holding the cake and handed it to Fenton. The boy looked at his parents and the rest of the family. They were all concentrating on the firemen and did not notice him scooped out a piece of cake on his finger and stick it into his mouth.

He turned away from the others to take a second scoop. He saw the black car slowly driving up the alleyway towards them. Thinking it may be the police. Turning back and caught by Garrett and Emily, his chocolate-covered finger entering his mouth. They pounced on him and scooped out some cake.

Dave and Sharon were still watching the firemen. It was only when Emily giggled in her treble pitch voice that Sharon turned and saw what they were doing. At first, she was angry but then took a scoop of cake herself.

The black car pulled up beside them, its back door opened quietly. No one noticed the man step out and walk up behind James. The white linen gauze placed over his mouth and they dragged him back into the car. The smell of the chloroform was the last thing James remembered as he fell onto the back seat of the car. The door closed, and the car drove away slowly.

Garrett turned and noted the car number plate. He loved cars, and this one seemed to be special with its tinted window and silent engine. That was the mark of a good BMW, a very classy car in his untutored eyes.

The family all dug into the cake and were licking their fingers.

Sharon looked around, she couldn't see James.
"Anyone seen James?"
"He was here a few moments ago," said Fenton, putting a piece of cake in his mouth.
"Sharon, he got out, didn't he?"
"Yes, I think so, did any of you kids see James once we were out of the place?"
Emily shook her head. The boys looked blank.
"Dave, I am positive he was with me when we came down the fire escape."
"Then where is he?"
Garrett was not as quick or street smart as his twin brother, so it took him a few seconds to realize why the car was there.
"They kidnapped him?"

"Whatdu mean Garrett?"

"The black car they took him."

"What black car, where?"

"Just now in the alleyway, a black BMW with tinted windows. It stopped and then drove off again."

Emily looked at her mother, a shocked expression on her face.

"What?"

"He was next to me, I offered him some cake. I took another scoop when I turned back to see if he wanted any. He'd gone."

"We keep this to ourselves okay."

CHAPTER NINE

Back Stabbing

Brian Pidgley flicked the curtains back into place on his Brighton Marina rented flat. The rain clouds were gathering out at sea. He sat down at the dining table and looked at the files on his computer. He opened one labeled 'Evidence JP' and scrolled down to find the picture he was looking for. The picture showed James standing on the back of the boat as he travels out to sea. The next picture was James and Brad standing very close together. Brian smiled to himself as he looked at the picture. It looked as though Brad was kissing James from the angle of the photograph.

He had found out that Brad was Julian Peterson, Jone's driver and possibly a onetime boyfriend. Therefore, James must have known Julian more evidence of James's sordid relationships. As they had found Julian and a teenage prostitute in the hotel, they were restoring. He realized and soon to the rest of the family would think it involved James in a gay sex ring. With this recent evidence, he would rid the property company and family of James once and for all.

Brian would wait to present the information at the next board meeting. Maybe by then, he would have found out more. Even better, they arrested James for his part in the sex ring. There was no other explanation for James's involvement with Julian, Brad, and the other druggie, sex-crazed party goers of Brighton.

He took a sip of the white wine he had just poured himself. He would show the rest of the family he was far better than James. He was sick of his younger sister Anne and her loser boyfriend telling everyone how clever James was. You have a problem let James solve it for you he is so clever. Well, after the next meeting James won't be able to show his ugly face in the Pidgley family again. He closed the computer until it was time for him to call his father and see how his mother was.

"Matthew Pidgley who's speaking."

"This is Brian."

"How are things in Brighton?"

"All is well down here, how's mom?"

"Your mother is complaining we are making too much fuss. She had a dizzy spell that's all, not the heart attack everyone was told."

"Are they sure it wasn't a stroke or heart attack?"

"No, we got a second opinion, and they confirmed she may have had too many chocolates or sweets."

"But she's not diabetic?"

"Not yet, but if she continues eating chocolates the way she does, she soon will be. So how is the hotel conversion project shaping up?"

"The work starts for real on Monday, I had to do a minor work to get it back on track. James had neglected a few things."

"That's not like James he is usually so diligent,

where is he anyway? I've been trying to get him on his mobile for the last few hours. I left him several messages when you see him, tell him to call me."
Brian played with something in his pocket and paused before answering his father.

"James is on a boat with some friends, he likes to party. I told him not to be late as we must be ready for the work on Monday."

"He is still young, and he's not let us down so far. Do you know we made seven hundred percent profit on those homes he built in Malvern?"

"I hope to do much better here in Brighton."

"I'd better go son, your mother is calling something to me. One second... She sends her love to you and James."

"Okay, dad, I'll tell James bye for now."

He closed his mobile and took James's mobile phone out of his pocket. He flipped it open and saw James had missed fifteen missed calls and had several messages unopened. Placing a newspaper on the floor, he took out the battery of the mobile phone. Putting the phone in the middle of the newspaper, he stomped on it with his heel. The phone broke into several pieces. He stomped on it again, then collected the pieces in the newspaper. On the landing outside his flat, he opened the rubbish chute. He crossed back to his door and threw the newspaper bundle into the chute. The bundle hit the back of the chute, causing the chute to bang shut.

CHAPTER TEN

The Manhole

James felt the chilly dampness before he opened his eyes. He wasn't sure where he was, except they tied his hands behind his back. He was wedged against a wall and he could hear running water. Although his legs still felt numb, he sensed he was standing on a ledge. From the way the water sounded, he was in a chimney. The water was a long way below him, as though it was a river rushing by.

He opened his eyes and let them grow accustomed to the surroundings. He assumed it was night as there was very little light. He took his left foot off the ledge and waved it around. He made a sweeping movement and found he was in a circular tube. He looked down and felt the wire tighten around his neck. He put his foot back on the ledge and shifted his torso to make the wire less constrictive.

First, he needed to get his hands free, then take the wire off his neck. Only he felt exhausted and hungry. Drifting in and out of consciousness. He awoke suddenly when he heard a thump above his head. A small shaft of light filtered into the chimney, only it wasn't a chimney. He was in a manhole shaft. The ledge was a ladder running down the side of the wall. They attached the wire around his neck to the manhole cover. Something was attached to the cover at the top of the ladder. Why was the wire attached to the ladder? A black object moved above, and more light illuminated the manhole. A circular grill pattern although very compact was in the middle of the manhole cover. The light was shining through this grill. James could now see the top of the ladder. It looked like rolls of some solid material. He pushed himself up and peered at them. They were rolls of dynamite. If anyone removed the manhole cover, they would cause an explosion. He would drop and hang if he was not already dead from the explosion. He needed to get his hands free and the wire from around his neck.

The light disappeared again and something metal hit the top of the manhole cover. If he shouted, they would try to open the manhole cover setting off the explosion. Then again, if he didn't call out, they would just open it, anyway. Whatever happened, he would be dead.

    He heard a deep male voice say, "It won't fucking budge."

    Another voice said, "Move out of the way, let a man do a man's job."

Again, the metal objects hit the top of the manhole cover. A foot covering the grill in the manhole cover moved and James could see what the problem was. He was grateful a small stone had wedged itself in the locking mechanism. The most council had put some locking mechanism on the manhole covers to stop them from being stolen. Especially the original Victorian cast iron covers.

The mechanism opened and closed a little as the man twisted a heavy key above. The stone didn't move. James didn't know how the stone became lodged in the lock, but it thrilled him. The man became very frustrated and stomped up and down on the manhole cover.

> "Hey, Dick you'd better stop that those kids over there are making fun of you."

The man on the manhole cover moved and roared at someone. The faint screams of kids running away. The man tried the metal key again. Still the stone wouldn't move.

> "Let's get the heavy stuff, it's the only way we will move this thing."

> "It's out at Hove, the rain will come before we get back."

> "Look, we got to check this out before the whole bloody place floods again."

The men left and James knew it wouldn't be too long before they returned. He needed to remove the rope tying his hands together. The ropes were tight and several knots had been used. If he had been awake when they tied the ropes, he would have used a trick his Uncle had taught him to escape.

He had been unconscious and hadn't used the trick. Closing his eyes, he ran his fingertips over the rope and knots. He hadn't come across this knot before. As a teenage boy, he had experimented with being blind and found he could see with his fingers. Although he didn't know this knot, he knew the basic principle knots followed. He found the end of the rope and pushed it back against the rope. Keeping calm was the most important thing he needed to do. If he panicked, his hands and arms would swell and he would have a hard time undoing the rope. The knot had a patterned to it; he traced over it with his finger, then in his mind tried to image it. If he were correct, he could undo the rope. Tracing the knot several times and then relaxed as he conjured up an image in his mind. The light had faded, either it was late in the day or something else had caused the light to disappear. The crash of thunder told him it wasn't night. Big black rain clouds had gathered above Brighton.

He tried to undo the knots. The sound of raindrops hitting the manhole cover made his quest to free himself more important than ever. He continued to play with the knot if he had imaged it correctly then he would soon undo it. The first knot came apart, giving him hope that he could get out of this mess.

The rain hit hard on the manhole cover. The first drips of water hit the top of his head. Working quickly on the second knot, he had been correct on the first one, hopefully the man who had tied it had used the same knot each time.

The water had gone from a few drips to a steady stream cascading down on top of him. Now he knew why the grill was in the middle of the manhole cover.

He tried to lean back against the wall, hoping the water would fall between his legs. Only he had forgotten to open them, and his jeans soon became soaked. He opened his legs and let the waterfall between them. He looked up. The water was becoming stronger. He was in a manhole used to elevate a flooding problem.

Wet all over except for his hands, he had kept the knots out of the water stream. He had untied two knots now he felt the knots left to undo.

The water was now flooding in and hitting the wire around his neck. This forced his head forward, and he was now getting a cold shower he didn't want. He had no clue where the water was falling. It was a long way down from the sound, as if hitting other water below. Working to free another knot, he realized the water had dried up a little. He could hear the water pounding the earth so the rain wasn't stopping. Something must have blocked the grill in the manhole cover.

His hands loosened inside the rope he was close to getting free. Wishing he hadn't cut his fingernails so short and understood why there was a craze for keeping one fingernail, usually the little pinky finger, longer. At the time he thought it a stupid craze, now he wished he had followed the fad. The last knot was tied differently from the others. It was tighter and from touch was a combination of several knots put together. He wasn't sure he could undo it before someone came to open the manhole. With all this water pouring in, he may drown before that.

For now, the water was only trickling in. The flash of lightning illuminated the grill in the manhole cover. Leaves had blocked the grill. He would never complain about leaves blocking anything ever again. If he came out of this alive. Maybe because he was hungry, he was having all these negative thoughts.

His patience was running out, his hands ached from bending backward trying to open the knots. If he pulled the knot, it would never untie. He stopped for a few seconds, closed his eyes and took several deep breaths. He had gotten this far, he could do it, he just needed to relax and let his fingers work.

Trying to push the rope back on itself so he could loosen the knot. It didn't budge. A splash of water hit his face. He spluttered the water off his face. The knot twisted around in his hand. He hadn't noticed and pushed the rope again. Suddenly the rope loosened and then fell off his hands dropping to the water below. He rubbed his wrists and arms. They ached from being tied together for so long. The danger wasn't over as he touched the wire around his neck. He found the clip holding the wire tightly around his neck. He tried to open the clip.

He held the wire in his hand and traced it up to the manhole cover. A clip connected it with two wires entering it. He traced the other wire behind the top of the ladder and felt something hard. Because of the lack of light, he couldn't see what it was. The clip had a slot on one side. The wires moved up and down the slot. Stopped from exiting the clip by a round ball on the end of the wire. He would have to pry open the slot to get the bulbous ball out. He searched his pockets for something to open the slot.

He found nothing that would work. As patience had been the watchword so far, he checked his pockets again.

In the small hip pocket of his jeans, he found a five pence piece. He pushed it into the slot, hoping it wasn't too thick. The leaves on the grill moved and water cascaded in at an angle, hitting the top of the ladder. The force of the water was so strong it pushed little stones from the locking mechanism dropping to the water below.

The coin fit and James twisted it. His index finger at the first knuckle took the brunt of the pain. He was sure he had cut himself trying to open the slot. Trying several times until it was wide enough for him to pull the end of the wire out of the clip. He was free to move about.

The water was now pouring in over him. He needed to get out of this manhole. He pushed on the manhole cover. He pushed the catch to open and tried again to open the manhole cover. Either there was another lock he couldn't see because of the water gushing in. Or the weight of the water was just too much for him to push against.

He looked down; he didn't know what was down below, but there may be a way out. He slowly descended the further he went down, the less light he had. His practice at being blind might just save him if he is lucky. He had traveled just over ten feet down when the ladder stopped. His left foot waved in the air, trying to find the next rung. He tried with his other foot, thinking the left one may have gone to sleep being cold and wet. He still couldn't find another rung to step on. The sound of the fast rushing water was a lot closer.

Hanging onto the ladder if only he could get out of the flow of water from above. Swing out from the ladder, holding by one hand. His hand stretched out to the side. He was trying to move so the little light he had would illuminate the bottom of the manhole. His right hand touched a metal bar. He grabbed it as the ladder continued on the other side of the manhole. It also seemed set deeper into the side. There would be a little shelter from the water above. He made sure his hand had hold of the bar before he pulled himself across. No longer in the line with water falling from above, he was wet and cold, but he wouldn't be getting any wetter. He took several deep breaths and slowly continued to descend this ladder. Looking below, he wasn't sure what to expect. With so little light, he didn't want to get himself into a more dangerous situation. His foot hit the rushing water and the force almost pulled him into the flow. He pulled himself up a rung and looked down into the water. His eyes had grown more accustomed to the lack of light.

A forty-eight-inch drainage pipe was full of gushing water. He wouldn't have a chance of survival if he fell into the flow. He climbed back up the ladder and stopped at the top, sheltered from the water above by this slight overhang.

He needed to rest and get some of his strength back. His stomach rumbled, "You can shut up too." Talking to himself, he gave a laugh at the absurdity of it.

The light from above disappeared, followed by metal hitting the manhole cover. The top of the manhole exploded, rubble falling into the water below. If he hadn't been under the overhang, he would have fallen into the water below.

He didn't move, if it were the kidnappers, they would have survived the explosion because they knew about it. Looking up, he saw no one looking down, and he heard someone moaning. The top of the ladder was twisted metal and would be hard to climb over. Was he making a colossal mistake, he thought as he

climbed the ladder? Looking around as his head appeared out of the manhole, he climbed out.

Two men lay on the ground, one of them was rolling
around. He wasn't sure if the other man was dead or
unconscious and he didn't want to stay around to find
out. Several lights had gone on in the house around
the small park. Running for the cover of some bushes
he almost tripped over. A woman carrying a bright
yellow umbrella ran from a house nearby. Her husband was calling to her from the front door of the
house. James was too far to hear what he was saying.
His legs hurt from standing on the ladder for so long.
He rested against a tree trunk, not sure if the woman
had seen him run over to the bushes. A Southern Water Sewerage Network team van stood on the roadside.

Several other people had joined the woman and were
tending to the two men. He wasn't sure if it was a man
or woman bending over, looking down into the manhole. Moving deeper into the bushes, he didn't want
anyone to see him. A tree had fallen, and he sat on the
horizontal trunk. The realization came to him. If he
had opened the manhole cover, he would have been
blown to pieces. Whoever planted the explosives
wanted him dead. But why was the question, what had
he done? It wasn't what he had done; it was something he had seen or heard. Unless it was Brian exact-
ing an act of ultimate revenge, his brother wouldn't go
that far. Would he?

It could be because he knew about the people smuggling. So why were they going to such lengths to kill
him, and in such a bizarre way? It was bizarre had he
died by being blown up, it would have been hard to
identify him. Had the sewerage men not arrived, he

would more likely have died from hypothermia or starvation. Then blown up which would have made finding out who he was even more impossible.

Why would anyone want to go to such lengths? He needed to turn the tables and let them think he was dead. The explosion would be on the news if one of the sewerage men had died, the news programs would report someone had died. Who could he trust and who was working against him? He needed to change his clothes, get a few things together and then do some detective work of his own.

The back staircase of his flat building although now hidden still ran from the third floor of the house to the basement. He arrived on his floor, someone had removed or covered the light sensor. The automatic light didn't switch on. He stood in the darkness listening to the sounds of the building. His door was closed and unless someone had placed a cover at the bottom of the door, it was lightless inside.

The people who lived on the same floor had made a big thing of telling everyone they were going to Paris. The wife had won a trip in a newspaper competition. James was dubious about it, and it had raised a red flag in his mind. They may have gone to Paris, but who paid for the trip? Was it just a ploy to get at him with no one as a witness? Had he suddenly become paranoid and every dark corner held a potential threat?

Opening the door to the closet between the two flats. He wasn't sure what it was used for in the Victorian days, now it was just empty. He had placed a plastic crate inside when he opened the small window a few days earlier. After his recent experiences, he had tried to be ready for the unexpected. They had caught him off guard and this was his time to turn the tables.

Standing on the crate he leaned out of the window and slide open the small window in his toilet. Slivering like a snake from one room into the next through the windows. Standing on the closed toilet seat, he listened for sounds in the flat. He had checked the floorboards to see which ones creaked when trodden on. After his naked beach nightmare, he had taken several precautions. Knowing he could get into the flat from the small closet, he had oiled the toilet door, so it didn't creak when opened. He swung the door open silently and stepped into the flat. From the light, he could see no one was in this room. Someone had searched the place and left various objects, books, and cushions in disarray. The kitchen was as he had left it, but the bathroom door was closed, and he remembered he had left it open as he always did. Listening at the door, he couldn't hear anything. He opened the door and relaxed when he found it empty. The bathtub was full of water. Maybe they had thought of drowning him and making it look like an accident. They had placed an empty mug on the small stool next to the bathtub.

This left only the bedroom to check. The door was slightly ajar and in darkness. He peered through the crack by the hinges. It looked like someone sleeping in the bed. He pushed the door open a little more and stepped into the room. Just inside, one floorboard creaked, so he stepped over it and then stood still. He listened for the sound of someone breathing. The room was so quiet it heightened his fear of someone jumping out and attacking him.

Approaching the bed, he looked around the room to
see if anyone was hiding in the dark corners. He could
see several bullet holes and a long knife slashed in the
sheets. He pulled back the covers, Bodo his childhood
teddy bear lay on the pillow, a knife sticking out of its
stomach. He picked up the bear and took out the
knife. With a little sewing, he could restore the bear.
James kissed it on its forehead and placed it on a chair.
This left the solid walnut wardrobe. He opened the
doors and stood to the side. No man or woman fell out
dead or alive.

Running back into the living room, he put the bolt on
the main door. While he was in the flat, he intended to
stay safe. James was organized and knew where he
kept everything he owned. Finding the flashlight and
backpack, he collected together a few of the things he
knew he would need. He lay some clean black clothes
on the bed, the black balaclava his grandmother knit-
ted for him would now have a use.

He emptied the bathtub and refilled it with hot water.
He placed the damp, dirty clothing he was wearing on
the clotheshorse, he would wash them later. Soaking
in the bathtub, he listens for any sound. Several times
he stood up quickly only to realize it was the wind off
the sea rattling the windows. His whole body ached,
his legs were stiff. He refilled the tub with more hot
water and soaked, almost falling asleep.

Dressed in black with his Doc Marten boots, he placed
a few more things into the rucksack. He was ready to
leave. This was his most vulnerable time. He unbolted the main door and quickly returned to the toilet.
He pushed the backpack out of the window, still holding he climbed onto the toilet seat. Below the closet

window, he had placed an S hook and hung the backpack on it. He slivered back into the closet and retrieved the backpack. He finally closed the toilet and closet windows.

He listens again at the door then had a panic thought had he unbolted the main door. Taken several deep breaths he remembered he had unbolted the main door. He didn't want anyone coming back and finding the door bolted on the inside and no one there. It was now important that everyone thought he was dead. The landing and stairs were empty as he crept down the back stairs. He left his building and hung to the ominous shadows. Deciding he would make his way back to the Beck's holiday flat and watch them. He just wasn't sure he could trust them. Dave had hinted he was connected to the local crime families in the East End of London. As most East End of London families claimed to be part of a criminal family. He didn't know if he could believe him.

The fire escape ladder of the building next to the Beck building was down. Climbing up onto the roof, he checked at the top to see no one was up there. Inspecting the roof to see if anyone was hiding and what other ways could someone access the roof. He found a corner behind a chimneystack and snuggled down to get a brief nap. Sleep he knew would have to wait until he could find somewhere safe.

Morning crept in and he woke in a fright. He was still alone on the roof. Rain clouds hung like curtains offshore waiting to blow into Brighton. The smell of bacon wafting up from a flat below made him feel hungry.

He walked around the roof, looking over the side at the building and street below. It was still a little too dark to see anything below. He could see into the Beck's flat the bedroom curtains were closed. The light was on in the living room and Emily was watching television. He had found his old watch in his flat. Not having his mobile phone, he didn't know what time of day it was. The watch said it was six-thirty in the morning. He settled down to spy on a family who had befriended him. For what reason, he had yet to find out.

He took a power bar out of his backpack and bit into it. It was not a substitute for bacon and eggs, but beggars can't be choosers, as his mother would say. The thought of his family and what they must think of him distracted him for a few moments. In the past, when any member of the family had a problem, they would rally around them and help them confront the situation head-on. He would do this once he had sorted out his present problem with the police and whoever else wanted him dead.

Daylight finally got out of bed and graced the earth. He checked over the roof, looking to see if anyone had been upon it recently. Someone had they had smoked from the number of cigarettes ends at least two packets. A half-eaten cheeseburger and soda lay dumped on the floor. Whoever had been here on the roof had left in a hurry.

He returned to look at the Beck's flat, surprised to see Dave at the window arguing with someone on his mobile. He seemed furious and even from the distance between them James could see Dave's bright red face. Still, in his pajamas, he paced up and down by the window. Watching from the roof, he wondered who in the Beck family was the weakest link. The twins were not as they both idolized their father. Sharon was as far as he could see a devoted wife. That just left Emily a quiet, almost forgettable child. He remembered how she had stared at him on the beach when they first meet. Then while eating the fish and chips she ate slowly, looking at him as though he was a ghost. Trying to contact her would be almost impossible as she was never far from her mother's side. Then again, if they met, would she give away the knowledge he was still alive?

Dave looked out of the window and up at the roof several times. James had positioned himself at the hole where the rain from the roof ran into the gutter. He could see Dave, but it would be very unlikely that Dave would see him. Emily appeared by her father and handed him jeans and a sweater. Dave still on the mobile put on the jeans and sweater. He turned into the room and shouted something again at Emily. The girl returned carrying a pair of trainers. She held them away from her as though they smelt. Then James remembered smelling dirty trainers when he had been with the Becks.

Dave was going out, but not very far because he hadn't put on a coat. From the rooftop, James could see one side, the back, and front of the Beck's building. As long as Dave didn't wander too far, he could spy on him. This was when James should be invisible, as it would give away his advantage.

It was time to decide which door Dave would exit the building. The front would be a little obvious unless he would get into a car. James went to the back of the building and looked down into the alleyway. Dave

emerged regretting not putting on a coat as the morning cold air made him shiver. He stomped his feet several times before walking up and down the alleyway
by his building.

The car pulled into the alleyway, then reversed out on
to the street. A few minutes later, a man entered the
alleyway from the direction of the car and entered. He
was a tall man in a black Crombie coat slung over his
shoulders. He wore an Indiana Jones hat pulled down
over his face. He walked as though he would meet no
one but taking a quick cut through the alleyway. Dave
ignored the man as he passed him and was surprised
when the man spun and spoke to him. Dave was animated when he spoke, his anger at the man gushing
forth. The man poked Dave with his finger sharply.
Dave pushed the man back and was off guard when the
man grabbed him by the throat. Dave took several
steps back until he was against the wall. This made it
a little difficult for James to see what was happening.
It was clear the man was very strong, and Dave could
do little more than a feeble struggle to get the handoff
his throat. The man slapped Dave across the face to
calm him down. Dave relaxed and stood looking the
man straight in the face. It must have been hard for
Dave with his I'm in control attitude. James had
learned a long time ago however tough you are there
will always be tougher men. After a quick speech, the
man let go of Dave, who moved away from the man.
From this angle, it was hard to see who the man was
and why Dave was so scared of him. The man waved
his index finger a few times before walking back down
the alleyway. James raced to the other end of the roof,
looking over the parapet.

The man had reached the end of the alley and was talking to two men. They were standing by a black car similar to the one that had driven into the alleyway before reversing out. One man entered the alleyway while the man took off his hat and coat. He placed them on the back seat of the car before looking up and down the road. James wanted to see his face, so he moved to the end of the roof. The man suddenly looked at the spot where James had been standing. It was the man who had been with Julie on the boat. He remembered the man's name she said he was using the name Karl Vektar. Pulling back from the parapet only to return and see the car drive into the flow of early morning traffic.

Dave had returned to his flat and was telling Sharon and Emily what had just happened to him. Sharon tried to calm her irate husband down.

James wondered what had happened to the man who had left Karl and gone into the alleyway. He checked over the side of the building. The man was trying to get hold of the fire escape ladder to the building. When James had climbed up, he had pulled the ladder up.

Gathering his backpack, James knew it wouldn't be too long before the man could get the ladder and climb up onto the roof. He checked to see if he had left any telltale signs he had been on the roof before heading for the door leading into the building. It was open, and he entered. Stopping and listened, he heard someone climbing the uncarpeted stairs a few floors below. James took two steps at a time and raced to the floor below. Like his building, it was a convert Victorian house. He opened the closet door between two flats.

It had several cardboard boxes stacked inside. He knew he wouldn't be able to hide inside there. Seeing a flat door open, he ran to it. Without looking who might be inside he entered and closed the door leaving a three-inch gap so he could lookout. The man reached the landing and was panting out of breath. He pulled himself up the next flight of stairs leading to the roof. James closed the door and gently fell forward, his head resting against the back of the door.

CHAPTER ELEVEN

Fenton

"You come to fix me telly?"
The old man sat in a winged armchair, a blanket over
his legs. The man's hands were thin and long, as
though they hadn't done a day's work all his life. His
face was the other extreme with deep lines and dark
shadows under his eyes. Wispy grey hair combed
backward because it needed cutting for a long time.
The few remain strands hung down over his bent
shoulders.

James nodded, put down his rucksack and went over to
the television. Though he did not understand what to
do, he looked at the back of it. The old man fell
asleep, his head falling on to one wing. Thinking it
would be best to play the part continued to look at the
back of the television. The problem a disconnected
aerial cable. James reconnected it and opened the television. It started loudly, the volume up high. Maybe a
neighbor had entered the flat when the old man was
asleep and disconnected it because of the volume. James turned down the sound. The old man
woke up, a smile appearing on the wriggled face.

"You fixed it. Wanna cup of tea I do, but you must make it."

James smiled and went into the old man's kitchen. He must have a daily helper to keep the place so clean. Finding the tea-things were simple as whoever looked after the man keeps the items in a logical place. Handing a mug of tea to the old man, he sat down opposite to drink his tea.

"When I was in the war, I had a corporal who looked just like you. He was a right bastard to us men, but do you know he saved our lives? I didn't serve in the next one. They said it was because I had a bullet in my head from the first one."

The old man sipped his tea and switched off the television. James wondered if he had disconnected the aerial cable so he could have visitors.

"I never got a bullet in me head it was my bottom straight threw me arse."

The old man fell asleep again, his mug of tea still in his hand. James took the mug and placed it on a table next to the old man. He wiped his fingerprints off it, then finished his mug of tea and returned to the kitchen. Washing the mug and then wiped everything he had touched leaving no fingerprints in the place.

Opening the door to the flat, he listened. Someone was talking either up the stairs or down a floor. James needed a disguise and began searching the old man's place.

In a closet, he found a pair of men's overalls. Although they looked very dirty, unwashed. He put them on over his black clothing. At the bottom of the closet was an empty aluminum toolbox. James pushed his rucksack into it, then stood by the door. He would have to improvise if he passed anyone on the

stairs. An unopened letter was on the sideboard by the
door James read the name. The old man was still
sleeping when James opened the door.

In a broad Birmingham accent, he said, "the television fixed now, Mister Tyler."
He left the door slightly ajar and walked towards the
stairs. Seeing the two men standing on the stairs below, he placed the metal toolbox on his shoulder. Ob-
scuring his face from them as he passed them. They
continued to talk, ignoring him. He continued down
the stairs, taking two steps at a time. He hesitated at
the main door, turned and walked to the back of the
building. He passed the building's laundry room,
stooped and retreated into it. Hanging on a peg was a
black and white flat cap. Taking it off the peg, he tried
it on. He pulled it down over his eyes before venturing
out into the alleyway.

He passed several people talking at the entrance to the
street. They took no notice of him. They wouldn't.
No one ever takes notice of a workman. Once on the
road, he walked away from the pier end of
Brighton. He needed to get some proper food and a
place he could sit down and think. After ten minutes
he felt it safe to slow down and look for a place to get
something to eat. The burger restaurant wasn't the
most exciting place around, but it was anonymous. He
ordered the friendly meal of cheeseburger and fries,
opting for a hot coffee rather than an ice-filled soda
drink. Sitting by an old fishing boat on the beach, he
made himself comfortable. From the roadway, it
would be hard to see him, but he could see anyone approaching him. Fast food had never been to his lik-
ing. His mother had been such an excellent cook, he
didn't desire it. So many of his friends had enjoyed

the quick and easy convenience of a fast-food restaurant.

He was hungry, so he devoured the food, savoring what flavors he could from it. The fried onions on the burger had tasted good. The coffee was hot and wet, and he relaxed as he drank it. What had he seen or heard that made these men whoever they were, want him dead? He could see several boats out at sea riding the waves. The sea was becoming rough as more darkening clouds moved inland. The first drops of rain fell from the sky. He had been wet enough recently, so he looked for a place he could run to and keep dry.

Several old fishermen had built storerooms under the promenade. He ran over to them and found one with the door open. The local drug users or drinkers used it from the state the place was in. Putting the toolbox down by the door he sat on it finishing his coffee.

He felt sorry for himself. His family wasn't talking to him and several men were after him for what he didn't know. He knew he would have to lose this feeling of self-pity if he would survive. The weather was also making him feel despondent. It was times like this when he needed a friend, someone to talk to. He had always been someone who didn't have many friends. The people he knew were his brothers or sister's friends, not his. The tide crashed onto the stony beach, making it difficult to hear anyone approaching.

It reminded him of his boat trip and the illegal immigrants he had seen on the small boat. They didn't look like they were important men, just ordinary refugees. Julie had said the man on the boat she was with had followed his boat out to sea and watched it. Next time he sees the man, he is talking to and threatening Dave.

The small person ran into the little tunnel and fell over James. The rain was no longer a drizzle but a pouring down. He pushed the person off, realizing it was Fenton. He grabbed the boy by the throat, anger growing inside him.

"Who is with you?"
Fenton hadn't realized who was holding him and screamed back,

"Bloody hell, you scared the shit out of me."
"I said who is with you?"
"No one I'm by myself."
Still holding the boy, James peered outside and looked up and down the beach. With the rain lashing the seashore, he was surprised he couldn't see anyone.

"Why are you spying on me?"
"I'm not who the hell are you, anyway?"
"Why did you come here?"
"I'm hiding."
"Who from?"
"Me dad, he's in a nasty mood so me and my brother did a bunk. We split up, and I came here."
"How did you know about this place?"
"You ask too many questions."
"Fenton I want to know."
"How do you know my name?"
James let go of the boy and stood in the doorway's light.

"Dad sent us out to look for you."
"Who sent you to look for me and why did they?"

"Dad told us to go find you. He is in one of his
moods when he panics. We end up doing things we
hate doing, so Garrett said let's do a bunk."
"Why does your dad want to find me?"
"He doesn't only two men told him because dad
had lost you, he had to find you and tell them
where you were."
"Why do the men want me?"

Fenton went pale and shook. James thought he might
faint. Grabbing the boy to stop him falling over, Fenton yelped like a dog. James pulled him up the boy's
shirtsleeve. The bruise marks were big and recent.

"Sorry I didn't mean to hurt you. I need to know
why those men are after me?"
"They told dad you had some information which
was very important to them. Some other men
wanted you dead, so you couldn't tell these men
what you know. I think that's right, anyway. It
was something like that."
"The men who spoke to your dad, do they want me
alive or dead?"
"Alive."
"The police, what about them?"
"They told dad you were a suspect in a murder."
James sat down on the toolbox again and expected the
boy to make a run for it. Fenton looked around the
tunnel seeing an old plastic milk crate he collected it
and placed it next to James.

"We Becks aren't the nasty guys."
"Fenton I can't trust anyone just at the mo-
ment. It's nothing personal against your family."
"I know you must be shit scared."
"I am and I don't want anyone to know I'm still
alive."

"Why you supposed to be dead?"
"The men who wanted me dead may think they
have done it. I want them to believe it."
"I won't tell on you."
"Not even your dad?"
Fenton thought for a few moments then looking
James straight in the face.
"Only if he hurts me."
"Does that a lot, I suppose?"
"Only when he gets angry Garrett had asthma so I
take the beating so he doesn't have a fit."

The boy was looking out to sea, his angelic face lost in
the thought of those beatings. Either of his parents had
beaten James. His father didn't believe it was the correct thing to do. After their conversation here in
Brighton, James now understood why.

He suddenly remembered something Brad had said to
him about overhearing something at the party. He was
unconscious, but someone thought he might have over-
heard something.
"Did I leave my mobile in your flat?"
"Not as far as far as I know if you had Emily would
have given it to mom and she would have told us
about it."
"Fenton don't tell anyone you've seen me. You
understand?"
"I ain't going to tell no one."
"Not even Garrett?"
"I wouldn't tell him he has a big mouth."
"And you don't?"
"Not unless you torture me and then I'll squeal like
a pig."
"What happened after I left?"

"Mom and dad went spare, especially mom. She said you were a posh bit of stuff, a bit of all right."
From the way Sharon had spoken and treated James, he was aware she liked him.

"Emily said mom fancied you."
James blushed, shuffling his feet in embarrassment.

"Then what happened?"

"We all went to this fantastic Indian place. As we sat down these two men sat at our table making Emily and Garrett sit at another table."

"Did your dad or mom know the men?"

"No, dad said we had this table first and one man opened his coat and showed dad something. I couldn't see, but mom did, and it scared her."

"What do you think he showed him?"

"It was a gun I heard mom ask dad if it could have been real. One man told dad as we had lost you, we had to find you, or we would all pay the price. The men left, and we had dinner. Well, I did, Dad didn't eat much, and Mom ate nothing. On the way back to the flat dad got real hansy and told us we had to find you tomorrow."

"So that was last night and this morning your dad met a man in the alleyway."

"How do you know that?"

"Doesn't matter, I just do."

"It was an unfamiliar man, according to Emily. Dad said he was looking for you and he said if we found you, we were only to tell him. Dad said he thought the man wanted to kill you."

"Are you sure it was a different man?"

"If Em says it was, then it was, she doesn't lie."

"And you do."

"Only to survive."

"How do you know about this place?"

"Last year when we came here, I found it and watched a couple make out."

Oh, the innocence of youth, thought James, remembering his first time watching a couple in Daffodil Park. The man couldn't get the girl's tights down. He ripped them and the girl got furious.

"I not going to tell anyone I saw you."

"I don't care anymore, I think I will be dead by tomorrow."

"No, you won't your one of us."

"I'm not a Beck."

"As good as my mom and dad would bring no one home, they wouldn't let us kids have friends over. Dad said we don't have strangers in our house or anywhere we might be."

James looked out to sea again, realizing how lucky he and his siblings had been with their parents. A seagull landed just in front of the door. He had not seen such a large bird, the beak looked so dangerous.

He turned and looked at Fenton. The boy had a way to make you relax with him. A red flag waving at James. He knew how gullible people could be.

"Why do you think he did it?"

"Because he could tell a con man a mile off and you're no con man."

"I might be."

"Not in a million years."

"Where's Garrett?"

"At the pier, he loves the place."

"I thought you two were never apart."

"Only when we are with Mom and Dad, I don't like his friends or his music."
The large hairy man appeared at the door. His clothes were old and very smelly. The man looked at Fenton, then roared. The boy ran past the man screaming. James picked up the toolbox and backed into the tunnel. He looked to see if he could find another way out of the place. He didn't want to have an altercation with the man. The second man appeared from behind James. He too was large and very dirty. He roared at the first man, then charged at him. They fell to the floor rolling over trying to punch each other. Each man roaring then grunting before ripping at the other man's clothes. James stepped back to the rear of the tunnel. There must be another way in which the second man had entered.

A stone stairway with water running down the steps went upwards. He took two steps at a time, emerging on the other side of the road. Stopped peering up and down the street from the pavement level. He could see Fenton running hard towards the pier. The street was empty of people and just a few cars parked. It was impossible to see if anyone was sitting in the cars. So, he retreats down the steps and sat on the toolbox out of the rain.

He couldn't risk being seen waiting until it was night. This was his time to think about the people involved. Speculating what part Julie played in this drama. She knew more than she was letting on. Maybe he should call her again, but he couldn't. If only he could remember where he left his mobile phone. Why had she been on the beach when he was naked and unable to move? She never really explained it, she just kept saying she was sorry for

screaming. Then again, her explanation of why she
was on the boat with the man calling himself Karl
didn't ring true. Did her mother ask her or a friend to
go on the boat trip? He would have to spy on
her. Then there was Brad something about him
wasn't, as it seemed. He had been in the army but
never talked about it as though he wasn't proud to
serve his country. The way he asked questions as
though he was interrogating you. It made James think
the man was an undercover intelligence agent, someone from MI 5. He smiled to himself. In the past, his
family had always compared him to an Agatha Christie
sleuth. Now he felt he was moving into the realms of
Ruth Rendell and her sophisticated investigators.

"Going upmarket," he shouted.
A woman walking her dog on the street above
jumped. The dog barked, then ran off down the street.
What was his plan of action, who was he going to spy
on first? If he found something out about Julie, it
would destroy his fantasy, so it had to be Brad.
He recalled where Brad had said he lived. When they
were driving to see Peterson Jones in Hove. Brad had
pointed to a house he said he lived in.
James was sure he would remember which house it
was. The angry shadows of night seemed to take a
long time arriving. His impatience was getting the better of him.
Finally, he felt he could leave his hiding place and
venture to his mission as a spy.

He slipped into an Indian take away shop and brought
their value meal. It was food he just wasn't sure if it
would be any good. The road wasn't hard to find.
Once he was close to the house Brad lived in, he
started looking for a place to hide. The only thing he

could see on the road was a small tent over a manhole cover. He shuddered at the thought of the manhole cover. Also, the tent was at least forty yards from the house. He was still wearing the overalls and carrying a toolbox. It wouldn't look odd if he entered the tent.

He lifted the flap and stood looking down into the manhole. Someone was climbing up a ladder from below. He exited the tent and ran a few yards up the street. The flap of the tent opened, and James darted behind a tall hedge. He was standing next to a port-a-loo in the front garden of a house under renovation. He opened the door and stepped inside. Expecting it to be very smelly and dirty, surprised how clean it was. Looking into the tank below, it looked as though the toilet was unused. He pushed the door a few inches open, realizing he was looking at the house he thought Brad lived in. Sitting on the toilet, he ate the Indian meal. If it didn't agree with him, he wouldn't have to go far to shed himself of it.

When someone appeared in the street, he would move his foot and the door would close the three inches. He was on his first Brighton stake out hoping he didn't fall asleep waiting for something to happen.

CHAPTER TWELVE

Saving Dave

Fenton arrived back at the flat, breathing hard. His upper chest hurt from running. Even though fit from exercising, he wasn't used to running that hard. Searching each room for the rest of the family. He was alone and no visible sign of a note where they had all gone. He slumped down on the sofa. Although twelve years old, he was still a little boy inside. Scared of the dark and larger bear-like men. The crumpled piece of paper lay beside one leg of the dining table. He opened it and spread it on the table. Flattening it several times with his hands. The writing was big and in capitals. He was grateful for that, as he wasn't the best at reading. He read the note out loud, stumbling over several of the words before he felt he had read it correctly.

'Meet me at Pascals on the London Road across from Baker Street. Go to the workshop at the back and be by yourself.'

He had seen the Pascals factory when he and Garrett had gone exploring on their first day. It was over by

the station where most of the buildings looked like
they had been abandoned.

Hesitating at the door, he speculated if he should leave
a note. Deciding not to walk, he ran to the station. The intensity on his face made several passers-by
give him a second look. Ignoring attempts to offer
him the help he kept focused on his goal. Pascal was a
red brick building boarded up, no longer a thriving
place of business. He ran from one end of the building
to the other. There was no way he could find a way to
get around the back of the building. The only place he
could see to get to the back was through a wooden
fence that blocked an alleyway between the buildings. He leaned against the wooden fence, his left
hand hanging down and running over the planks of
wood. He caught one as his hand brushed over it. The
plank was fixed by one nail at the top. Facing the
fence, he moved several of the planks in the same
way.

Looking up and down the street before sliding the
planks, he stepped into the alleyway. Walking the entire length of the side of the building, he couldn't see a
way inside. Towards the back, there was a window,
dirty and with several panes of glass broken. He was
just too small to see inside. The plastic five-gallon
paint drum filled with water. He tipped it on its side
and let the water run out. Placing the upside-down
drum by the window, he climbed up and peered inside
the building.

His father was in the middle of the room on his knees
with his hands tied behind his back. The large bear-
like man had his hands around Dave's throat. Fenton
acted quickly, running to the back of the building. He

looked around and found a three-inch-thick plank of wood a little over three feet long.

The workshop door was open about seven inches, just enough for Fenton to squeeze through. The man had his back to him and covered his father from seeing him. Realizing he couldn't hit the man on the head because of his height. He crept up behind the man and aimed the blow to the back of the man's knees. The man crumbled down on to his knees. The second blow hit him on the back of the head, cutting it open. Falling to the side of Dave but splashing him with blood. Fenton attacked again, hitting the man on any part of his body he could. Anger had taken over the boy and he went out of control.

Dave shouted several times "Fenton Stop."
Finally, the boy stops, tears running down his face. He hugged his father, sobbing hard.

"Untie me, son."
The words didn't sink in, Dave repeating them before Fenton understood. Dave held his son until he had calmed down.

"Stand over by the door and see if anyone is around."
While Fenton stood at the door Dave approached the man. From the look of the head wound, he didn't expect the man to be conscious. He checked the man's neck for a pulse, trying hard to find one. The man was dead, his son had just killed a man. Searching the man's pockets, he took the wallet then picked up the plank of wood Fenton had used.

They walked away from the workshop and out on to the street. The road was deserted to Dave's relief. They crossed a piece of derelict land, stopping by a group of homeless men who had built a fire. Dave placed the plank of wood on it.

The flames licked around the wood and sizzled the blood still on it. Not until the wood engulfed in flames did Dave walk away from the fire, his arm on Fenton's shoulder.

His son had just saved his life, never again would he hurt either of his boys. After the way, he had taken his frustrations out on Fenton. Knowing the boy had covered up because of Garrett's asthma. He was a hero and one day he would tell the world or at least the family how brave Fenton was.

The warmth of his father's arm comforted Fenton. He loved his father regardless of how the man had treated him in the past. Nothing would stop him from helping the man who had given him life and taught him so much.

On the far side of the derelict land, they found two red milk crates. Dave turned them on their edge and they both sat down. Fenton's head hanging low. What if he had killed the man he would go to jail and not see his family for a very long time?

Neither spoke nor looked at each other in the face. Fenton shuffled his feet in the dusty earth. Spots of blood were visible on his Doc Marten boots. He would clean them when he got back to the flat.

Taking a deep breath, he looked at his father, knowing he must know the answer, or it would haunt him in his dreams.

"Did I kill him?"

Dave looked at the boy's face, so innocent yet so worldly. He knew the wrong answer here could

destroy him inside forever. It would be better to lie
than let him know he was a murderer.

"When we left, he was still alive. The other man
who kidnapped me would be back soon and find
him."

Fenton could tell his father was lying and he would
have done the same. He would only believe what his
father said.

"Why was he trying to kill you?"

"They want to know where James was."

"Why what has James done?"

"I think he was in the wrong place at the wrong
time. He saw or heard something making them
want to kill him."

"I hope they don't kill him, I liked him."

"Me too."

"So did Mom."

"Oh, she likes all young attractive men."

"But she loves you."

"I know that's what makes us the Beck's from the
East End."

"The Beck's."

"Did you find James?"

"No, Garrett might have he went to the pier."

His father had lied to him to protect him from the pain
of knowing the truth. Now he would protect his family from knowing. As they say what you don't know
you can't tell.

"I don't think we should mention what happened to
your Mom or Garrett and Emily."

"You're the boss, what you say goes."

"Fenton."

He hugged his son the emotion of what had occurred
had finally hit him.

As they walked back to the flat Fenton reasoned in his mind why he had lied to his father. If the men who had almost murdered his father had got hold of James, they would have tortured and then killed him. Although he would feel guilty for several weeks, he knew he had done the right thing.

Dave put his arm around Fenton again. Something special had just happened between father and son. Something he would never in a million years have thought would happen. He was so proud of his son, twelve years old and already a man. He wouldn't ever tell him the man was dead at twelve. It was unlikely he could handle it and later he would lose respect for his father for lying to him. It was a no-win situation and therefore best left unsaid.

Sharon, Emily, and Garrett sat at the dining table eating. Fenton went into the bathroom. He needs to wash his face and gargle. Sharon knew something had happened from the way Dave avoided looking at her. Over the years of her marriage, she had learned not to ask but wait until they were alone and broach the subject slowly. Returning from the kitchen, she carried their food and placed it on the table. Fenton sat down next to Garrett, not looking at him or any other member of the family.

"I want to go home."

The words from Emily seemed to bring the whole family back to the table.

"Me too," said Dave, "I miss home."

CHAPTER THIRTEEN

MI 5 Connection

James practiced moving his foot, so the door closed and opened easily. He was thinking buying the Indian food might have been a mistake. It wasn't the food only his stomach seemed not to like such rich spicy delights. He burped several times, the taste of his meal hitting his taste buds a second time.

Looking out on the street, he wondered where Brad's car was. When he entered the street, he hadn't seen it parked. Maybe he had a garage at the back of the house and put the car inside. Brad might not have arrived home. The man worked strange hours as a driver.

His stomach continued to make noises. He laughed, at least he was in the right place if he had a problem. No searching around for a toilet to use. The house was a nineteen-thirties building the owners were having it completely renovated and adding a third floor. Converting the loft into several rooms. This brought his mind back to why he had come to Brighton. The hotel conversion was his father's idea, and Brian had just

come in and taken over. Maybe Brian had something
to do with his present situation. It was for him incom-
prehensible that a brother would do something like
it. Then again, he had never really got on with
Brian. It wasn't just jealousy; Brian had become
greedy wanting more. At the board meeting about the
houses they had built in Great, Malvern Brian had
complained they sold the properties too
cheaply. James knew this was just greed. Overprice
them and you could hang onto them for a very long
time. Just after they had sold the last one, the housing
market started its downturn.

Brian had joined the money set wanting to have as
much as possible regardless of how you get it.

Two very young teenagers walked past the house.
They returned, the boy opening the port-a-loo
door. Seeing James, he let the door close. They were
looking for somewhere to kiss and cuddle. It was unlike James thought they were looking for somewhere
to make out. They were too young, except these days
who knew what a thirteen-year-old got up to.

> James heard the boy say to the girl, "some old perv
> in there, possibly wanking."
> "Bloody cheek." Shouted James then realized he
> shouldn't say anything.

He didn't want to bring attention to himself.
On films and television programs, characters doing
surveillance didn't have to wait long for something to
happen. In actual life, he realized things were different. He had been sitting on this toilet for over two
hours and all he had seen was two kids. It scared him
he would fall asleep and miss what he was hoping to
see. His eyes closed and his mind drifted off.

If it hadn't been for the honking of a passing car, he would have missed Brad. He parked his car two house up and sat talking to someone on his mobile phone before climbing out of the car. Not dressed in his driver's uniform, but jeans and a black sweater. He looked up and down the road before crossing and entering a house. It wasn't the one James thought he lived in, but the one next door. Giving James a better view.

The house already had lights on and James remembered seeing someone enter the house when he arrived in the street.

Because the Port-a-loo was next to a very high privet hedge, the streetlight didn't illuminate the toilet. As long as James didn't move it would be hard for someone to see him sitting inside.

It was moments like this he needed his mobile phone. If only he could remember where he had last used it. When he confronted Brian, had he placed it on top of his car. After Brian had gone, he couldn't remember if he still had it. If Brian had taken his mobile phone what good would it do him? Except it would be difficult for James to call the family and vice versa. Except Brian had said the family didn't want to speak to him. Was Brian telling the truth, that was the question he needed answered.

The movement from Brad's house brought James back to reality. He picked up the toolbox and crept out of the toilet. He slipped down between the port-a-loo and the hedge. Because of the lack of light, it would almost be impossible for anyone to see him. A man came and opened the door of the port-a-loo. He was the same build as Brad, only he had a beer belly that hung over his jeans.

He spoke into a walkie-talkie.

"He has gone I know he was here I saw him when I came home."

Brad answered through the communicator. "Where do you think he went?"

"Not sure I saw some kids looking inside the port-a-loo, maybe they scared him off."

"I think we should contact London and let them know the situation."

Brad appeared from behind the hedge. From James' vantage point and the overhead streetlight, Brad looked exhausted. It could have been a trick of the light.

"We need to find him before they do, he is the only person who knows what happened."

"If he saw something and we still don't know if he did."

"You read the report about him in Malvern last year."

"I did and still don't understand how he stumbled across so much information."

"He may be an amateur, but he is clever at being in the wrong place at the wrong time."

"The Brigadier said we should bring him in. He would be a very good operative. After spending time with him, I realized he has a logical mind."

"At least we know he is alive."

The two police cars braked hard, stopping outside the house. Four young policemen came into the garden and confronted Brad and the other man.

"And what may we ask, what are you two up to?"

"Nothing officers."

Brad took out his wallet and showed the officers his MI 5 card.

"MI 5."

A smaller policeman stepped forward and looked at the card.

"A little far south for you boys."

"We are everywhere, not just in London." Noting the officer's sarcasm.

The other officer realizing this could escalate into a problem if he didn't stop his colleague from speaking said.

"Sorry, gentlemen, we had reports of suspicious going on here."

"We understand we too saw something very suspicious active here, hence why we came to investigate."

A tall thin policeman who had stayed back and watched suddenly stepped forward. He had been at the scene where they found Julian Peterson Jones.

"You're Peterson Jones driver." The words came out so quickly it surprised the officer himself.

Brad's co-worker sensing a little friction developing took control of the situation.

"Undercover work and now if you gentlemen wouldn't mind, we have to report back to our superiors in London."

Brad and the other MI 5 operative cross the street and entered the house. The officers stood for a few seconds before retreating to their cars and driving off.

James waited before moving his position he wouldn't leave but get a few moments of sleep. Brad was MI 5, not James's favorite organization but then again possibly better than the American equivalent. If Brad was undercover watching Julian, then what did James see which everyone wants to know about. His head rested against the port-a-loo. Unaware of the cat that came and sniffed at him during the night. Or the homeless woman who used the toilet then went into the house to find somewhere to sleep. She was unaware of him.

CHAPTER FOURTEEN

ANG Security

Waking to the noise of hammering and BBC Radio One James took a few seconds to realize where he was. He slid out from beside the port-a-loo. The workmen were showing the homeless old lady out of the house and on to the street. She was screaming at them about her lost baby left in the house. James could slip out into the street without being seen. The workman overalls had worked so far, but he needed a change in his clothing and look. Something that would let him blend into the background without too many people noticing him.

It was still very early and the thrift store wasn't open. He hadn't decided on the look he wanted, but he knew it had to be drastic.

The greasy spoon café next door to the thrift store was serving breakfast. Even though the Indian meal still lay heavy on his stomach he needed to eat. Standing at the counter, he saw Romeo standing behind the counter. They looked at each other in the eye, neither acknowledging the other. James ordered breakfast and a cup of tea and paid. Romeo took the money but put the change on the counter, not handing back to James. Searching for an empty table, wondering if he should have left the change on the counter. Romeo watched him and then took a deep breath.

Sitting at a table at the back of the café, he assumed there would be a back entrance if he needed one. He realized Romeo's glances at him. He wasn't sure if they were friendly or I will call the cops on your looks.

When James's food was ready Romeo sent the other counter server over to his table. Having to keep one eye on the door, he didn't enjoy the meal. Being hungry made him finish the meal. He knew he couldn't predict when his next meal would be. His next plan of action was to get a change of clothing, then go down to the marina. He needed to know who owned the boat Julie had been on. Know thy enemies had been something his grandfather had always told him. Until now, James hadn't thought it was good advice. Today it was the best advice he could have.

After finishing the meal, he was contemplating ordering another cup of tea. The thought of confronting Romeo again he changed his mind. The street was empty, although he had expected it to be full of police pointing guns at him.

Romeo appeared at the café door and called him back.
    "You forgot this." He handed James a sealed envelope.
    "Oh thanks," said James, pushing it into the pocket of the overalls.
Romeo's face showed pain and fear.

The tall thin charity shop lady was changing the sign on the door from closed to open. She looked at James and opened the door for him. Rummaging through the rack of men's clothing, James found what he thought would be a good disguise. He paid the lady. She suggested a pair of trainers to go with an outfit. James looked at his money and then at the shoes. It wasn't because he didn't have enough money. He wasn't sure if he needed the trainers. The lady misunderstood and taking the coin change she had handed him the trainers. He thanked her and before guilt came over him; he left the shop.

Brighton being a tourist place had several public toilets. He found one and entered a stall. Changing into the new disguise and placing his other clothes into the bag provided by the thrift shop. In the cracked wall mirror above the washbasins, he checked his appearance. He kept the cloth flat cap. Finding the spectacles with clear glass in the thrift shop had been pure luck.

He entered the toilet a workman and exited a student geek. Only the toolbox and plastic bag gave him away as the same person. He needed somewhere to hide them. The workman's outfit had proven to be very useful.

He walked into the railway station with no fear of being recognized. To his disappointment, they had removed the lockers on one wall. A notice read 'because of the ongoing terrorist action the lockers have been removed for safety reasons'.

Sitting outside the station, he thought about where he could hide the toolbox and other things. Then remembered the envelope given to him by Romeo. He opened the envelope, not sure what to expect. It contained an address and a key.

Cautiously James found the building, realizing it was Romeo's flat.

Once inside the flat, he checked to see if anyone had followed him. No one had followed him so he relaxed, then looked around for a place to hide the toolbox and clothing. He left a note thanking Romeo and said he would see him later. Suspicious of Romeo's behavior in the café, he would spy on the waiter later to see whose side he was on.

When Brad took him to the marina, he hadn't had time to look around. Making it more of a friendly place with shops and restaurants. Flats above them opened the place up to more than just a boat parking place. As a student, no one paid much attention to him. He blended in without being obvious that he was trying to.

They moored Seadog Four closer to the parking structure than he expected. Remembering the name of the boat from when he had seen it on its way out of the marina. He wasn't a boat lover, but it was a cute little craft you could have fun on it. If you had the money and time. The boat was empty and looked as though they had not used it since the day he had taken a boat out to sea.

"Nice isn't it. Only one owner."
The man was in his late fifties and looked as he was a salesman. His suit showed a fleck of cigar ash on the collar and a grease stain on the old school tie. From the accent, the man had been to a public school. If he knew which school the tie belonged to, he could have mentioned it, and hopefully, the man would be very forthcoming with information.

"Looking to buy?"

James smiled to himself. He had over the years been able to pass himself off as more than an ordinary secondary school educated man.

"Possible. My father said I could have a special present if I passed my exams."

"Jolly good show. Well, this little beauty is up for sale."

"Oh, I thought the owner would never sell. That's what he told my girlfriend Julia when he took her out two days ago."

"That can't be the owner, he is dead."

"The man was lying."

"Your girl is Julia...?"

"Julia Brooke, Lady Julie Brooke if you know her."

"I know of her family and you said she went out on the Seadog the other day."

"Yes, with the owner she said Karl something or other."

"He's not the owner good God, no just a friend of the owner's father I think."

"Really and you said the owner was dead, would that be Jules PJ?"

"Julian Peterson Jones yes his father brought the Seadog Four as a gift for his eighteenth birthday I think."

"Sad news that about Jules I like him even if he was a little you know Ac Dc."

"Quite."

"Do you have a card and if my father thinks it appropriate, he will be in touch."

The man produced a business card out of a small leather wallet.

"I didn't catch your name."

"James Clayton St. James. One of the Dorset St James's."

"Right, I look forward to hearing from your father." James hated this kind of snobbery but knew it had its place in a well-ordered society. Without it, con men couldn't scam the rich and famous that so desperately wanted to rub alongside royalty even if it was minor unimportant ones.

They shook hands and James wandered back to the shops. So the man Karl was a friend of Peterson Jones senior. Everyone knew that Peterson Jones wouldn't be the first millionaire to get his money from illegal sources. Then there was Julia. What part did she play in this hideous drama? Had she just befriended him, had sex with him just to find out what he knew? The lovemaking must have meant nothing to her. He had as always given his heart to the moment and for what so she could take advantage of him. He was hopeless at understanding how a woman's mind worked. He could have fallen deeply in love with her.

Brian Pidgley walked past his brother and didn't recognize him. For a second James wanted to call after him. He watched as Brian entered the condominium building. This is where he is living and he had the audacity to question James renting a flat in the center of Brighton.

Looking at the names on the doorbell button, he found next to number three Penthouse suite Brian Welsh. That was his mother's maiden name and the one Brian had used.

A security man gave him a quizzical look, so James looked at the back of the place. A group of homeless men were searching through the rubbish bins. Several black plastic bags of rubbish ripped open, and the contents were thrown on the floor.

One man picked up the mobile phone, tried it and then threw back onto the floor. James recognized it immediately as his mobile phone. He picked it up, then walked away from the homeless men. The security guard came around the corner of the building shouting at them. Brian had taken it, even smashed it so it wouldn't work. The inside of the phone seemed intact, the cover and the LCD screen damaged. At least with the old phone, he could retrieve some phone numbers stored when he purchased a new phone.

The way his mind jumped from one thing to another sometimes scared him. He needed to see the Beck's again, maybe not talk to them, but at least to see them. He didn't know why something was drawing him to them.

He found it hard to think they had been part of this drama. Hoping they only became involved because he had sat too close to them on the beach. Standing near to their flat building, he watched as they loaded suitcases into a taxi. They were leaving, so maybe he would never know what part they played. Fenton noticed the student standing watching them. He somehow looked familiar, but that is what all students look like isn't it. Then suddenly he realized it was James and wrote in his notebook.

The family climbed into the taxi and drove off. Fenton pushed a piece of paper out of the window. It fluttered to the ground and blew towards James. As the taxi turned the corner Fenton was at the window his index finger across his lips. Did this mean the boy had kept quiet or was James to keep quiet? In very childish writing James read; Call this number tonight around eight. Tell whoever answers the phone you want Fenton. I'll tell you all later, Fenton your fiend. James hoped the boy meant friend.

James felt he was going around in circles. He had achieved little, only answered some of his questions with more questions. At least now he knew what happened to his mobile phone. Maybe his family weren't angry with him, he only had Brian's word for it. Then again, his father wouldn't just take Brian's word he would contact James if he wanted to.

Sitting down at a table outside a café in the Lanes, he thought about what he should do next. The owner of the café with the grey-haired and dirty grey beard stuck his head out of the door.

"If you're not buying move on. You bloody students think you can park your bums anywhere."
James smiled and went inside the café, ordering a sandwich and a very large coffee. The man's attitude changed, asking James if he wanted a dessert to follow.

Although the recent rain had cooled the temperature of the air he sat outside. This was a reaction he thought to the manhole experience. Something he hoped he would never repeat, even if he found himself in a similar situation. The owner reappeared and placed a sandwich and large coffee on the table in front of James.

"Would you like to read the newspaper?"
Taking it with a nod of his head, the owner felt forgiven for his assumption earlier. They had made the sandwich with great care, and he wondered if every sandwich was as good as this one. He had always tried to eat at the same time each day, maintaining he would

get the right amount of blood sugar and energy needed to function properly. The coffee was boiling hot, so he sipped it and picked up the newspaper to read.

Folded inside out. So he had read several articles before he reached the front page. The shock of seeing the man he had met on the boat. Who introduced himself as Read Simpleton that is Read with an A had been found dead. Only in the paper, it gave his name as John Trinkle.

The newspaper said he washed up on shore further along the coast, naked and with a bullet to the head. Police believed he was killed out at sea and dumped. He read the article several times, making sure he missed nothing. It didn't mention any family, not even a wife. The man knew he would die when he said goodbye. Hence why he said remember me. Why he had called himself Read Simpleton was a mystery. Just another to add to the many mysteries he had already accumulated. How did the police know his name, someone must have identified him?

A teenage girl and boy ran down the lane, hitting the café table as they went past. Following them was a tall, well-built ANG Security Company guard. He was already out of breath from chasing the pair. When he reached James's table he stopped for a second to catch his breath.

He had forgotten about the security company involved in the party and the hotel conversion. They deserved further investigation, as he didn't believe in coincidences.

ANG Security Company operated out of a port-a-cabin near the rail station. The fence around the property

needed repairs, making security impossible. Not a
very good advert for a company boasting itself as the
best in Britain for personal security. Dante Hoble was
enjoying his first week working for ANG. He had
hoped to be out at some store or building site acting as
a security guard. Instead, placed at headquarters man-
ning the communication system. The only problem
was no one called in, so he had nothing to do. This
was his sixth night of waiting for something to happen. Shocked out of his daydream by a student entering the Port-a-cabin. It wasn't the sight of the man but
he had locked the door so how had the student just
been able to walk in.

"Can I help you?"

"Are you hiring?"

"Yes, fill out this application and the owner will do
a complete background check on you."

James took the application form and filled it out. He
used a false name, address, and age. Dante twisted his
pen between his fingers. If they gave a job to this student, he would work at the office, then maybe he could
go out and be a real security guard.

James handed Dante the application form, pleased his
disguise as a student was working.

"What type of security does ANG do?"

Before Dante could answer the door opened. Standing
five foot nine inches in a brown pin-striped suit, Viktor
Angskian stepped into the port-a-cabin. His suit may
have made him look the businessman his white trainers
didn't somehow match. The jacket coat was open ex-
posing a very large expensive beer belly. Perched on
top of the trouser waistband proudly.

"Who's this?"

"New applicant Mister Angskian."

Dante handed Viktor James application to remove the
pen before it fell to the floor. Viktor lifted his John
Lennon imitation glass placing them on his forehead. He read the application, then stared at James.

"Err Adam, can you start now?"

Without hesitation, he replied, "Yes."

"Good, you're hired. Dan, you have ten minutes to
show Adam what you do. Then get down to the
Brighton Centre on the King's Road. Use the back
entrance and find Martha Mogen."

Viktor dropped James's application on the desk.

"And Dan shows him where to file the applications."

The door banged shut as he left the port-a-cabin.

"The names Dante."

James remained seated and watched as the confused
Dante tried to put together his thoughts. He looked at
the application form upside down. Reading the false
name James had written.

"Mada it's simple."

"Adam."

"What is?"

"My name Dante is Adam."

"Really?" He picked up the application and, turning, read the name correctly.

"Sorry I was…"

"You were showing me what I had to do."

"Yes, that's right, it is very easy you sit here in this
chair and if anyone calls in you take a message."

He pointed to the microphone on the desk.

"You are on channel four and we only use that for
emergencies. The rest of the company uses channel
two. If you need to relay a message to Mister Angskian, then please dial zero one on this dial pad and

holding down this button when you speak. Remember to let go or you won't hear the reply."
"No problem."
"You lock up at midnight and lock the door after I
have gone. We get some strange people around
here after dark."
"You have a set of keys for me?"
"Oh yes, I almost forgot. There is coffee over there
and maybe milk in the fridge."
Dante stood and put on his coat as he pulled a set of
keys out of his pocket and handed them to James. At
the door, Dante turned as though about to add something. He stared at James, his brain already excited to
be going to an actual security job.
"Questions?" before James could answer he continued, "Good remember to lock this door after I've
gone."
Remembering the only way to lock a port-a-cabin door
was with the key. He found the correct one and locked
the door, checking it several times. Closing the blinds.
He didn't want anyone to see him go through the company files. The coffee was instant, and the milk was
less than a day old. This must be the most incompe-
tent security company in the world, he thought. He
had just got a job looking after its headquarters without a proper background check.

Sitting at the desk he opened the drawers the top two
were empty. The bottom drawer contained the remains of a cheeseburger and an open can of soda.

He went to the window and checked outside before
checking the filing cabinets. If anyone appeared, he
would say he was filing his application and Dante had
forgotten to tell him where it went. One bank of filing

cabinets locked with four drawers, each labeled part of the alphabet.

He checked each key until he found the one that opened the cabinet. The top drawer contained a folder labeled applications. He stuck his inside and checked the other files in this drawer. In the second he found the Pidgley Properties folder. Along with his letters hiring them to protect the hotel and remove any unwanted personnel, he also found two letters from Brian.

The first was the canceling of the contract to secure the hotel. Thanking them for their services and accepting their request of release from the contract. The second letter from Brian was again thanking Angskian for finding information about James Pidgley. The family worried about James's activities in Brighton. Attached is an agreed payment for this service. Attached was a copy of the letter from Angskian to Brian. He described James as a sex-crazed party animal who enjoyed being out of it on drugs. The information came from being at a party given by one of Brighton's wealthiest families. He photocopied the letters and replaced the files.

He couldn't find anything on Peterson Jones or his supermarkets. They were the security firm for Peterson Jones, so it was strange under the P's he hadn't found a single file.

In the next drawer down he found the answer. They devoted the entire drawer to Peterson Jones. He flipped through the files, surprised at the extent of the work they had done for the millionaire from Hove. They labeled the last file 'Julian's Birthday Bash'. It contained a list of the caterers and who

would be at the house, including the waiters and host-
esses. The next list was the guests and their home address. In case any of them needed taxis. Again, he
made a photocopy of each document and replaced
them in the drawer. Locking the file cabinet, he wipes
it clean of his fingerprints.

After placing the photocopies in his rucksack, he took
out a paperback to read. His coffee had gone cold, so
he warmed it up in a small microwave oven.

The door rattled as though someone was trying to get
in. At the window, by the door, he looked out and saw
Angskian starting to search his pockets for his
keys. James unlocked the door and opened it.

    "You locked it. Very good most of the others who
    man the office never found out how to do it."
    "Common sense."
    "I suppose so. Anything happened?"
    "No, Mister Angskian."
    "Oh, that is good."

Angskian crossed the room and opened a small
closet. Inside stood an old pre-Second World War
Two heavy safe. Taking a large key out of his pocket,
he opened and placed a packet he had been carrying
into the safe. From where James was, he thought the
safe was empty before Angskian had placed his package. He closed the safe, locking and replacing the key
in his pocket.

Standing up, he quickly turned and looked at
James. He expected him to be looking at the
safe. James was sitting in his chair reading his paperback.

    "Don't open the door to anyone and when you
    leave tonight push the keys through the

letterbox. Here's fifty pounds for tonight. Your
mobile number is on the application form, right?"
James nodded, knowing it was a dud number.
"Good your too good to in here I think I'll put Dan
back in here and have you out at the Centre tomorrow. Okay with you?"
"Whatever you want, Mister Angskian."
Before leaving, Angskian checked the door of the
closet and then with a wave of his hand left. James re-
locked the main door looking out of the window and
watched as Angskian climbed into the passenger seat
of a car. The streetlight wasn't bright, so he couldn't
see who was driving. It didn't look like Brad's car, so
he assumed it wasn't him.

Contemplating whether he should try to open the
safe. He gave it a miss from the size and shape of the
package he could assume it was possibly drugs. Although he didn't approve of drugs, he would never crit-
icize others for them using it. He was upset because
they drugged him. The millions countries spend on
trying to stamp it out, they might as well just give in
and tax it to the hilt. Eventually, the drug users will
kill themselves with it. The uses might die out natu-
rally once all the users are dead.

He looked at the closet again, the last safe he had like
that had a secret drawer. Only this safe was too small
to have one. He wouldn't waste his time and if he got
caught, he would blow his cover.

Understanding why Dante had been so bored nothing
was happening he dialed the channels on the communicator. Channel two was the only one active with
loud rock music playing and what sounded like someone say he had found a naked woman in the men's

toilet. Brighton was the happening place for finding people naked.

The clock on the wall ticked to nine-thirty and suddenly remembered he should call Fenton.

A man who sounded as though he had marbles in his mouth answered the phone.

"Can I speak to Fenton?"

"I'll get him."

In the background, he could hear something being hit or beaten.

"This is Fenton."

"Fenton its James."

"I wasn't sure you saw me drop the note. So, your still safe?"

"For now. How are things at your end?"

"They tried to kill dad. I stopped the man, but I think I killed him instead. Dad said he was still alive when we left, but I know from the tone of dad's voice he was lying to protect me."

"I haven't heard of them finding anyone dead since you have left."

"Maybe I didn't kill him."

"I'd believe your dad and he won't be taking stranger's home again."

"I guess not. The reason I wanted you to call was that Garrett found something out about the man in the restaurant."

"Tell me."

"He runs an old record and CD shop. Garrett said it was a front for drugs."

"Go on, I'm interested."

"You ask for a particular CD and get a CD case full of the drug you ask for. Say you want cocaine then you ask for White Snake's 'Slip it in.' or marijuana would be Bob Marley's Star Power. And heroin would be The Best of China Crisis. Clever really, if you think about it."

"I won't ask how he found out."

"Why not he saw this guy hooting up and followed him to the record store? He stood watching for a bit, then followed one druggy. He asked what the score was and was told about the CD."

"I wouldn't know what to ask a druggie about how to get drugs."

"Me neither but that not my scene, it's Garrett's."

"The reason you don't mix with him."

"Correct. Drugs are stupid, they cloud the mind and you can't think straight. That's why Garrett is a dunce at school."

"How old did you say you were?"

"Twelve going on thirty according to mom."

"Which record shop?"

"Moggies records."

"I've seen that place. Anything else?"

"Only keep in touch for mom's sake."

"Does she know you're talking to me?"

"No, but I'll tell I've heard you're safe."

"Where are you speaking from?"

"The boxing club I'm learning to box so when I get more meat on me bones, I'm ready."

"For what?"

"To go professional."

"How is your dad taking all this?"

"It scared the shit out of him. Me and him have a unique relationship now, it's like I more a brother than his son now."

"Do you like that?"

"Sure, he doesn't hit me anymore. They calling for
me, I've got to go call me again."
The phone went dead and James hung the phone handset on the cradle. Maybe he should call home and talk
to his father.

The door handle rattled and then someone tried to push
against it. They continued, then they hammered on it.
"Open up Dante boy it's us let us in it's cold out
here."
James lifted the blind by the door and looked a teenage
boy in the face. He screamed and shouted something
at two other boys. They ran off, giving the finger to
whoever was watching. He took a piece of paper and
wrote a note sticking it on the back of the door.

To lock this door, you need to use the key.

These kids had bullied Dante, and they expect him to
be there. It would be several days before they ven-
tured to visit again.

When you want the time to go fast, it never does. Earlier he hoped the time would go by quickly. Then
when it didn't seem to, he gave up expecting an inter-
minable night. The clock ticked to eleven fifty-
five. His shift as a security guard was over and now,
he needed to find somewhere to sleep. He switched
out the lights and stood peering out to see if anyone
was approaching the port-a-cabin. After a few minutes
of waiting, he opened the door quickly, stepped outside, and locked the door. The letterbox was one of
those you could fit your hands inside. He held it open
and once his hand was inside throwing the keys across
the room towards the desk. Stepping into the shadow
by the port-a-cabin, he watched. With his disguise, he

couldn't be too careful. Someone still wanted to kill him.

His rucksack on his back and his hand in his pocket for warmth, he found Romeo's key. He would go to the café the waiters go to at night and see if it was okay to stay at Romeo's.

The light rain had been promising to appear during the day and never did until now as he walked towards the café it started. Without thinking, he turned into the street Romeo lived on so to get out of the rain he took the chance and went in. The flat was empty as expected. He would wait for Romeo's return and ask him if it would be okay. His head hit the cushion on the sofa and he was asleep. Only just conscious of someone had placed a blanket over him in the middle of the night.

The bright sunlight streamed into the room and James woke out of his deep sleep. The smell of toast being cooked made him feel hungry. He had taken a second to realize where he was. A woman was in the kitchen making tea. She looked at him as he entered.

"Sorry I thought this was Romeo's place, and he lived alone."

"It is Romeo's apartment." She said in a South American accent.

He wasn't sure which country she came from.

"Romeo has gone to work, and he told me to make you toast and tea for your breakfast."

"That was nice of him."

"My lover is a gracious man."

"Your lover?"

"I am joking we are not lovers, Romeo doesn't like women for love. We are just friends. One day he

will fall in love with me and we will get married
and have many children."

"You love him?"

"Yes, and he says you are a very special man, are
you his lover?"

"No, I'm not gay, I like ladies."

"Then why does he say you are a very special
man?"

"I don't know, I'm not special."

"You must be if Romeo says you are."

She handed James a tray with toast, and tea neatly
placed.

"I too go to work now."

"Thank you."

"No problem goodbye, very important man."

He didn't know what to say and watched as she left the
flat. The toast was hot, and she had spread plenty of
butter. He ate, taking the papers out of his rucksack. He would start the day by spying on Moggies.
What he needed was to know more about the man calling himself Karl. Then later in the day, he would
search out Gordon Tuff and Miss fix it, whose name
according to the guest list was Patrice Sickle. The list
gave them an address so it wouldn't be too difficult to
find them. As he perused the list, he found his name
alongside Julia Brooke. It gave a Brighton address he
didn't know for her. She was someone else he wanted
to talk to.

Someone had added a few names at the end, one of
those names was John Tinkle, the dead man. So, he
was at the party and then on the boat. Everything was
coming together. The entire thing was to do with the
smuggling of people, but certain types of people.

He sat back on the sofa, closed his eyes and wished he had watched more spy movies growing up. Spying on someone, or as the American call it, staking out a subject wasn't as easy as it seemed. Most people are oblivious to others watching them. Those who live on the edge of crime are always aware of the watchers.

He showered and prepared himself for the next part of his understanding of what happened to him.

Finding a place to sit and watch in the street would not be straightforward. The record shop was in the middle of a line of shops. The café or to give it the correct title Olde Royale Tea Shoppe wasn't open when he arrived. It also didn't look like the place to have chairs and tables in the street. The bus stops on the other side of the road was thirty yards from the record shop. He could pretend to be waiting for a bus. He stood leaning against the lamppost, hoping a bus didn't arrive too quickly.

"You waiting for the number thirteen? If you are then you've just missed it and the next one isn't for an hour." The old woman chuckled as though she was happy about giving unwelcome news to strangers.

"Thanks. I was waiting for the number thirteen. It must have been early."

"You're not from around here or you'd know the number thirteen is always early on account the driver has a bit of how's your father with a lady at the other end of the route."

James nodded, he didn't want to get into a conversation with this woman. She could distract him from his mission. He stuck his hands in his jeans pocket hunched over his shoulders and gave a sad face. She just laughed and carried on down the road.

Several buses arrived, then departed each time as the door opened. He told the driver he was waiting for the number thirteen. They nodded in sympathy, most saying at least the rain stopped.

The record shop had just opened, only one man had entered then left. It was too early for the school kids to buy their favorite CD's. The teashop opened, and they placed two tables on the pavement. He ordered a ham and cheese toasted sandwich and a pot of tea. Although it was only ten-thirty in the morning, he was hungry. Sitting down, he was aware of who was in the street and what they were doing. Traffic to the record shop had increased and the man calling himself Karl had arrived.

The taxi pulled up next to the teashop and James' table. The man immediately sat at James's table. Brad smiled as though he was genuinely pleased to see James. Dressed in very casual clothes and having not shaved for a few days, Brad too had a fresh look.

"I had a report you were dead."

"I would like it to stay that way."

"When did you realize I wasn't just a driver?"

"Not sure when but on the boat something didn't seem right to me."

"So, we can agree I keep quiet about you being alive and you keep silent about me being you know what."

"Brad, you're a dead man's driver unless I understand what you and your friend told the police last night wasn't true."

"So, you were there?"

"Right next to you, listening to everything said. Tell the Brigadier I'm not interested in being one of

his operatives, I remember meeting him in Mal-
vern."
"I think he already knows that from when you last
met."
"So why are you here?"
"I think we are watching the same person."
"Maybe, but I think you know his actual name."
"I do."
"Did you know he was watching us when we went
out to sea."
"No, I didn't you are good at being in the wrong
place at the wrong time."
"Meaning what?"
"The show begins later."
"Do I have a front-row seat?"
"Best seat in the house it was mine."
"It surprised you to find me here?"
"I didn't recognize you as we drove by the first
time, then when I did, I knew I needed to speak to
you."
"Why?"
"Do you remember on the boat I argued with a guy
who then got off the boat."
"The one who washed up on the shore dead with a
hole in his head."
"Yes, him, he was the man we had on the inside."
"Did he know you?"
"No, that was the plan that way if someone was
watching they wouldn't see anything which would
make then suspicious."
"And now he is dead."
"With some very important information dead with
him."

"Do you want me to leave before the show begins?"

"No, just sit tight and enjoy watching."

As he spoke, several police cars raced up the street
and stopped outside the record shop. They dragged
Karl out in handcuffs and placed him in a police
car.

"Candy store has been closed."

"What was special about the men we smuggled
in?"

Brad stood and walked away from James and the record shop. Seeing two policemen walking towards him,
James followed.

CHAPTER FIFTEEN

The House of Cobham

Brad was standing twenty yards from the corner of the adjacent street. He was talking to the man James had seen the night before, looking into the port-a-loo. They were in a heated discussion, standing very close to each other. Neither of them noticed him approach, surprised when he spoke.

"You didn't answer my question."

"I can't."

"Why? Because you don't know the answer, or is this one of Britain's top secrets?"

"Something like that."

"I helped smuggle them in, don't you think I have the right to know who they were."

"You should have asked when you were on the boat with them."

"Would you have told me then?"

"Probably not."

They stood in an awkward silence, staring at each other. A young mother pushing a pushchair broke the impasse by asking them to move out of the way.

"James this is Simon, my colleague."

The man held out his large bone crushing hand. James didn't take it. The man would squeeze his hand hard. If the man punched you, the pain would stay around for days. Simon looked at his hand, then at James who gave him a nod of the head.

"Simon's a pussycat, he just looks like someone who wants to kill you."

"Brad can't answer your question nor can I. Some information can get you killed."

"I already know that someone wants to kill me for something I know, but I don't know what it is I know."

"You've gathered these men were not ordinary refugees looking for asylum. The man you know as Karl, the man who just got arrested for drug dealing. Well, he paid a lot of money to have those men smuggled into the country."

"So that was why he was watching us on the boat." Simon gave Brad a look of surprise. Brad had not told him this information.

"Why did he smuggle them in?"

"Sorry, that's all we can tell you."

"You said the man I know as Karl. What was his actual name, can you tell me that?"

"Carolle Brockner his origin of birth not known. He spent several years in Ukraine. I knew him as the man who could get you anything you wanted for a price."

"Another fix-it person."

Brad continued after Simon gave him a nod.

"Interpol thinks he may have been supplying young children to a pedophile ring here in England and America. Over a hundred children under ten years old had gone missing from a Ternopil a tiny village in the Ukraine. It was the last place he was before moving to Brighton."

"So why didn't Interpol arrest him?"

"Not enough evidence."

"So now he will buy his way out of jail selling his information."

"If he lives that long."

Brad turned and faced James directly, his expression was one of serious intent.

"James, when we were on the boat, did John Tickle say anything to you?"

"Only for me to remember him, he picked that fight with you so we would all remember him. He knew he would die."

"Only I didn't know who he was."

"Would it have made a difference if you had?"

"Maybe not, it would have compromised the operation."

"It feels like I am living in some American television series. Not even a good one."

"The men who are after you will more likely go underground now that Brockner is arrested."

"You know who they are?"

"Not only who they are, but are trying to find the men you smuggled in."

"They've gone missing too?"

"Not missing, just into hiding."

"Ah, you have them."

Simon interrupted, "I wish we did, sadly they alluded us."

A taxicab pulled up at the curbside Simon opened the door and climbed in.

As Brad started to close the door he said, "If you remember anything about John let me know, please."

"It works both ways," James shouted as the taxicab
pulled away.

He wondered if he should have told them about the
name John Trinkle had introduced himself as. It was a
clue to something, but they were holding something
back from him. This was a game of bargaining that
you know for what you need to know. He would store
the information away. He might even find out what it
relates too.

The street had become busy with people shopping. He
needed to blend in and move on.

Arriving at the address Gordon Tuff and Patrice Sickle
had given, he found it was a junior school. They were
the people who would give an address near the place
they lived. So as not to walk too far after a taxi had
dropped them off. If they needed to give an address to
someone, they would give this one. Then meet them
outside the school rather than have them go directly to
their home. He looked around the area and see what
struck him as the place they might live. Their lifestyle
was middle-class suburbia. One problem of post-war
Britain was the similarity of houses built. Replacing
the bomb-damaged properties was the major consider-
ation. So many of the houses looked the same. If it
weren't for the homeowner's individuality. Painting
the doors and windows frames of their houses in a
unique color, it would be hard to differentiate. Sometimes, the creation of a beautiful garden made the
house stand out. Twice he wandered up the same
street before realizing he had. An old white hearse
was the only thing that stood out, parked next to the
school. He gave up, he would find another way to
track down this elusive pair.

Julia Brooke or should it be the Honourable Lady Julia Brooke was next on his list. She lived according to the list from ANG Security on the other side of town. It was moments like this he wished he had used his car.

The problem was he wasn't sure if it was being watched, and not just by Brad and his cohorts. The student disguise was working well, he hadn't realized how ordinary people treat a student. After the fifth man had shouted at him to get a job, you lazy bum and why aren't you in college. He created phrases in his head he could shout back at them. When a middle-aged man who was supporting an ulcer shouted 'Lazy git get back to the classroom'. He retorted with one phrase 'I can't my college teacher got a student pregnant and had to resign.' The man stopped, his mouth dropped open and then replied, 'Figures what fucking perverts teachers are.' The man's reaction shocked James. The words didn't match the expensive suit or car the man was driving.

The hotel was one of the smarter, more expensive hotels in Brighton boasting of four stars. Julia Brooke ran down the steps at the front of the hotel and into James. She apologized, then recognized him. Looking back at the hotel, she took his arm and walked him into the alleyway at the side of the hotel. Her first reaction was to slap him across the face, then she pulled him to her, kissing him on the lips. Both these reactions caught James off guard. He just stood looking at her.

"I was told you were dead."
"I want to keep it that way."
"Why?"
"Who told you I was dead?"
She didn't answer but looked back towards the road.

"Julia, I thought we had something special now I realize you were just using me."

He placed a hand on her cheek and pulled her face to face his. She said nothing, lowering her eyes.

"They tried to kill me, so who told you I was dead?"

She stood, not saying a word, looking again down to the road as though she was expecting someone to appear.

"I know you know a lot more than you're letting on. If that night was just another one-night stand of sex for you then walk back to the hotel otherwise tell me."

"You looked so different I didn't recognize it was you."

James stared at her. She was prevaricating he didn't need this just at this moment. He walked away down the alleyway.

"James comes back I'll tell you what you want to know."

He returned and leaned against the hotel wall, looking off into the distance. He didn't want to make eye contact. Knowing she could melt his resolve.

"Gordon Tuff told me they had killed you in a manhole explosion."

He could no longer keep his eyes off her. She was beautiful. Under normal circumstances, he would have dragged off into the hotel. Booked a room and made love to her for the rest of the day.

"That night meant a lot to me too, so don't think it was just a one-night fling."

A man appeared at the entrance to the alleyway. He was wearing an old-fashioned Norfolk jacket and

heavy green and brown tweed trousers. He strutted up
the alleyway to them.

"There you are my dear, for a moment it worried
me where you were. The doorman said you had
gone around the corner."

"Sorry, daddy, I was just catching up with an old
friend."

"Ah yes, nice to meet you…"

"This is James's daddy, he is a friend of mine."

"It's a pleasure to meet you Sir, your daughter and I
haven't seen each other for some time."

The reply by James took Julia's father by surprise
most of the men he meets these days had no manners.
In fact, they found it difficult to have a conversation
with their elders.

"It's a pleasure to meet one of Julia's friends. My
daughter keeps her Brighton life a secret."

"Oh, daddy, that's not true."

"So what do you do?"

"I'm a student, Sir. My parents own a property
company, so I'm studying architecture and property
management."

"Very smart at least you're not one of these idle
young men we see in the papers every day. Julia,
we need to get back, you know how your mother
fusses."

"Yes, daddy. James, I'll catch up with you some
other time."

"I'm sorry James but her mother and I are giving a
party this weekend our twenty-fifth wedding anniversary. Julia, why don't you invite James down
for the weekend? Most of the people there will be
your mothers and my friends. Having someone
your age will make life a little more bearable I'm

sure."

"Say you will come, we can continue where we left off and catch up on all the gossip." She took a business card out of her pocket and handed it to him.

"If you arrive at around eleven in the morning, we could have lunch together. The party starts at seven and will go on all night. I'll find a room for you so you can stay overnight."

She gave him a peck on the cheek and then put her arm around her father's and walked back up the alleyway.

"What a very charming young man my dear."

James smiled if only the old buffer knew what had taken place between them. Then again, he possibly already did. He went back to the thrift shop and found some more appropriate clothing for his weekend trip. Brighton was one of those places where you could get the upper-middle-class clothing in a thrift shop. He would stay at Romeo's flat again tonight and leave early in the morning. Passing the railway station, he checked on times of trains to the nearest station to Julia's country home. There were no trains to that area of rural England.

The Cobham estate had seen better days. Now reduced to a few acres. They maintained the grounds around the house. It was a large Victorian house with four floors and an attic. The paintwork on the windows and doors needed repainting. It looked as though some windows had cracks and even broken on the upper floors. He arrived five minutes before eleven o'clock after a struggle, opening the gates to the long driveway up to the house. One of Romeo's more mature men friends had rented James a car for the weekend without asking too many questions and accepting cash instead of a credit card.

Julia was waiting for him, her dress reaching down to her ankles. He suddenly had a vision of entering the world of the Brontes. She gave him a quick kiss on the cheek and then taking his elbow guided him up the steps to the house.

"Should I get my things?"

"Don't worry about them, Brigs will bring them in."

She took his car keys and once inside the house hung them on a hook inside a little cupboard hidden behind the door.

"We are having a cozy lunch in the conservatory, just the two of us. Mommy's put you in the blue china room on the second floor. Brigs will take your luggage up and put your clothes away. Did you bring a dinner suit?"

"Full tux for the occasion." Another friend of Romeo owned The Best Dressed Man in Town Shop. He rented James a tuxedo for the weekend. Again for cash with no questions asked.

"Brigs will press it for you or whatever he does with men suits. Sorry James but this is old-world England as though everything is out of one of those Victorian novels. My family hasn't moved on very far from those days. Hence why we are short of money although daddy is trying to put that right."

They walked through the house, passing a magnificent staircase. The conservatory was someone of passion as it had every kind of flower growing in it. The table and chairs placed strategically in the middle, reminding him of a school trip to Paris. A small bistro and

two lovers holding hands drinking hot chocolate. He
was fourteen and Susan Ellis was just fifteen. They
were in love vowing to marry and have many children.
Sadly, a week after the trip they broke up after James
found her behind the school boiler room with Robin
Duckstone. It took several months to get over it, and
even to this day he feels sad when he thinks of it. Julia
saw his facial expression change.

    "Something wrong?"
    "No, this is beautiful, so romantic."
    She removed the silver covers off the two plates.
    "I hope you like salmon, it's pouched. Daddy
caught them last week in Scotland."
    "I love fish and Scottish salmon is one of my favor-
ites." He was lying and hoped she didn't see it. He
liked fish, but he had eaten quite a lot that week already.
    "Would you like some wine?"
    "No thank you, water would be nice."
Someone had gone to a deal of trouble to prepare this
meal. The presentation was exquisite and the taste or-
gasmic. He liked to think of food like sex sometimes.
The meal could be pleasurable or like having a very
terrible time a with girl.

He watched as Julia ate her food. She had been to a
finishing school. The way she put the food on her fork
and then in her mouth. She had been trained to do it
correctly. It was such a delicate operation he became
fascinated by her. She didn't speak with her mouth
full of food and the other thing he noticed she kept her
mouth closed while chewing. He had noticed these
days that many girls ate as though they wanted to show
what they had inside their mouths. His mother would
love to see this. The last girl he took home his mother

declared after she had gone that the girl was as common as muck. He hadn't taken another girl home since.

She cleared away the plates, placing them on the small trolley. The Apple Tarte Tatin prepared by an expert pastry cook and melted in the mouth. He hoped he could have more. She offered none. After she had served the coffee, she moved her chair closer to him.

"Well now, you're fed, I'd better tell you what I know."

"Julia all I'm after is the truth about what happened to me and who killed Julian."

"Why do you care about him?"

"His father asked me to find what happened."

"I would have thought he would leave it to the police to find out who did it. Not someone who almost died themselves."

"I thought it strange too, but then so much has happened that is strange."

He drank some coffee it tasted bitter, and he looked at it.

"It's one of mommy's favorites, for me, a little bitter, but you get used to it."

She took his cup and drank some.

"You didn't need to have done that."

"I didn't want you to think I was trying to kill you. If I was, I wouldn't have gone to so much trouble over the meal."

"It was excellent."

"Did you ever wonder why I was on the beach when I found you. You saved my life."

"How I was naked, stabbed in the groin, and at the time believed to be dead."

"People, ordinary people, thought the aristocracy, have everything. Money, power, and privilege, the wonderful life. I don't starve and we haven't run out of money."

"At least that's good."

"True, I can only equate this with a famous actress, actor or celebrity. You are in the spotlight and everything you do they watch. Even if you are not doing something people are watching you waiting for you to step out of line. I hate it."

"So why were you on the beach?"

"Grandfather is a brilliant man if what he says he has done works we will be very rich again."

"Legally?"

"Good God, my family would do nothing illegal."

"I'm glad to hear that."

"According to my father, grandfather already know he has been successful but won't let on. Once again, we will be in the spotlight and I just couldn't take it anymore. People telling me how they would like me to be and act. I was going to walk down into the sea and drown myself. Only this handsome prince was lying on the beach "

"Only I was naked and dead."

"The shock of seeing you brought me back to reality, so I screamed."

"Did you see who dumped me on the beach?"

"No, although I thought I saw a hearse drive away."

A man wearing white gloves and black tailcoat entered the conservatory. A young rosy face girl about Julia's age was one step behind him. Julia looked at him, gave a nod of the head. The man and girl removed the lunch things. The girl checked the coffeepot and quickly left the conservatory. Just as the man was about to wheel the trolley away, she returns and placed a fresh pot of coffee on the table.

"Don't you speak to them?"

"Oh yes, only when we have guests they seem to be reticent to speak to us. That was Brigs, the Butler, he has been with this family since he was a boy. His father was the butler before him. If you've ever watched Up Stairs, Down Stairs television series, then you will know what goes on in a house like this."

"Even in the twenty-first century?"

"In old families, nothing changes."

"What can you tell me about Gordon Tuff and Patrice Sickle?"

"Dangerous people, into drugs and I think the occult. They supply the Brighton rich with whatever they want. I only know them because of Julian. His father is coming tonight, another ruthless man."

"What did his father think of his gayness?"

"In denial, Julian wasn't gay, just going through a phase like all young rich men. The fact he was dead with a naked boy and fifty ten pounds notes ram up his backside. His father still maintains it was just a phase."

"Where did Julian's money come from?"

"He worked for his father. Doing what, I never found out."

"Did you like Julian?"

"Yes, very much he didn't take stick from anyone. He once said if he ever married a woman it would be me. He added, I would have to have my hair cut and dress like a boy."

"He was gay?"

"Gordon got him drunk one night and had these

two girls strip off. They danced naked in front of
him until he vomited when one girl stuck her fanny
in his face. Julian was a homosexual through and
through."

"I wonder if his father put Gordon up to it."

"Maybe my only sadness is Julian, and I argued before he died."

"What about?"

"You."

"Me."

"He was furious when he found out I had found
you naked on the beach."

"Why?"

"I wouldn't tell him what you looked like naked.
Convinced I had taken a picture of you."

"You didn't, did you?"

"No, I have a photographic memory." She smiled
and then gave him a wink.

A mature version of Julia entered the conservatory.
Dressed in a silk dress that reached her ankles, although it had a slit up to the knees.

"Mommy, this is James."

James stood and took her hand and gently shook it.
The soft white hands hadn't ever lifted a finger to do
manual labor, not even dust the family china.

"I'm so glad you could make it, Julia has so few
friends. Now poor Julian is dead, I was worrying
she wouldn't have any."

"Oh, mommy I'm not that hard up for friends I just
don't like to be with them all the time."

"Just like your grandfather. I am sorry to break up
this little lunch party, but I need your help, Julia."

It wasn't the tone of her voice, just the infliction of the
way she said little lunch party. James felt this woman

didn't care about her daughter or what she was doing with her life. As long as she, the mother, could manipulate the daughter to do her bidding.

"It's the seating arrangements for tonight, they are in a complete muddle. Jessica Ponsanby Smyth is refusing to sit next to her husband."
"Why mommy?"
"She says not until he apologizes for the little indiscretion with the waitress and the Champaign cork." Without taking a breath she continued, "I'm sorry to take my daughter away, but she is so good at organizing things for me."
"That is not a problem, your wedding anniversary is an important occasion."
"Oh, how nice of you to say, James, wasn't it."
"Yes, ma'am."
"Julia, I like this young gentleman."
"If it is acceptable to you, Lady Brooke, I would like to have a walk in your beautiful garden."
"Julia where did you find this perfect gentleman. James, you have my permission to look at the garden."

They left the conservatory talking, their heads almost touching like two gossiping schoolgirls. He poured himself another coffee and drank. Briggs the Butler arrived and stood to the side until James had finished drinking.

"Sorry to keep you waiting."
"Does sir require anything else?"
"No, thank you, I will have a walk in the garden."

They hid the door from the conservatory behind a large bushy plant. Briggs pointed it out to him. Once again James thanked the Butler.

When he was young, he would stay with his Aunt Eileen on the Yorkshire seacoast. She would take him to country houses in Yorkshire and Lancashire to look at gardens. She had no interest in what was inside the house. For her, the garden made a house. At the time he had hated it but as this was his favorite Aunt, he attempted to please her. Now years later he realized it gave him a foundation of how clever the Victorian gardeners had been.

He strolled around the Cobham house garden. Someone had spent a good deal of time and money making a garden to provide the house with flowers, fruit, and vegetables. He found a quiet spot next to a running brook. Someone had nailed a notice to a tree naming the place as Poet's Dell.

Sitting on a sawed-off tree trunk, he looked into the water. There was something about running water that seemed to inspire the imagination. Maybe the bad thoughts float away, only leaving pleasant ones. Taking out his notepad, intending to write a few lines on how he felt. The first page already had two words written on it. He didn't remember writing them, but he must have as it was in his handwriting.

'Reed Simpleton' he remembered the man had introduced himself as Read with an A. That was such a strange thing to say, then Read had added "my parents like to play with words."

Was he telling James to play with his name? Read Simpleton was it an anagram, but for what? He played with the letters. It was moments like this a computer with an anagram program would help.

The soft hand cupped his eyes, and he felt the soft lips kiss his neck. Smelling Julia's perfume, although he hadn't heard her approach.

"What are you writing?"

"A poem in Poet's Dell."

"Oh, James, how romantic are you writing one?"

"Would I lie to you? I am contemplating a word poem using as few letters as possible. Once they are an anagram and used repeatedly."

"How clever you're not just good looking."

"How are things at the house?"

"With my mother, everything is a drama. You were very ingenious to win her over so quickly. What a charmer you are, you had her eating out of your hand."

"Your mother likes to be the center of attention, it's easy to give her that position."

"Few men know or understand how to treat a lady. I'm disbelieving you came from the gutter in Birmingham."

"It's all true me Lady."

"My brother Benjamin has just arrived, so the entire family is fussing over him."

"Where has he been?"

"Cambridge."

"I didn't even know you had a brother."

"Two the youngest William is at boarding school and can't be here which is a drag as he the only one I like."

"Do you have any brothers or sisters?"

"Five sisters and four brothers."

"What! Your mother and father must have liked bonking."

James smiled, he had heard this so many times it was no longer funny.

"We'd better get back to the house, it's an informal tea in the library. My brother may ask if we are bonking, tell him yes."

"I will tell him a gentleman doesn't divulge a lady's secrets."

"Oh, how perfect I can see why mommy likes you."

They meandered back to the house, Julia putting her hand in his. He could forget why he was here, or that he had other problems just hoping this moment would never end. Once they were in sight of the house Julia let go of his hand and step two feet away from him.

"Have I suddenly got the plague?"

"No, sorry, it's that grandfather doesn't like to see affection in public."

"Or lady's ankles, I suppose."

"You noticed, I hate it, but to keep the peace you sometimes have to compromise."

"Sad, I like your ankles."

She laughed and squeezed his arm.

As they crossed the recently cut lawn, the house was full of light. He wanted to ask how many bedrooms there were but knew it was one of those insensate questions you don't ask. Had Julia not been with him, he would have found the family from the light chatter emulating from the library. As they entered the talking stopped and all eyes focused on them. Lady Brooke rushed across the room and taking James led him to meet Lord Cobham. James's ability to blend in with any class of people had he believed derived from his father. The Pidgleys had always regarded themselves as classless. Even though the great British populous would put the Romany below the working class. The

old aristocrat eyed James with suspicion. He had seen
many a mountebank as he called them to try to win a
place in the Cobham family. James answered his
questions with polite honesty. When the Lord asked
what James's, intention was to his granddaughter, his
reply brought a smile on the old man's face.

"I have no intention, just the moment sir, we are
friends. If it is to go further, then we need to know
each other a little longer. Then I would ask you
and her father's permission."

Julia's brother Benjamin was more forthright and as
predicted by Julia asked if they were bonking. James
gave his reply to the amusement of those around.
Lady Brooke monopolized him with her friends. Julia
stood back and watched as he skillfully played the
aristocratic game. At each attempt by Benjamin to
make fun of him, his replies twisted it back on the
questioner. The light sarcasm and wit were something
Julia hadn't seen in any of her other friends.

Tea was over and everyone drifted out of the library.
Lord Cobham called Julia over to him and whispered
in her ear. She seemed delighted with what he said.

"James let me show you to the China Blue room."
They climbed the grand staircase and walked around
the landing to a less impressive staircase. On the second floor, Julia skipped along to a blue door. She
opened the door and let James step inside. They
painted the entire room in unique shades of blue with
what looked like willow patterns on the walls. He had
expected to see a four-poster bed and was a little dis-
appointed to see an ordinary queen size bed. The silk
bed covers and pillows matched the wallpaper.
Julia closed the door and pulled him to her. The kiss
was long and loving. Locking the door, she took off

her clothes. Pulling back the silk cover and throwing the pillows on the floor, she lay naked on the blue cotton sheets. He wanted to take pictures or paint a picture of this vision of beauty. From a stripper's point of view, he had never been fast at taking off his clothing. Always placing them neatly on a chair or table. Julia watched as he stripped down. A flash of him naked on the beach resurfaced in her head. She shuddered to dispel the thought.

Opening a small drawer in the bedside table, she took out some condoms and threw them at James.

He laughed and climbed onto the bed. She smelt of roses as though her white soft body had laid in a bath of rose petals. He kissed her lips, and she gave an imperceptible moan. He lay on top of her and taking her wrists and restraining them so her arms were outstretched. He kissed her neck and down to her breasts. She remembered the first time he had done this and how it had excited her beyond belief. The passion flowed the only sound was the squeaking of the bed. Worried that others in the house might hear the sound. So he made love slowly. She had never had sex with anyone who took it at this pace. It was rare for her to have an orgasm with most of the other men. They had their orgasm and were sleeping in less than three minutes. He was taking his time, giving her the pleasure she so desired from a man. They fell asleep nestled into each other, Julia feeling secure and ecstatic. The knock at the door woke them both. The clock on the wall read five forty-five.

"I've run a bath for you, sir." A man's voice James didn't recognize.

James climbed off the bed slightly disorientated. Julia giggled and gathered a sheet around her body.

"It's time to get ready, go have your bath, I'll see
you later."
He leaned over and kissed her lips, the smell of
roses mixed with the smell of sex lingering on her
body.
They had placed a white toweling bathrobe and towel
over a chair. It was just like a hotel everything thought
of for the comfort of the guests. Lying in the bathtub
enjoying the warmth of the water and the softness of
the bath salt. He had slipped in time and was inside a
D H Lawrence novel.

A note on the back of the door read 'Please close the
light when finished'. Someone had played with word
and crossed out the letter in trying to be funny. It now
read 'Please lose the light hen fished'. It reminded
him of the anagram Read Simpleton. The problem
was he didn't know how many words should be in the
answer. Without a computer to help, he could only see
how many words he could create. It might give him a
clue to what words he was looking for. If only Brad
and his friend Simon had been more forthcoming with
information, he might have solved the anagram by
now.

The door to the china Blue room was slightly ajar. He
entered cautiously even though he thought nothing
would happen to him here he still needed to keep his
wits about him. The bed remade and his evening
clothes laid out. His black shoes had been polished
and placed next to the chair. It was good he was only
visiting he could get used to this luxury. The British
Empire had gone. The memory still lingered in the
hearts of those that ran it.

At fifteen, his mother had insisted all her boys knew how to tie a bow tie. Even his brothers objected to the lesson. What was the point they asked people don't wear bow ties anymore? He was glad she had forced them to learn. This was one occasion when knowing how to do it was important. He stood looking at himself in the mirror. His Aunt Eileen had called him her little Lord Fauntleroy. At that moment he felt like a lord. Maybe when this is over, he would spend some time with his aunt. She kept asking him when he would visit her.

Standing on the top step of the grand staircase, he wasn't sure what to do once he was down in the hall. He had always taken the advice, if in doubt watch others and follow them. Julia's parents were standing outside the door of the family Ballroom. From this advantage point of walking down the stairs, he could see inside. They had placed round tables around the outside of the dance floor. A quick count told him each table could seat ten people. He hoped he was on a table with friends rather than snobbish people. As the guests arrived at the front door, Briggs and other members of the staff took their coats and hats. They then proceeded to the ballroom and shook Lady and Lord Brooke's hand before entering the ballroom.

Easy enough to just follow the leader and nothing could go wrong. At the foot of the stairs, Briggs approached James. He seems impressed with the way James looked.

"Miss Julia is in the Library waiting for you, Sir."

"Thank you, Mister Briggs."

"Just Briggs, Sir."

James felt a little embarrassed by this mistake. He should have remembered to call him Briggs. The loud

bang as a car backfired outside James fell to the floor.
A small Pekinese dog ran over to him and sniffed at
his nose. One servant rushed across the hall and
helped James stand up. He knew he had gone red with
embarrassment. Saved by a man in a General's uniform who had just arrived.

"Appropriate reaction young man you must have
been in Iraq." He then continued talking to his wife
loudly. "You know my dear, I always say you can
tell a military man by the way he acts to loud
noises."

James took this opportunity to slip into the Library.
Julia was waiting for him. Her face showed concern.

"What happened?"

"A car backfired, and I shot to the ground. A natural reaction these days."

"Not surprising under the circumstances."

She brushed his jacket and picked a piece of cotton
thread off his trousers he had picked up off the floor.

"I wanted to meet you in here because I want you
to escort me into the ballroom."

"It would be my pleasure, me lady."

"Grandfather said you were the perfect gentleman
and therefore had grown up in an aristocratic
household."

"I liked him straightforward, unlike your brother."

"He's just a silly fool who thinks he knows it all.
Do you dance?"

"Depends on the dance."

"The old stuff like the waltz and grandfather's favorite, the Military two-step."

"I'm a little rusty on both, but I have been known
to cut a mean waltz in the past."

"Then you are my knight in shining armor as grandfather said."

"Your grandfather said a lot."

"He liked you."

Briggs entered the library.

"Everything all right, Miss Julia."

"Yes thank you, Briggs."

"Then if the gentleman is ready, they are waiting for you now."

James took Julia's arm in his and led her out of the Library.

CHAPTER SIXTEEN

Conspiracy Ball

Their entrance to the ballroom was as though Cinderella and Prince Charming had arrived. The room went silent, and all eyes looked at them. The sound of whispering grew until her grandfather Lord Cobham approached and kissed Julia on the cheek. Surprised he did this as James had been told, the old man didn't like the show of affection in public. He shook James's hand, then led them to meet some of his friends. Benjamin scowled at the scene and then spoke to his friends. Watching this, anyone would have thought a plot was being hatched.

Her mother led away Julia to meet one of her old school friends. Seeing James standing looking around the room, Hector Peterson Jones spoke to him in a loud voice.

"James how nice to see you again."

"Mister Peterson-Jones, what a surprise."

"I don't think you have met my wife. Madeline, my dear, this man is a friend of Julian's."

"A fine young man, many of his friends will miss him."

"Oh, thank you, you're the first person to say something nice about my son. Were you one of his lovers?"

The forthrightness of the woman took aback James. He searched for something to answer that wouldn't sound patronizing.

"No Madeline, James swings for my side," said Julie, joining James.

"My wife is a liberal and was a lot more understanding of Julian's friends than I was."

"I just felt the boy needed support, not criticism. Hector, I need a drink."

"Let me take you over to the bar Madeline, we ladies can have a brief chat."

"My silly wife encouraged Julian to fester in that lifestyle. I'm so glad you're not a nancy boy, James."

He took James by the elbow and led him to the side of the ballroom. Several people looked at them and whispered to those who they were with.

"We should have lunch soon I think I have a position in my company for someone with your expertise. I don't know anyone who has outwitted the Tibbs brothers and stayed alive."

"I'm not sure what you are luring to, but I am alive that is true."

"Clever and discrete, very good, the qualities of a man of honor."

"Depends who is being honored."

"Quite. With Karl in jail, it will of interest to see who takes over his game."

"The record store, you mean."

"I like your cautious at all times."

"You never know who is listening or if you are being bugged."

"Oh, no fear of that here, this household is too high
for that."

"I'm glad to hear that."

"As for Karl, as long as he keeps his mouth shut the
top man will be safe."

James stopped listening to the words 'Top Man' suddenly jumped out of the anagram. If the letters left
were a name, then he would know who was behind the
smuggling and maybe more.

"We don't have to worry about Karl, he knows the
score. Ah, the ladies are returning."

"Hector did you know James is in property."

"Yes, my dear, this man is brilliant and I hope I can
persuade him to join my company. I see Seidler
has just arrived with his wife. Come, my dear, I
think I need to have a talk with him."

"Sorry, Julia, but you know what men are."

Julia stood next to James, her hand slipping into his.
They watched as Hector and Madeline greeted the
other man and his wife.

"He was friendly to you."

"He thinks I know what is going on."

"Don't you?"

"Maybe. Julia, who is Seidler?"

"Donald Seidler and his dreadful common wife,
Carlotta. She is really from Rotherham but puts on
airs and graces that just make me sick."

"Wow, a bit of snobbery."

"Not really, when you meet her, you'll understand
what I mean."

"Tell me about him."

"A very rich and dangerous man who thinks he can do just as he pleases and is above the law."

"You don't like him either."

"Him, his wife and their bitch of a daughter thank God she is not here or I wouldn't be. Their son just died."

"Tell me what you feel about her and how the son died."

Before she could answer a man in a livery uniform announced that everyone should take their seats for dinner. Julia whispered in his ear, 'table four'.

Table four was close to the top table and far enough away from Peterson Jones for him to relax. He found his name place and stood behind the chair waiting for the other guests to arrive and take their places. The other table guests arrived and introduced themselves to him. He seemed the only one who they didn't know. As soon as they all sat down, an army of waiters arrived with the first course. The food was nothing special, except he noticed his portions were slightly larger and looked more appetizing. Obviously, Julia had a hand in this when he caught her eye during the dessert. She gave him a smile and a wink of the eye. Other than small talk, he didn't speak to anyone at the table. After the speeches that seemed to go on forever, the ladies left the room. The men who smoked cigars retired to the patio outside the ballroom.

James retired to the library and away from the endless chatter. After an earful of complaints about how bloody awful it was, they couldn't fox hunt anymore. Then the cost of a new Bentley these days being so expensive the old one would have to do for another five years. He was glad to get away and think.

Sitting by the fire, his back to the door. He realized he was vulnerable in this position, so he moved to a seat by the window.

Peterson Jones and Donald Seidler entered the library.
"Donald, you haven't met James yet, a very promising young entrepreneur who knows the score."
"Julia's new manservant."
"Hardly I serve no man but myself."
"Well, put I'm Donald Seidler I heard about you obviously from Hector."
Donald held out his hand and James shook it. The freemason handshake was so obvious James could resist giving one back. His cousin Terrance had been a freemason and boasted to the entire family about it. One night when he was drunk, he taught his cousins the various handshakes. James had found it most useful in dealing with certain businessmen. He suspected that Brian had become a freemason.
"James, what do you do?"
"Donald, James took Julian's place in the last shipment. He is trustworthy and safe."
"Be it on your head if he isn't Hector. I just want to know what's happening now Karl has shut up shop."
A man and his wife entered the library looking suspiciously at the three men.
"Someone else has to open a record shop. Where else will the teenagers of Brighton buy their CD's?" said James.
Donald laughed out loud and gave James a friendly punch on the shoulder. The man and his wife returned to the hallway.
"I see what you mean Hector, we could do with a quick thinker around here."

"He is very discrete too. As for Karl will we replace him and then move forward. We cannot allow the Eastbourne boys or a London mob to move
in."

"What about the Birmingham mafia would they be
welcome?" said James playfully.

"Depends on who. What do they call the leader of
the mafia?"

"The Don."

"The Don I thought that was a professor at Cambridge or Oxford."

"Hector, I don't care as long as our ship is water-
tight with no leaks."

Several couples arrived in the library to sit and talk.
Donald and Hector left and went into the garden.
James watched as the two men's heads were very close
and they carried on talking. Simon the colleague of
Brad peered at the door and seeing James retreated
quickly. Was he here to watch James or someone
else? The noise level in the library had grown as more
people arrived.

Returning to the Ballroom, he found Julia sitting by
herself, a glass of water in her hand. She smiled as he
approached her. The band played a waltz as Julia
stood up and stepped closer to James. On cue, he took
her hand, and they waltzed around the room. The by-
standers applauded to bring others back to the ballroom. Others joined them on the floor, and soon the
room was a swirl of dancers.

"I can't sleep with you tonight, but I will tomorrow
night."

"Don't force yourself Julia just let it happen when
it does."

"I'm not alone, I have my cousin Rebecca sharing my room. If I'm not there, she will blab to the entire family in the morning."

"What time does this finish?"

"About two in the morning, why?"

"I'm getting very sleepy."

"Too much sex in the afternoon can do that to a man."

James led her to a table, and they sat down. Looking around the room, he saw Simon again. He was sitting very close to Hector and Donald, close enough to hear what they were saying.

"Who's that man?" asked James, showing the direction with his little fingers.

"Which man there must be hundreds of them?"

"The one sitting next to the girl in the lilac dress."

"I'm not sure who he is, he came with Brigadier Thaw."

"Who's Brigadier Thaw?"

"The man in the uniform treading on the toes of that poor girl who is half his age."

James watched as Simon pretended not to be listening to Hector and Donald but made it so obvious he was.

"Why do you want to know who he is?"

"I've seen him before, but I'm not sure were."

"According to Cynthia Padgett, he is not an agreeable man. Throughout dinner, he didn't say a word and even took her bread roll when she wasn't looking."

"Oh God, what a complete swine do you want me to throw the blaggard out sis."

Benjamin Brooke had arrived at the table drunk and looking for some fun.

"You two bonking tonight I need to find someone I mean I can't go to a party and not get my leg over now can I."

"You must think of your reputation, Ben."

"Absolutely Jimbo. I like your new fellow Sis he's okay."

Benjamin stumbled off on the dance floor, bumping into several of the guests before his mother stopped dancing and took him outside.

James felt a wave of sleepiness wash over him. For a few seconds he wondered if he had been drugged again. Where would he end up naked this time on the phallus of Helith at Cerne Abbas in Dorset?

"You look exhausted."

"I am, I haven't had a good night's sleep for some time."

"Why don't you go to bed if you want to just slip away no one will notice."

"I think I will, and it gives the girls a chance to interrogate you about me."

"They've already done that several times. I've stopped going to the bathroom down here, I get waylaid each time."

"What did they say?"

"Now that would be telling, and I'm not doing that. Except I should tell you you're on the list because of your connection to Peterson Jones."

"So he carries some weight and not just on his stomach."

"Let's just say knowing him will open doors."

"And close a few I'm sure. I going to bed, enjoy the rest of the party."

He kissed her on the cheek and slid out of the ball-room. Several people saw him leave and while some of them didn't care, one watcher wondered where he was off to.

Opening the door to Blue China room James saw a young naked girl sitting on top of a naked middle-aged man. They had thrown the bedclothes on the floor along with their clothing. Both were drunk and unaware of his presence in the room.

At the top of the staircase, he pondered if he should return to the ballroom. He yawned and went to find another place to sleep. Although the attic room wasn't used anymore, they were still technically bedrooms. In a room in the middle of the line of former servant quarters. He found a bed complete with mattress and blankets. The sound of music still playing from below gave a smoothing lullaby effect to the night. He curled up on the bed wrapped in the blankets and fell asleep.

Waking the daylight flooding into the room after a slight panic, he remembered where he was. He felt refreshed after the full night's sleep and he hadn't woken in a sweat over some nightmare or the sound of someone entering the room.

The house was eerily silent only the old grandfather clock in the main hall made any sound. The constant ticking told the world life must go on regardless of what happens. They had restored the ballroom to its mausoleum status with dust cover covering the furniture. The library gave the same impression without the dust covers.

He entered the dining room expecting to find it full of people eating and talking at the same time. The room was empty of people, although breakfast was on a sideboard. They had left empty plates and cups on the table. Lifting the lid of a salvo, he piled his plate with kedgeree and bacon. The scrambled eggs had turned to rubber. Popping some bread in a toaster, he sat down at the long dining table. The coffee pots were empty, but someone had placed a fresh pot of tea on the table. He ate and wondered where everyone could have got to.

After finishing his meal, he sat for several minutes. A trolley near a door used by the servants had several plates and cups on it. Placing his used plates and cup on the trolley before looking out of the window. The sky was a grey wash, but at least there was no sign of black rain clouds. He would go to his room, wash and change his clothing before going in search of the family.

Guardedly opening the door of the Blue China room, the unwelcome guests from the night before had vacated the room. The room smelt of sex. The bed clothing was still on the floor, as was a white bra and a pair of pink panties. He and his siblings grew up being told to leave the place as you find it. After making the bed, he placed the lady's undergarments in a drawer. The notion that one servant would see them and report back to either Julia or her mother was the last thing he wanted. The smell in the room suddenly became stronger. Opening the window to let the morning fresh air in, he thought he saw someone enter the house below.

He put on the dressing gown given to him the night before by Julia. It felt a little damp as though someone had used it. Using the same bathroom, he had the night before he soaked in the bath. It was then he noticed the paper sticking out of the dressing gown pocket. He leaned across and took the paper from the pocket. Unfolding the paper, it said, 'James, you're not in your bed? Gone shooting with the family, see you later. Julia.'

She knew he hadn't been in the China Blue room. Maybe she too had walked in on whoever was having the passionate night.

Back in the Blue China room he changed his clothes and packed the dirty clothes into his suitcase. It was then he saw the piece of paper. Slipped under the door and pushed to the side when he opened the door. If this is how the aristocracy communicated, then it was no wonder Britain had lost its empire.

The note read, 'Just to let you know I don't think Julia heard you bonking last night. The girl was pubescent though, you lucky bugger.'

He knew immediately it was Benjamin who had written the note. Finding him and telling him it wasn't him would be important if he wanted a relationship with Julia. Folding the note, he placed it in his back pocket.

After placing his packet suitcase in the rental's boot car, he returned to the library. Deciding in business had always been easy. Making them in his personal life had usually grounded him to a halt and then disaster. Picking up a coffee book on a table inside the library, he sat with his back to the windows. For several years he and his siblings had discussed if anyone brought the high gloss, very expensive coffee table books to place on a table. This family made his constant argument only the rich can have coffee table books correct. He would never be sure if it was a quick flash of light that made him look up. The reflection in the glass doors of the bookcase saved his life. Slipping to the floor as the two-barrelled shotgun fire twice into the back of his chair. The white stuffing and red leather of the high-backed winged chair covered him. The glass from the bookcase door had landed on his legs. Peering around the side of the chair, he saw a man walking toward the front door of the house. He ran to hide behind the library door, his heart thumping. Expecting the man to enter the library, it surprised him when two ladies dressed as though they were in a kitchen scene in a Christmas pantomime entered. As they crossed the room to examine the chair he stole out of the room and ran to the back of the house via the kitchen. Creeping around the side of the house, he saw the man running down towards Poet's Dell.

When Brig's had parked the rental car at the back of the house, he was a little annoyed thinking they only wanted Rolls and Bentley's parked in front. Now he was glad the faithful Butler had parked it around the back. Leaving the Cobham estate was the only thing he could do. If he stayed, maybe whoever was trying to kill him would. He had relaxed a little too much and let his guard down. This had allowed the gunman to try and kill him. Maybe he had seen the gunman before. He was sure it was at the party last night.

He returned to the car after dropping his suitcase off at Romeo's. Sporting the student attire and with the added white stuffing and red leather from the chair, he looked just like a budding academic.

Aware of the traffic on both sides of the road, he watched as the car raced past, then made an illegal U-turn. The driver stops the car a little ahead of James and scrambles out of the car, screaming.

"What do you look like? You're out of the Pidgley family." Brian takes a picture on a small digital camera. "And this picture will seal it."

"Do whatever you like Brian, you're pathetic."

"I want the checkbooks and all the documentation for the hotel conversion."

"Buy me out and you can have them otherwise go to hell."

"No way I'll go to the police and say you stole them."

"Do that brother and I'll drag your name through the press so Pidgley Properties becomes the laughingstock of England."

"You wouldn't?"

"But I would if only to teach my sick older brother a lesson. And next time you steal my mobile phone and trash it make sure you wipe your fingerprints off it before you throw it away."

Brian's face changed from anger to a stunned silence. How had James known he had taken the phone, let alone smashed it?

James continued to walk down the street with Brian still shouting after him. Knowing Brian would follow, he entered the Lanes district. It would take Brian some time to find a parking space before he could pursue James on foot. As he walked down the Lane, he passed two men he thought he recognized. They were the two men off the boat he had helped smuggle into the country.

They saw him and followed him.

"Please, we need to speak to you."

James stopped and faced the men.

"We have a consignment of two hundred arriving
in two days."

He wasn't sure what they were talking about, but at
that moment he saw Brian running towards him.

"Stop that man from following me and I'll help
you." The men turned and seeing Brian blocked
his path.

"Excuse me, I need to get by," shouted Brian trying
to push past the men.

They pushed him back. James continued down the
lane. At the first intersection, he turned left and
walked into the first open shop he found. He could
hear Brian screaming at the men.

The New Age shop had the smell of incense and
homemade soap. It was very gothic and an ideal place
to hide as Brian would never enter such an establishment. The owner of the shop peered over the countertop and then sunk back into her chair. She didn't want
to have contact with this man. She hoped he would
just browse and then leave. She hated answering questions from students. They were usually silly ignorant
questions about black magic.

James looked out into the lane the shouting had
stopped and he saw Brian running by. He counted to
ten, then left the shop and turning into the lane, and he
met the two men. One thing he knew was these men
would have some answers about why his life was in a
mess. He had help smuggle them into the country now
they wanted to get help.

"We talk about our delivery, we use your hotel for
our consignment, yes."

"What consignment I don't understand?"

"Two hundred beautiful ladies and you can have
anyone of them for free. Some are still virgins you

like virgins, all men like virgins. Now you come to our hotel."

"Sorry no if we will talk it will be in the open with people around."

"Then we go to the pier."

"No, I need to keep away from there. Do you like football?"

"Yes, very much we like football."

"Brighton and Hove Albion are playing at home tonight. We meet at the game and talk."

"We can't talk now, please."

"Sorry I have a meeting soon see you later tonight."

"Okay, what time is the game?"

"It starts at seven forty-five, so we meet seven-fifteen outside the ground."

The two men conferred in a foreign language James didn't recognize.

"It is all right, we meet tonight and please no tricks."

"The same goes for you too."

They shook hands. James could see Brian retracing his steps, so he ran up the lane away from him.

Sitting by the fountain in the old Steine. He had just agreed to meet two men who might be after him. Or tell those that are where he will be later. This time he took a few risks. "As if I hadn't already," he said to himself. A pigeon splashed in the top bowl of the fountain, making the water flow over the side of the bowl to the one below. He'll never know what made him think of the beach, but he did, and the naked men murdered on it.

Luck had been on his side but why, what made him different from the other men. He needed to know more about them and why they had been so unlucky.

The Jubilee Street Library was a very impressive building. The main part of the library lacked adequate lighting along with bookshelves that seemed strangely depleted. Maybe the locals read a lot, or the more likely reason was the town and county cutbacks in spending.

Finding the back issues of the Argus newspaper had been a little challenging.

Scanning the paper for anything to do with naked men found dead on the beach. The police told him the first murder had taken place in June. Unlike his own horrific experience, the first murder didn't have a picture of the body on the beach. The victim Graham Smith was an unemployed nineteen-year-old that likes to go nightclubbing. Known as a drug user they had arrested him for selling them. His girlfriend told the paper he had gone to join some religious group in Hove.

The second murder victim Joseph Kent like Graham was nineteen years old. The picture showed a police forensic tent on the beach. He worked in one of the Marina restaurants, having dropped out of school at sixteen. His distraught mother told the newspaper reporter he was a quiet boy who likes horror movies. Co-workers described him as weird and into anything gothic and dark.

The third victim was found two weeks later. The picture of Oliver Metcalf on the front page of the paper showed an angelic seventeen year old. The article reported very little about him and even asked for anyone with information about Oliver to call the police. Police had found he spent time at an Internet café. He too was naked and stabbed in the groin. His clothes never found and the only jewelry he had was a silver chain and pentangle. James made a note to see what else they had found since finding the body.

A woman walking her dog discovered two days after they had found Oliver the body of Nigel Jenks. The paper mentioned Oliver in passing but added nothing to his story. Nigel's mother wasn't surprised they had found her son dead. He couldn't read or write. And he had two Anti-Social Behaviour Orders against him. Nigel was due in court again the following Monday. His mother's boyfriend Ron Clipsum said, 'Nigel had upset someone, and they had done him in'.

Police had linked his murder to the other naked bodies on the beach. One comment struck James was from the woman who had found the body. She had said at first she thought it was a girl lying naked on the beach. He didn't seem to have any genitalia.

Scott Bowen, the fifth victim, tortured before they murdered him. They found his naked body under the pier, laid out as though he was already in a coffin. They reported he was dead before being placed on the beach. Unlike the others, they had left behind his clothes in a neat pile. Scott was a student at a local college and was studying history. His thesis was on the infamous Hell Fire Club, and it's linked to Freemasonry.

Except for Nigel Jenks, all the victims had some quasi-occult connection. James wrote Black magic on his piece of paper, then added the word chocolate after it.

Reading about yourself being found naked on the beach by a titled lady seemed bizarre to him. He felt detached, as though it had happened to someone else. The reporter had gone into detail about his naked white body. The description was bordering on being pornographic. One thing he didn't know when Julia found him. They placed him in the Vitruvian man pose. Legs spread apart and arms stretched out. He felt a twinge in his groin, the scars of the stabbing reminding him of his ordeal. Michelle Didmouth, the reporter claimed after the police had gone. She had found a stone on the beach painted white. Placing them she said at Pidgley's head, hands, and feet producing a pentangle.

James had very little experience with the occult. A former girlfriend Monique De La Motte had tried to introduce him. The encounter with the black magic rituals was more of a theatrical farce than something mysterious. The murderer of the naked bodies on the beach could have something to do with someone dabbling in Black Magic. The odd quasi-occult anomalies were the common thread between the dead men. Except with Nigel Jenks, the report of his death had focused on his behavior rather than the actual murder. He would dig a little deeper into Nigel's death unless this was a copycat crime, then there should be something occultish to his murder.

That opened up many questions for him. Who picked him and why he wasn't into the occult? Had the newspaper reporter seen those white painted stones or had they just been invented for sensualism.

He closed the paper, then realized he had left his pen inside it. He flicked through looking for it, knowing it would have been easier to just lift the paper, shake it and let the pen fall out. The picture of Julian Peterson Jones was a few years old. The paper hadn't been very kind to the Peterson Jones family. It started with the

homosexual son of... The article explained how they
found him dead. His undressed body lay next to the
adopted teenage son of London property tycoon Donald Seidler. He was naked and his clothes were still
missing. Morten Seidler who liked the name Mobi
was sixteen years old. He had run away from his public boarding school two weeks earlier. A spokesperson
for the family had said Donald regarded the boy as his
son and the death had upset him.

Although the forty thousand pound a year school
wouldn't make a comment. The reporter had found
out from several of Morten's classmates that he said a
Master raped Morten.

The recollection of Donald Seidler and Hector Peterson Jones neither show signs of any grief at the loss of
their sons. The Great British stiff upper lip attitude
never display your true feelings in public.

He found his pen and replaced the newspapers on the
shelf. He would speak to Brad about Julian and
Morten.

He sat back in his chair and closed his eyes. Something was formulating in his mind. It wasn't very clear
and he would have to let it grow rather than forced into
creation. His inner senses told him to be careful. It
felt like he was being set up. The friendliness of Hector Peterson Jones and Donald Seidler was very suspicious. If they were the impressive businessmen, they
claimed to be, why would they accept him too easily.
Even checking him out he wasn't a big player like they
were. So far, he had ignored those traits his family always claimed were Romany. He would let his imagination flow and heed any warning he felt.

The librarian walked by him. The smell of her perfume reminded him of Julia. He wished he had stayed
rather than run from the Cobham estate. Not that he
just wanted to have sex with her. He felt something
deeper and wanted to explore it. He looked at the librarian as she sat behind the inquiry counter. Above
her head, the larger hand on the round clock jumped to
the next second. It was time for him to move, get
something to eat and then make his way to the football
game.

Arriving at the Withdean Stadium in Tongdean Lane
and surprised at the amount of police present. Hoping
his disguise was good enough so one of the keen-eyed
police officers wouldn't recognize him. According to
the local radio station, they were expecting an enormous crowd. He stood by the home team entrance,
trying to blend in with the others who were hanging
around. There was no sign of the two men and a
thought struck him. Maybe they had gone to the Away
Team entrance on the west stand.

He watched as the supporters in the blue and white
shirts filed into the stadium. Several police officers
passed him. The only one gave him a second look, but
it was enough for him. He would buy a ticket and go
into the stadium and look for the men inside. The line
to buy tickets was small. The problem was the man in
front of him. He was carrying a box with Brighton and
Hove Albion blue and white shirts falling out of it.
After the shirts fell several times onto the floor, the
man finally placed the box on the floor and pushed it
along by his foot.

James arrived at the ticket window and bought his ticket. As he turned to leave a young blonde-haired girl in a club shirt spoke to him.

"I think you dropped this," handing him a club shirt.

The man with the box of shirts was causing a problem at the gate and several police officers had arrived. James took the shirt off the girl and thanked her. It had fallen from the man's box.

The extra-large shirt went over his clothes and he felt he blended in with everyone else. He found his seat in a sea of blue and white tee shirts. Unless you knew what, he looked like it would be hard to find him among the other fans.

He had ignored his inner senses for the last few days. Maybe that was why he had found himself almost killed and on the run. The powerful urge for caution washed over him. He may have picked the place to meet the men that didn't mean it couldn't be a trap. He scanned the crowd, looking for the men. It was un-likely they had club shirts and therefore would stand out from the crowd. He couldn't see them, and the game started. The first twenty minutes seemed to drag with very little excitement to get the crowd aroused. After a challenge to Nicky Forster, he scored a goal and sent the home team supporters into ecstasy. The supporters were elated at the end of the first half. Leaving his seat, James wandered around looking for the men. Suddenly he saw them shaking hands with Donald Seidler. He quickly hid behind a group of fans and watched as the three men talked. Donald seemed agitated with the men and wagged his index finger several times before he relaxed. The fans James had hidden behind moved back to the seats. Moving quickly, he leaned against a brick wall with the cover of two police officers in front of him. Donald shook the men's hands again and left the two men turned and found some seats in the stadium. James went back to his bank of seats only to find someone had taken his place. He sat down in the first empty seat he could find. If he leaned forward, he could see the two men. The second half of the football match started. The two men from what he could see were not interested in the game. They sat facing each other and talked.

He couldn't understand why they hadn't been looking for him. They had wanted the meeting and yet they seemed uninterested in looking for him. The crowd roared and James looked at the pitch. It wasn't a goal, just a near miss. When he looked back at the two men, they had left their seats. He stood and ran towards where they had sat. He couldn't see them as he ran to the men's toilet, finding them empty. Someone shouted Jim, and he looked in that direction. The man shouting wasn't calling for James, but behind him, he could see the two men leaving the stadium.

He cautiously followed them and watched as they got into a taxi and drove away. The next cab moved forward and James climbed in.

"Follow that taxi, please."

"You taking the piss mate?"

"No, I need to follow that taxi."

"Okay, I hope you have the money if they are going a long way."

"I wouldn't get in your cab unless I did."

The taxicab pulled away from the curb and raced after the first taxi. James sat back in the seat, trying to work out which way the men were going.

For a few seconds, he wondered if he was being taken on a fool's errand. The taxicab in front seemed to drive around in circles.

Then headed for the marina.

CHAPTER SEVENTEEN

The Missing Piece

The taxicab had followed the two men's cab only to find when they arrived at the marina. They had been following the wrong taxi. Somewhere along the route the driver had either lost them by mistake or deliberately followed the wrong taxi. He had spent some time talking on his mobile phone as they drove along. James wasn't sure what language he used, but it wasn't English. Consequently, he hadn't understood if the driver was talking to the taxi they were following or someone else.

The sea thrashed at the beach a rage building beneath the waves. Far out in the English Channel dark formidable clouds were forming. Another storm was gathering whether it would aim for Northern France or England was undetermined. It matched James's mood. He wasn't sure if he was depressed or maybe becoming depressed. Lost in a maze of his mind, the puzzles answer eluding him. He couldn't see the complete picture in his head. It was like watching a digital film on an analog television. The wooden beach seat needed a fresh coat of paint and some screws replaced. He enjoyed the breeze blowing over him as he sat listening to the music of the waves.

He stomped his feet, so they didn't fall asleep. This made a draft sending a fast-food restaurant red wrapper floating across the ground. The town council hadn't cleaned this part of the seafront for some time. Between his feet, he could see a piece of a child's jigsaw puzzle. He bent to pick it up and saw several other pieces under the seat. The wind kept blowing his hat off, so he took it off and put it in his pocket.

He stooped to collect the jigsaw puzzle, counting seven pieces altogether. He arranged them on the bench seat by his side. The jigsaw was seven inches by six inches and one piece was missing the most important one. Without it, the picture wasn't complete, although he could guess what was missing.

He deduced a fire engine ladder and fireman. Stooping again he looked under the seat again. A boy he assumed had abandoned the puzzle, maybe because he had lost the one piece. Or his baby sister had eaten it while he was paddling in the sea. As a baby, his sister Anne was always destroying her sibling's toys when they weren't around. Remembering his sister brought back memories of his family. He needed to call them and see if his mother was getting better and to talk to his father about Brian.

Looking back at the puzzle, it was as if a curtain drew back for a few seconds and an idea had formed. The puzzle was like his own problems something was missing. He had lots of information, but the central piece was missing. Like the puzzle, maybe he could deduce the missing piece or pieces. He searched his pocket for some notepaper and a pen. The pen was easy, the ballpoint pen clogged with ink and fluff from his jeans, a slight problem. A small scrap of paper was all he could find. He picked up one piece of the jigsaw and turned it over. The white card back was perfect for making notes. He wrote furiously to get all he could remember down. Cramming as much as he could onto each piece of the jigsaw puzzle.

On one piece he wrote Peterson-Jones and Donald Seidler what is their connection. This he followed by putting names or subjects on the pieces. His mind drifted off into thought when he wrote Julia's name on a piece.

Each piece became crammed with writing and he put the puzzle together, the picture side face down. Studying his notes, a pattern emerged. Like the puzzle, the centerpiece was missing the thing which joined everything together. The answer he knew was in front of him, only obscured by his inability to sift the facts from the emotions.

Lost in thought, he didn't hear the approach of his brother Brian.

"Still playing with kid's toys you never grew up did you, James?"

He ignored the croaking voice and quickly dismantled the puzzle, pushing it into his jean pocket.

"If you're interested, Mom is doing fine now. Although it would be nice if you had called to see how she was."

"I've already heard she is out of danger."

"Who from?"

"Brian, despite your efforts, I still have friends."

"Your friends came to see me wanting to rent the hotel for two weeks. As we are delayed on the

conversion because of your antics I told them yes.
The money they offered was good, and they paid
upfront."
"What friends?"
"Two Russians, I think."
"They are not my friends, did they tell you what
they needed the hotel for?"
"Some visiting schoolgirls from Russia on an edu-
cational visit to England."
"Haha that is hilarious, and you believed them?"
"Of course, and it's very good money."
"Your visiting schoolgirls are illegal under-aged
school girls, immigrants, here for prostitution."
"What!"
"Don't call me when they arrest you for running a
brothel. You will be the first pimp in our family
and Brian think of the publicity."
Brian's mouth dropped open and then quickly closed.
James watched as his brother ran down the promenade
towards the town. At first, the slight laugh grew until
he was laughing so loud that an obese man walking his
small dog stopped. Retreated the way he was walking
dragging his dog.

He took a piece of the puzzle out of his pocket and
read what he had written. *What is Julia's connection?*
He needed to remove the emotion from his thoughts.
Love and sex were clouding his thinking process. She
knew everyone, and he realized she had played him for
information. Then there was Carolle Brockner known
locally as Karl. What was her relationship with the
man, maybe they were lovers? He stopped himself as
his jealous streak was clouding the thoughts. Had they
been intimate on the boat. She had denied that there

was anything between them and she was just doing a favor. Could he believe her?

The hand on his shoulder didn't make him jump and without looking up he said, "What's wrong with Brian, you need my help?"
He stood up and turned to see Brad and two other men.
    "Time to come in, James."
Sitting between Brad and another man in the back seat of the unmarked car. For the first time in several days, he felt relieved. It was over and whatever happened now, he could at least hope to get some sleep. One piece of the jigsaw puzzle had twisted in his pocket and was pushing into his leg. He didn't want to move it or they will see him try to do something in his pocket. They would misunderstand and search him or shoot him, then search his pockets.
The car suddenly pulled into the curb, Brad jumping and running over to a metal door in the grey concrete building. This side of the building didn't have any windows and looked as though transplanted from Russia. They led James down a flight of steps to a dark, cold passage.
    "Sorry, James, but we have to put you in a cell."
James nodded, he had expected something like this and was looking forward to resting.

The room in the same grey concrete as the corridor and was only eight feet wide by ten feet deep. A glass block window set high in one wall. One block had cracks and several pieces of glass were missing. He could feel an icy stream of air blowing in from outside. A World War Two type metal bed with a plastic-covered mattress looked inviting. In the middle of the bed was a folded blanket, a white cotton pillow lay on top. The only other thing in the room was a stainless-steel toilet bowl. A roll of toilet paper precariously balanced on the metal seat of the bowl.

James stepped into the room and the door closed behind him. He took his shoes off and lay on the bed. Covering himself with the blanket and fell asleep.

Waking from his sleep in the dark, the sound of a raging storm filled the room. A whistling, screeching scream bellowed through the crack in the broken glass brick. The room was chilly. He imaged he could see his breath as he exhaled. Thumbing noises sounded either outside or in the building, he wasn't sure. Then the single light above flickered on. Then as the noise stopped, and the light went out. The sequence repeated itself self and after the fourth time he concluded, it must be some torture technique. He lay on his stomach, his face buried in the pillow so he couldn't see the light. The first clang of bells made him sit up. He always thought bell ringing should at least sound like a tune. He curled up into the fetal position and tried not to listen. They wouldn't break him, not with this game. Tortured as a child by his older brothers and he survived. This would eventually get to him, but not immediately. If this continued all night, then it would break him. The room became silent, and he relaxed. He lay for a few minutes on his back before the cacophony restarted. The light flickered, and he searched the room for the speaker. If he found it, he could rip out the wires and stop the noise. As the light strobed slowly, he scanned each wall, then the ceiling. If they had placed a speaker in the room, they had hidden it extremely well. He sat up and looked around the bed, lifting the mattress to see if they hid the speaker beneath it. Sitting back on the bed, he tried to see if he had missed anywhere. The metal toilet was the only place he hadn't looked. Could they hide a speaker in the base of the metal bowl? Crawling on his hands and knees, he searched around the bowl. When the cell door opened forcibly, he was peering down into the bowl, wondering if it was under the water.

Brad stood looking at him, his expression was complete amazement. The light went out again, James staring where Brad had stood, only seeing a black shape.

"Sorry about this, you'd better follow me." James sat on the floor and wondered where he'd go. The lights flickered on again, the screaming noise rising to a high pitch, screeching. Brad was no longer standing in the doorway, but the door was still open. He hadn't imagined it until he remembered a film he had seen as a teenager. It was about a man in the jungle being tortured with water. Then imagined he saw people and things, which were not there. As if out of an old horror movie Brad slid into the doorway again. His smile looking more like an evil grin.

"Come on, James, or you will freeze to death down here." James crawled on all fours to the door before standing. Brad had raced ahead and in the flickering light, he tried to see where he had gone. The lights went out and using the wall to guide him; he tried to follow. He didn't see the stairs and fell on to them. The handrail of thick rope hanged loosely between hooks on the wall. If someone else was using the stairs and was grabbing the rope, the person behind would find it difficult to heave themselves up the stairs. Brad was putting all his weight on the rope. Making it almost impossible for James to use it to climb the steep stairs. At the top, a soft glow was visible at the end of a corridor.

Entering a large room glowing in candlelight. Its similarity to a living room than a government office surprised James. Several easy chairs around the room. In the middle two large sofas had been place on either side of a glass coffee table. Simon, Brad's partner in the investigation, lay on one of the sofa's a bottle of beer in his left hand. He nodded towards James and pointed for him to sit on the other sofa. Sitting down slowly, looking around the room and the candles that illuminated the place. He once had a girlfriend that would only use candles at night to light her home. Although very romantic when her house caught fire he wasn't at all surprised.

"The powers out and our small generator doesn't seem to work very well."

"There's a storm?"

Simon nodded then continued, "we thought you would have come up once you found the lights out."

"I couldn't the cell door was locked."

"No it wasn't, did you try it?"

"No, I just thought…"

"James you're not under arrest."

"I'm not?"

"No, we just needed to talk to you."

"But I thought the police and your organization were looking for me."

"The police are no longer looking for you, and we never were. We always knew where you were, well almost before you vanished, and then we heard you were dead."

"For the second time in my brief life, I thought I
was."

"So have you worked it out yet?"

"What?"

"Who tried to kill you or at least embarrass you?"

"Not really, I was just beginning to see a pattern
when you came along and threw me into the cell."

"We didn't throw you and we only placed you in
there while we cleaned this place up. Brad's a bit
of a pig and left the place a mess."

"So, you weren't torturing me with the sounds and
light show?"

"No those were the good old days, that's right isn't
it Bradley."

"Don't listen to him James the man is full of his
own bovine excrement. There is a storm raging
outside."

"Like the one in October nineteen eighty-seven?"

"Not as bad. Did you think we were giving you the
old mind-changing control torture?"

"Well, to be honest, yes."

Brad laughed before grabbing a wooden dining chair
and swung it around. He sat on it, resting his arms on
the back, his thighs clamping the sides of the back of
the chair. Controlling his laughter, he tried to speak
but stopped as he laughed again.

"Sorry, James, we know who put you on the beach
and why. We also know about the smuggling of
people and the prostitution."

Simon leaned forward on the sofa and took over the
explanation from Brad.

"They have sent us to deal with smuggling. Our
problem is we know all the minor players but can't
seem to get a fix on who is behind it."

"So, who put me on the beach naked?"

"Gordon Tuff and Patrice Sickle."

"The drug dealer and his moll, why did they do it?"

"Oh, she was more than just his girlfriend, she had some power in the relationship. First, she would lure young, vulnerable men to their house. Then plied them with drink and drugs. We are not sure if Gordon raped them, someone had raped them. Then Patrice would become the high Priestess and they would have a satanic ritual sacrificing the victims."

"So why didn't they do it to me?"

"Well, first it wasn't full moon that night. More importantly, they thought you had a connection with Hector Peterson-Jones."

"Julian's father?"

"The police arrested them this afternoon. Someone called the police saying their son was missing and the last time anyone saw him he had entered Tuff's house. The police raided it and found the boy tied up, naked and drugged."

"I tried to find their house, but all I found was a school."

"And that is where they lived, he was the school caretaker."

"Says a lot for background checks."

"I doubt they ever did one."

"So gentlemen, what do you want from me?"

"Information."

"About what, I don't think I know anything."

"Is there a connection between Hector Peterson-Jones and Donald Seidler?"

"I'm not sure exactly but they are up to

something."

"We need hard evidence, will you help us get it?"

"I have my price."

"We expected that."

"First did Tuff and Sickle kill Julian and Taylor?"

"The police say not."

"So who did?"

"We don't know and to be truthful we don't care."

"Because they were homosexuals?"

"No, if we followed every crime we came across, we would get nothing finished."

James looked at the two men, he didn't believe them. Sensing this, Brad quickly commented.

"We are only interested in the people smuggling. Any information we find out about other crimes we pass on to the authorities who are investigating it."

An awkward silence closed in on them. James sat looking at the floor, not sure what he should say. Brad and Simon gave each other knowing looks, which meant nothing.

"What about the smugglers?"

"I suppose James that must include you and me."

"I suppose it does, only you were acting under orders."

"And you were helping me, it is in my report."

"Thanks. You know they are using the hotel I came to convert."

"Yes, and your brother is about to get a visit from the vice squad."

"Oh, he will just love that and then cry to our parents it was all James's fault."

"He can try, but the police have him on tape talking to the Russian."

"Shit poor Brian, it gets deeper and deeper. At least the family might know the truth."

"We will step in before it goes to court, but Simon and I believe your brother needs a little lesson."

"A big lesson."

"Julia?"

"What about her?"

"Was she…"

"… Nothing personal. I don't kiss and tell."

"I wouldn't ask anything personal I heard enough when you were together."

"You taped it."

"No, we just listened in. Sorry, but I could just say it was all part of our job too."

James sank deeper into the sofa. He was now bright red with embarrassment. Brad left the arm of the other sofa and entered a kitchen area.

Simon changed the subject, but not without giving James a smirk.

"What we know is she or her family are involved in the smuggling?"

"I'm not sure she knows everyone who is involved."

"Her family is old money. Nazi sympathizers during the Second World War."

"It doesn't surprise me you were at the party. Looking around the ballroom, you could expect Hitler or one of his henchmen to enter at any moment. And everyone was in corners in some conspiracy."

"Wheeling and dealing everything from small-time drug deals to bank raids."

"Are you serious?"

"I don't know, but they were doing deals criminal or not, I couldn't say."

"So why were you there?"

"The same reason you were, getting information. It surprised me to see you there, I thought you would blow my cover."

"I wasn't sure you had a cover."

Brad returned carrying three bottles of beer. He handed one to Simon and another to James. Both Brad and Simon looked at him as he inspected the top of the bottle. Brad handed him the bottle opener, smiling.

"What's funny?"

"Simon said you would check the top of the bottle before opening it."

"Damn right I will, at this moment I trust no one. I hope you understand."

"We do."

"So, can I go back to my flat?"

"Sure once the storm has stopped."

Three hours later, James pushed the key into the lock of his flat. The storm still raged outside, but he had braved the weather and got to his flat. He had checked the secret seals he had placed on the door before leaving. They were still intact. No one had gone through the door. Switching on the light, pleased to see that in this part of town the weather had not affected the electricity. Closing the door, he slid the two bolts into place. Then he checked all the windows before locking the one in the toilet. He hoped he wouldn't need that entrance or exit again. The flat was as he had left it, but he checked for obvious bugging devices and found none.

His joy of electricity was short-lived as the lights died. He searched for his torch and found candles in a drawer in the kitchen. Placing one on each corner of the bathtub. After lighting them, he stripped off his clothes and ran the water in the bath. Gas fueled the water heater, so the water came gushing out hot.

He lay soaking in the tub, the flickering candles giving the bathroom an eerie glow. Listening as the wind outside lashed at the building. Thinking it would be his bad luck to have the roof and side of the building ripped off while he was still in the bathtub. As he soaked the wind seemed to die down and he listened to the noise in the building. Several times he thought he heard someone moving around the living room. Straining to listen, but each time he gave into his imagination. He was paranoid, and the people who had left him naked on the beach were now in jail. There were always the people who had put him in the manhole. He stood up quickly and dried himself. He found a clean pair of pajamas, dressing in the darkness. Returning to the bathroom, he blew out the candles. Using the torch, he searched for something he could use as a weapon. Suddenly he realized he wasn't safe, Brad and Simon didn't know about the manhole. Someone was out there and could still try to kill him. The metal golf club in a closet would be the best weapon he could have. It would be his bed companion tonight. It wasn't as soft and as curved as Julia had been. The golf club wouldn't hurt him emotionally unless he rolled over on top of it while he slept.

Checking the flat again, even looking under the bed to see if anyone was hiding there. The sheets were cold, he would have to wait for his body heat to warm the bed up.

His mother had always traveled with an electric blanket. Now he understood why she was a wise woman, and tonight he missed her. He would call in the morning and see how she was. With this thought, he fell into a deep sleep.

The gloved hand gripped the door handle and tried to open the door to his flat. The man pushed hard against the door, but it wouldn't budge. For tonight, James was safe. The man crept down the stairs, unaware of the pair of eyes staring through a spyhole in the flat below James.

Sitting at the dining table in his pajamas drinking a cup of tea. He wished he had milk, but he hadn't so he would just have to make do with what he had. Trying to think what he should do next, only his mind came up blank. Forced out of his daydream by the hammering on his door. Grabbing the golf club, he approached the door. Standing to one side, having watched several American television programs when the victim stood behind the door. The gunman had sprayed the door with bullets, killing his victim.

"Who is it?"

"Dad and Donald James open up."

He quickly unbolted the door and still with a security chain on, opened the door a little. He saw his father standing holding a brown paper bag.

He took the chain off and let his father and brother into the flat. Neither said anything but looked around the place. James could see they were checking on him.

"What were you expecting, a drunk orgy or a posse of male prostitutes?"

"You don't have to be rude, James, but after what Brian told us we didn't know what to expect."

"I'm sure Brian painted a horrific picture and my

family who I grew up with believe the lying bastard."

"Language James."

"Sorry, Dad, but you force your way into my flat. Treat me as though I am some kind of criminal without finding out if what you have been told is true."

"James, after they found you naked on the beach, I'm sorry but I wondered what kind of life you lead."

"And my jealous, selfish brother plies you with a tale of horrific portions and you fool believe him. Well, I'm not the one they arrested today for running a brothel with illegal under-aged schoolgirls from Russia."

"That's why we are here. They arrested him last night. It upsets your mother, and it is obvious it involves you," said Donald.

"What?"

"Look James, just tell Dad and me what you know so we can get the solicitor to get Brian out and clear this mess up."

"I know nothing you should ask the brothel keeper."

James returned to the dining table and sat and continued to drink his tea.

Matthew looked at his son. He had found it hard to believe what Brian told the family. James was either a talented actor or he was telling the truth.

"I brought some breakfast according to the radio news you had a storm here last night and most places are without electricity."

Matthew placed the containers on the table. James went into the kitchen and returned with two plates and

two forks. Donald laid the plates out and realized
there were only two.

"There are three of us."

"But only two will eat when I have the last meal,
I'll choose what I want to eat."

He left them and went into the bedroom and dressed.
Sitting on the bed, he heard a third voice talking in the
next room.

Brad was sitting at the table when he returned into the
living room. He smiled when he saw James but
quickly changed his facial expression when he saw the
scowl on James's.

"Dad this is Bradley with MI-5 you know the government secret agency. He has been following me,
knows all about Brian and the girls, why don't you
ask him. I am going out, when you leave, close the
door behind you."

James left before any of them could speak. He ran
down the stairs and almost bumped into the old
woman from the flat below him.

"You had a visitor last night, they tried your door."

"When?"

"After you came home, it was a tall, fat man. I
didn't like him, and I told Pickles my cat that man
was up to no good. You need to be careful."

She picked up her cat, who had been rubbing itself
against James's legs. And went into her flat, closing
the door behind her.

"Thank you."

James ran down the stairs and into the street. Dodging
several cars crossing the street, he ran into the alleyway opposite. The town had signs of storm damage.
A tree had fallen on one corner, the hoarding of one
shop hanging precariously further along the street.

He wandered until he arrived at the seafront and reached the bench Brad had met him on the day before. Sitting down with a thump, he looked out towards the sea. How could his family treat him like this? Why had Brian poisoned the minds of the family against him?

The wind off the sea was cold, cutting and very refreshing. The surf was high and pounding the stones on the beach. He looked down at the floor and saw the missing piece of the jigsaw puzzle. It was wet and the layers of paper separating.

Was this an omen for him, would he now put the last pieces together and solve the mystery of...? What? That was the point of what did he need to solve. First, who had tried to kill him in the manhole? Second, who had killed Julian and Taylor? Why was he worrying so much about their murder? Because of their link, if he solved the one, he would know the answer to the other. He shivered and went in search of a café for something to eat. Why had he been stupid to refuse his father's gift of breakfast? But he was, like his father, very stubborn about certain things.

The café was warm and full of workmen eating either a late breakfast or an early lunch. He ordered and found a table at the back of the café. If he needed to solve Julian and Taylor's murders, he needed to find out who wanted them dead. Donald Seidler and Hector Peterson–Jones must be a link.

A tall thin girl who looked anorexic and depressed delivered his breakfast to the table. She placed the food in front of him and returned to the kitchen without speaking or looking at him. He still felt angry with his father and brother Donald. How could they believe what Brian had said without finding out his side of things? Stabbing at the sausage fat squirted out and landed on the back of the workman on the next table. James gave a brief snorting laugh and relaxed. It was enough to make him reconsider his attitude toward his father. Was he, James, being unreasonable? How often had he jumped to conclusions not knowing the complete picture? So why was he being so hard on his father, a man who he respected and loved? What had Brian said to make the family come to such a conclusion that it involved him in criminal activity? They involved him. He had helped smuggle illegal immigrants into the country. Now he was at the mercy of the British Secret Service whether they would prosecute. Even though Brad had said he had already cleared it with someone above.

James felt very uneasy. His life once again was in the hands of someone else. All his life he had allowed others to control him. He looked around the café, it had suddenly filled with people standing waiting for a table. This was one of his pet hates. He always felt he needed to rush his meal so someone else could sit and eat their meal. A very large building site worker stood and left the café. While the depressed, anorexic waitress clears the table and wiped it arbitrarily. He saw Julia's brother Benjamin on the opposite side of the café, his head sagging down as though he was asleep. From this angle, James couldn't tell if it was drugs, alcohol, or a lack of sleep. As the waitress passed Benjamin on her way to the kitchen, she kicked him. He awoke, muttered something and fell back into his stupefying pose.

Another workman obscured James's view. The man desperate to get his breakfast or early lunch and sitting down at the vacant table.

"You finished?" asked the depressed, anorexic waitress in a monosyllabic tone.

"Almost," replied James, taking his plate from her clutching hand.

He quickly finished the meal and drank the remains of his pint-size mug of tea. He lightly tapped Benjamin on the shoulder, expecting the boy to jump awake.

The boy didn't move but in a slurred voice said, "Okay, I'm going." He tried to stand and missed colliding into the waitress.

"Let me help you, Benjamin."

"Thanks, you know my name, do I know you?"

The waitress held the door open and in her tuneless tone said, "Good ridden."

On the pavement, James didn't wait for Benjamin to say where he wanted to go. In his most authoritative voice, he asked the boy.

"Where do you live?"

Benjamin looked at him, then pulled his wallet out of his pocket. James opened it and stuck inside was a note saying if found please return to this address. Benjamin was leaning against him but pointed up the street and said again in his slurred voice, "Two streets that way."

James placed the boy's arm over his shoulder so he could help him walk along the street.

They walked slowly, stopping every few yards while Benjamin straightens himself up and tried to walk unaided. It didn't last, and he soon put his arm on James's shoulder for support.

"Heavy night."

"Heavy life I'm not drunk or drugged if that is what you're thinking." His slurred voice controlled.

"I wasn't thinking you were. You just look exhausted."

"I am, I have been awake for seventy-two hours and I now need some sleep."

"Almost at home."

"How do you know me?"

"I'm a friend of Julia's."

"Julia my sister?"

"Yes."

"Were you bonking her, she likes to bonk only she screams and wakes everyone up. Once when she was doing it at Cobham grandfather sent a servant in the middle of the night to tell her to stop fucking her brains out."

They stopped outside a very expensive block of flats. It differed from the one he had seen Julia enter and exit. Benjamin gave James a bunch of keys and pointed to the building's main door. He leaned Benjamin against the wall and tried several keys before finding the correct one. Opening the door, a cat dashed out.

"Oh, shit you're in for it now, that was Miss Crumples little cat. If she finds out you let it out, she will make you find it for her. She's a real bitch, but filthy rich."

The lift was an old-fashioned wire cage with wooden concertina sliding gates. He placed Benjamin against the back wall of the lift while James closed the gates. The boy slid down and lay crumpled on the floor. The note in the wallet stated the flat was number thirty-seven. He pressed the third-floor button and turned to help the boy stand.

"Sorry I am so tired."

The lift arrived on the third floor and James opened the
sliding gates. Benjamin stepped out onto the landing,
walked unsteadily towards number thirty-seven.
James quickly followed, looking at the keys. At the
door he pushed the doorbell it rang several times. He
hoped that Julia would be home. No one answered, so
he tried the keys until he found the one that unlocked
the door.

Benjamin stumbled in and fell into a dining chair next
to a sofa. He had fallen asleep and looked as though
he would fall off the chair at any moment. James
pushed the boy's body, so it leaned towards the sofa.

Looking around, this was the father's flat the children
could use when daddy wasn't in town. Oil paintings
of members of the family hung on the walls. Some by
famous artists, others looked like members of the family had tried to paint. They covered every surface in
the room with picture frames. Some big while others
tiny miniature pictures. Each picture portraying members of this English aristocratic dynasty. On the piano,
the present family stood as though on parade, ready for
inspection. He looked for Julia's picture but could not
locate it.
    "Who you looking for?"
Benjamin stood next to him, swaying back and forth.
    "Julia."
    "She's not there nor is she here."
    "Do you know where she is, I really would like to
see her."
    "Need to bonk her again?"
    "No, but I need to ask her something."
    "She runs away the silly bitch scared of…"
He tottered backward and landed on the sofa.

"What's she scared of?"

"The dark and big fat men who will come to get her
in the night."

He suddenly keeled over and was asleep. James
scanned the picture one more time before moving to
another table. There was no sign of a picture of Julia
on any of the tables or sideboards. The drawer of a
writing desk near the window was just a fraction open.
James opened and peered inside. The silver-framed
picture of Julia was in the drawer. Several pieces of
broken glass fell to the floor as he took the picture out.
The black-and-white photograph was several years
old. The girl in the picture was in a school uniform,
her teeth braces visible as she smiled. Even then you
could see the beauty that would blossom later in life.
He didn't hear the key being put into the lock of the
door. Only aware that someone had entered the flat
when he heard the footsteps on the wooden floor of the
hall.

CHAPTER EIGHTEEN

Benjamin Brooke

Donald Seidler entered the room as though he owned the place. He was breathing heavily, having run up the stairs. Seeing James, then Benjamin, he asked, "Julia here?"

"No, according to Benjamin she has gone away."

"Bloody typical, did the idiot say where?"

"No, just she went away."

"Damn and blast, I suppose he's out of his head again? Let's hope he causes no more trouble."

"Do you know some bloody idiot didn't close the gate, and I had to walk up the three flights of stairs? Some people are so inconsiderate these days."

Donald turned and left the flat, banging the door behind him.

"That was me or should that be I," said James a grin on his face.

Looking out of the window on to the street, he watched Donald cross the road and climb into a chauffeur-driven car.

He looked at Benjamin on the sofa, a grin formed on his face.

"It should be I. Has the old bastard gone?"

"Donald, yes."

"Good, the bloody fool, and that are what he is. Soon and very soon he will find out how much of a clown he is."

"Why what will happen?"

"His world is about to explode."

"How?"

"Do you know he is my Godfather, whatever that means? He never goes to church or spends time with me unless he wants me to run one of his stupid errands."

"Donald and Peterson-Jones are friends."

"Not friends, it's all business with them. Money is the only thing that matters. Money is their God."

"And your sister Julia."

"Julia, Julia, why is it always about my sister doesn't anyone care about me."

"Should they care about you, Benjamin, you seem very irresponsible."

"I should become an actor, I think I would be good at it."

"So, this is all an act?"

"They should care about me, I have all their secrets. If I told you or even better the police what I know so many people would go to jail. Shit, that would be hilarious with my parents in jail."

Suddenly Benjamin fell to his knees in a praying position and crossed himself.

"Bless me father, for I have sinned. It has been six days since my last confession. I have done the

usual sex, drinking, and stealing, but Father, I have
also committed a mortal sin. I have…"
He stopped, opened his eyes and looked at James
"You're not a real priest, I need a real priest."
He stood up and ran out of the flat, letting the door
bang behind him.

At the window, James watched as Benjamin ran up the
street, stopped and changed direction before disappearing out of sight. What had Benjamin done to make
him think it was a mortal sin?
"Come to think of it, what constituted a mortal
sin?"
He said to the picture of an old general on horseback.
Running through the list of mortal sins he could think
of starting with murder. He tried to conjuror up others
but not being a catholic. He hadn't had the religious
education to know the answer.
Taking a quick look around the flat, he wanted to see if
it was empty. What was he going to do now, leave the
flat but with nowhere to go. On the hall floor, an
opened letter had fallen. It must have blown down
when Benjamin slammed the door. He picked it up
and saw it was addressed to Julia, turning the paper
over it was from her father. The phone in the hall rang
and without thinking James automatically picked up
the handset.
"Benjie it's Julia get the fuck out and hide."
James listened, he didn't want to speak, just hear her
voice.
"Benjie is that you?"
After a pause, he said, "No, it's James."
Julia was silent this time the pause dragged on until
James couldn't take it anymore.

"Julia you still there?"

"Yes, where is Benjie?"

"He just left to find a priest I think."

"Oh God, he is on his religious act again, was he drunk?"

"I don't think so, he said something about being up for seventy-two hours with no sleep."

"My brother went to a private Catholic Boys School. He thinks by staying awake and praying for hours on end it will solve all his problems."

"Donald Seidler came looking for you."

"Bloody hell don't trust that man James."

"I don't except he seems to be very important around here."

"He wished he was the fool."

"Your brother called him a fool."

She went silent again, and he listened to her breathing. She gave a long deep sigh as though she had come to some conclusions.

"James what I am going to tell you could get me into a lot of trouble. What the heck you're in enough of your own. Donald Seidler and Hector Peterson-Jones put it about they are the big bosses in this part of the world. They are just puppets of who is running the show."

"So who are the people at the top?"

"I can't say that would get me killed like Julian and Taylor. God, I miss them, they were so much fun, two silly queens."

"I never knew them."

"Your loss. Anyway, it's the person who I can't talk about that wants you dead."

"Why what have I done?"

"Nothing only you were at the wrong place at the

wrong time. Heard something you shouldn't, and
the rest will play out in time."

"What place when?"

"I've said too much already this phone might be
bugged and we both know whom by. I always
thought a chauffeur should know their place."

"Give me a clue Julia please."

"It's where all this started for you."

"The beach."

"No before that, they thought you heard something,
and it scared them."

"What did I hear?"

"I don't think you did, they drugged you, passed
out on the floor. I've got to go if you see my
brother, tell him to go to grand mamma's. He'll
know what that means."

She hung up, and he stared at the handset, hoping she
would continue. His desire for Julia returned she had
got under his skin. Sitting on the gold-painted wooden
chair next to the phone table, a wave of despondency
filling his body.

What had she meant before the beach and on the floor?
He looked at the letter in his hand. The thought of all
the letters his father had written to him over the years.
He read the letter from Julia's father he was telling her
how much her mother and he loved her. One line
stuck in his mind '*you're our daughter and whatever
you do we will love you forever.*' He thought of his
parents and the number of times they had said that to
him. That morning he had shown disrespect for the
man who had stood by him all his life.

His father was only reacting to a pack of lies given to
him by Brian. No one in his family would expect one

son to lie about and another son. He needed to say
sorry and mend a few bridges.

As he was going back to his flat, he rehearsed what he
would say to his father. The main door had been
locked, and the flat was empty. Either his father or
Donald had straightened the place. The teacup he had
left on the table, washed and placed on the drying rack.
In his bedroom, the bed made, and his dirty clothes
neatly folded on a chair. This was the work of his father, tidying up after someone was his way of releasing
his frustration.

They must have gone to the hotel if he rushed, he
could catch up with them there.

The old hotel locked up and looked more depressing
than he remembered. They strung blue and white police tape across the front entrance. He wasn't sure if
this was because of the murder or the place used as a
brothel. At the back of the hotel, he found the place
the homeless used to gain entry. One of the security
men they had used when first taking over the property
had shown him the way.

There was a warmth to the building, and it smelt of a
perfume shop. The reception area cleaned up and several chairs and tables neatly arranged. They had converted the registration desk into a bar. Looking at the
bottles, most of them were empty or smashed in
pieces. He ran up the central staircase to the first
floor. The marble pillars had been polished and heavy
red velvet curtains hide the entrance to the bedrooms.
This looked more like a Victorian brothel scene out of
an old film. He pushed aside one curtain and entered a
bedroom. The room contained a full-size bed with
satin-type sheets on it. A small bedside table with its

drawer open stood next to the bed. In the drawer, he saw several tubes of lotions and oils. Hundreds of silver foiled wrapped condoms neatly packed into the drawer. The Russians meant business. This was a well-planned operation. He ran up to the next landing and into another room. It was just like the one below. Except someone had left a small, neatly dressed doll in the center of the bed.

He missed out the third floor and checked out the rooms on the fourth floor. They were empty too high to bring a client. The window in the room he entered was open and lead onto a flat roof. Stepping outside, the cool sea air wrapped itself around his body. He felt as if it was lifting him off the floor. Energy seemed to re-enter his body. He needed to regain his positive attitude and solve the problems he was facing. He couldn't allow the quagmire of depression to engulf him. It was time to pull himself together and move forward.

The Old Stein with its water fountain and newly planted trees stretched out below like a carpet. The tops of the domes at the Royal Pavilion sparkled as jewels dropped on the carpet. He needed to see his father, to apologize for the way he had behaved. If only he could forget the complete mess as though it never had happened. Then there was Brian and his insane jealousy corrupting the picture. Maybe if he could control his emotions and watch what he said, he could repair the bridges. He closed the window and descended the stairs. The first voice he heard was his brother Donald's. He lent over the balustrade and saw his father and Donald talking in the entrance hall. He went to shout to them but heard his name and stopped. Quickly pulled back he crept down the stairs to the first floor trying to listen to what was being said. The acoustic of the hotel lobby gave a little echo to the sound emanating from it.

They were talking about the mess the hotel conversion was in. It seems neither James nor Brian had helped in the confusion.

On the first floor, he slid along the wall until he was over them and behind one of the marble pillars. Unfortunately, the pillar blocked the voices, so he had to move to the side of the pillar. Donald was pacing up and down. James had to move back when Donald looked up. Donald returned to his father's side and James resumed his position by the side of the pillar. He had not heard the beginning of the sentence, but the words of his father hit him.

"He is no son of mine."

"James."

He turned and saw Brian standing on the other side of the landing. James ran through the red velvet curtains and raced down the corridor to the fire escape. He pushed open the door and descended the metal staircase two steps at a time.

As he ran down the street, his emotion took over and he fought off the desire to cry and scream out.

The man who had spent his life being his idol had just said he was no longer a son of his. The world as he knew it had just collapsed. Out on the street, he ran one way then another, not sure where he was going. He soon lost his breath and slowed down.

He needed to control his breathing and his emotions. Arriving at the beach he walked out on to the stones and sat down looking out at the sea.

What was he going to do without the support of his family? He had always known they were there for him. If his father stopped caring, other members of the family would follow. One of his fears as a child was not having his father around him, and now it had come true. The thought welled up inside him and burst forth as he let out a sob which converted into crying. A woman on the promenade saw him and when she realized he was crying walked swiftly away. Not even a good Samaritan wanted to come to his help. He was now alone with someone wanting to kill him for something he didn't know.

He couldn't do anything about his family. Time might heal the rift. However, he could find out who is trying to kill him. Julia had given him a clue if he knew what it meant. He sobbed and pulled a handkerchief out of his pocket. He wiped his eyes and blew his nose. At seven years old, when his older brothers had taunted him to a point. He screamed at them, wishing he were an orphan. Now he felt he was, so what he needed to do was get his act together and start afresh.

Julia had said before the beach, he was on the beach. He looked around and saw he was in the place they had placed him naked. His sob became a laugh at how ironic that he would end up here of all places. So where was he before he ended up on the beach, at the party in that house in Hove. That was it, that's where his nightmare began. She had said remember the floor he wasn't sure what that referred to. It was Peterson-Jones who gave the party for his son according to the estate agent Mike Gammon. Lying back on the beach, he looked up at the sky, a cold grey texture. Mike had said they had given him money to rent the place. No, that's not what he said they had given him money to keep his mouth shut. If Peterson- Jones were so indifferent to his son, as Brad had said. Then why did he give the boy a party to cover up the actual reason for the gathering of so many people? It was to hide the truth behind something else. There was a meeting at the house, so they put on a party. The special guests could come as though they were attending the party. Julia had said he had heard something, but she thought he was unconscious. So, he was in a room on the floor, the floor now he could see what she meant. He was maybe behind a piece of furniture or something, so those attending the meeting didn't see him. That wasn't it someone, possibly Romeo, had said they opened the door. The light was off, and two men were talking. The men then could see James lying on the floor, they didn't know he was unconscious.

"Okay," he said to himself. Why that house? Who owned it? Mike Gammon would know, and maybe that is what they wanted him to keep quiet about.

CHAPTER NINETEEN

Miss Heard Words

Matthew and Donald looked up when they heard Brian's voice. They didn't see James but heard him run from the landing. Brian ambled and defiantly down the staircase, a grin on his face.

"Who was that?"

"Your beloved other son the little Lord Fauntleroy."

"James, where did he go?"

"He ran off after he heard you say, 'He is no son of mine.' I think he may have been crying."

"Donald, we've got to find him. Brian, I don't know what your problem is, and I don't have the time to find out just at the moment."

"I'm not the one they found naked on the beach."

"Maybe not, but you have caused all the problems since. I've talked it over with the lawyer he has been told by the police you can return to Birmingham. They will call you when you need to appear in court."

"Birmingham why would I need to go there I have my hotel to convert."

"Not any more Donald will take charge until we

can find James. I should never have allowed myself to listen to you. I thought your sister Anne was
the bad egg. How wrong could I be?"

"Donny, you will not let him do this?"

"Sorry, Brian, you have only yourself to blame,"
said Donald.

"Pack your clothing and you can drive me back to
Birmingham once we have found James."

"Try some sex club, I'm sure you will find him hiding in one of them."

"Brian shut your mouth now or it will force me to
do something I vowed I would never do. Hit one of
my children."

Brian stepped back, away from his father. He knew he
had gone too far and would need to be quiet until he
reached home, and he could talk to his mother. She
would be on his side.

"And don't think you can talk your mother to your
side of things. I have already put her in the picture
to what you have done and the lies you have told.
If it hadn't been for the MI-5 guy Bradley, we may
never have known the truth."

"Dad, tell Brian mother's comment, it's very apt
just at the moment," said Donald

"I'm not sure."

"Well, I am down on the floor right now so you
might as well kick me further."

"You only have yourself to blame. Your mother
said you remind her of your Uncle Robert."

"Uncle Robert, the one who went to Zambia when
it was Rhodesia."

"The same."

"He ended up going to prison, almost beheaded."

"Ha, I can see the comparison and why Mom
would think that. Brian, you are such a fool."
Brian looked at his father and brother before leaving.
"So where do you think James will go?"
"I'm not sure, but let's leave a note for him at his
apartment.

CHAPTER TWENTY

Gardener's Tale

The estate agent's office was empty except for Mike Gammon. James peered in the window before entering the shop. He walked up to Mike, who gave the usual slimy estate agent's smile.

"Good afternoon, sir," he suddenly realized who James was and changed his expression.

"Mr. Gammon, I need some information."

"You want to buy a property, then you have come to the right place."

"No, I don't want to buy a place, I want to know who owns one."

"I'm sorry we can't give that information out to the public."

James had stepped closer to Mike and grabbed him by the throat before he could move.

"Don't mess with me, just tell me who owns the house the party was in."

"I don't know?"

James tightened the grip and panic washed over Mike's entire body.

"Look I don't know." The grip got tighter.

"Don't make me hurt you because just at this moment I have so much anger I could lose control."

"Shit, I can't tell you, if I did, they would kill me and you."

"They already want to kill me, so I have nothing to worry about do I."

Mike's body shook, and he urinated in his trousers. James released the grip and held Mike by the arm.

"Now let's you and me get the file."

He pushed Mike towards the bank of filing cabinets at the back of the shop. Opening the drawers, Mike searched for the file, the sweat rising on his forehead.

"I can't find it. Oh, God."

"Calm down."

"But it's not here." Mike sobbed someone about to cry from fear.

"When did you last see it?"

"Mr. Haberman, he had it on his desk, but he gave it to Miss Bunnell the secretary."

"So, where does she sit?"

He points at a desk next to the filing cabinets. Each desk had a brass plate on a wooden block with the name of the person sitting at the desk. Rifling through the folders on the desk of Miss Bunnell. James unconcerned what order he left them or whether they ended up on the floor. Looking at the picture and the address, he found the folder he believed to be the house.

"Is this the place and don't lie or you're dead?"

"Yes."

James opened and read the file one page contained all the details relating to who owned the property. James took the paper and threw the folder on the desk.

"Thanks for your help."

"Please don't take it, let me make a copy."

James watched Mike copied the double-side sheet.

"If I find you have told anyone I came here, I will be back and it will be the last time you see me or anyone. Understand?"

"Yes, please don't tell them it was me who gave you the information."

As he left the shop, he saw Mike hurriedly picking up the folders from Miss Bunnell's desk and replacing them neatly. The man was terrified, and it wasn't just James.

Klauss Oberlin, the owner of the party house, lived in Hove in a large property with extensive grounds. The security system around the place was state-of-art. Two enormous dogs patrol in front of the wrought-iron gates. This place was a fortress, and no stranger could get access. James walked past the entrance, aware the security camera was following him as he proceeded past the house. They had seen him and maybe they would make a move on him. At least it was a way out of his problems. The dogs barked at him, so he crossed the road. The gate swung open. He stopped and watched as a car with black-tinted window drove out. The dogs, he realized, were on chains so they couldn't rush out into the street. They were for show and an early warning system.

Looking around, he couldn't find anywhere to hide. The design of the street made it impossible to watch any of the houses without being noticed. It must screw up police surveillance.

Continuing to walk away from the house, he turned into another street with the same impressive houses.

He would need to work out a strategy and look at all the possibilities that could go wrong.

Turning into another street, he found himself on the street where the party house was. Clever the house was so close to the owner's house but far enough apart. The party house looked deserted, so he approached. He wonders if the cleaning lady was in. He would use the same excuse he and his father had used about buying the place. He pushed the doorbell and as expected, no one answered. Walking around the back he found some white painted wooden garden chairs neatly arranged around a square white painted wooden table. He pulled one chair out and sat down. The garden had been kept immaculately. The lawn, cleverly mowed, so a pattern appeared.

He took the middle piece of the jigsaw puzzle out of his pocket. This was a missing link to the complete picture and why he was in danger. He wrote Klauss Oberlin on the piece and twisting it in his fingers looked at it.

The voice from behind made him spin round and stand up.

"You come to look the place over. The estate agents have been and gone and he said he wouldn't be back today. I don't have a key to the place so I can't show you I only do the gardening."

Composing himself, James said, "It is a beautiful garden and must be one of the house's selling points."

"That's what the owner says."

"Mr. Oberlin?"

"You know him?"

"I meet him for the first time the other day and he

told me about the place." James sat down again.
"He wants to sell it, not sure why, he doesn't need
the money."
"I know little about him?"
"Not much to tell, a very wealthy German, came
here after the War. That's World War Two, before
your time. Funny we were fighting his kind and
now they seem to own so much."
"That is what my grandfather tells me."
"Well, your grandfather ain't wrong. Anyway, Mr.
Oberlin is very secretive about what he does. He
lives around the corner you know."
"Yes, I know I have just come from there but he
had gone out."
"I used to do his garden now he has someone who
lives on the premises to do it. Another German
who looks like a real Nazi in his brown gardeners'
uniform."
"My name is James."
The gardener pulled one chair away from the table and
sat on the edge of the seat.
"Bernard me name, been a gardener all my life since I
was a lad and left school."
Taking out a self-rolled cigarette from a tobacco tin
and lit it using a cheap plastic lighter.
"You should be proud of yourself, this is a magnificent garden. When my father and I first came to
look at the house. We both said it was the best
thing about the house. It is the reason I came
back."
"So you're thinking of buying it?"
"Thinking is the word. If we can get Klauss to
lower the price."
"Good luck that's the one thing I don't like about

him, he is such a scrooge. Oh, he pays me the going rate, but my other customers at Christmas give a great bonus. He gives me twenty pounds and expects me to be grateful. Mean I call it."

"Maybe his show of opulence is just a fake. He is, as my grandmother would have said, all fur and no knickers."

"No, he has the money, he has a bloody big safe at the house. One day when I was trimming a bush by the window it could see inside it. There must have been thousands of pounds stacked inside."

"Hence the tight security."

"That's because his painting is worth millions." Bernard looked at James as an expression of suspicion came over his face. "How do you know Mr. Oberlin?"

"Hector Peterson-Jones introduced me." It was a gamble because he wasn't sure if Peterson-Jones and Oberlin knew each other.

"I do his garden too, sad about his lad. Julian was a bright kid when he was growing up. My misses said he was a little queer, you know effeminate, but he was always laughing."

James takes a big gamble, "I found him and Taylor Seidler."

"You mean dead?"

"Yes, my family is the owner of the hotel we found them in."

"That must have been horrible."

"It was, I don't think I shall ever forget it."

"No, you wouldn't, and is that how you met Mr. Peterson-Jones?"

"Yes, and he introduced me to Klauss."

Bernard sat back in the chair and relaxed. James had passed the test he now hoped he could gain some information on how to get access to Oberlin house.

"You married James?"

"No, my girlfriend is thinking about it, I asked two days ago and she asked me to give two days."

"Pleasant girl, is she?"

"Lord Cobham's granddaughter Julia Brooke."

"Miss Julia, she's a real cracker, she would come over to and play with Julian in the summer when they were tiny kids."

"Why does Klauss have two houses?"

"Now that's funny you should ask that because I was wondering myself the other day. Then I remembered this was his mother's house when she came over from Germany after the war."

"I see nothing to do with this place being difficult to have such tight security around it?"

"Tight security my ass. If a burglar wanted to get into Mr. Oberlin's place, all he would have to do was go around the back of the next-door neighbor's house. Climb the big oak and over the wall, you go. I kept telling Mr. Oberlin that they should cut the branch. He said no one would break in that way as they didn't know about the tree."

"Well, if he got any sense, he would have cut it now."

"Not him, stubborn as a mule. Look, it's been nice talking to you, but I've got to get back to work. If you buy the place, think of me when you pick a gardener."

"Bernard, when we buy the place you will be the gardener."

"Thank you, sir, that is most kind of you."

James watched as the old man walked to a small shed and went inside. There were no windows in the shed, so James raced across the lawn and stood at the side of the shed. He listened and heard Bernard on a mobile phone.

"Hello, its Bernard had a youngster over here asking questions. Said his name was James." There was a pause then he continued, "Yes that sounds like the man."

James pulled the door open and grab the phone out of Bernard's hand before the old man could react. He listened to the voice at the other end and smiled.

"Thanks, Brad, for the glowing testament."

"James, what the hell are you doing?"

"Trying to find out who wants me killed and why. Although the why is not important."

"I've told you no one wants you anymore."

"Not true and I intend to live a long life, so I need to find out."

"You'll get yourself killed."

"Not me, I have nine lives and I've only used two of them. Bye Brad."

James closed the mobile and handed it back to Bernard.

"I'm sorry sir, I was only following what they told me to do if anyone came around asking questions."

"At least Bernard, you were on the right side."

"I would never tell that Nazi bastard anything. You have no worries there. If you are planning to break into his house, watch out for the dogs, they run wild at night. Give them a bone or something."

"If I am, I will."

James left the house and strolled back towards the Bright town center. Julia had mentioned about an oak tree when she left the note, was this the tree she was talking about. Possibly wasn't the big tree in Poet's Dell, an oak tree.

If only he could remember what he might have heard, it would make sense of this mess. Too many people telling too many lies, that was what the problem was, and it sounded like a government plot. Whatever he overheard must be something so dangerous to the people concerned they wanted to kill him.

He felt exposed out on the streets anyone could take a pot shot at him. He needs to change his look again. The starving student was his best so far, and he had left other clothing at Romeo's place.

He still had the key and let himself into the flat. The place was empty although from the warmth of a coffee cup on the table. Whoever had been there has just left. He found the clothes where he had left them and after taking a bath, he changed into them. He placed his other clothing into a plastic bag. Wrote a note on it saying the property of James Pidgley do not throw away. It surprised him at how much a baseball cap changed the way a person looked. If pulled it down to cover the eyes, it was almost impossible to recognize the person.

He made himself a cup of coffee and relaxed. Here at least he felt safe and could think without interruptions.

"So, what's my next plan?" He said out loud, expecting an answer to materialize out of thin air. Standing up, he searched his pockets. He had left his credit cards at his flat and he only had an insignificant amount of cash left on him. Although he didn't want to return to the flat just in case, he saw his father he needed to get his other wallet and some more cash. The man leaning against the wall of his flat complex seemed familiar, but he didn't recognize him. As he came closer, he could see it was Dave Beck. The man looked very anxious and something troubled him. He looked at James but didn't recognize him immediately.

"James is that you?"

"Yes, Dave, what's the problem. Fenton, okay, I hope."

"The boy is doing well, and he told me about what happened. I need to talk to you, but my train leaves soon so could we talk on the way to the station."

"I need to the run-up to the flat and then we can go."

James ran up the stairs and opened the flat door expecting to see his father or at least his brother. Neither was there. He quickly grabbed the wallet and some money, then left the flat. The note his father had left still lay on the table, unread. As he closed the door, a draft caused it to float from the table and under the sofa.

Dave was standing waiting for him, James wondered if this was a trap. Last time he had seen this man in this state it was when he was waiting for a car in the alleyway.

"Dave what's the problem."

"You were so good to Fenton, my wife said you were salt of the earth. Coming from her that meant a lot. I almost sold you down the river."

"I don't understand."

A police car drove down the road, both James and Dave felt uncomfortable and walked towards the station.

"I had not told you the entire truth, and it's been playing on my mind. I couldn't sleep, shouted at the kids and even raised my hand to Sharon. Now that's something I have never done in my life, hit a woman. I talked it over with her. She said there was only one thing I could do and that was come and confess to you."

"Interesting, I suddenly have become a priest to so many."

"Sorry I…"

"You the second person who wanted to confess to me in the last twenty-four hours."

"Really it must be something about you that makes people think you are holy," said Dave, giving a nervous laugh. "Any way to get back to what I did wrong by you. A long time ago I did something not important for what it was. Only this man, a policeman called Michael Hampshire helped me out of the problem. He came to me just after we had met you and told me I was to hand you over to some men. I was to trap you and they would do the rest."

"So, what happened?"

"It went wrong they came and took me then beat me up. Fenton came along and…"

"And what?"

"James swear you will tell no one. Fenton didn't mean to do and still thinks he didn't."

"Didn't what?"

"Okay, Fenton found me in a warehouse and hit the man who was beating me up. Fenton killed him. He didn't mean to, but it just happened. I told him he hadn't kill the man."

"I won't say anything and as for what you did, you

were protecting your family and I would have done the same. So, who were you supposed to hand me over to?"

"Some guy names Seidler and another Oberlin. I've heard of him supposed to be a big shot in financing stuff."

"So has your debt to Hampshire been paid in full."

"Yes, thank God. He was angry when he found out they had tried to beat me up. I didn't tell him about the other."

"Wise not to once a copper, always a copper bent or not."

"What about you now?"

"Dave someone still wants to kill me. I said someone but I now know its Klauss Oberlin."

"Shit, that heavy you need to get that sorted out he's not a man to play with."

"That is precisely what I am trying to do."

They arrived at the station and stood looking at each other. Words had to stop, and neither knew how to finish this brief meeting. Dave looked at the platforms to see if his train had arrived. The train had arrived, and passengers were boarding it.

"Dave go carefully and give my best to your family. Be proud of Fenton, he is a chip off the old block."

"If you ever get to London look us up, there will always be a welcome at the Beck house for you."

"I will, now go get your train before you miss it."

Dave ran towards the platform, not seeing a man who had been pursuing them towards the platform. James ran toward the first railway employee. Pointing to the man said he had just seen the man trying to molest boy in the toilet. The railway employee ran after the man, grabbing several employees and apprehended the man. The train pulled out of the station, the man still trying to explain to the employees. The police arrived and James smiling left the station.

Simon leaning against one of the cast-iron columns. He nodded to James and smiled.

CHAPTER TWENTY ONE

Safe Breaking

James sat covered by a bush in the garden next door to Klauss Oberlin's mansion. He was no stranger to sitting in a bush watching others. It wasn't long ago he had learned that as a boy his father had done the same thing. He felt safe not because he hid in the bush, but the night was very dark. The moon hadn't appeared and a coastal mist was creeping over the town. The only setback was with this mist came cold dampness penetrating any thickness of clothing. The house whose garden he was hiding in wasn't as big as Oberlin's. The family who lived in the house wasted money. Every light in the house seemed to be on when he arrived. He had taken extra care to ensconce himself in the bush without being seen.

He watched as the night unfolded and the house light distinguished one by one. The family was going to bed the children first. From what he could see inside the house, they were not so many children as teenagers. The boy was slow and seemed on drugs, although without being up close James couldn't confirm it. The daughter who was younger than her brother was loud. She banged doors before settling in her room at the front of the house and played heavy rock music. She appeared at the window and stared at the spot James was hiding. He froze and knew he must not move a muscle to remain unseen. She was arguing with someone in the room. After a few minutes, she turned down the music. He wondered if he or his siblings had ever behaved like that as teenagers. As he couldn't remember he assumed they had not, or his mother would have reminded them as they got older.

Two squirrels ran across the lawn from behind him. Maybe this was what the girl had been looking at. A very large tomcat ran from the front porch of the house and hissed at the squirrels. A sensor light above the main door switched on and illuminated the front garden. Relieved he had dressed in black, James hoped he blended into the bush.

No one came to the window so obviously this was a usual event and after seeing it a few hundred times even the children would get bored by it.

The last light to go out was the bow window to the right of the main door on the first floor. The parent's bedroom with its en-suite bathroom with his and hers dressing rooms.

He waited for at least an hour before making his move towards the oak tree. Therefore, found himself surprised when an ominous figure ran across the driveway to the side of the house, then up to the tree. As the figure ran across in front of the house, it surprised him the light sensor didn't switch on the lights. He watched as the figure climbed with easy and rested on one branch. Taking his small night sight binoculars from his pocket, he looked at the man in the tree. At first, it was hard to distinguish who the figure was. Then the person turned to face the street, and he glimpsed a full face. The night for him was he thought would be scary and difficult. Seeing who the person was up the tree, he smiled and left his hiding place to join the person sitting astride the branch.

He reached the oak tree and found that someone had placed heavy nails into the tree so it was easier to climb. It reminded him of the time he had climbed a tree to rescue his sister Anne. He reached the branch before the other person realized he was climbing.

"Benjie nice to see you again."

"Does my sister know her beloved climbs trees in the middle of the night?"

"I doubt it as we have never discussed it. So, what's your plan for the night."

"I think the same as yours only for different reasons."

"Well, I am sure you know mine so what are your reasons for being up a tree on a cold damp night?"

"As you know most of what's going on according to sister dear, I might as well tell you the rest. My God Father Klauss Gottfried Oberlin has something of mine, and I need to get it back."

"Gottfried!"

"Yes, that is his full name, a true German with very Germanic ideas. Anyway, he has something which could get me into a lot of trouble. So, I want to get it back so he can't blackmail me anymore."

"What has he got you so desperately want you will break into his house in the middle of the night to get it?"

"Ah that's something I can't tell then you'll know everything. I think I should leave some things unsaid."

"Is that why you wanted a Priest?"

"No, that was just to get out of the house did you
think I was confessing to you."

The emphasis on you made James think before he answered. Benjie was acting the whole time. Maybe
from the time they met in the café until he ran out of
the flat.

"You saw me enter the cafe and pretended to be
druggy because you couldn't slip out without me
seeing you."

"Very good my dear Watson. It was hard because
the sweet innocent waitress had just agreed to sleep
with me if I left. Hence why she kept kicking me."

"She wanted to sleep with you?"

"Oh yes, I am very desirable, it's the title. The
lower class thinks sleeping with a titled person the
fuck will be better."

"I hope you don't disappoint, we can't have the
lower class upset."

"Don't care just another one-night stand for me."

"What about them?"

"I like to think it was the best night of their pathetic
insignificant lives. They will want me again, only I
never repeat performances."

It was this attitude that James found so obnoxious and
could see his brother Brian being like this. The dogs
in Oberlin's garden were barking at something near the
gate. James looked through his night sight binoculars
and saw Brad peering into the garden. Disappearing
into the darkness and mist.

"Why were the dogs barking?"

"Some old tramp just walked past the gate."

"Smelt the bugger did they."

"What happens now?"

"We crawl along with this branch, drop into the garden and get into the house."

"That simple?"

"Not quite there are the dogs and the alarm system but as I know a way around both it should be a doddle."

Without waiting for a reply, Benjie crawled along the branch and dropped into the garden of the Oberlin mansion. James followed, but instead of dropping into the garden, he hung from the tree before dropping. The dogs sensed the intruders and raced around the corner of the house towards them. The chain restraints were only for the daytime at night the dogs had the run of the garden. Seeing and smelling Benjie, they immediately made a fuss of him. One dog broke away and approached James, he sniffed then suddenly bit into James' leg. James cried out, pushing his hand into his mouth to stop his voice from being heard. The dog tossed its head from side to side, James' leg still in its mouth. Fumbling through his pockets, he quickly found the raw meat he had brought with him and threw it at the dog. The animal let go of his leg and ate the meat.

The other dog left Benjie's side and attacked the meat on the ground. Benjie took some bones out of a plastic bag he had hidden inside his black hooded top.

James limped away from the dogs, hoping they wouldn't attack again. The meat disappeared quickly and searching for some more raw meat both dogs move towards James.

Benjie waved the bones, and the dogs looked at him and then back at James. One dog trotted over to Benjie and sniffed the bones. Benjie threw the first bone across the garden. The dog that had sniffed the bones chased after it. The second dog in an attack crawl approached James. Benjie quickly stepped in between James and the dog. Allowing the dog to sniff the bone. Once the dog seemed interested Benjie threw the bone. The dog chased after it, then stopped, looked back at Benjie and James before continuing the chase.

Benjie hurried towards the back of the house. James limped as quickly as he could, the pain in his leg beginning to increase. They reached a small, low building with a ladder onto the flat roof. James monitored the dogs, hoping they wouldn't get bored with the bones and come after him. Benjie climbed the ladder and helped James when he reached the top. At least up there, the dogs couldn't get him. He could feel blood running down his leg and into his black trainers.

Whispering Benjie said, "We have to climb this drainpipe." Pointing to a black metal drainpipe. James watched as his partner in crime climbed the pipe with ease and then disappeared at the top. With an effort, James followed, each movement of his left bitten leg hurting more as he climbed. He reached the top and saw a window open Benjie was leaning out and helped him inside.

The attic room was very warm. The smell of wood permeates the air because of the heat-generating up from the house below. Once inside Benjie sat James down by the window. Putting his index finger to his lips, signaling James not to make any noise. Then he pointed across the room and the darkness to a little red flashing light. James was looking up at the light as Benjie tapped his arm and pointed to the wooden floor. Someone had placed a piece of glow in the dark

material on the floor. Using mime, Benjie told James
he couldn't go beyond that line. Whatever Benjie
thought the last thing on James' mind was to move
about. His leg was hurting, and he needed to look at it.

Benjie leaned over almost as if he would kiss James on
the ear, whispered.
"We have to stay here until morning. Once the
family is up and out of the house, we can move."
"If they leave, won't the alarm system be on?"
"Too loud lower your voice. No, the cleaning lady
will be in and she knows me, so we won't have a
problem. Now try to get some rest we are going to
need our strength to get through tomorrow."
Benjie turned away and curled up just like a
baby. Slowly James lifted the leg of his jeans and tried
to look at the dog bite. There was not enough light.
He would have to wait until morning to see the damage. He tried to relax and sleep, the pain in his leg
kept waking him just as he was dozing off.

Benjie was quickly asleep and snored light almost like
a cat purring. He could hear strange sounds in the attic. The first was a scurrying sound as though some
tiny creature was running around the room. A clatter
of claws followed this on the wooden floorboards. James imaged giant rats running around who
would sense his bitten leg and want a piece. In the
darkness, he saw something, a very faint shape creep
towards him. He lifted his right leg in preparation to
kick whatever it was away. Wondering if he should
wake Benjie but decided not to as whatever it just vanished. His imagination was creating monsters. Being
tired, he dozed off, the heat of the room covering him
like a blanket.

Waking with a start, something soft and furry was sitting on his lap. He placed a hand on it and felt a very furry cat asleep on him. Obviously, this was the creature who had crept across the room he felt like laughing out loud at his stupidity.

He looked out of the window. The dawn was breaking, and he could now see the attic room. Benjie was still asleep. The cat had changed positions but was very content to sit on him and let him stroke its fur.

Careful so as not to disturb the cat, he dragged his left jean leg up and looked at the bite mark. Blood had congealed, but the teeth marks were deep and would need some medical attention. The cat woke up and cleaned itself. This feat had always amazed James, and he wished humans could do the same. He supposed they could only not as efficiently as a cat or dog.

Benjie woke not long after he seemed refreshed and smiled at James, who was still cradling the cat. Sitting up next to James, Benjie once again whispered into James's ear.

"We have to wait for the little light to go green before we move."

To watch a tiny light turn green was all James needed to complete this madness. The cat bored with just sitting there or maybe sensed there was food down below for it. It stretched and walked away and out of sight on the other side of the attic.

Both Benjie and James became focused on the little light. It was like watching the turning on of the Christmas lights in Oxford Street. The anticipation was becoming too much. If James didn't move soon, his legs would never move again.

Benjie was fussing with a newspaper and didn't see
the red turn to green. James tapped him on the leg and
pointed to the little light. Benjie gave the thumbs-up
sign and stood up. James using the wall slowly stood,
the pain in his leg intensifying.

Any breaking and entering will increase the blood
pressure and tension with his bitten leg, James felt like
running away. He had not slept and now the morning
had arrived, and he was feeling nauseous and
pained. Dawn had broken and the morning sun was
trying to break through rain clouds. He lifted the jean
material and looked at his leg for the first time in the
proper light. It horrified him at what he saw, the deep
bite marks and congealed blood. Bruising around the
bites had deepened to an angry purple and the entire
leg throbbed with pain. The bleeding had stopped, but
only thin scabs covered the teeth holes. If he hit or
moved the leg wrong, the bleeding would start
again. He needed a bandage of some sort to cover the
wound. Searching his pockets he only found tissue paper handkerchiefs.

Benjie was on the other side of the room, looking out
of a window. He was on his tiptoes and peering
down. Without straightening up, he motioned James
to join him at the window.

Limping slowly, James crossed the attic floor holding
on to the low beams of the roof. Benjie pointed down
toward the driveway of the house. A large black
chauffeur-driven car parked by the main door. The
back door was open, waiting for its passenger to arrive
and get in. Unable to put any weight on his left leg,
James tried to steady himself as he looked out of the
window. He fell against Benjie, who didn't seem to

object. The chauffeur climbed out of the driving seat and ran around to the open door. Ready to close once the passenger and been seated inside. A tall thin man with balding grey hair came into view. He was wearing an expensive Crombie style coat and black leather gloves. Before getting into the car, the man turned and looked up at the house. James and Benjie pulled back, unseen.

"That's Klauss."

Feeling uneasy about the look at the house, James suddenly had doubts about his companion. Why would the man look up at his house unless he thought there was someone up here looking down?

> Benjie sensing the mood change in James said, "It's okay he does that every morning as if he is saying goodbye to his property."

Nodding James became cautious. That was just too rehearsed to be true. Leaning against the wall for support, he looked around the attic. There must be a piece of cloth he could use to bandage his leg with.

> "What are you looking for?"
> "A piece of clean cloth to bandage my leg."
> "Is it that bad?"

James showed his leg to Benjie, his expression told James it was bad. He had diagnosed it correctly.

> "Shit, that's bad we need to cover that before you get infected."

Benjie searched the boxes and suitcases in the attic. Finally, he stood to uphold a white cotton shirt. He ripped the shirt into long thin bandages and handed them to James to apply them to his leg.

> "Where did you get the shirt from?"
> "When we were kids, we played dress-up with the Klauss children, Julian and Taylor sometimes came

too. We had this old suitcase full of clothing, I just found it and saw the shirt. Julia always called it the Romeo shirt from Romeo and Juliet."

"You've known them for a long time?"

"Most of my life."

Carefully wrapping the torn material around his leg, he hoped this would support it and stop any immediate problems. The cotton fabric pressed against his leg, increasing the pain. Slowly the pain faded away, and he felt the strength returning to the weakened limb. Benjie had returned to looking out of the window. James hoped his sidekick would understand and not take an attitude with him when he was slow in moving.

"His wife leaving. First, she'll go to the spa and have a massage, she will follow this by getting her hair washed and set. Next, she goes to get her nails cut and polished, including her small piggy like toes. Finally, lunch with one of her nouveau riche society girlfriends. Then into the car and some secluded lane for a quickie in the back with the chauffeur."

"You're kidding right?"

"Not at all and to look at her you wouldn't think she came from a Basildon council estate."

James looked out of the window and saw a beautiful woman. She would not have been out of place on a Paris fashion runway. Her hair was blowing gently in the breeze, cascading down over a beige camel-hair coat. She was stunningly beautiful, even at this distance. The chauffeur helped her into the car, holding her hand just a little too long. So, part of what Benjie had said was true. The car drove out of the driveway and the big wrought-iron gates closed.

"We can go now, the kids are at boarding school or finishing school in Germany, poor sods. That just leaves the cleaner and she should be in the kitchen. Stay here and I'll check it out."
He went down the small staircase and onto the landing below, disappearing out of sight. James sat down on the top step of the stairs. He had always hated being made to wait, scared he would miss out on something. He hoped this would not be a trap and Benjie had set him up with Klauss. He didn't have his watch, so he did not know how long Benjie had been gone. When you're waiting for someone like the doctor or dentist, a few seconds can seem like hours. Becoming impatient, he slipped on his backside down a step. He still couldn't see anything on the landing, so he took another step down. More of the landing below was visible, but there was no sign of Benjie.

This time he took two steps down and could see the entire floor below. The image of being six years old and sitting on the stairs at home waiting for his father flooded his mind. It was always because he had done something wrong according to his brothers. He bumped down some more steps until he was on the last step. Standing, he found the bandage helped and he could put weight on the leg.

There were several doors on the landing, and he assumed they led to bedrooms. He tried the first door next to the attic stairs. It was locked after trying several others he gave up and went to the main staircase. They hung on the walls, oil paintings of military men, mostly on horseback. They looked German, but he was no expert and therefore only assumed they were. Descending to the floor below, he stopped and listened. Hearing nothing, he continued down. Whereas they had carpeted the floor above, this landing's floor was highly polished old wood. His sneakers squeaked as he walked to the first door. It was, as he expected, a family member's bedroom with an en-suite bathroom. It was more like a hotel room than a family house. He closed the door and heard other squeaking sounds coming towards him.

Opening the first door near to him, he stepped inside. The walk-in linen closet was full of sheets, pillowcases, towels, and tablecloths. Several towels fell on top of him, so when the door swung open towels covered him. Expecting to see the cleaner looking at him, it surprised him to see Benjie's smiling face greet him. Relaxing, he removed the towels off his head before he left the closet. Benjie put his index finger to his lips to stop James from speaking.

Benjie then signals to James by pointing down to the floor below. Using his first and second finger in a walking motion to go downstairs. James turned and headed for the main staircase. Benjie grabbed his arm and stopped him. Again he pointed to the other end of the corridor. Treading carefully to eliminate as much noise as possible from their trainers. They built the house in the nineteenth century and had a servant staircase. This ran down the back of the house towards the kitchen. The stair treads had no carpet, luckily the wood had no varnish, so their trainers didn't squeak.

The staircase twisted three hundred and sixty degrees so you ended up at bottom directly below where you started. Halfway down, Benjie stopped and pulled James closer to him.

"Uncle Klauss's study is the second door on the right. Opposite the stairs is the kitchen, so we have to be very careful."

James nodded he understood, and they continued down. The kitchen door was open a little and a woman's voice was singing along with the radio. James tries to work out what language the woman was singing. He couldn't as most of the time she just 'la la' to the song.

At the foot of the stairs, Benjie put his arm across James. Stopping him on the stairs, while Benjie tried the study door. James took a few steps up the staircase, still being able to see Benjie and the study door.

Benjie crept on his tiptoes so his trainers wouldn't squeak on the floor to the study door. He tried the handle. The door didn't open. He tried again and then shook his head. The door was locked.

The kitchen door swung open and a small rotund lady with her head looking at the floor entered the corridor. Mrs. Gladison had worked for the Oberlins for twenty years and noticed nothing. She lived in her own world. James pressed himself against the side of the staircase. Benjie crouched down beside a table next to the study door. The woman turned left and opened a cupboard. She mumbled to herself and took something out before returning to the kitchen. She closed the kitchen door behind her.

Benjie rushed to the staircase and pushing James upwards and stopped halfway. He was breathing heavily and sweat had formed on his forehead.

"Shit, that was close, I was sure she had seen me."
"She is one of the old domestics, see nothing, hear nothing, say nothing."

"Just like grandfather's butler. He must know a lot
of family secrets."

"And they pay him to keep it to himself."

"I don't understand Uncle Klaus never locks his
study door."

"Well, Benjie he did this time."

"So how do we get in, he must have the key with
him."

"No, the cleaner may need to get in or his wife so
he would hide the key where they knew to look."

"Okay, Sherlock, but where?"

"Try the drawer in the table and if it's not there,
then it will be under that clock on the table."

"I hope your right."

They crept down the staircase and James watched as
Benjie checked the drawer. He shook his head and
closed the drawer. Picking up the French ormolu
clock, he smiled back at James and picked up a
key. The clock slipped in his hand and chimed. He
caught it before it hit the table and replaced it carefully. They both froze just in case the cleaner had
heard the clock chime and came to investigate. She
didn't, so Benjie put the key in the lock and opened the
study door. James rushed in behind Benjie and closed
the door as quickly as he could. Taking the key from
Benjie, he locked the door.

It was a private library lined with books except over
the fireplace. Where a picture of a man in what could
only be a Nazi uniform without the swastikas was
hanging.

"Uncle Klauss."

Several brown leather chairs with small tables next to
them scattered around the room. Over by one window
a solid oak desk and a large high back brown leather

chair behind it. In front of the other window was a glass cabinet containing German souvenirs from the first and second world wars.

"Where is the safe?"

"I don't know."

"What do you mean you don't know? You said last time you saw the safe it was full of money." Then James remembered it hadn't been Benjie who had said that.

"Did I say that I don't remember I was seven years old when I last saw the safe."

"What! I don't believe it, you got us to break in and you didn't know where the safe was."

"It's in this room somewhere."

"He might have changed the bloody safe by now."

"I doubt it, he is a mean old bastard."

"So where was the safe when you were seven years old?"

Benjie pointed to the wall where most of the books were on very solid looking bookcases. Sitting opposite, they both studied the bookcases.

"Oh, it had a wooden door."

"It's not a metal safe?"

"The safe's metal only it was behind a wooden door. I remember because Uncle Klauss opened this door and said abracadabra or something like that."

"A hidden safe behind a bookcase. Clever, but not a genius. We need to look for a secret door in the bookcase."

They started at opposite ends, carefully checking to see if the books were real or fake. Benjie gave up after a few minutes, his attention span being very low. James painstakingly checked each shelf on each bookcase. If these are actual books, they must have made the door with shelves in it. He moved away from the bookcase and sat on the arm of one of the brown leather chairs. He was looking for any imperfection, which might have occurred because there was a door. Doors sometimes sag, especially under the weight of books. After a few minutes, he rose and checked out one set of shelves that seemed to be out of line with its neighbor. He pulled the shelves, and they swung towards him. Behind the door stood a black metal safe five feet high by four feet wide. He couldn't see how deep it was. In the center of the safe door was a silver dial.

"I told you I would find the safe."

"Do you know the combination?"

"Of course, and you won't believe how I know."

"So, tell me."

"Uncle Klauss got the safe the day I was born, so he used my birth date as the combination. He told me once when I was about seven or eight, I assumed he thought I wouldn't remember."

"I hope he hasn't changed it."

"So, let's open it and find out what's inside."

James sat in one of the leather chairs. He had never really been a fan of leather chairs. They always seem cold to him. This chair felt strangely warm and comfortable. Benjie knelt before the safe, twisted the silver knob one-way then other. He tries to open the safe. Only the door stayed closed. He tried again, with the same results.

"Okay, this time it will work." He tried for a third time and after it failed, he hit the metal safe.

"I can't understand it, I know I have the right number so why didn't it open up."

"Let me try, I'm a little more patient than you are. What is the combination?"

"My birth date five three eight seven."

James mentally worked out he was twenty-two, therefore younger than Julia. He had assumed she was the younger one. Stooping next to the safe, his bitten leg hurt. It took him a few minutes to get comfortable. He knew if these were the numbers, he would have to move the dial carefully. He turned the dial, so the zero was at the top. Then he turned it to five to the left, three to the right, eight to the left and seven to the right. He pulled on the door handle, it stays shut. He reversed the process, starting with turning it to the right. Again, the door remains shut.

There was some writing on the center of the silver dial, although it was almost polished away. 'Six digits required.' He immediately tried again, adding one and nine before the eight. He pushed down on the handle and pulled. The safe door opened.

Benjie joined him and they both looked inside.

The center shelves were stacked with money. The top shelf had items wrapped in bubble wrap and a zip-lock plastic bag. Benjie grabbed at them, hiding one, then after an inspection of the others returned them to the safe. In the safe's bottom drawer, James took out the papers held inside. He carried them limping now because of the position he had been in when on the floor.

Sitting in the leather chair, he read the papers. Benjie had removed the items from the middle shelf and was searching behind the money.

The first few papers were household contracts and invoices. The next group paper clipped together were contracts to sell guns and ammunition. Klauss Oberlin was an arms dealer and from what the papers read maybe uranium. He continued to read and realized that the deals were with countries like Iran and Cuba. One contract alone was worth twenty million pounds.

Was this what they thought he heard and why they wanted him killed? One document quoted a price for the uranium shipped from America to Iran. Someone had written on the document. 'Check with the CIA contact to see if we can use the US military to deliver the stuff.'

If this was the reason for the contract on his life, then he could understand their frustration.

Benjie was replacing the money into the safe. He was muttering to himself about not finding it.

James returned to the documents the next group was about a charity that helps childless couples adopt children from other countries. The first question into James's mind was why would Oberlin be helping a charity. Attached to the back of one document was a handwritten page. It contained babies' names and ages. The next column was the names of a couple, and the last column contained amounts of money. Some amounts were vast while others were in the thousands. Oberlin was stealing or buying babies and selling them on the black market.

The last bundle of documents was in a thick, large size envelope. James opened the package and read. It was blackmail material used against politicians, top policemen and many corporate businessmen. Each person's name contained a reason for the blackmail sometimes with evidence attached. Amount asked and if they paid it in money or favor.

This was incredible, armed with this information James could ask for protection from Oberlin. He felt ecstatic at last he was on top.

Benjie suddenly said loudly, "Don't move the security system on."

James turned his head slowly. The little light on the security sensor had turned red.

"So, what happened?"

"How should I know the cleaning lady might have gone out?"

"Well, she must have."

"She never goes out."

"I'm sorry to say she has."

"Maybe she has gone shopping and will be back."

"Then Benjie, we must sit and wait for her return."

"And be still one large movement and the alarm system will activate."

"Correct so get comfortable she may be some time."

"Shit, I wish I was sitting down."

"Well, you're not so don't move or we both could be in the shit."

"It's all right for you James, you're sitting in a nice comfortable chair. I'm stuck standing next to a metal safe with nothing to sit on."

"Can you lean against the safe?"

"Oh yes, I could do that."

"Did you find what you were looking for?"

"No, it must be somewhere in the room."

"Are you sure Klauss had it in the first place?"

"Not really, he said he had, so I believed him."

"You could call his bluff."

"What if I'm wrong and he has it?"

"Not knowing what it is, it could screw you."

"Okay, I owed some guys a lot of money and my father wouldn't help me out. Uncle Klauss said he would take care of it after I did a thing for him."

"Figures they always want something."

"I saw it as a business only then my sweet uncle Klauss kept something and hence the blackmail."

"Sorry to hear that but he is a despicable man even though he is your Godfather."

"James, did you find what you were looking for?"

"Oh yes, and it's dynamite."

Benjie's shoulder hurt where it was resting against the safe. He tried to reposition himself without moving. He had never stayed in one position for very long. This was becoming agony for him and he tried to roll over to the other shoulder.

James was glad he had been sitting when the alarm activated. He was in a comfortable chair and could rest his head against the back of it. He couldn't turn the paper over because that would be a very substantial movement.

"How long do you think before she returns?"

"Assuming she has gone shopping, I don't know."

"My legs are beginning to hurt and I'm not sure how much longer I can stand here."

"What time does Klauss usually come home?"

"I think around six, but his wife should be home before that. Oh God, where is the cleaner, why hasn't she come back yet."

"Want some cheese with that whine?"

"James I'm hurting don't make funny remarks."

"So is my leg, but you didn't give me much sympathy."

"I didn't know it was as bad as it was."
The little red light turned green. Benjie saw it first and raced for one chair. James turned around and looked up at the alarm sensor he relaxed. He took one of the large zip-lock bags out of the safe and emptied its contents back into the safe. He then placed the papers he was holding into the zip-lock bag. Placing it inside his shirt and pushing the bag around to his back. He crossed over to the safe.

"Benjie help me put these things back in the safe so we can get out of here."
They quickly returned everything to the safe and closed it, twisting the dial as they did.

Benjie was closing the bookcase when a sound made them both turn around. Klauss Oberlin and his chauffer stood just inside the study. They had entered by a hidden door disguised as a bookcase. Klauss had a gun in his hands and was pointing it at them.

"Trying to break into my safe Benjamin, what would your grandfather say to that."
"Uncle Klauss I was just trying to get back what you have of mine."
"Silly boy, you only had to ask. Well, it's not in the safe."
James realized that Klauss didn't know they had been in the safe. He thought they were just breaking in.

"Mr. Pidgley, I presume, we finally meet after you have caused me so much trouble."
"I'm sorry, Mr. Oberlin, I can't think why."
"Well, you got drunk I think and heard too much."
"That is where you are wrong. I wasn't drunk, someone drugged me, and I didn't hear a thing."
"Really so why are you at my house?"

"To meet you. To see the man who wants me dead face to face."

Both men stared at each other. Only Klauss showed surprise on his face. If James kept his head and didn't let his emotion take control, he might just get away with this.

"Okay, Uncle Klauss, if there is nothing else, I'll be on my way."

This brought Klauss back, and anger seems to develop in him.

"Not so fast you have been very disobedient for the last time. Both of you sit on the chairs."

He handed the gun to the chauffeur.

"If they move, shoot them."

James sat facing Klauss. Benjamin sat at an angle so he would have to turn to see his Godfather and the chauffeur. Klauss stood behind his desk, picked up the phone and punched in a number.

"It's Klauss be at the marina in one hour."

He didn't wait for a reply, disconnected, and dialed another number.

"This is Klauss." He paused while the other person on the other end spoke. "Could you get him for me, please?" Again, he paused then when someone spoke repeated, "Be at the marina in one hour."

He replaced the receiver and came around the desk and took the gun off the chauffeur.

"Going somewhere nice, Uncle."

"We are all going on an enjoyable trip."

"You two get up and move." Using the gun, he pointed to the hidden entrance. Nodding with his head, he told the chauffeur to go first. They left the study, Klauss closing the hidden door behind him.

CHAPTER TWENTY TWO

Justice Executed

James and Benjamin sat in the lower cabin on the boat. Although the size of the boat was very much like the one James had taken part in the smuggling of the two men. This boat's design was different. There was no upper deck, it only had the main deck with the steering and controls and a lower cabin they sat in.

They had left the house and driven across town to the marina. Oberlin, once James and Benjamin herded inside the boat, released his chauffeur for the night. James was sure the man knew what would happen. His facial expression was one of those for a perfect straight man to any comedian. Never had James seen such an expressionless face. He left quickly after they had arrived at the marina.

The only thing James found a little strange was a very large fireman's ax by the steering wheel. It seemed so out of place at the same time with what James thought was about to occur, maybe not. Klauss Oberlin had made two calls to tell two persons to meet him at the marina. If James was correct, then it would be Hector Peterson-Jones and Donald Seidler.

Klauss was on deck doing something and was just out of sight. He would pounce quickly if anyone tried to dash it. Benjamin sat lost in his world as though nothing bad could happen.

It had struck James that they had not tied them up, or at least handcuffed together. Relaxing, he would see what played out before making his move to escape. His leg was still hurting from the dog bite.

The boat swayed in the water as someone had come on board. He strains to hear who was speaking.

"Klauss, what's all this about?"

Donald Seidler peered into the lower cabin and sneered. Benjamin stood and hand-stretched out said, "Donald, how nice to see you have you come for this brief trip."

"Sit down, Benjamin, we will talk later."

Donald retreated on deck to join Klauss.

"What the hell is going on Klauss?"

The men moved to the stern of the boat so neither James nor Benjamin could hear. After Donald had left Benjamin stayed by the opening to the deck trying to listen. Once he realized he couldn't hear a thing he sat down next to James again.

"Who do you think the other member of our party will be?"

"I don't know Benjamin but if Donald is here, then it could be Hector Peterson-Jones."

"Oh gaud, that awful man I don't like him. He is so pompous and thinks he owns the world."

"So you don't like him."

"I've just told you I don't weren't you listening, I'm hungry do you think we will have some food on this trip."

"I doubt it."

Benjamin sank back into the seat, a childish, petulant sulk on his face. So, he knew what would happen. Interesting how he hadn't reacted to anything. Maybe he thinks he is safe. Exempt from anything because of his connections. What happens when he finds out, how will he react? Like a little boy and cry, then beg for mercy.

The boat swayed again someone else had joined the men on board. He didn't know who. Only they could hear raised voices. Only Klauss's raised voice seemed distinguishable, the others' voices were nothing more than mumbling.

"What's going on, why haven't we left yet?"

"I don't know, maybe now the fifth person has arrived we will set sail."

"The boat hasn't any sails, it uses a motor."

"I know it was just a metaphor."

"I want to go on deck, I don't like it down here."

He stormed towards the stairs, Donald blocked him coming slowly down them.

"Sit down Benjamin, we are setting off now and Klauss doesn't want you wandering around on deck. Who knows, you might fall overboard and we can't have that, can we."

Benjamin returned to the seat next to James, the sulky face returning. Donald sat in one of the leather round back chairs. He felt awkward and couldn't make eye contact with James. Benjamin was a stupid boy, nothing but a fool. James, he felt, was shrewd and would have something up his sleeve. He needed to have a cover story just in case something went wrong. Klauss was a clever man, but had he underestimated James. From what he had learned so far, James Pidgley had run rings around everyone. Even escape from a manhole with no injury. He had been there when they put James inside the manhole. The expert said no one could survive, then James had outwitted everyone. They all turned and looked at the stairwell as Hector Peterson-Jones descended below.

He also didn't make eye contact with James and avoided looking at Benjamin. The boy turned and faced the window. He was not pleased to see this man.

The only sound was the throb of the motor as it took them out to sea. Through the window, James had watched as the boat maneuvered out of the marina into the open sea. Slowly the shoreline became smaller and smaller until nothing was recognizable. The boat stopped and they heard the splash of the anchor dropping into the sea. Donald and Hector rushed up the stairs to the deck. Another heated discussion was taking place, this time more raised voices. The odd word distinguishable, but it was still hard to understand what the argument was actually about.

Hector and Donald seemed at odds with Klauss. Donald stood at the top of the stairs and said. "If you do that, then we are all ruined."

Benjamin crossed to the stairwell his impatience had gotten to him and he wanted out. He was just like a caged rat and couldn't take being confined. Without waiting, he ran up the stairs onto the deck.

After a few seconds, he called down to James, "Hey James come on deck it so nice up here."

James stood and walked at a funereal pace once on deck he saw Klaus sitting in the driver's seat. Benjamin sat next to him, a smug grin on his face. Hector and Donald on the stern seat, looking more like

twiddle Dee and twiddle Dumb. James took the port
bow seat so he could see land.

"We will have to wait a little while before the fes-
tivities begin, I am sorry to say. I believe they are
better conducted at night." said Klauss.

For the first time, James heard his German accent pro-
truding into his English.

It was dusk and the light onshore shined like little pin-
pricks of light. The promenade lights strung from
lamppost to lamppost looked as if they were a string of
glowing pearls around the coastline.

"Do you swim, James?" asked Donald.

"Not very well, so I hope we don't have any acci-
dents."

"I can't swim at all, I hate going into the water."

"We know Benjamin every time you came to my
house, we asked if you wanted to swim, you said
no."

"Donald that is because I couldn't swim but I didn't
want anyone to know or they would make fun of
me."

In those few minutes, the light had gone, and it was
now night. The land seemed even farther away than
before.

"Okay time to start everyone down in the cabin."

"Shall I keep watch just in case?"

"What for Hector pirates? I said everyone."

Once down in the cabin Klauss ordered everyone to sit
in a particular place. Once again Benjamin and James
sat on the two-seat couch. Donald sat on one of the
leather chairs to the right of them, and next to him was
Hector.

Klauss sat on one of the high bar stools. Placing it in front of the couch so he was facing James and Benjamin.

"Are we going to play a game like charades?"
No one answered and from Benjamin's face, James realized the boy was playing a game he wasn't stupid. Klauss disappeared up the stairs and the four looked at the stairwell, each with his own expectation of what was to come.

Klauss reappeared, dressed in a judge's gown and carrying a gavel. Benjamin opened his mouth to speak, only Donald put a finger to his lips to shut his mouth.

Klauss banged the gavel on the bar counter and
shouted, "All stand this court is now in session."
They all stood and faced him. He bowed to Donald and Hector, who bowed back. Benjamin turned and bowed to James and then took his arms as though he would waltz around the room. Klauss hit the bar again. James had this feeling he had just walked into a Marx Brothers movie. He would have a problem keeping a straight face if Benjamin continued the clowning around.

Klaus then sat on the high bar stool, having difficulty getting his balance. James had to hide a laugh, as it was very comical.

"You may sit."
They all sat down and then Klauss with some frustration beginning to shout "not you two." Hector and Donald stood then sat quickly, James and Benjamin stood then sat down. Benjamin couldn't control himself anymore and fell to the floor laughing. Hector and Donald tried to stifle a laugh, only to snort and cough.

Klauss lost his temper and banged the gavel on the bar counter until it broke. This sent the four others in the room into fits of laughter.

In anger, Klauss produced his gun from his pocket. He ordered Hector and Donald still shaking with laughter up to the deck. He shouted at them, which sent Benjamin into even more laughter.

The trio returned and took their place, none of them looking at James or Benjamin.

Using just the hammerhead of the gavel, Klauss hit the bar top.
"Order. Now will the prisoners stand." No one moved and Klauss leaned forward and pointing at James and Benjamin continued. "You two."
James rose, but Benjamin defiantly sat in his seat.
"I said stand."
"I know, but what did you mean prisoners? Am I a prisoner?"
"Benjamin just stand you've had your little fun now we must be serious."
Hector and Donald looked at him still sitting defiantly then at Klauss then back again to Benjamin. Their heads turning one-way than the other in unison.
James suddenly got the image of Wimbledon tennis and desperately tried to control a laugh. Misunderstanding this Benjamin thought he was laughing at him so he slowly rose from the seat.
"Finally, we can now begin."
"Standing before the judge Klauss Oberlin are the Honourable Benjamin Royston Herbert Brooke of Cobham House and James Pidgley of no fixed abode. The jury is Hector Peterson-Jones and Donald Rubin Seidler."

"Sorry to interrupt, but what are we charged with?" asked Benjamin once again trying to upset the procedure.

"I'm getting to that, don't be so impatient. I must swear the jury in first."

"Uncle Klaus, Grandfather says you shouldn't swear."

"I will not swear."

"You just said you would swear in the jury."

"I'm not going to swear at them."

"Oh, I thought you meant bloody hell jury or something like that."

"Benjamin stop all this nonsense."

"You should say what you mean."

"Member so the jury will you in good faith and honesty reach a verdict in accord with the law."

In unison, Hector and Donald said, "Yes."

"Now for the charges. Benjamin Royston Herbert Brooke, we charge you with the murder of Julian Peterson-Jones and Taylor Seidler. How do you plead?"

"I was only following orders."

"That I suppose means not guilty."

"No, I did it, but I was told to."

"We will get to that later. James Pidgley, we charge you with aiding and abetting in the said murder. How do you plead?"

"Oh, guilty, but like him, I was just following orders me, Lord."

Benjamin and Donald understood James' irony. Hector and Klauss looked blankly at him.

"You plead guilty is that what you're saying."

"No, your honor, I am saying I was told to do it."

"Who told you?"

"Now that would be telling, wouldn't it? What is worth?" James's Birmingham accent suddenly appearing and added to comedy being played out.

Klauss was beginning to become irritated by the frivolity of the procedure.

"Prisoners you do not seem to understand the seriousness of your crime. If this court finds you guilty, we will put you to death."

"I think both Mr. Brooke and myself understand the seriousness of murder. We don't understand the legality of this quasi kangaroo court."

"The fathers of the dead men, Mr. Peterson-Jones and Mr. Seidler want justice."

"Or is it revenge and an eye for an eye?"

"Enough. Mr. Pidgley sit down, we will deal with you later."

James sat amused at the stalling tactics he and Benjamin had created. Benjamin's hand next to James gave the thumbs-up sign. Even if it were true about him murdering Julian and Taylor, he was warming to the man.

"Benjamin Brooke, we charge you with the willful murder of Julian and Taylor, beloved sons of these two men. You have pleaded not guilty the court will now present its evidence."

Klauss climbed off the stood and reached for something from behind the bar. The envelope he produced was thick, reminding James of what he had under his shirt.

"First, we have a confession statement you wrote the night of the murder."

"You told me to write it so I wouldn't feel guilty."

"Next we have two pictures of you with the bodies

of the men taken by you just after you murdered
them."

"Peterson-Jones told me to take a picture to prove I
had killed them."

Peterson-Jones shook his head but remained silent.

"What happened to the murder weapon?"

"I got rid of it even though Donald had told me to
bring it back and he would dispose of it."

Donald shook his head and then looking at Hector
mouthed 'not true.'

"The evidence against you is substantial, what says
the jury."

James jumped up he had heard enough. "Stop the
Prisoner has rights to. He will present his defense."

"We are at sea, Mr. Pidgley, those laws don't apply."

"Under maritime law, they do so as a lawyer for the
prisoner I would like to call out the first witness.
Benjamin Brooke."

"Don't be ridiculous."

"Your Honour if you want this trial to be recorded
as fair and just you must let us cross examine the
witnesses."

"Oh, very well, be quick about it."

"Benjamin Brooke, do you swear to tell the truth,
the whole truth and nothing but the truth."

"I do."

"Why did you murder Julian Peterson-Jones and
Taylor Seidler?"

"Because they blackmailed me to do it."

"What do you mean they blackmailed you?"

"Last year I was involved in a minor accident with
my car."

"You bloody well murdered a little girl in a hit and run." shouted Peterson-Jones.

"They found out about my minor accident and said if I didn't do as they asked, they would tell the police."

"Who gave the instructions to murder the two men?"

"Peterson-Jones and Donald took me to their club for dinner and laid out the plan."

"Bloody lies," shouted Peterson-Jones.

"I must protest your Honour Mr. Peterson-Jones can have his say later."

"Hector, keep your mouth shut."

Hector bowed his head, Klauss wasn't the kind of man he wanted to upset.

"So, you carried out the instructions given to you and murdered the two men."

"Yes."

"How did you feel after you had murdered the two men?"

"Bloody great such a rush Donald opened a bottle of Champaign saying all his worries are over."

"Do you know what he meant?"

"Taylor wasn't his son, he adopted him and said he was nothing but trouble. He called him a gutter-snipe and the world would be best without him."

"Thank you, Mr. Brooke, I now call my next witness, Mr. Peterson-Jones."

"I protest," said Peterson-Jones.

"Just answer the question so we can get this over with."

"Hector Peterson-Jones, do you swear to tell the truth, the whole truth and nothing but the truth."

"Klauss I must protest you said nothing about this."

"Just get on with it."

"Hector, why do you think Benjamin murdered your son."

"I don't know?"

"Do you miss your son?"

"Well yes, he was a good lad at heart."

"You said he was a dirty little queer who should disappear off the planet," said Benjamin.

"Is that true Mr. Peterson Jones?"

"My son was homosexual, and I didn't like it."

"Why not after all he was your son. Someone to be proud of, surely."

With venom in his voice, he replied, "He was a dirty little queer bringing down the family name. It was the kissing and the fondling of Donald's son Taylor in public for my friends and business colleagues to see. Everyone talking about it behind my back, I was becoming the laughingstock of the town."

"So, you wanted Benjamin to kill your son?"

"I wanted the problem to go away. Julian was becoming a problem, especially with the business side. Talking, no he was boasting about what he had done."

"So, you blackmailed Benjamin to murder your son."

"That was Donald's idea, he wanted Taylor off his back."

"Don't bring me into your sordid little tale. I know nothing about any of this."

"Don't lie Donald we are up to our neck in it and you know it. If we don't dispose of these two, then it's over for us."

"Then let's get on with it rather than playing this stupid game."

"It is not a stupid game, I have my standards and I will not put any man to death without a trial."

"Very honorable Klauss, but the longer we drag this out the more problems we may have."

"If I am to die, don't you think I should know why?"

"That's correct James, if your intention is to kill us, we should know why."

"With you Benjamin, that is easy. You killed a little girl in the hit and run, then you murdered their sons."

"And me what have I done?"

"I think the expression is in the wrong place at the wrong time. You know too much for your good."

"Meaning what?"

"You heard things on the night of Julian's party."

"I think that was your son's last supper. I heard nothing that is my point I may have been where I shouldn't have been. Gordon Tuff and Patrice Sickle had drugged me for one of their sordid rituals."

"But you may have heard something, and we can't trust you. I'm sure you understand it's just business."

"A dirty business from what I can see."

"Maybe, but if it wasn't us, then others would do it."

"And that justifies murder."

"We do what we have to."

"I am sure that would have been Hitler's defense."

"Do not bring that honorable soldier into this."

"Don't you mean murderer?"

"They never proved he murdered anyone."

"So, you all admit you convinced Benjamin into murdering Julian and Taylor."

"It justified the end to what was becoming a nightmare."

"Who was it tried to have me killed in the manhole."

"That was Klauss's idea and brilliant it was too. We still don't know how you got out of it alive."

"Divine intervention and a lot of cleverness on my part."

"It was at that point we felt you needed watching, we had underestimated you."

"And your son Julian, he knew what he was doing, he despised you for what you were. He told someone you were the worse scum on the earth, and he would do everything to bring you down."

"He would never say that, I know he wouldn't."

"Ever thought of talking to Julian and explaining."

"He wouldn't listen, spent more time with his chauffer than me."

"Oh yes, Brad the chauffer and MI-5 operative."

"What, you're lying."

"No, I'm not. You are all being investigated by the police and MI-5."

"I'm clean they have nothing on me," said Klauss, confident he wasn't being investigated.

"Sorry to disappoint you Klauss but you are. According to Brad for arms dealing with Iran and blackmail of high-ranking police officers."

"They have no proof."

"They must have something for Brad to tell me about it."

"You're bluffing."

All three men looked worried for the first time. Donald sank back into his chair and rubbed his face with his hands.

"Shit, this is for nothing."

"Donald I don't know how this man learned of these things. I would know if the police or MI-5 were investigating us. Now we have a job to do so gentlemen lets adjourn upon deck and come to a verdict."

The three men left the cabin, only Peterson-Jones looked back at James and Benjamin.

James sat down. He would now have to work out his plan to escape. He had lied about swimming at school; he had been a school champion. Although he had never swum more than a mile and he had calculated, they were over two miles out.

Benjamin was opening the small portholes and looking outside. For the first time, he showed signs of fear. He knew what they intended, and it scared him.

Voices raised again on the deck above. An argument followed. Donald and Hector didn't like what Klauss was saying.

James, at last, knew the truth and hoped he could tell someone once back on dry land. First, he needed to get off the boat.

Benjamin searched the cabin as he lifted the cushions off the couch before opening cupboards. He pried open the locked cupboards. From behind the bar counter he produced a bottle of scotch. It was unopened, so he ripped the seal off and took a long swig before offering the bottle to James.

"No thanks."

Benjamin relaxed back on the couch, taking swigs from the bottle. He had consumed about half when Klauss came down the stairs.

"For God's sake, Benjamin."

He took the bottle from him and placed it on the bar counter.

"In a moment I will call the jury back with their verdict. James, I am sorry this has happened to you but that's life."

"It's not over yet, Klauss."

"For me no, you yes."

Standing at the foot of the stairs he shouted, "would members of the jury return."

Donald and Hector came down the stairs. They looked like the condemned men. Taking their seats, Benjamin patted Donald on the knee.

"Want some whiskey Donny baby? It's bloody excellent stuff and quells the nerves and everything else."

He laughed hugging a cushion of the couch.

"Not now, Benjamin."

"Ah go on it is bloody good stuff from Scotland."

He was drunk, and it looked like he was a loud drunk. This could be used to James' advantage in his aid to escape.

Klauss climbed onto the high bar stool and this time fell off. Benjamin laughed out loud and fell to the floor, rolling about. Klauss perched himself on the edge of the bar stool. Donald and Hector picked Benjamin off the floor and sat him on the couch.

"Gentlemen of the jury, have you reached a verdict?"

"Yes, your honor."

"Prisoners stand."

Defiantly, both James and Benjamin sat. Realizing it was a lost cause, Klauss ignored and continued.

"Members of the jury in the case against Benjamin Royston Herbert Brooke, what is your verdict?"

"Guilty."

"So say all of you?"

"Yes, your honor."

"In the case against James Pidgley, what is your verdict?"

"Guilty."

"So say all of you?"

"No, you Honour one member of the jury abstained."

"May I ask who abstained?"

"No, James you may not."

"Why I would like to know who felt sorry for me."

"I did," said, Donald.

"I would have, only you have become a problem, James."

"Thank you, Donald and Hector you need to get some actual balls."

Benjamin fell to the floor laughing again.

"Enough. Guilty it is then."

Benjamin slides back onto the couch. "Condemned men that's what you and I are James old chap for the chop. Err your Honorable Judge I thought we had done away with the death penny, a penalty that's the word. I think I may be a little drunk, only a little will the court consider that…" he gave an enormous burp and giggled.

"We are at sea."

"I know bloody water everywhere and not a drop to drink, only a bottle of scotch."

"The jury has reached its verdict, so that only
leaves me to pass sentences."
Klauss produced a square piece of black cloth and
placed it on his head.

"Under the law, we have found you guilty of murder Benjamin Royston Herbert Brooke. We will
take you from this place and execute you for your
crimes. And may God have mercy on your soul."
"Alleluia and amen to that, can I have some more
whiskey now, uncle Klauss?"
"Under the law, we have found you James Pidgley
guilty of aiding in murder. Likewise, we will take
you from this place and execute you for your
crimes. And may God have mercy on your soul."
"He is mad you know, my grandfather thinks it is
German inbreeding. Brilliant man my grandfather
did you ever meet him. You should I think he
would like you. Do you know what my grandfather
told me once very interesting it is too? He said,
never show a person who you are especially close
friends they could turn to be your worst enemy.
Good isn't it."

Klauss handed Donald the gun and nodded his head
for him to proceed.

"I think we should go a little further out to sea before we, you know, do it. Hector, you steer while
Donald gets these two ready."
Donald pointed the gun at James and Benjamin and
pointed for them to go on deck. Hector sat in the driving seat and started the motor. Benjamin was trying to
stand, but he had too much to drink. Klauss had
stayed down in the cabin. He had decided the other
two should carry out the execution.

The boat motored out to sea, the lights of a big ship were visible. The sea was choppy and Benjamin couldn't control his balance. He fell into Hector, who swung the boat towards the enormous ship. Donald grabbed hold of Benjamin and a struggle between them began. He was trying to grab the gun, only he was too drunk to have the strength to get hold of it. Benjamin grabbed the Red Fireman's axe and swung it at Hector. He missed and struck the steering wheel and sheered if off. The key in the ignition also broke. Donald reacted by firing the gun and shooting Hector. James didn't wait to see what happened he dived into the water making sure he knew which way land was first.

He swam as fast as he could away from the boat. He stopped when he thought he had covered enough distance. The boat was on a collision course towards the ship. Hector had fallen over the controls and Donald was trying to pull him off them. He saw Benjamin descend in the cabin, carrying the ax. The explosion must have been seen from the shore as the small boat plowed into the ship. It would surprise him if anyone on board the small craft had survived.

On the ship they switched on enormous arc lights and searched the water. From what he could see, there was nothing left of the small boat. He swam again towards the shore. It would be a test of endurance. The water was chilly, and the waves had increased in size. He would have to put all his energy into making it to the shore. He saw two emergency craft leave the marina and race toward the ship.

The moon was playing a game with him and hiding behind the clouds. At one point he thought he was only a few hundred yards from the shore. Only to find he must still have a mile to go. His arms and legs were hurting, he needed to get into shape. The cold sea-water was attacking his bite wounds. A helicopter with a bright beam swept the sea, looking for survivors. He needed to get to the shore before they saw him. He didn't want to have to explain what he was doing on the boat.

His feet suddenly hit the seabed he had reached the shore and staggered up on to the stony beach. Exhausted, he collapsed lying face down and passed out. How long he lay there, he wasn't sure. He woke in the early morning. The sun drying his back. He felt the plastic zip-lock bag dig into him.

The girl screamed, and he jumped up and faced her. She looked at him and screamed again.

"What's wrong, I'm clothed this time."

The ten most played CD while writing
Brighton Ho!
Music is an inspiration to create pictures in your head.

Edvard Greig	Holberg Suite Op 40
Ennio Morricone	Cinema Paradiso Soundtrack
Yanni	I.n. M.y. Ti.m.e
Liang Bo	Best song of Liang Bo
Hua Chen Yu	Mountain and Sea
ANU	GaGa
ANU	Tianya Songgirl
Les Yeux Niors	Balamouk
U2	October
Madness	Mad not Mad

ABOUT THE AUTHOR

Edward Arno was born in a field in Frankley Beech, Birmingham, England. His father was a milkman and his mother was a house parlor maid. They met during a bombing raid at the end of the Second World War. Growing up on a council estate, he attended the local public schools. The Issigonis Mini auto plant at Longbridge was the symphonic sound of his childhood. He moved to America to pursue a screenwriting and directing career.

He resides in Burbank, California and is also an active member of the Mystery Writers of America.

Website: www.edwardarno.com
Facebook: Edward Arno Author
YouTube: Edward Arno